WHO HAS THE TIME TRANSFERENCE DEVICE?

Ali asked this of Dr. Lindstrom, and now she was frightened by his revelation that it was in the hands of the Iron Men, KGB hardliners pushed out by Glasnost. Every hour . . . every minute . . . every change they make in the past gives them a stronger hold on history.

Desperately she asked, "Can Jim go back there and do something?"

"No. There's nothing he can do without new information. These events are only happening now and Jim can't possibly know about them."

Suddenly Ali had a very unpleasant but necessary thought. Someone else would have to go back. Someone who knew what she had just learned. She was terrified. . . .

TIME WARRIOR #1

Time of the Fox

Matthew J. Costello

A ROC BOOK

ROC
Published by the Penguin Group
Penguin Books USA Inc., 375 Hudson Street,
New York, New York 10014, U.S.A.
Penguin Books Ltd, 27 Wrights Lane,
London W8 5TZ, England
Penguin Books Australia Ltd, Ringwood,
Victoria, Australia
Penguin Books Canada Ltd, 2801 John Street,
Markham, Ontario, Canada L3R 1B4
Penguin Books (N.Z.) Ltd, 182-190 Wairau Road,
Auckland 10, New Zealand

Penguin Books Ltd, Registered Offices:
Harmondsworth, Middlesex, England

First published by Roc, an imprint of New American Library, a division of Penguin Books USA Inc.

First Printing, November 1990
10 9 8 7 6 5 4 3 2 1

PRINTED IN THE UNITED STATES OF AMERICA

To Harry McShane.
After D-Day + 3, he had enough stories to last
a lifetime . . .

1

“Give me a break,” Alessandra said to Jim, laughing full and loud. The late fall breeze sent her long brown hair flying behind her.

She's much too beautiful to be hanging around with me, Jim Tiber thought. There's something wrong with this picture.

“No,” he said, quickly skipping in front of her, then walking backwards. *“Look at it,”* he said, gesturing to his right. “Go ahead, take a good look.”

Alessandra nodded, humoring him the way she always did. She glanced quickly left. “So what? There's a fence. A nice big fence. It makes me feel secure.”

Jim grinned. “But that's just it. You see, Columbia University wasn't always surrounded by a fence. No. It used to be open to the world around. Now it's like an armed camp.”

“And I'm just as glad,” Alessandra said. “Don't tell me that you'd actually like the campus open to Morningside Heights, would you? Do you have any idea how many murders there are out there in *one week?”*

“Right, exactly,” he went on, as if she was agreeing with him. “That's precisely my point. The cities weren't always like this—decrepit, filled with no-man's-lands where even the cops don't go anymore. And Columbia University wasn't always filled with armed security goons.”

"Will you stop walking in front of me?" She laughed. "You're making me dizzy."

He moved back to Ali's side. It was a short walk from the great brick library building to the grad student's gleaming high-rise dormitory.

No one lived off-campus. Not anymore. You'd have to be crazy to do that.

Of course, the Board of Trustees, in their wisdom, considered moving the school out of Manhattan. There were stories of Rockefeller land up-for-grabs in Westchester.

But a potent squad of well-healed alumni protested, many based in the financial ghetto of lower Manhattan. Columbia University's history was tied to Manhattan, they argued, and that shouldn't be changed.

The alumni, needless to say, rarely made it uptown to check out their besieged alma mater.

It was important for Jim to make Ali see that this was all wrong. . . .

"But nobody seems concerned about this. Certainly not your profs in the Physics Department. They're too busy measuring dingleberries on subatomic particles to worry about real problems."

She turned to him, some of her amused smile melting.

There, he thought. That got her attention.

Now it was his turn to grin. "Though there are some bright, beautiful exceptions in the department . . ."

But Alessandra looked really annoyed at him.

"And I suppose the stuff you study, all that nosing about in the screwed-up history of the Twentieth Century—the bad old days when everything went to hell—that's doing some good?"

Alessandra stopped walking, her face set, angry, and Jim knew that she was terminally pissed off.

"You're living in a dream world," she said.

"So what's so bad—"

"And I'll tell you what's wrong with it. There are real problems, problems that are getting worse every day, problems that no fence or security guards or wishful thinking can help."

"What is this? The physicist as Mother Teresa? How quantum physics will save the world?"

She shook her head and started walking again. "It's a hell of a lot better than wasting time studying the stupidity of the past."

"Do I detect a slur on the respected field of Contemporary Studies?"

"It's just an excuse to lose yourself in research."

"Those who forget the past—"

"Are probably better off," Alessandra finished.

They passed the Central Security Building, near what was once Teacher's College, Columbia's primo Education School. Like Education Schools at many Ivy League universities, TC was phased out as the electronic classroom—with its banks of computers—became king. The Electronic Education Act of '98 finished the teaching profession. Teachers wore lab coats now, and they could sniff out bugs in programs like microchip hound dogs. Inspiration was discarded in favor of something called "Continually Moderated Educational Progress."

Even most of Jim's profs preferred showing old lectures on laser disc.

The result was a system where everyone grew up to either slip behind terminals, processing data for the rest of their insignificant lives, or vanish into the forbidden lands of the sprawling cities, with their fiefdoms of crime and violence.

Jim didn't say anything for a moment. And he wondered whether he had succeeded in the impossible—actually getting the unflappable Ali mad at him.

He looked at her quickly, a side glance, as they neared the dorm tower. All the students acted oblivious to the security guards posted outside, outfitted with the finest black Nauxite—secure against any shell fired from a handgun. The students streamed into the buildings, laughing, talking, having a great time.

They ignored the dark hulking shapes perched on

the building's steps like grim stone figures. Human gargoyles.

Jim reached out and grabbed Alessandra as they reached the bank of elevators.

"Mad?"

She shook her head and forced a small smile.

"No," she said. "Worried." Her smile broadened. "What's to become of you, Jim? You and all your research. Who'll give a damn . . . out there?"

"I hope you do," he said.

She nodded. "Yes . . ." she laughed, "almost as much as I care about understanding Hawking's last theorem."

"Last *unproven* theorem," Jim added.

"Unproven for now," she smiled. "I'm working on it . . ."

"Dinner later?" he asked. "Chez Dining Hall? I believe they're serving your favorite—erratically chipped beef drowned in gluten sauce, served on a bed of nearly new bread."

She laughed again, her final admission of defeat.

"Yes, but I have to work tonight. No—"

An elevator arrived, and they hurried inside, packed tightly with a dozen other students.

He leaned close to her. "You were saying . . . no . . . what?"

She rolled her eyes. She looked at him, put her lips right up to his ear and whispered . . .

"No fucking . . ."

"It's on your bed, Tiber. You better check it out."

Jim rushed past his roommate, Richard Blau, an agreeable electronics business major who managed to nail down respectable grades and still party every night.

Jim went to his bed and picked up the envelope. "Who brought it over?" He tore it open.

Richard finished toweling himself. "Dunno. Some undergrad flunky." Richard paused. "I couldn't help but notice who it came from. . . ."

Jim saw that too. It was Dr. Pomford, his nemesis, the man who stood between Jim and everything he wanted to do in college. He read the letter, skipping through the niceties in the first paragraph. Richard come closer to Jim, peering over his shoulder.

"Bad news?"

Jim read the last fatal sentences aloud. "The Doctoral Theses Committee feels that, without any substantiating documentary evidence to support the candidate's proposal, approval for the intended thesis subject must be regretfully denied." He paused. "Shit."

"Tough break, Tiber. Wanna go off-campus with me tonight? Nothing like a bit of party-party to chase dem blues away."

Jim shook his head and crumpled the letter into a ball.

"Ob-la-di, ob-la-da, life goes on . . ." Richard hummed, stepping away from Jim. "Don't let the blue meanies get you down, Jimbo."

But Jim threw the crumpled piece of paper right at Blau's face.

"Pomford turned me down," Jim said, leaning across the tray. "The idiot . . ."

Alessandra looked down, playing with her evening meal as if it might suddenly spring to life. She grimaced at her food. "You weren't far off guessing tonight's dinner. What the hell is this stuff? Cedar chips in plaster?"

"Ali—are you listening to me? I've been shot down. Pomford—the old toady—has just blown my proposal away. He's kissed off my thesis."

Alessandra finished the rest of her meal, then looked up at him. "I know," she said. "I heard you, Jim. Evil old Pomford turned down your proposal. But it's not like you didn't expect it. Don't worry. You'll think of something else."

"But I don't want to do anything else. What gives him the right to do that?"

''You want me to tell you? Okay, I'll tell you . . . but you won't like it.''

''Go on,'' he said, tightening his fingers around his unblemished fork, not at all sure now that he wanted to hear what Ali was about to say.

''Okay, here goes. First, you say you want to do a thesis on the Beatles, on late twentieth-century pop music . . . on the birth of the rock and roll art song, if there is such a thing.''

''There is,'' he grumbled.

''Sorry, but I have a problem putting Los Beatles in a class with Mahler. But hey, that's my taste. And that's okay. That's what the Contemporary Studies department was set up to do, to sift through the past hundred years of dreck and decide just what—if anything—has any lasting value. Your paper on the Beatles certainly wouldn't be the first.''

''So, what's the problem with my proposal?''

''The problem, dear Jim, is that you're hung up on this idea of yours . . . this mysterious 'influence,' a behind-the-scenes benefactor . . . a mystery man—''

''Or woman.''

''Or *woman*, someone who performed a Pygmalion-like transformation of the scruffy pre-fab four. Do I have the basics right?''

''Yes, except—''

Somebody came up behind Jim and put a heavy hand on his shoulder. ''You're working tonight, Ali, right? Not wasting time with our medieval scholar, old Jimbo here?''

Jim turned around, looked up, and saw one of Ali's fellow physics students, a big, beefy guy wearing a dopey smile.

It was Martin.

What a load!

Jim shook his shoulder, dislodging Martin's hand.

''They're going to give the positron inversion another shot, babe . . . should be lots of laughs,'' Martin said.

"Yes, Martin," Ali said. "I'm going to the lab right after dinner."

"Ooops," Martin said, slapping his gorilla head in mock horror. "There I go, forgetting the social niceties. Went and interrupted your dinner." He nodded his head and winked at Jim. "Catch you later, Ali."

Jim shook his head. Martin did little to improve his appetite. He speared a forkful of whatever was hiding under the smeary yellow sauce and he stuck the now-cold food in his mouth. "Hard to believe that jerk is a budding physicist," he said, while chewing resolutely. "God help the universe . . ."

"He's good, too," Alessandra said, stinging Jim with her quick defense. "He's been working in the Red Building. There's something very special going on in there."

The infamous Red Building was located in the northeast corner of the campus. He knew that it was once Spencer Hall, part of the Lit Department. But it had been greedily taken over by the sprawling, well-funded physicists from Columbia's Nevis Lab. It had its own security fence, its own guards.

Very special stuff was going on in there . . . so the rumors went.

The entire building was covered with massive red tiles, ugly flat red tiles. Whatever was going on in there had to be important stuff, there was no mistaking that. Still, most of the grad students called the Red Building "the scab."

"You were telling me—in detail—what was wrong with my proposal," Jim said, talking through the food. It's amazing such a cruddy diet actually supported intelligent life.

Ali dabbed at her mouth. Jim then watched her put some lipstick on—the femme fatale as particle physicist. He felt the slow, discomforting burn of jealousy.

Ali and Martin . . . Martin and Ali. He didn't like the sound of that. Not at all.

She stood up, scooping up her tray.

"My problem?" Jim repeated, realizing that he'd let a nasty edge creep into his voice.

"The problem is that you lack any—by 'any' I mean just that—*any* evidence about this mysterious influence on the fabled Beatles. You have dates, and you have all the musicological stuff you need." She had her tray hoisted. "But where's your evidence? It's a guess, Jim. A hunch. Maybe you're right . . . maybe you're not."

Jim stood up, surprised at how mad he felt toward Pomford, and now toward Alessandra for supporting him. He grabbed her arm.

"But that's the whole point in doing the research. You're a scientist. That's the whole damn point, isn't it? Why research things we know? I have some good clues, I have dates, comments about Hamburg, the Star Club, lines right in the music."

He shook her arm a bit as he talked, not noticing her fork and knife slipping to the tray's edge. Then, as he went on talking, they clattered to the floor.

"Will you let go, Jim? Christ, sometimes I don't understand why the hell you're here. It's a school. You play the game, you get your diploma, then get away." She knelt down, racing him to recover her utensils. He saw some nearby students enjoying the show.

"If that old fart Pomford would just let me do the work, I'd be able to prove it."

Ali stood up and shook her head. "I've got to go."

He stood there, ignoring the snickers of the other students.

"See you tonight . . . when you're done?" he asked, too loudly.

Too desperately? he wondered.

She kept walking, and shrugged. "I don't know . . ."

Shit, he thought. Do I have a way with the ladies, or what?

He sat down, pushing his entree to the rear of the platter and moving a jello-and-fruit combination to the place of honor.

Way to go, he thought.

He couldn't believe his luck in getting someone like Ali as a friend. They weren't lovers. They were both too guarded for that. She described them as friends who fuck.

But the way he had acted, she'd probably end their relationship.

Enter Martin.

He pushed a spoonful of the jiggly dessert into his mouth, thinking about what he'd do for the rest of the evening. Look for another angle for his thesis. Something less controversial. Maybe another look at the autobiography of George Martin—the "fifth" Beatle, the genius producer who was credited with creating the phenomenon of the Beatles. Then there were the recording notes from the Abbey Road studio . . . the tape transcripts . . .

But the answer wasn't there, Jim thought. The Beatles were transformed long before they cut their first hit record. Something made them experimenters. they came back from Hamburg ready to turn the recording studio into a sound lab.

Yeah.

If it started anywhere, it was in Hamburg, sometime during their second trip there. 1962. The Star Club. Right on the infamous Reeperbahn.

Whatever weird alchemy had occurred already happened by the time they came back to the UK. Something changed them from screechy-voiced scruffy rockers—no better or worse than a dozen other bands gigging at the Reeperbahn clubs—to musical poets, artists, pop visionaries whose music defined an age.

He knew he was right. And if he could only prove it, Pomford would have to let him write his thesis.

But how the hell can I do that? Jim wondered.

2

The wind bounced nastily against the permanently sealed windows of Jim's room. He was too high to hear the rustle of the few trees still left on the overcrowded campus. The oafish sound of the wind was all that was left to experience of this chilly fall evening.

Jim got up from his bed, carefully stepping over scattered piles of papers and books, and he looked outside. The message—the illusion, he thought—was obvious. Columbia's students are above it all, towering above the college itself, high over Morningside Drive, above the city—so high you can see from the George Washington Bridge down to the Twin Towers, hulking, fortresslike, to the south, down to Wall Street.

He stood there, looking out, breathing against the glass. His breath made a tiny foggy patch. He rubbed it away and returned to his work.

There was no joy in his work tonight. With his proposal firmly rejected, there was nothing to do except dump all this junk on the floor and scramble around for some approved area of research. The Nouveau Existentialism of Jay McInerny? Or, *peut-être* the *fin-de-siècle* New York club scene? The Catholic Experience and its influence on Andy Warhol?

Why punk stunk?

But he looked at the pile of books, paper, and microdat discs sprawled across his bed. Here was Paul

McCartney's speech when he resigned as PM. And Ringo talking nonsense about a "silver grey submarine" from his senior citizens' resort in north Scotland.

George—the wealthiest of the lot, a new age movie mogul—said nothing, of course.

Jim had letters and taped interviews with dozens of people, most of them with their already frail memories severely damaged by age and a lifetime of pharmaceutical excess. There was no tape from George Martin—Pomford's nominee for the musical guru behind the Beatles. He was unfortunately, deceased.

But even George Martin admitted in his autobiography that before the first recording session on Wednesday, June 6, 1962, "Something had happened to the boys' music."

Something indeed. Something that took what was just another skiffle band and made them the driving force of a decade. But what?

Jim reached over and snatched a beer from the half-dead six-pack lying nearby.

Pomford! he thought. The silly ass. The complete new age academic. More of a cautious technocrat, a figure out of Gilbert & Sullivan. One eye on grants, another on the door.

The university wasn't a place for learning. Not in his department. It was a place for regurgitation.

Of course, Jim knew what he should do. Pack all this junk into boxes, and scramble around for another topic . . . *prontissimo.* Kiss Pomford's butt. Grease the wheels.

Yes, sir, Dr. Pomford, you were certainly right. You sure saved me from wasting a lot of time researching something that was clearly hopeless.

Yeah.

Thanks a heap. Now can I pick you up and bounce you on your bald head?

He looked at his watch. Nearly midnight. Gotta bag my American History seminars for tomorrow. He guessed he could cancel his freshman class without too much trouble. No complaints from those goal-oriented dweebs.

He took a slug of the beer.

He just hoped that Alessandra might stop by, after she was done dicking around in the lab with pug-faced Martin.

That would be nice.

Except Jim realized that he'd been more obnoxious than usual—for no apparent reason. There were limits to what Ali would put up with. He knew that, having crossed *that* line many times. Still, he thought, my boyish charm, my brilliant intellect and general sense of fun should win out in the end.

I hope.

He smiled at the thought . . . and then belched.

As if in answer, the wind outside pushed against the glass again.

He thought of turning out the light. She wasn't going to visit him tonight. Then he heard footsteps in the hall.

The doorknob turned.

Jim had no chance to clear his bed of the chaotic jumble of papers, books, and tapes before his guest arrived.

"Well, James, it certainly looks like you've been working hard all night," Alessandra said. She walked over to the bed and pushed aside the remaining beers with her foot.

"Like one?" he asked. She shook her head. "Some green tortilla chips? I think that there are some—"

She shook her head again.

He sat up in bed. "I still can't believe Pomford blew me off," he said, by way of explaining the state of his room. "Look at this. Does *this* look like no documentary support to you?"

"The asshole."

Jim grinned. "Didn't know you knew words like

that. Most becoming. Anyhow, it's back to the old drawing board. Unless I come up with some miraculous source of hitherto unrevealed information. Got any ideas?''

Alessandra sat down on the bed, pushing aside a chaotic pile of his reference material. She looked preoccupied—half here, and half somewhere else.

''I'm sorry for you, Jim. I know that it meant a lot to you.'' She reached out and touched his hand. I know why she likes me, he thought. It's her sick puppy instinct. She'd like to put me in a cozy cardboard box with some milk-bones and a warm fuzzy.

Maybe a dog chewie if I was a real good boy.

''Oh, don't worry about me.'' His fingers sneakily closed around hers. ''What's wasting a few years in research? Hey, it was just a theory I had. I'll find another.'' He sat up beside her, the beer giving him enough of a foggy distance from his now derailed academic career to focus on encouraging Ali to comfort him in a more direct way.

He put a hand on her shoulder, letting his fingers separate the shimmering strands of her auburn hair.

Then he tried to pull her close. But she sat stiff, upset, looking somewhere in front of her, miles away.

Belatedly aware that something was wrong, Jim asked, ''What's bothering you?''

''I saw Martin tonight . . . at the particle lab.''

Jim let his hand slip away.

''Oh. . . .''

She turned toward him. ''No, not like that. Not at all. Sure, he came on to me . . . you know, he always does.''

''Such scientific persistence.'' Jim looked at her. ''You know, if he wasn't such a big bastard I'd like to—''

She raised a hand, cutting him off.

''He started talking about the Red Building, bragging. He said that he works there three nights a week.''

''Ah, the infamous Red Building. Where endowment money disappears faster than a magician's rabbit.''

She turned to him, her face excited. ''No, you've got to listen to this. Martin works there. And he said some of his friends told him what's going on. And a few of the other assistants know what's going on.''

His current can of beer empty, Jim reached down and searched for a new one. He picked it up and held it, tilting it toward Ali. ''Sure you won't join me?''

She shook her head. ''Will you listen? Martin says they're doing something there with time—he actually said the words 'time travel'—''

''Time travel? And they won't give me permission to research the Beatles. Now, there's common sense for you.'' Jim stood up, laughing. ''Quick, let's call the alumni association. We'll put a quick end to this nonsense. We'll have sit-ins, just like the Sixties. Right outside the—'' he started laughing and couldn't say the words—''Outside the Time Travel Building. 'Hell no, we won't go!' ''

''Jim! Damn, there's no talking to you anymore, is there? You just do whatever you want, and to hell with listening to anyone.'' She stood up.

She was on the verge of storming out of the room. He quickly stopped laughing and grabbed her arm.

''Hey, there I go again. Screwing things up. My natural tendency. Please,'' he said, struggling to sound as earnest as possible, ''don't leave.''

She froze there a moment, and then turned and walked over to the window. ''He says that they've had some success . . . that the machine works. That's why it's all covered in red—some kind of shielding, or something.''

''A time machine . . . and it works?'' He felt giggles beginning to percolate up from his belly. But he quickly cleared his throat to suppress them. ''Ahem, well, that certainly would be something. Yes, sir—''

She looked at him. His desk lamp splayed across his rumbled bed, throwing a faint light onto Ali. Behind her it was black, with only the distant lights of the city outlining her. She looked tired, drawn. But, as always, breathtaking.

Why the hell she puts up with me, he thought, is something I'll never know. . . .

"Martin says it's not a time machine—not exactly. He hasn't seen it or been there during the tests. But one of his drinking buddies *has* helped the scientists. He says it's more like a transmitter. It tunes in the time-space frequency—the 'radio waves of causality,' Martin calls them. It can transmit your thoughts to that frequency."

"So it sends your thoughts through time?"

Alessandra nodded unconvincingly. "I . . . I think so. Something like that. Martin doesn't really know how it works—"

"Not surprisingly."

She frowned. "But his friends told him that it does work. There have been experiments, successful experiments."

"Sounds like they're yanking Marty around." Jim shook his head and walked over to Alessandra. He put his hands on her shoulders. "I'm no physicist, but even I know the logical difficulties with time travel. It's open season on coherent history, with goofy paradoxes, endless loops, practical impossibilities, and—let's not forget my favorite—multiple instances of the same object or personality. Lots of fun for stories but absolutely crackers as a real possibility."

Ali walked away, thinking, obviously bothered by the same thoughts.

"You're right. I mean, what you're saying about traveling in time. But this could be different. Look, Martin said that you don't really go anywhere. Nothing moves."

"Well, better living through quantum physics has always been my motto. Now," he said, once again trying to direct her to his rumpled bed. "Why don't you step into my office for a consultation before my roommate comes back?"

She reached out and took his hands. "You don't see it, do you? You don't know why I'm telling you all this?"

"To make interesting conversation?"

That brought a small smile. "No. Your thesis, Jim. Your crazy ideas about the Beatles."

"Yeah," he said, thrust back into cold, hard reality. "What about it?"

"If the machine works—if it's real—you could go back there, back to whenever you think they first got their act together. You could get your documentary proof."

He pulled her toward the bed. "Yeah, and I could tell John Lennon to stay the hell out of New York City. . . ."

Jim felt his lovemaking, at least for tonight, was unusually perfunctory. Sometimes Alessandra inspired him to tremendous heights of erotic dexterity. But tonight he just wanted to get close to her, close, and quickly. And for her part, she acted just as pleased that it was done quickly. When it was over, she settled comfortably into the crook of his shoulder.

Maybe his roommate wouldn't come back tonight. That would be nice, he thought. Then Ali could stay.

But after he nearly tumbled into a deep snoring sleep, he felt her stirring, slipping from him, sliding away.

He turned the light on.

"Going?"

She nodded. "I've got a lab to run at seven A.M. I need some stuff from my room."

Jim leaned back against the pillow, watching her put on her clothes, enjoying it almost as much as when he had undressed her. She padded into the small bathroom.

He looked at his papers, now discarded, abandoned on the floor. And he started thinking about what she had said.

What if . . . he wondered. Yeah, what if there was something to it?

The Red Building was the most secure joint on the campus. No question about it. It had its own electric fence, and a special armed goon squad with their own security badges.

Okay, he thought. Obviously, something big is going on inside there. Really big.

But time travel?

Time travel . . .

Now wouldn't that be something? What an incredible thing for historians, even if it was only a matter of tuning in the past, like some old radio show, and studying it. The ultimate firsthand research, for everything from Napoleon to the Beatles. That would be neat. And it sure could make a difference in my life, he thought.

Ali came out of the bathroom and slipped on her pumps.

Jim started to get out of bed.

"Don't get up. I'll just disappear into the wind. Your phantom lover."

He swung around, his bare feet touching the cold linoleum floor. "Ali . . . could you learn some more—"

"More?"

"About the Red Building . . . about the time travel thing . . . ?"

"You're actually asking me to talk with Martin? Could be dangerous, Jimmy." She laughed. "I might fall in love with him."

He blinked and pushed some errant strands of hair off his forehead. "I'll take that risk," he answered. "Find out what you can. Maybe they need some guinea pigs, some volunteers. . . ."

"I'm seeing him in the morning," she said. "I'll see what else he knows."

Jim nodded.

"Just don't tell him it's me who's interested."

She opened the door. The sound of an ultraviolent holo-movie echoed from down the deserted hallway.

"Want me to walk you back to your room?"

"No." She laughed. "Go back to sleep."

She shut the door. Jim turned off the light and curled up in the still-warm sheets.

But he didn't fall asleep.

Not for a long time.

3

"Don't you have about two dozen hungry freshmen waiting for you, Tiber?"

Jim painfully opened one eye and saw his roommate Richard looking down at him, so disgustingly awake and bright-eyed it made Jim want to bury himself in his blanket and hide from the world forever.

"What time is it?" Jim mumbled.

Richard made a show of looking at his watch. "Oh, about ten to eight, Jimbo." He grinned. "It's going to be one mad dash to make it, me boy . . . hope you don't have a long wait for the elevator."

Then—like a spectral harbinger of doom—his roommate left, leaving Jim to wonder what the hell he was going to do. He could cancel the seminar, but he had already been tersely summoned to Pomford's office for pulling that trick one time too many. Of course, he could just show up—make an appearance—and then release them for some "independent study."

But no, that wouldn't fly, either. Most of the wide-eyed freshmen were just taking the course to complete their token humanities electives, a cultural bone offered to Western Civilization before unleashing the thoughtless, pragmatic desperados with their new-age technology. Columbia, like most universities, eagerly served the far-flung interests of the space community, the microchip mavens, and good old U.S. business.

It was a new era of prosperity. *If* you were part of

the game. A lot of citizens were permanently out of it.

Take the cities, for example. The urban wonderlands were filled with roving, dangerous armies of the disenfranchised. Riots didn't last long—the new technocrats, with their efficient riot control, didn't allow that. But there sure were a lot of them.

Jim's freshman students weren't bothered by such things. In fact, most of them didn't seem bothered by anything, other than maybe getting a job. Our great cultural heritage? Why, that had about as much relevance to their lives as great-grandma's attic filled with dusty toys and yellowed clothes.

Jim sat up. He looked at his watch. Six minutes to get to his seminar.

He looked around his room. Rumpled clothes on the floor. His ragged toothbrush in sight (though he wasn't above using Richard's in a pinch), and half of a toasted burrito oat bar sticking out of its wrapper.

Hadn't tasted too good last night, but it would have to suffice for a breakfast.

Five minutes.

Plenty of time he thought. Plenty. He got out of bed to begin a dash to the hallowed halls of Columbia University.

A single hand rose from the sea of bland faces. One single blade of hope in the withered field of the lecture hall.

A young coed, all sparkling, bright. Jim felt like he needed sunglasses just to gaze upon her early-morning brilliance. He tried to remember what he had been talking about that could have inspired her to actually stop and ask a question.

He pointed at her hand.

"Mr. Tiber," she addressed him sweetly, "I thought you said that the current cultural repression, the subversion of the normal cultural process, was an inevitable result of the complete meshing of business, and technology, and government."

Jim cleared his throat. Did I say that? he wondered. Wise words.

"Yes . . ."

The girl looked around, acting flabbergasted, stunned, shocked—

All Jim could think of was a nice tall glass of orange juice—ice cold, loaded with little bits and pieces of genuine orange. Yes, that would put some life back into his body.

His tongue felt like a tattered carpet.

"Well," the girl finally went on, "if that's true, then why didn't anyone see it coming? I mean," she said, letting a tiny condescending tone creep into her voice, "*you* said that it was a progressive process, over the past hundred years, and *nobody* saw it happening?"

She froze, her eyes locked on Jim, while the imprisoned audience seemed to stir.

Ah, they smell blood.

Now, what was the student's name? A moment's reflection demonstrated to him that recovering that fact was impossible.

Too bad. It might be helpful in deflecting her attack.

For a second he thought of telling her to go to the window—go to the fucking window and look outside. Look at the goddam university, look at the city, look at the whole screwed-up country. If no one saw life disintegrating, year after year, then the inhabitants of the Twentieth Century must have had their heads up their assholes.

He would have loved to say that.

It might not even matter now, careerwise. Now that his project was dead, his academic life at full stop.

But, as his father used to say—speaking from experience, he added—it's best not to burn your bridges.

"Not a bad point, miss—not bad at all. Except you're making two . . . very . . . incorrect . . . assumptions." He walked down from the small platform, a wooden teaching perch worn to a concave shape by decades of other ill-prepared graduate assistants running seminars. "One, you're assuming that there was no one who saw it all coming. I can direct you to a dozen books from the late Sixties, all of—"

There was a bit of snickering at this. Jim's obsession with the Sixties, his belief in its absolutely vital importance to understanding the current state of world affairs, was a source for much amusement on campus. He was treated as though he'd made a fetish of studying the collected works of Chuck Jones, the genius behind the Looney Tunes oeuvre.

"Dozens of books," Jim snapped. He stood right in front of the girl. "And you're making another, even more fatal assumption—that those who created this new world didn't know what they were doing, didn't understand how it would change the face of the country, of the world," Jim smiled, enjoying his turn to be condescending. "The Twentieth Century technocrats knew exactly what they were doing—and why. The big question—"

He turned and walked back to his perch.

"—is why did everyone let them? And do all the new technologists, circa 2000, have a clue what they're up to? I doubt it."

Jim looked at the sea of faces. Dubious faces. Shocked? Bored?

He looked up at the clock.

They're all waiting for the same thing I'm waiting for, he thought. The ancient clock's minute hand—a soothing anachronism—seemed to quiver, poised between one moment and the next. Then it clicked.

Another minute farther from the past, another minute lost forever.

Unless, yes, unless Alessandra wasn't talking through her hat . . . unless the wonder boys of the new technology inside the Red Building had really done something . . .

Interesting.

He smiled at the students.

Jim scooped up his books and his few pages of scribbled notes.

"Class dismissed."

He waited outside the Trump Physics Lab, a solid black building that—it was rumored—had cost ex-President Trump nearly half his wealth. State-of-the-art research financed by condo development and gambling casinos, thank you.

Jim watched for Alessandra to come out.

The building was, of course, restricted.

She came bouncing down the steps talking animatedly with another young woman and breezed past Jim as if he were invisible.

"Ali . . ." he said quietly. Then, louder, "Ali!" She stopped and turned, squinting in the brilliant fall sunlight. Her friend waited a moment, but then Alessandra turned and told her to go on. She walked over to Jim.

"Haunting the Physics Building? You look like the Phantom of the Grad School."

Jim looked down at his rumpled clothes. He rubbed his chin, feeling the stubble. "Busy morning. I was in a rush."

She smiled. Maybe she wasn't giving up on him after all.

He asked, "Can I join you for lunch?"

"Sure."

He walked alongside her, noticing how some of the better heeled students looked at them, probably wondering what such a beauty was doing with such a disheveled loser.

"I've got an idea," he said.

"Congratulations."

"No," he said. "You know what you told me last night, about the Red Building, about Martin?"

She fixed him with her laser-blue eyes. "I thought you couldn't stomach Martin."

"I can't. But if he's not just blowing wind, if there's

something to what he says, well, it could make a hell of a lot of difference."

"*If* it's true," she said offhandedly.

"Right. And if it *is* true, it shouldn't be left in the hands of some needle-brained physicists—"

Alessandra sighed.

"Present company excluded," he added, not quickly enough.

"Look," she said, "it's just a story, Jim. Rumors . . . Who knows what's behind it? It all sounds more than a bit unlikely to me. And by the time anything is released to the public, we'll all be very, very old."

He grabbed her hand and pulled her close to a maple. Its leaves were all burnt orange, a fiery tree, brilliant against the metal blue of the sky.

"That's just it, Ali. If there's something there, *now's* the time to see it . . . to try it."

She laughed. "I can't get you in."

"No. But your pal Martin could."

"Ah, but Martin hates your guts."

Jim squeezed her hands. A breeze sent a scattering of leaves swirling around them.

"Yeah. But he *likes* you . . . likes you a lot."

"Wait a minute," she said, pulling away. "What are you talking about here?"

"Nothing." He saw she didn't believe him. "No, not what you're thinking—honestly! Just, I don't know. You could be nice to him. Then ask him for a favor. One favor. You. Him. And me. Inside the lab."

"You're corrupt. You're worse than the gang of creeps running the city."

"Yes," Jim grinned. "But it's corruption with a noble purpose. It's a quest for truth." He grabbed her hand. "It could save my thesis."

She looked away, across the quadrangle, over to the library, one of the few buildings left intact from the old university.

"Martin could do it," Jim said. "He could get us in. If you get him to . . ."

She looked back at him. "Maybe," she said slowly.

"Maybe he could. Though it would take a lot of work to get him to drag you along."

"But there you go," he said, grinning. "It's possible. You can do it. Right?"

She took a breath and, after an eternity, she nodded. "What the hell. I can try. But in that case, we'd better cancel our luncheon plans while I track down Martin."

"I wasn't really hungry anyway," Jim laughed.

"I was." She turned and started back to the Trump Building. "I'll call you at the dorm and let you know what happens . . . if anything."

"I'll start packing my bags."

She kept on walking, turning around, walking backwards now, laughing. "I told you—you don't really *go* anyplace."

"Just a toothbrush, then," he said.

He heard her laughing all the way across the quad.

"Uh-uh," Martin said, continuing to refill the printer with scanpaper. "I'm sorry, Ali. Really. I'd love to show you the place—honest! But if I sneaked you in there, why, they'd toss me right out of the project, maybe out of the department. I'd have to be absolutely crazy to try it."

"Martin," Alessandra cooed, keeping her voice low. The Particle Physics Lab was a noisy place. At least a dozen experiments on the unexplained random activity of subatomic particles were in progress, ranging from the mundane—how to best produce unstable neutrons—to reversing the polarity on positrons. All lab time, crucial to the grad students' career, was booked months in advance. And there was a healthy black market selling suddenly liberated lab hours.

She touched Martin's bare arm. He had played football in high school—as he was fond of reminding everyone. But a shattered knee ended his glory days of contact sports.

"Martin, you know everyone's constantly bending the department's rules, using labs they're not supposed to and uplinking to restricted datanets *all the time.* If we got caught—and I don't think that's going to happen—it would just be you showing us the lab. Professional curiosity.''

She gave his arm another tentative pet.

It was probably cruel manipulating the poor thing this way. It was also surprisingly enjoyable.

The physicist as tease.

''And I tell you, we're not going to get caught.''

''Oh?'' he said, snapping the lid down on the paper carrier. He hit a button and yards of data started streaming out, onto the floor, printed on laser-readable scanpaper. Hard copy was rarely used unless you needed to jump all around searching the printout for some lost numbers.

Ali looked at the mountain of paper as it built.

The more primitive types still liked to touch their work.

''How do you figure that?''

''No problem,'' she smiled, trying her best to make it all seem like a lighthearted romp, hoping he wouldn't dwell on the Red Building's security fence and special cadre of armed guards. ''You can borrow some passes. Just for a few hours tonight . . .''

Now he looked at her, at the same time pulling his arm away from her hand. ''Passes? What do you mean—'passes'? You mean *a* pass, don't you? I already have mine and—''

''I want to bring someone with me.''

Martin's face became all scrunched, as if he'd just bit into a lemon. ''Who?''

Alessandra raised her eyebrows, smiled, thinking, If this works I can become a used car salesman.

''Jim,'' she said brightly. ''Jim Tiber.''

Martin walked away, shaking his head. ''Jee-zus!''

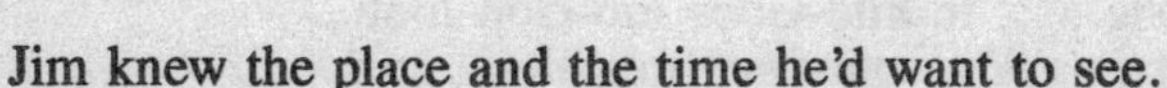

Jim knew the place and the time he'd want to see.

No question about it.

To him, it had always been obvious. Something had happened to John and Paul on their second trip to Hamburg. They were a hit, playing at the Star Club, five sets a night of primitive rock and roll. They partied until dawn and then slept until they had to drag themselves out of bed for the first show in the smoke-filled club.

Later, when the craziness set in, each of them said the same thing. It was the best time of their lives.

But after Hamburg, when they went back to good old Liverpool, they were different. The rhythms were still a plain-and-simple four to the bar, and the chord changes weren't anything that unusual. But from that point on every Lennon-McCartney song was an experiment, something new, novel—and, for its time, completely unique.

It was magic.

Whatever set them apart from all the other Merseyside bands began in Hamburg.

Jim popped a microdat chip into the remote player. He slipped the two cushioned earplugs in place.

"Roll up! Roll up for the Magical Mystery Tour."

"The Magical Mystery Tour" was not, perhaps, the height of the group's musical career. But still, it was interesting enough, with an exuberant, naive atmosphere of psychedelia and pseudomysticism.

It would all end so quickly. . . .

He leaned back and spread a small map out on the bed. It showed Hamburg, the main roads, the parks, the Aussenalster harbor, the infamous Reeperbahn.

He didn't believe it was possible. Not really. Time travel. It was illogical.

But it sure had his imagination working overtime.

And he sat in the dark room, listening to the music, drifting with it . . .

The phone beeped. Jim ran over and turned off the music . . . in mid-Goo-Goo-Goo-Joob.

It was Ali, sounding breathless, annoyed.

"Meet us outside the Physics Lab . . . in ten minutes."

"You did it?" he said. Incredible woman, he thought, and he started feeling the first tinges of guilt over his pressing her to use her considerable charms on Martin. "Way to go, Ali."

"He doesn't know."

Jim paused. "Doesn't know what?"

She took a breath. "Martin doesn't know that you want to use the machine—if there is any machine."

"Let's just keep that our little surprise."

"Right," she said, without any conviction. Then, she added, "Ten minutes," and hung up.

Jim shot out of bed and looked in the mirror. He was wearing a T-shirt with the word "Imagine" on it, his once-white painter's pants, now long overdue for a rhumba with the campus laundry machines, and generic Korean sneakers.

Well, he wondered, what does the well-dressed time traveler wear? If he was going to the court of Louis XIV, he guessed he'd be completely underdressed.

But the Sixties?

No problem . . .

He waited outside, feeling uncomfortably cold now that the wind was whipping through the corridors and alleys made by the buildings. Students hurried past him, some hustling to all-night cram sessions in the library, others to the dull social clubs that were the administration's feeble attempt to provide some on-campus social life.

He waited. More than ten minutes.

Where the hell were they?

A flurry of odd thoughts ran through his head. First, he remembered that Ali said that the machine—the rumored machine—didn't actually take you anywhere. It all happened, appropriately enough, in the mind.

And he knew that he should have a name from the past, someone in mind that he'd like to spend some time with, borrowing his brain for a bit.

That gave him a moment's panic. Outside of the major players in the Hamburg part of the Beatles' life, he didn't know whom to choose. Certainly not Jurgen Vollmer, the German photographer who idolized the Beatles. Not Astrid Kircherr, the self-proclaimed existentialist who wore her angst and her art on her sleeve. Then who? Klaus Voorman, another art student from Hamburg's Institute of Fashion? Stu Sutcliffe, more of an artist than a musician—fated to stay behind in Hamburg and die?

They were all key players in the Hamburg road trips. But they were all too close.

Even if this was all perhaps a game of pretend, Jim knew he'd have to pick some minor character, some nebbish who could see what was going on with the Beatles, who they hung out with, without drawing too much attention on himself.

And then he came up with a name. Someone mentioned by George Harrison. A waiter in the Star Club, smack in the center of the red light district. George had called him a "good old sod." A bit player from the Beatle's Hamburg days. Just a name . . . Wolfgang Prater.

Wolfie, they called him.

Good enough, Jim hoped. Good enough to get close to the Beatles.

But as he waited, watching people come and go,

dark shapes bundled up against the gusty wind, Jim started to think that maybe he was getting yanked around.

It would serve me right, he thought. Alessandra is sick of my ranting.

Then he heard the great doors to the Physics Lab open. A pool of bright white light shot across the steps. Two people walked out and hurried down the steps toward him.

It was Martin and Alessandra!

Pug-faced Martin walked right up to Jim.

"Tiber, I want you to know one thing. I'm doing this for Alessandra. A favor, from one physics dweeb to another. You," Martin said, jutting a meaty finger into Jim's chest for emphasis, "are just along for the ride."

It's amazing, Jim thought. Absolutely incredible that this gorilla has a degree! And he's actually doing graduate work! Why, it's as if he were some new kind of genetic mutation, combining the intellect of a normal person with the couth and bearing of a lower primate. Martin was the modern intellect perfectly suited for the fast-food era. A belching Albert Einstein with a six-pack.

"Come on," Alessandra said, nervously looking right and left at the quad, dappled with the brilliant bright blotches made by the tungsten lamps. "Let's get going."

Jim would have enjoyed firing off a quick fusillade of *bon mots* at Martin, a positively crushing salvo of repartees and put-downs to make the boor stagger away, permanently damaged by truthful observation cuttingly delivered.

But since Martin was their ticket into the lab, he just smiled and kept his big mouth shut.

He kept it shut, even when he saw Martin put a chunky arm around Ali's shoulder, guiding them toward the northeast corner of the campus.

* * *

''These are the passes,'' Martin said, handing two plastic cards to Jim and Ali.

Jim looked at the all-white card with the small, indistinct photo. He laughed. ''This doesn't look anything like me.''

''They just check to see if you have a card,'' Martin barked. ''Then it's up to the computer card reader to open the main door.''

''We can do that by just sticking the card in?''

Martin shook his head. ''No, you need PINs, but I got the numbers for both of your cards.''

''I'm impressed,'' Jim said sarcastically.

They stood under a fat maple, still clutching most of its leaves. But even in that mottled light, Jim saw Martin redden. ''Look, Tiber, will you just keep your mouth shut?''

On cue, Alessandra touched Martin's arm, soothing the savage beast. At the same time, she shot Jim a warning glance.

Jim nodded, holding the white card. He looked ahead.

There was the Red Building, a bright, cherry color ringed with a half-dozen powerful lamps. Two security guards stood at the entrance gate, and Jim saw a few others patrolling the back.

''I think I once saw a World War II movie like this,'' he whispered to Alessandra, ''except they were trying to get outside instead of in.''

Martin looked around. ''Here are your PIN numbers,'' he said. He handed them each a slip of paper. Martin started off toward the building. ''And whatever you do, for Christ's sake, try to look like you belong.'' He looked back at Jim, his sneakers, his sweatshirt. ''Geeez!''

As they neared the gate, though, Jim felt comforted to have big, burly Martin walking up to the guards. Martin easily outweighed either guard, and he was nearly as tall. Jim watched Martin flash his badge to them. Alessandra hurried up to the fence and showed hers. The guard seemed to linger a moment looking at the card, and Ali's face.

Slowly—perhaps too slowly—Jim came up to the fence.

"What are you folks up to tonight?"

"We have to check the data spools," Martin said, obviously referring to some activity he'd done before. The questioning guard nodded knowingly. Don't tell me the guard's an expert in quantum physics too, Jim thought.

Jim held up his card, hoping to catch the light at just the right angle so that the glare would make the picture indistinct.

Instead, the card flipped out of his hand, sailed back and forth, before landing on the ground.

It was half on one side of the fence, and half on the other.

"Oh, I'll get it for you," the guard said.

"No, that's o—" Jim started to say, but the guard was already crouching, snapping up his card, picking it up, looking at it.

Jim felt the intense heat of Martin's eyes boring holes into him. Martin mouthed a word.

Ass . . . hole . . .

Then, the cavalry to the rescue. Alessandra spoke.

"You guys must get cold out there, spending the whole night."

Right, Jim thought. Poor babies . . .

The guard with his card gave it a quick glance. Then he looked up at Alessandra. "It's a job," he said staring into the fatal pools of her wide eyes.

Aren't women great, Jim thought. They're like some kind of secret weapon against men.

The guard handed him back his card through the gate.

"Okay," he said to his compadre. "Open the gate."

The gate slid open, and Martin thanked the guards as they hurried through. When the gate quickly clicked shut again behind them, Jim tried not to wonder whether it would be as easy to get out.

Martin walked up to the main door, and he inserted his card, hitting the keys for the security card. Then Alessandra followed, having memorized her number.

Jim had to stick the card in and dig out the now-crumpled piece of paper.

"Unbelievable . . ." Martin muttered, exasperated.

"Isn't it, though?" Jim said.

When all four numbers were entered, Martin hit another key that signaled the security system to open the door.

The door opened with an ominous whoosh. They walked inside. And then the door closed behind them with a disturbing finality.

They walked down a long corridor. Martin opened another door to some steps leading down, then went down two flights.

"There's an elevator," he whispered, "but then we'd risk running into anyone else working."

Martin led them to a generic corridor with brown metal doors, deserted, lit by powerful lights.

"I've only been here three times," Martin said. He sounded scared. "I'm not even sure we can get into the lab itself."

"Don't worry," Alessandra said, touching him again. "We'll figure out something."

Martin nodded, and Jim leaned closer to Alessandra.

"What did you have to promise that gorilla to get him to take us inside here?"

"Let *me* worry about that," she hissed back.

A funny thought occurred to Jim. Maybe Alessandra wasn't doing this just for Jim. No, this risk was too big for her to put her career on the line just for a friend.

It had to be something else.

She wanted to see the machine for herself. Maybe see it work.

He looked at her differently then, feeling that things weren't exactly under his control. Thinking—

This isn't just my junket.

After leading them through the mazelike patterns of rights and lefts, Martin stopped opposite two harmless-looking brown metal doors. The sign simply said Lab 217.

"Go ahead," Jim said. "Try the door knob."

Martin reached out a tentative, if meaty, hand and gave the knob a good twist.

It moved a few millimeters before coming to a dead stop.

"Shit," Martin said. "Damn thing's locked."

"Well, you wouldn't think they'd leave a time machine lying around, unprotected, like a floor waxer, do you?" Jim said.

Martin ignored the remark.

Then Alessandra dug a hand into Jim's arm.

"Someone's coming," she hissed.

"Great," Jim said, beginning to lose all faith in their venture.

Martin groaned.

"What should we do, Martin? Can we hide somewhere?"

"I—er, we—"

The footsteps were closer, just there, turning the corner and—

It was someone in a starched green custodial suit.

The man stopped and looked at them.

"Help you kids?"

For the longest moment no one said anything. Then Jim took a step forward. "We've got to get our Fibonacci sequences out of the computer in there, but this meathead," Jim said, indicating Martin, "forgot his key."

The custodian seemed to study them.

Alessandra stood beside Jim and spoke. "We were just trying to think if there was someone who could let us in . . . so we didn't have to go all the way back to the tower and then come back here."

"I can let you in," the man said, struck by his brainstorm.

"Would you?" Jim asked.

"Sure, why not?" He dug out a retractable key chain loaded with dozens of keys. "I've already cleaned up in there, but that's no problem. Just don't make a mess. . . ."

The custodian opened the door and switched on the light. He held the door open while they walked in.

"Just make sure the door is locked when you leave," he smiled.

Jim nodded. "Don't worry, we'll take care of everything."

The custodian left, shutting the door behind him.

Alessandra grabbed Jim's arm. "Whatever happens, Jim Tiber, we don't say a word about how we got in here." She turned to Martin. "Not a word?"

Jim nodded.

He walked to the center of the room and looked at the object in the center of the floor.

Feeling like a perfect fool, the most gullible idiot in the world, he touched it.

Then he turned and asked, sneering—

"Is *this* it?"

5

Henry Deems looked at the mirror inside his locker and gave his almost-vanished hair a quick combing, arraying the sparse strands in a uniform pattern that he hoped covered most of his bald head. Then he took out his black lunch box and the tightly wrapped bundle that contained his dirty uniform.

He shut the locker, and the slam echoed in the deserted basement of the Red Building.

Henry was happy with the way his last years of work—the daily grind, as he called it—were turning out. After nearly twenty-five years pushing real hard, he finally had a chance to take it a little easy.

Not that his job was all *that* easy. No, being custodian of the Red Building—with all its important scientists and labs—kept him hopping. Yes, sir. But not as much as his old position, cleaning the three big buildings in the center of campus.

Yes, this was much more . . . manageable.

And he enjoyed the special feeling of importance attached to this building. Special things went on here, and he was part of it.

It was a nice way to sail into the golden years, ready for his cozy condo in Boca Raton.

There was one drawback, though. The scientists in the Red Building kept real late hours, crazy hours. Why, tonight some of them just took a few hours off after nearly two days of working around the clock. They just left that lab, Room 217, looking like shit.

And then some students come in to do some more work!

If you ask me, Henry thought, it's the eggheads who do the hard work. Me, I got my shift and a six-pack. Just as long as my work got done, Henry thought. His supervisor always said, you know your business, Henry.

That he did. He gave a good day's work for an honest dollar, always had. Always would.

I'm from the old school, he told his wife. Not many like me—not in the U.S.A., at least.

He started up the stairs, preferring to walk up rather then take the elevator. Time to think . . . to shift gears.

Henry had two children.

Had.

They were gone, both in a different way. And even a passing thought of them—like now, after helping those students—caused him terrible pain. He felt it in his chest. A scary, empty feeling.

Jack, his boy, had died in the Texan Border War. No one called it a war. There were no wars anymore. Just like that Vietnam thing, they just called it some small skirmishes between the Americans and our neighbors to the south. Only when it threatened to blow up into a big problem, then the President—an old hand at such things—gave the Mexicans just what they wanted.

And that was a big chunk of Texas and California.

Nothing to it. Nothing at all, not when you're used to selling off your country in bits and pieces.

Only—

He thought, reaching the top of the steps and the door outside, why did my boy have to die? If it was hopeless, pointless to begin with, why in God's name did my boy have to die?

And then there was Sissy. His princess. Spoiled her rotten, his wife told him. But she was his sunshine, the one thing he looked forward to when coming home, even more than that first sip of cool beer and a Jersey Yankee game.

(Hell, he didn't blame the Yanks for leaving. How could they stay in the city? Who was there to come and see their games?)

But he lost his Sissy, too. First she just drifted into things Henry didn't understand. Some good things, he supposed, like the New Earth movement. Then something else, music that sounded like shrieks from hell. She started speaking a slang, a whole new language that closed him out from her world.

She left home.

Then, every now and then, she'd call for credits for her Moneycard, then *actual* money—which meant only one thing.

He stepped out into the air—so cool, cleansing, briefly blowing away the terrible thoughts, like insects buzzing around.

They found her body, small, withered, curled up in an abandoned building near the old Lincoln Center.

The drugs had left almost nothing to bury. She was skin and bones. A hollow, dead thing long before she died. They became drug-taking machines, the police told him. That's all they do. That's all that matters.

His princess.

He walked to the gate. Slowly, he forced himself to smile.

The guards turned toward him.

"Evening, boys. Getting a bit nippy, isn't it?"

"At least you're heading home, Henry," Toland, one of the guards, said.

Another guard pressed a button and the gate started slowly sliding open. And Henry waited. The quad was deserted.

"Everything okay in there?" Toland asked, as if just making conversation.

'Oh, sure. Fine. Some students came in before—" Henry smiled, glad to work someplace around young people, hard-working young people with a future. A real future. "They forgot their key to one of the labs so I let them in."

The gate clicked completely open.

Henry felt Toland looking at him. The air was colder. Then Toland came close to him. The faint light picked up an unpleasant scowl on his face. "You're not supposed to do that, are you? It's not procedure."

Henry shrugged. "I guess not. But what's the harm? They'd have to go all the way back to their dorm and—"

"*What* lab did you let them into?"

"Two-seventeen. On the second sublevel. I don't think there's anything wrong—"

Henry watched Toland hurry over to a small kiosk and pick up a phone. He stood there, frozen, wondering—

Did I do something wrong? I was just trying to be helpful, help the kids out—

Harry heard the gate closing before him. Slowly. Until it latched shut, locked, with an ominous click.

Jim laughed.

A time machine. Oh, sure.

It was a large, spacious lab, impressive with a bank of computers off to one side, and one wall completely filled with flat black equipment, dark and inscrutable.

But in the center of the room there was a chair. The supposed time travel device.

"I think, guys," Jim said, "that we've just wandered into the dental research department. It looks like they're trying to crack the painless root canal problem."

But then he saw Alessandra look at the chair. She ran her fingers up to a small cap near an adjustable headrest. Then she turned and walked to the wall and looked at the enormous black boxes. She reached out and touched the dials, letting her fingers run along the smooth, black surface. A few lights were on, including one small red light that blinked on and off.

"Unbelievable," Alessandra said. "It's really true."

Martin, standing right near the door, looked uncomfortable. "Okay, we can go now. You've seen it. It's real. Now let's get the hell out of here before anyone—"

"Real?" Jim said, turning from Martin to Alessandra. "What are you talking about? You mean this?" He tapped the chair. "*This* is a time machine?"

"No," Alessandra said. "Not a time machine." She walked over to the computers. From the green glow reflected on her face, Jim saw that one screen was on. "I explained that to you, Jim. You don't go anywhere."

"C'mon . . . let's go," Martin stammered, looking nervously at the door.

"This is it?" Jim said, pointing at the chair.

Ali nodded.

Martin edged near the door. "Let's—"

"Disintegrating neutrons," Alessandra said.

"What?" Jim responded.

"It's based on the principle of disintegrating neutrons. Miller's Theory of Causality."

Jim smiled, trying not to seem too doltish. "A brief explanation, if you wouldn't mind."

He saw Martin standing closer to the lab door, ears cocked for the sound of anyone coming.

Ali stopped her prowl of the lab, and Jim could almost hear the synapses firing in her mind as she pieced together all the elements in the lab.

"Time is made up of events," she said. "And to a physicist, the fingerprint of an event, the trail, is the change in the status of subatomic particles. Electrons are exchanged, or released. Neutrinos are produced."

"Neutrinos?"

Alessandra grinned and looked right at Jim. "An elementary particle that pops out when other particles decay. Don't you know *any* quantum physics? It's the primal action of every event, the bedrock of chronology, according to Miller."

"So . . ." Jim said, trying to hurry her along to

some explanation of how this odd-looking chair might have something to do with moving through time.

"The neutrino is a tracer particle. Each point in time—at a specific location—produces a unique, telltale tracer of neutrinos. If Miller's theory is right, the sequence of time—the subatomic events—are a loop. A big Möbius strip—like the expansion and contraction of the universe."

The beginning of an idea bloomed on Jim's face. "And if it's a loop, you can tap into it at any point?"

Ali grinned at Jim's offering. "Sort of. But then," she said, turning away, studying the computer screen again, "I'm no Stephen Hawking, Jim. But that machine over there," she said, gesturing at the solid wall of flat black hardware, "looks suspiciously like a tachyon generator."

"It is," Martin added, risking a glance away from his watch at the door.

"Thanks," Alessandra said, without much sincerity.

"Come on, Tiber," Martin bellowed, trying to reclaim his authority in their expedition. "You make her get the hell out of here. It's my neck and—"

"Hang on, Martin. We're just getting to the good stuff. You were saying, Ali . . . a tachyon—?"

"It's the golden egg of quantum physics. A subatomic particle that travels faster than the speed of light. It can move in any direction in the Miller Time Loop—theoretically, that is. And my guess is—"

Martin opened the door.

"Will you shut that?" Ali snapped at him.

"I thought I heard—"

"My guess is that the scientists here have found—or are close to finding—a way to tie brain waves to tachyons. Shouldn't be all that difficult." She looked up, thinking it over. "That is if they found some way to bind it to the Cerenkov radiation—"

"Piece of cake," Jim added.

"Amazing," she said, lost in wonder. "Then that

would mean that they've solved the imaginary mass problem. Incredible . . ."

"That one always bothered me too, babe. So now that you got a handle on what's happening here, are we ready to give it a go?"

That was all Martin had to hear. He stormed over, his face flushed, a colorful mixture of fear and anger. He looked, Jim thought, like he was going to explode.

"What did you just say, Tiber?" he said. "What the fuck was that?"

Jim smiled at the hulking Martin. Bad knee or no, Martin could do a good impersonation of a charging rhino.

"We're going to give the machine a try, of course. That's the whole point in coming here, Martin me boy."

"The hell you are." Martin reached out and grabbed Jim by his shirt. He effortlessly whipped Jim close to his beet-red face. "You touch anything here and I'll—"

Alessandra started hitting the keys of the computer.

"Sure looks like it's up and running . . ." she said, staring at one of the monitors. "Sure . . . it's all been left on . . . for some reason."

Martin, seeing her, quickly released Jim.

"Hey, what are you doing, Ali? Stop that."

But she ignored him and hurried to the black boxes, the suspected tachyon generator, and checked a few of the switches.

"Yup, everything is up and running."

Martin took giant steps toward her, his fist balled.

Jim went to stop him. Not that he had any real chance of doing *that*.

Martin took another step, and then the room was filled with the sound of an alarm. A high-pitched sound, loud and shrieking.

"Oh, shit," Martin said. "I'm getting out of here."

Alessandra looked at Jim, a glum expression marring her beautiful face.

Martin dashed out of the lab.

"What do you think?" she asked.

We could leave, Jim thought. But this was a once-in-a-lifetime opportunity. Go for it, a small, impractical voice inside his head suggested. After all, what did he have to lose?

"Hell . . . we're already here. And I doubt we could get out of the building with that alarm blasting."

She smiled. "Right. Let's give it a shot."

Jim tried to settle himself in the chair.

The alarm made it sound like the building was on fire, or ready to self-destruct.

"If you say 'open wide' I'll bop you one."

Ali laughed and pulled the bowl-shaped cap down snugly onto Jim's head. "Just relax, Tiber. I'd guess that this has a sonic sleep inducer so once it's running—"

"I won't feel a thing, right, Doc?"

"Hopefully."

She went back to the computer screen.

"What's your date?" she asked.

My date, he thought. He had wrestled with that for a long time. It boiled down to a case of figuring out where, and when, the Beatles had changed, when they had become so different from all the other English pop groups.

It wasn't during their first outing to Hamburg, even though that's when they met Astrid Kircherr and Jurgen Vollmer. No, they came back from that wild and woolly engagement in the Kaiserkeller, still just another band.

The big change came, quite clearly, after their second gig in Hamburg. Their fabled run at the infamous Star Club. They came back to the UK for a tryout with EMI set up by their adoring manager, Brian Epstein. And from that moment on, they were a different band. They wrote their own music, toying with rhythms, melodies, and sound in an untutored but completely experimental way. Their producer/den mother, George Martin, held their hands through their first recordings.

But from those first sessions, the Beatles claimed the recording studio as their creative domain.

Right after Hamburg . . .

Jim knew what date he wanted.

"May 7, 1962," he said. "Do you know how to punch that in?"

Alessandra's fingers moved over the keys. "No. I've just got to hope that they have some built-in prompts." She spoke loudly, ignoring the high-pitched tweet of the alarm. The computer made a bleeting sound in answer. "Oh . . ." Ali said. "I see how they have it set up. Each point in time is assigned a frequency. It's like using a shortwave." Jim couldn't see her too well. But he heard her hitting the keys. "There. Alright. Now, the place, James?"

"Hamburg, *mein fräulein.*"

More tapping. "No. That's not right. I must be—" She hit the keys with lightning speed, the clackety-clack competing with the alarm.

"What's wrong? Can't you—"

"Got it! They're using sidereal coordinates. Okay. . . . Not so bad. I guess they expect a lot of business once they get the bugs out."

Bugs? thought Jim. Who said anything about bugs? What kind of bugs . . . ?

The siren kept wailing.

He thought he heard footsteps.

"Ali," he said quietly.

She looked up from the terminal, her face unmarred by any concern over the alarm or their fate.

"Yes?" she said, smiling at him.

"I appreciate this. Even if we do have to transfer to Miami State U."

"Sure. What's life without a little adventure?"

She went back to the keyboard.

There were definitely footsteps outside.

"A name, Jim. And a birthdate. Quickly."

Jim said, "Herr Wolfgang Prater, *bitte*. Born November 12, 1937."

Ali hit the keys.

Just as the lab door opened.

Dr. Elliot McManus pushed past the growing crowd of students at the gate, all of them drawn by the piercing sound of the alarm. Some wore heavy fall coats while others stood sleepy-eyed in robes and slippers. They were talking, laughing, craning their necks to see what was going on.

McManus roughly pushed past them and up to the gate.

"Come on," he snapped at the guards. "Get a move on. Open it up, will you?"

He had to wait for the gate to lumber open, slowly, deliberately. And he wondered, then, whether this was the work of that other lab . . . whoever the hell they were.

We shouldn't have left, McManus thought.

As soon as the gate had opened wide enough, McManus slid through and ran up to the door. Toland, the head security guard, held it open for him.

"Dr. Jacob and Dr. Beck are already inside," the guard said, joining McManus on his jog into the building, hurrying to the elevators.

McManus wanted to tell Toland that he was in big trouble, that whatever idiot was responsible for this was going to get crucified. But that could wait for later. If the Time Lab was sabotaged it would all be academic anyhow. None of it would matter. Not a bit.

He already assumed that the machine was damaged, perhaps destroyed. It was the shielding he was worried about. If that was damaged, if that was destroyed, then it *really* was all over. McManus could ignore all the changes outside the lab, all the chaos, the besieged city, the fence around Columbia—a fence!—and the new world order.

He, and the rest of his team, treated it as an illusion . . . temporary. Glitches and snafus—changes that could be corrected.

Except if they weren't corrected soon, the changes would last forever.

Now he started blaming himself. They never should have left the lab. Even if it helped for them to leave and actually *see* the extent and the speed of the changes.

It was incredible.

And dangerous. The existence of the Time Lab—in terms of their own memory of it—was at risk every time they left the building. Outside the shielded building, their memory was hostage to all the changes. Only a computer link to the Time Lab kept them posted about what was and *wasn't* real . . . they had to take what the datalink told them on faith. It told them the way things were supposed to be.

McManus marveled at his memories . . . how many of them were new . . . false . . . .

I grew up with the Euro-Asian Compact, McManus thought. Except it never was supposed to happen. *Hadn't* happened, actually, until two days ago.

I was teaching college when the Mexican conflict broke out, McManus thought, still trying to accept the reality of the situation.

Except that the Time Lab computer—linked to the shielded lab—told him that the Mexican fiasco was also a brand new rewrite of history.

It was terribly disconcerting.

After their brief tour outside—to an increasingly alien world—McManus and his team had made an important decision. They couldn't afford to go outside any longer. They were vital to the project—only they could save time as it was supposed to be. It was just too risky to go outside . . . to absorb the quickly accelerating changes.

They would have to stay in the lab. Live there. All the time. Until it was all over.

And McManus didn't even have an idea what their chance of success might be. They were alone. Against a better-organized, better-financed—a more powerful—enemy.

And he had another fear.

Would enough changes occur so that the university might abandon them, stop food and water? How long could the Time Lab survive then? That was one of the things McManus had been working on, checking last-minute things before bottling the team up in the Time Lab.

Fortunately, the Time Lab was self-sufficient as far as supplying electricity. But it was otherwise completely vulnerable . . . increasingly so as lab assistants drifted in and out of the building, constantly suffering the sudden absorption of rewritten history.

Soon the doors would have to be locked.

It was just too risky. . . .

And—as if that wasn't enough of a problem—now there was this break-in. What was it? Spies, sabotage? Just what the hell was going on here?

He waited for the elevator. He looked at Toland.

Was he an innie or an outie? McManus wondered. Had the head security guard been outside during the past twelve hours, missing most of the violent changes that had taken place outside. Had he blithely—and unknowingly—had his memories, and his world, changed?

Or had he been on duty in here? Protected.

McManus decided to test him.

"Nice fence," he said.

"Excuse me?" Toland answered.

"The fence . . . around the university," McManus said. McManus had an altered memory that the fence had been there for years, well before he had arrived on campus.

But the Time Lab's computer told him that it wasn't true. It wasn't real history.

The guard looked at him.

"Excuse me, Doctor . . . what *fence?*"

McManus smiled. Thinking . . . well, at least the shielding is still up and running.

And then the elevator was there.

6

"We don't have to do this—not if you don't want to."

Alessandra pulled the metal cap tight against Jim's head, fitting it as flush as a beanie.

"Getting nervous?" shc asked.

"No, I just thought that the alarm might be causing you some concern."

She hurried back to the computer terminal. "As if we're not already in big trouble? Might as well see"—she threw a switch—"what this thing can do."

Jim muttered, "I just hope it doesn't have any lethal side effects. . . ."

"Hmmm?" Ali said, not really listening. "What's that?"

"Nothing. I just said—"

The black boxes against the wall—the suspected tachyon generators—blinked to electronic alertness. Suddenly the flat black face of the wall was filled with assorted digital readouts, all in various muted colors—pale green, faded magenta, washed-out yellow.

Jim felt a tingling on his head. He wished he could scratch just under the cap.

The alarm kept shrieking. It occurred to him that possibly it had nothing to do with them. Maybe there was a fire, or something.

But then he heard the sound of lots of steps coming down the hall.

"The jig is up, sweetheart," he said, imitating the hard-boiled Bogie.

He heard another switch being thrown—an ominous sound, terrifyingly loud amidst the quiet hums and whistles of the lab.

"There," Alessandra said. "It's all ready—I think."

"What happens now?"

"Just say 'when,' " she grinned.

He heard the lab door fly open, smacking rudely against the wall behind him. And he heard angry voices.

But he kept on looking at Alessandra.

"When."

Ali watched the doctors run in, followed by a small army of security guards. They all stopped at the entrance, expecting, perhaps, to face mad terrorists.

She looked down at the computer screen. The cursor blinked a prompt to "Press Enter to Transmit, Esc to Abort Program."

"Stop! Right there!" she heard one of the doctors yell.

I never was too good at taking orders, Ali thought.

She smiled, nodded, and then pressed Enter.

Jim's first observation was that Ali must have done something terribly wrong. Nothing was happening. Absolutely nothing. He heard the doctors yelling something, though it sounded indistinct, almost muffled. He turned and saw Ali standing, looking over at the doctors, then back to her computer screen.

In fact, Jim was just about to sheepishly slide out of the dentist's chair, pop off the metallic beanie, and take his medicine. What category would this fall in? he wondered. Collegiate hijinks . . . or something far more serious and irrevocable?

Then, for no reason, he felt sleepy.

He fought to keep his eyes open but it was impossible. They were too heavy, and the chair suddenly felt so comfortable. Cozy. Just for a moment, he thought. I'll just rest my eyes for a tiny . . . moment.

As soon as he closed them he realized that this

wasn't sleep. He was completely aware of everything that had happened, aware and worried. There was none of that pleasant drifting away to dreamland.

No losing consciousness.

He couldn't see anything, just a murky blackness irradiated by the neon-red flashes of what he supposed were the blood vessels of his eyelids.

Then there was a light.

A big, bright light. Indistinct at first, then slowly resolving itself into a brilliant, piercing, almost painful light.

A brilliant white light. It reminded him of something.

That's it! he thought. That's the whole ball of wax. It's all over. Sure. A bright white light . . . that's right out of the Tibetan Book of the Dead. I'm about to cross over to the other side.

A bit prematurely, he thought glumly.

If he had been walking to this light, he would have tried stopping. But as far as he could make out, he was just floating. He looked down to where his body should have been. But there was nothing. As far as he could tell he was seeing without any means to see. No body. No eyes.

Great. He wondered just what the hell he had found so damned important about the Beatles. They certainly didn't seem all that important *now*.

Something was *very* wrong. Maybe dummo Martin picked the wrong lab. Yeah, maybe they went into the Illegal Experiments with Humans Lab. To the Zombie-Making Machine. A cheering thought, that! His only hope might be if the good doctors knew how to turn the thing off and get him back . . . and out of here. . . .

Wherever *here* was.

"Don't touch anything," one of the scientists barked.

Ali backed away from the terminal. She saw Jim sitting in the chair, blacked out, sleeping like a baby.

The scientist, a short, gaunt man with a great, bald spot on top of his head and longish, unkempt hair dangling down in the back, looked at the terminal.

"Christ, it's too late. Dr. Beck, would you please take a look at him?"

A burly, no-nonsense woman in a white coat walked over to where Jim sat and leaned over the chair. She pulled back Jim's eyelids and flashed a light into his eyes. Then another scientist—his eyebrow furrowed—went to the side wall and examined the colorful readouts flashing there, muttering to himself like an old farmer counting eggs.

The security guards seemed ill at ease, standing there with their heavy pulse rifles slung, ready for kick-ass action. One of them coughed.

Finally, the wizened scientist at the computer looked up.

"Oh, you may go," he said, looking at the guards, ignoring Ali. "Perhaps post someone outside. . . ." He nodded at the security officers, who didn't immediately react. "Go on . . . it's okay," he insisted. "We're obviously too late. You may go."

"And the student?" Toland asked, gesturing toward Alessandra, with the butt of his chunky rifle.

"She'll need to stay here . . . for a while." The doctor forced a quick smile. "You may leave. Thank you."

Then the guards backed away and trudged out.

After a long silence, the gaunt scientist turned to Ali, as if seeing her for the first time. "You have no idea what you and your friend have blundered into, Miss—"

"Alessandra Moreau," she whispered.

The scientist—his plastic security badge identified him as Dr. Elliot McManus—nodded. "It is very unfortunate for you . . . but much more unfortunate for your friend there," he said, gesturing at the chair. "But it may be the most beneficial mistake of your thoughtless young lives."

McManus turned away from her, back to the terminal.

"But now let me see just where you've sent the boy. . . ."

Jim was in the light, swimming in it. A faint warmth surrounded him. He saw that it was made up of hundreds of shimmering strands, like optical fibers, glowing, brilliant. They all seemed to be moving.

Then he turned around.

At least it felt like he turned around. There was no sense of motion, of turning his body.

He turned and saw that now he was moving along one of the strands. And there was no feeling connected with it. No fear, no sense of motion, no wonder, no amazement. It was completely undreamlike. He was numb.

It felt similar to Buddhist detachment. He wanted nothing, he needed nothing.

I *am* nothing, he surmised.

But just as that stupendous thought suggested itself—in a curiously detached way—the movement ended, the light faded.

It was dark. Hazy.

No. It was smoky. He could smell it, the smoke, and—

He blinked. He felt himself blink. Felt the eye close, the lashes touch.

And when he opened his eyes he was looking down on a porky man wearing a forest-green cap that looked lifted from the spring collection of Robin Hood.

There was a loud knock on the lab door. Ali watched Dr. Beck hurry to open it.

Ali stood in her place on the floor, not knowing where else to put herself, while Toland came in, clasping a ragged-looking Martin.

"Dr. McManus, we caught this one trying to get out the back."

McManus barely looked up from the terminal.

"Yes, fine . . ." He waved his hand. "I won't have any need of him—at least not now. Keep him in the building, though." He crouched down, close to the monitor. "Just in case."

Ali watched Martin start to say something through his pulpy, bruised face. But the guard quickly whisked him away.

Ali decided she'd better try to resolve just what her status was. So far this building seemed to be a law unto itself.

"Dr. McManus . . . perhaps I can explain. My friend, Jim Tiber—"

"Elliot!" Dr. Jacob called from across the room, sounding horrified. "Transmission is complete."

"Successful?" McManus asked.

"It appears so."

"Dr. Beck, is the boy all right?" McManus asked.

The woman bent over Jim's body. She checked his eyes again, and then his pulse. "Everything is normal, Dr. McManus."

McManus stepped back, rubbed the back of his neck, and nodded. "Good . . . good. Well, at least your friend made it . . . made it to—" He leaned back toward the monitor. "To May 7, 1962." The scientist shook his head and turned to Ali. "What in the world could be the importance of that date?"

Ali watched him walk up to her. McManus was a little man, his skin tight over a skeletal face. There were great puffy bags under his eyes and a crazy network of red lines in his eyes. "An odd choice," he said tiredly. "And tell me, Ms. Moreau, what is the location?"

She cleared her throat. "Hamburg. The Star Club."

McManus looked confused.

"Hamburg?" McManus pulled a chair away from the desk and sat down tiredly. "Hamburg? Why on earth did he go to Hamburg?"

Ali smiled, hoping to evoke a similar reaction from the scientist.

Instead he sat there, morose, preoccupied, and distant.

"You see," she said, "well, it's hard to explain. But the reason he wanted to go to Hamburg is—"

She looked around the room. The other two scientists—while still going on with their work—were looking over at her, their ears cocked for the explanation.

Then she just came out with it.

"It has to do with the Beatles. He wanted—needed—to meet the Beatles."

McManus shook his head back and forth. "Poor boy. Poor stupid, silly boy." Then McManus made a small, breathy laugh, an ominous laugh. "Is he ever in for a surprise."

Alessandra quickly looked over at the other scientists to see if they, too, were laughing. But their faces were set, grim.

Whatever humor McManus had discovered in the situation was clearly lost on them. Then McManus reached out and took her hand. His fingers felt cold, undernourished. "Now, tell me dear. Everything. About you and the boy, this Jim Tiber, and why he wanted to"—McManus sighed—"travel in time."

Jim stared at the man. Porky the Pig as Robin du Bois. The man's face was—for all the smoke—glowing beet red. He displayed a mouthful of teeth, gleaming, and his tongue danced around crazily in his oversized mouth as he spoke.

In German.

"Ich hätte gern ein Dinkelacker!"

From the look on the man's face, it wasn't the first time he had issued the request. And the man, a wood sprite gone to seed from too many tankards and creamy pastries, turned to his companions. He said something that Jim couldn't make heads or tails of.

Jim's German—sufficient to obtain a hotel room with a nearby toilet—was lost. Gone.

Jim brought his hand to his face. And he knew that Ali had done it.

He felt a moustache. I've got a moustache! he thought. Unbelievable! He looked around the room. The place was filled with loud customers, and waiters hustling great mugs of beer through the maze of tables, surrounded by billowing smoke and music.

Jim looked at the stage. A band. Four guys singing. "Good Golly Miss Molly."

And none of them looked like the Beatles. He looked at the drum. Big swirling letters.

Cliff Bennett and the Rebel Rousers.

Uh-oh, Jim thought. I screwed up.

The man at the table stood up, rising majestically to his troll-like height of five feet, two inches. Jim expected that the man would have to look up at him, except they were nearly eye to eye.

I'm somebody else, Jim thought. Somebody much shorter.

"Will you get me a beer or will I have to get the manager?"

The man had plastered his face right up against Jim's. And after Jim took a step backward and wiped the spittle from his cheek, he realized something.

I just understood the man, he thought. One minute it was nonsense. And then . . . I *understood* him. Perfectly. Even though the man wasn't speaking English . . . I just *knew* what he said.

The man's head, meanwhile, looked like it was going to pop off his rotund body.

"*Yah, yah,*" Jim said, and he turned around. In the back he saw a long wood bar, crowded by people taking their liquid nourishment closer to the kegs. But he also saw the other waiters walking to the side and getting service from a woman who slapped the frothy steins down with frightening speed.

Jim hurried over there, happy to get away from the angry customer. And as he walked, Jim tried to deal with the weird sensations.

It felt real. All of it. The smell of the beer-stained wood floor, the loud, blunt rock and roll. The sound of people laughing . . . talking. Real.

Almost.

It felt just a bit off-center, like the time he went back to his family's house in Falmouth, the town he spent his wonder-years in. His family had been long gone and another family lived there.

Same house, same porch, same block. Even the same trees lined the street.

It was all the same, but different . . . as though it was filmed through some gauze constructed of equal parts nostalgia and barely perceptible changes. A touch of fresh paint here, some new bushes there.

This felt the same way. It wasn't like a holo-movie. But, man, it wasn't normal life either!

Then there was this new body. This new *short* body.

It was out of shape, for one thing. The guy had no muscle tone. There was a nagging heavy feeling in the chest, a dry, foul taste on his tongue. It took Jim a moment to flash on what that meant . . .

Jeezus, I'm a smoker.

The moustache was okay. At least, until he got a look at it in the mirror. But his new size! I'm a shrimpy waiter.

It could be worse. I could have plugged into the bartender. That would have made for some mighty angry customers while I fumbled with their orders, he thought as he anxiously surveyed the clientele.

He got behind another waiter.

"Some night," the man said, turning to Jim.

Jim nodded.

Then the waiter picked up his drinks and flew away. The bartender, her face framed by dry tight blonde curls, spoke.

"Yes, Wolfie?"

Jim looked at her. Wolfie . . . Right, I'm Wolfgang Prater.

And she's—

The name came to him from out of the blue. Trude. She likes to hump the waiters. She's humped me.

Jim smiled. "Four Dinkelackers," he said in

smoothly delivered German. She smiled, and deftly filled four mugs.

Jim turned around and looked at the small stage. It looked like the Star Club, just like in the photos he studied. And it was obviously Hamburg—or at least someplace in Deutschland.

Cliff Bennett and his Rebel Rousers segued into a bland rendition of "Kansas City."

But—he wondered—

Where were the Beatles?

Trude slapped the mugs down on a tray.

He turned around and decided to ask her.

"Where are the Beatles?"

Trude laughed.

She shook her head. "Wolfie . . . don't you remember? You told Weissleder that they'd be here just before their show . . . you had such a time with them last night."

Right, Jim thought. Weissleder. A nasty son-of-a-bitch. The Beatles should be here. After the Rebel Rousers. That's what *I* told Weissleder.

And despite his total confusion, Jim smiled.

I *know* the Beatles. I'm one of their pals. A confidant.

Neat-o. He grinned to himself. *Neat-o*. . . .

He picked up the tray and hurried back to the table and his sputtering, impatient customer.

7

Bits and pieces of someone else's memories started to creep in.

Someone shouted, "Hello, Wolfie," and Jim turned, responding quite naturally to this new name, hearing the German as if it was his mother-tongue. He saw someone waving, and Jim raised an arm and waved back.

For a second he didn't have a clue who the person was.

Then there was a name.

Frederick. He works on the docks. He favors the Star Club for its fabled ability to attract young *frauleins*. The music, though, he always complains, is "too loud."

It was as if some trace memories in the host's mind were left over, like forgotten crates left behind after a big move.

Jim smiled at burly Frederick but kept on tending to his tables. It would be a mistake, he thought, to get into any protracted conversation. He was having enough trouble just taking drink orders and getting people their change.

For the first time he felt scared.

What if I don't get back? he thought. What if I'm stuck here, circa 1962? There were probably worse places to be—but he wasn't too happy with Wolfie's humble station in life, or his physique. What did the next decade hold? Beatlemania, of course. The Kennedy assassination. Vietnam. The end of the American century. The Nixon Years. The Reagan Years. The Quayle Scandal.

And I'd be middle-aged at the time of the final assault on the planet's environment, he thought.

I could go to Woodstock. The thought made him grin.

That might be interesting.

But it didn't seem real . . . not the way real life was supposed to feel. There was something artificial . . . something distant about how this felt to him.

No. He didn't want to stay here.

But, okay . . . that was no problem. Alessandra would probably only give him three, maybe four hours before yanking his wayward mind forward in time. She wouldn't let him languish in the past for *too* long. If he was lucky, he'd get some great background information on the Beatles. If not, well, they could always try again.

Maybe.

"Ein schnapps, bitte," someone barked from a smoke-shrouded table.

Jim turned, still amazed how natural the German sounded. Must be something to do with borrowing someone's brain, he figured.

"Ein schnapps?" Jim said.

The man nodded, and Jim hurried to Trude. For the first time Jim looked at the big clock hanging above the bar. It was circular, outlined with blue neon, almost hidden on a cluttered wall filled with shelves groaning under the weight of ornate Bavarian beer steins, colorful serving trays, and a scattering of record sleeves from groups that had played the Star and gone onto some minute degree of fame.

It was ten-thirty.

Perhaps, Jim thought, the Beatles won't show up tonight.

Great. Then I'd get to spend a pointless evening

serving northern Deutschland's finest lager while listening to a band that didn't make it.

"Why so glum, *liebchen?*" Trude said, caressing Jim's cheek, drawing him out of his reverie. It seemed clear that he and Trude—as improbable a couple as they might make—enjoyed an intimate relationship. Looking at her pleasant, round face mounted above a well-packed dirndl, Jim hoped that his visit to the past didn't stretch too far into the wee hours.

"I'm just wondering where the Beatles are . . . I hope—"

She smiled. "You didn't hear? They just showed up! Just minutes ago, Wolfie." She leaned close. "And a good thing for them, too," she said, gesturing to a morose-looking figure sitting at the other, darker end of the bar. "Mr. Weissleder would not have taken too kindly to their disappointing all their fans."

Jim smiled—the act feeling strange, the way the face curled itself into a pleasant wrinkle, the small whiskers touching his lips.

It's not my smile, he thought.

Cliff Bennett and the Rebel Rousers finished their lackluster set to polite, if not prolonged, applause.

Jim hustled the schnapps over to his customer, who rewarded Jim with a two-deutschmark tip. He didn't know whether that was generous or not. If I stay here for long, he thought, I'll have to get a handle on the local currency.

The stage lights went out, and then quickly came up again. A man was there, dressed in a sleek gray suit.

The crowd stirred unpleasantly as he started to tell a goofy joke.

"Guten abend, meine damen und herren," the comic began. "I can see we have a very intelligent crowd at the Star tonight. Very intelligent. Now, if the waiters will please see that no one tries to leave during my act. Just a few jokes, and then the Beatles—" The audience started applauding at the mention of the group.

"Why, thank you! Yes, we have trouble getting these Beatles to come back here every night. . . . Seems like they get lost about a block south of here."

There was some laughter at this, confusing Jim. Then he remembered where he was. The Reeperbahn was known for its raunchy clubs, but it was more renowned for its wild and woolly red-light district. And all the Beatles admitted sampling its pleasures.

Some more people entered the club, talking loudly, ignoring the unfunny comedian. Jim turned and looked at the newcomers. There was a woman with dark, straight hair. And a shorter man, wearing a skullcap.

The woman's face was oddly familiar.

Jim stared, barely able to see her as she navigated the dark aisles to a table right next to the stage. Some of the stage light spilled on her face. And then Jim knew who she was.

Astrid Kircherr.

Jim felt the powerful aura of the woman from halfway across the room. It was Astrid Kircherr . . . and she was beautiful. She had met the Beatles through Klaus Voorman during the group's first visit to Hamburg in 1961. And she had fallen in love with Stu Sutcliffe, a sometime Beatle.

Now, it was a year later. Stu was dead from a tumor pressing against his brain. There could be little joy in her coming to see the Beatles.

The comedian, sputtering, as eager to be off the stage as the audience was to see him go, finished to scattered applause and donkey noises.

He paused at the curtain . . . and announced the Beatles.

The stage lights went out again, then on.

And there they were. Looking so young . . . Paul's baby face, and George still a kid. And Jim saw the drummer, Pete Best, arranging his drums, not knowing what he was about to miss.

Only John Lennon radiated something else. He came to the microphone—there was only one on the small stage backed with a black curtain.

"Und now," he barked out in a wild parody of a Prussian general, "you vill hear a bit of rock und roll."

On cue, Paul counted.

"One, two, three . . ."

George's guitar spat out a clean, if straightforward, lick. Pete Best slapped the drums lackadaisically. John leaned close to the mike again. He opened his mouth . . . and wailed—

"Well shake it up baby, now . . . twist and shout . . . Come on, comeon, comeon, comeon, baby, now . . ."

Lennon's voice was electric—a perfect, razor-sharp rock and roll voice. Supposedly, he never liked his singing, preferring to do one take of a song and forget it. But it was a powerful instrument for rock and roll.

The other Beatle boys gave choirboy support behind him, repeating "twist and shout . . . shake it up, baby." The girls at the nearby tables were moving, shaking, ready to jump out of their seats.

Just wait, Jim thought. You guys ain't seen *nothing* yet. In about a year you'll have whole countries wriggling in their seats.

They came to the middle eight bars. George and Paul, grinning at each other in what became the Beatles trademark—joy through rock and roll—and did their best to lay down some killer riffs.

But it was their raw energy, and not their musicanship, that made the song so damn exciting. When John finished, squealing the last note of "shout," everyone at the Star Club started cheering, whistling, banging their mugs on the scratched-up wooden tables.

And Jim stood there, clapping, grinning from ear to ear—(With someone else's face!)—thinking that this was the greatest moment in his life.

They were alone. There were just Dr. Beck, who was keeping a close watch on Jim's body, and Dr. Jacob, who drifted in and out of the conversation while examining the tachyon generator on the wall. McManus seated Alessandra in a chair and sat down facing her, a very serious expression on his face, not interrupting as she tried to explain why she and Jim snuck into the lab.

"I guess—I don't know—I guess I thought that since I'm in the Physics Department, what harm could there be?"

From behind her she heard Dr. Beck quietly laugh. McManus nodded.

"You, er, didn't wonder about all the security? Didn't that tell you something about what is going on here?"

Alessandra smiled. Sitting here, like this, reminded her of countless heart-to-heart talks with her father. Dad always tried unsuccessfully to reason with her. The family's summers in Bar Harbor were wonderful idylls interrupted only by an endless stream of fatherly lectures on responsibility, maturity, the importance of obeying rules and doing what one should.

All stuff she didn't give a damn about.

Like the time she took the sailboat out all day . . . worrying everyone sick, showing up at sunset with a nasty, brilliant red sunburn. "Now, Alessandra, you know you're not supposed to take the boat out on your own. I'm very disappointed . . . very—"

There was always disappointment . . . and always punishment. Nothing too severe. Her father loved her too much for that. And, after a while, even she wondered why she always pushed against the walls, testing the limits of her world. She had everything—the best schools, summers in Bar Harbor, week-long trips to Europe for the various opera festivals which were her father's passion. Money was no object. Never would be.

So why did she make so much trouble?

Then she realized the answer. Later, after she had left home.

All the money, all the houses, all the cars. All of

Daddy's golden horde, all that happened because of how her father was, how he *acted*.

And later, she learned that his nickname—in Washington, on Wall Street, in London—was "the Pirate."

The nickname created a picture in her mind, a picture from an old Burt Lancaster film—in brilliant technicolor—of a buccaneer hanging rakishly from the mast, the skull and crossbones flapping in the air.

He had taken chances. Risked things.

And so had her grandfather . . . a resistance fighter in France who stuck it to the Nazis and lived to laugh about it.

It was in the blood. She knew that staying safe and cozy wouldn't take her where she wanted to go.

She listened to McManus talk to her. For all the man's consternation, he was having a difficult time being tough on her. The thought that she might be kicked out of school didn't fill her with any great terror. With her family name, and her grade point average, almost any school would accept her even if she was a time bandit.

"This is all very confusing," McManus said. "Why would you do this—this breaking in?" The tired-looking scientist paused and smiled sadly. "But that's all irrelevant now. I'm afraid I have to explain everything . . ."

Alessandra nodded. She sensed the other doctors shifting uneasily, looking over at her, and she suddenly felt anxious. She could see Jim's body, the rhythmic rise and fall of his chest as he went on peacefully sleeping.

Dr. Beck checked the insulin rack that stood next to Jim.

Alessandra blinked. She looked at McManus. "Coma . . . ?" she said quietly. Then louder. "He's in a coma?" she asked. She stood up and started to walk over to Jim. But McManus quickly reached out and grabbed one of her arms. He shook his head.

"No . . . he's not in a coma." The scientist looked

away. "It's something else I have to tell you. Something—"

There was a knock on the door. "Come in," McManus ordered.

Toland, the security guard, walked into the lab.

"My two men at the main door are sending me some pretty funny reports, Doctor. They tell me they can see stuff going on outside, things changing."

McManus nodded. "Yes . . . I know." Alessandra looked at McManus, looked at the man's sunken eyes. He looked as if he hadn't slept in a week.

"Tell them not to look," McManus snapped.

"But they want to go out and—"

"No one leaves!" McManus ordered. "Not anymore." He turned to the guard, his strength suddenly fierce, overwhelming. *"No one.* No matter what. Do you understand?"

"Yes, sir," the guard said. He started to leave.

"And please bring Professor Lindstrom down, for Christ's sake."

Then the guard was gone.

Alessandra felt cold pinpricks of gooseflesh across the back of her hand. It's getting cold in here. Either that, or—

McManus looked at her, and she swore there was something close to pity in his eyes. "A little knowledge, eh? As they say, very dangerous. Yes, the time transference apparatus works. A major breakthrough . . . I suppose. But do you know why this building is covered in red tiles?" He gestured at the air.

She shook her head.

(So cold.)

"And do you have any idea why we've turned the building into an armed camp, a small fortress?"

She shook her head again.

"So you don't have a clue as to what's going on—out there?" he said, indicating outside the building.

Another shake.

"Interesting . . ."

Then he reached out and held her cold hands. And she felt how cold the man's thin, tapered fingers were even as they held her tight.

"So you don't know that your friend, this Jim, can never, ever be brought back, do you?"

8

Jim would have liked to just stand there, a giddy grin on his face, and enjoy the show.

This was, after all, an absolutely incredible moment. Up there were the Beatles, all decked out in black leather, looking like rejects from the cast of *The Wild One*. The songs they were singing were an odd collection of rhythm and blues and standards from Carl Perkins, Buddy Holly, and Larry Williams.

Jim was beginning to wonder if he'd hear even one original Lennon/McCartney tune when they began a dirgelike ballad that threatened to put the raucously inebriated audience soundly asleep.

Paul sang the song, with the same syrupy voice he used for "Till There Was You" from *The Music Man*.

The melody was familiar, even in this primitive form.

Paul stopped before the payoff phrase, rolled his eyes, and then droned, "Love me do-o-o . . ."

The crowd grew restless, eager for the Beatles to get back to bashing out some good old rock and roll. John wandered off stage just as Paul finished to scattered applause and a few boos.

And then John returned with a toilet seat around his neck.

"I 'ope you nice people aren't eating the bleedin' food in this place." He mugged a horrified look at his oval collar. "Me and the boys know where it comes from."

Some of the younger people in the audience laughed. Others, who obviously didn't speak English, turned and looked around, asking for a translation.

Authentic Beatles humor, Jim thought. The irreverence, the wit, was already there. Even if it was more Three Stooges than Spike Milligan.

The laughter ended, and John broke into a shattering version of Larry Williams's "Dizzy Miss Lizzy."

Yeah . . . Jim grinned. It would be great to stand there and take it all in. But that was not to be. First, there were the customers, loudly insistent in their not unreasonable desire to be served prompt refills of their mugs of beer. Some of them seemed to know this Wolfie character, joking around, asking what could be wrong with him tonight.

Others just banged their mugs loudly on the rough wooden tables, catching Jim's attention but also drawing the glare of Manfred Weissleder, the bullheaded manager. Of course, Jim didn't know too much about Weissleder except that even a casual look told you that he looked like bad news. His gray, shimmering suit all but screamed "mobster."

It was probably wise to stay on his good side—if he had one.

Then there was Trude.

Obviously, undernourished Wolfie had tested the waters in that ample sea of flesh one time too many. The female bartender with arms like mutton legs clearly looked upon Wolfie as her love object—whether the feeling was reciprocated or not.

And—Jim thought, grinning, as he took tray after tray of drinks away—maybe it was reciprocated. Hell, I don't know Wolfie's taste. Maybe he *likes* them big. It gave him a momentary buzz to think about the two of them together, in the sack . . . looking sort of like an exclamation point and a big, fat zero. . . .

But how does this guy come off knowing the Beatles?

It was in Paul's autobiography, *Yeah, Yeah, Yeah.* Paul had told interviewers about some people they knew in their Hamburg days—and good old Wolfie was right there among them.

But how did he get to know them?

Where was there a chance for Wolfie to hang out with proto-moptops? The Beatles were on stage, and Wolfie was stuck here, down on the crowded floor.

It didn't make sense.

As the evening wore to a close—the patrons staggering away to perhaps taste the other pleasures of the Reeperbahn—Jim began to panic. The Beatles were concluding a wild Buddy Holly set, finishing with the classic "Words of Love."

Trude was making cow eyes at him.

Good grief! Jim worried. How long do I have before Ali yanks me back? What an opportunity to waste. I've learned nothing. Nothing, except what a bitch of a job the Beatles had playing four to five hours straight. In a year, they'll be doing half-hour sets for what most people earn in a year.

I gotta do something, Jim thought.

He put down his tray. A customer called him, but Jim wiped his hands on his apron (God . . . an apron!) and walked toward the backstage door.

Jim had a feeling that this set—the last set—was nearly over. There was something about the song the Beatles were doing—Carl Perkins's "Honey Don't"—and the way George kept looking at his watch that told Jim that they'd soon be out of there.

He moved quickly, but not quickly enough.

All of a sudden the song ended. And Paul leaned into the single mike.

"Goodnight, ladies and gents."

"And all you bears and rabbits," John said.

Pete Best did a final roll and comic cymbal crash. Then they had their instruments unplugged, hurrying off the small stage, out some back door, before Jim could get to them.

Hurrying away.

To oblivion, because if I don't get to them now, it will be too late, Jim thought.

And what about Alessandra? How did she deal with the security people or the scientists or whoever showed up? Had she screwed up her career just to satisfy his whim? Were both their careers about to go down the toilet?

Not that she needed a career. Not with the money in her family.

A job was the *last* thing Ali needed.

He pushed his way to the stage, past couples getting up to leave, young women dressed in some odd echo of the fifties, still with the totally unflattering puffy hairdos and tube dresses. There was some leather, some denim, but the Star Club crowd seemed mostly middle-class.

Jim pushed past the exiting people like a salmon swimming upstream.

He heard someone calling to him, yelling from the back of the club.

But Jim kept moving, watching the four subjects of his thesis hustle out the back . . . about to be lost.

Alessandra stood up.

"One way? What do you mean, one way? I thought that nothing really happens with the machine. Look, he's still there," she said pointing at Jim, who was still in a very deep sleep. "What the hell are you talking about?"

McManus didn't answer her immediately. Instead Ali watched him look over at the other two doctors, searching for moral support.

What is this? she wondered. What the hell is going on here? And then she began to feel an incredible fear growing, a terrible sense that she was about to learn something that would change her life forever.

What have I done to Jim? she thought. Oh, God, what in the world have I done?

And, as if Jim sensed her thoughts, his sleeping body heaved as he took a big breath of air.

And McManus came to her.

"The machine works, Alessandra. At least, we believe it does. But we can't be sure, not absolutely—"

He paused again maddeningly, and Alessandra, never one to tolerate pregnant pauses or thoughtful prevarications, raised her voice.

"Tell me. Tell me what's wrong!"

The doctor turned back to her, his face sad, weary. Dr. Beck, a motherly-looking woman with an electronic stethoscope hung around her neck, walked over to him, standing there, ready to lend support.

To McManus.

Or.

Or, she thought, to me. After he tells me.

"It works, based on the telemetry readings," he said, gesturing toward the machinery. "Works fine, apparently. But—but when we brought people back they were hopelessly insane."

Alessandra moaned. She brought her fist to her mouth. She started shaking her head.

"No," she said. Then again, "No."

But McManus, a wizened, weary elf, kept nodding. "Yes. Only three times. The apparatus only works with humans. There was no way to test it with animals."

"Oh, god," she said. Alessandra staggered back.

There was Jim, lying in the chair, as if he was just catching some Z's. Conked out, as if he had spent the night bull-shitting about the decline and fall of Western Civilization.

He looked blurry. All out of focus.

Why, she wondered.

An eye felt full, itchy. She rubbed at it. She felt her tears.

Dr. Beck put a hand of Alessandra's shoulder, but Alessandra pulled away and walked over to Jim, touching him.

"Please," Dr. Beck said, arranging an IV bottle near Jim. "It's best you don't touch him."

"Jim," she said quietly.

Then she heard McManus talking to Beck about something, about their machines, their damn machines

. . . as if they were done talking about Jim, as if—*that was that!* It was all over. She and Jim had made a mistake and now, well, they had to live with it. She turned on them.

"What the hell is wrong with you?" she barked at them.

McManus looked up from the bank of monitors.

"Hmmm?" he said.

Alessandra walked back to them. "You said two? Two other people have been used."

Out of the corner of her eye she caught Dr. Jacob walking away from the tachyon generator, his clipboard held tightly in his hand.

They're worried about me, Alessandra thought. And they damn well better be.

"Two people go crazy and you leave this thing hooked up and operational? What in the world is wrong with you?"

McManus glanced at the screen, pointed at it. "Have it print out," he said to Jacob, who had just moved closer to him. Then Ali heard him say, quietly, "And see where the hell Lindstrom is . . ."

"What kind of machine is this?" Alessandra said, yelling, shrieking at the doctor who was acting so unflappable, hiding by his computer.

But McManus left the safety of his bank of monitors and walked over to Ali. Now his eyes glowed angrily.

"Listen, Miss Moreau . . . it was you and your friend here who came into this lab . . . unauthorized—broke in, for Christ's sake." He walked up to her, looking right into her tear-smudged eyes. "You *broke* in here. I should have you arrested. Thrown in jail. Kicked out of the university."

"Elliot," Jacob interrupted. "We're getting more changes. . . . "

"Damn. . . ." McManus stopped, and went back to the monitors.

Dr. Beck took Alessandra's arm. "Perhaps you'd like to lie down somewhere, get some rest. I could give you something, maybe a—"

Ali shrugged her off. "Changes? In Jim? What does that mean?"

She walked over to the monitors.

Jacob looked up, startled by her approach. The portly scientist tapped McManus's arm, warning him.

But McManus kept looking down. "No. Let her see. It doesn't matter—not now."

Ali looked at the monitors. They were flat displays, unenhanced by holographic windows. If speech recognition was being used, McManus had it off.

One monitor read, "Variations in Known Chronology."

The other listed, "Chronology Previous to Insertions." That screen also featured a digital window, with numbers spinning wildly, careening out of control. She looked back at the first screen.

It was a list of museums. The Prado. The Louvre. The Met. Each followed by the names of pieces of art, all in parentheses, all marked by a + or a −.

What is this? she thought. A learn-at-home art program?

She grabbed McManus's arm. "What is this stuff? What does it have to do with Jim?" The scientist kept watching the screen. "You didn't answer my question. Why did you leave the machine connected? It's a failure. You should have shut it down!"

McManus nodded. "Oh, I might have done that. Might have. Except for one thing."

Jacob was shaking his head, trying to get McManus to stop.

"Elliot," Beck said, "the boy's pulse is going up."

McManus nodded.

"You see," he said gently, turning back to Alessandra, "two of the subjects went insane. But I'm afraid we have someone else still back there."

"Besides Jim?"

McManus nodded. "Besides Jim . . ."

Jim had almost reached the back door, the door that he knew—another chunk of memory—led to two dingy dressing rooms, a cramped bathroom, and a narrow entrance to the kitchen, filled with the spicy aroma of overcooked sausages and reheated strudel.

Jim reached out, grabbed the doorknob, and gave it a turn.

But someone grabbed him and, without the slightest bit of effort, snapped him back, spinning him around, smashing him against the cheap wood door. His head made a loud crack against the wood.

His attacker—bald, with beady blue-green eyes—put his toothy mouth right up to Jim.

"Well, Wolfie, I thought today was the day. That's what you told me, eh? On Friday, Helmut. That's when you'll get your money. That's when we'll be square. That's what you said."

The bull-like man drove a knee into Wolfie's groin. And Jim wished, as he gasped and coughed, trying to suck down some urgently needed air, that his use of Wolfie's mind didn't also involve hooking into the apparent deadbeat's nervous system.

"Friday, Wolfie. And I'm still—" Helmut brought the other knee up—"waiting for my money, liebchen."

Jim nodded, wishing that Wolfie's slowly percolating memory would supply him with some answer to get this behemoth off him. Do I have the money? Jim wondered, in which case, it would be a simple matter of saying, hang on, Helmut. I have your deutschmarks right here. Or there. Or wherever.

On the other hand, if Wolfie had, rather unwisely it would seem, stiffed Helmut, then surely he must have prepared some clever ruse to dodge the loan shark.

But at present Jim didn't have a clue just what Wolfie had planned.

He looked out at the nearly deserted Star Club.

Trude was there, serving the last lingering customers at the bar. Manfred Weissleder was still sitting in the shadows, talking to one of the waitresses while he and Helmut were doing this nasty little dance in the shadows. And Jim's partner was giving him one wicked case of blue balls.

Helmut wrapped his fingers around Wolfie's windpipe. Jim wished that Wolfie wasn't such a wimpy character. And he wondered what would happen if Wolfie were to die.

Where does that leave me?

"Hey, come on," Jim said, pleading. "I'll get the money for you . . . no problem."

Jim heard a click.

It took him only a few seconds to figure what Helmut had planned for him.

"You had your time, you little shit." Helmut grinned. And Jim saw a thin, shiny knife in Helmut's free hand.

The stage lights went out. The knife disappeared.

Now he and Helmut were in complete darkness.

And then a tiny pinching sensation in his stomach told Jim where Helmut had placed his knife. . . .

9

The reassuring thing about dreams is knowing that they aren't real. In fact, Jim thought, at those moments of intense fear, during his worst nightmares, he could be surprisingly cool-headed; he could step away from it all and enjoy the grisly proceedings.

After all, it's just a dream.

That's all.

But this experience, this weirdness of occupying someone else's mind, feeling everything his body felt—which at this point included a pig-sticker of a knife pressing into Wolfie's midsection and the beginnings of a definite loosening of the bowels—didn't have that reassuringly fuzzy feel at all. In fact, it resembled reality in nearly every detail.

(Nearly every detail . . . except for the soft, burnished glow everything had . . . like a Kodachrome just beginning to fade to pale yellow and orange.)

Jim had the misfortune of selecting the body of someone in debt to a very nasty man.

He considered calmly explaining the situation.

But the man spoke again.

"I don't like being screwed over, eh, Wolfie? And now everyone will know it."

Was he really going to do it? Jim wondered. Was this dullheaded gangster really going to push the blade home? Screw the Beatles. This was the only thing that concerned him.

"Hey," Jim tried, smiling at the gorilla. "Ease up. I'll get you the money, honest."

That, apparently, was the wrong thing to say. The bald-headed man—who reminded Jim of a minotaur, more of a human bull than a primate of any type—gritted his teeth, obviously angry at hearing such words one time too many.

The man's muscles tensed as he squeezed Wolfie's underfed body a few more centimeters.

Now, he thought. Now would be a good time for it to end, for Ali to shut the machine off, or whatever she had to do to bring me back. An interesting experience, thank you . . . but I really must go home now. Jim thought of a gasping Lou Costello, facing Bela Lugosi's Dracula who, for some strange reason, had Frankenstein's monster in tow.

Hey, Abbott!

"Nice . . . ," the man-bull said, "and slow. . . ."

Jim recognized that they had come to some kind of end point in their conversation. He frantically tried pulling away from the vicelike grip of the man, but to absolutely no avail.

What a wimp this guy was!

He felt the blade cutting into his skin. Just a prick at first, a paper cut, a splinter. Then genuine alarms went off in his head.

He started to scream. Unmanly, he knew, but trapped in this underpowered body, there was no more self-reliant course.

But the man's hand swiftly covered his mouth, pinning his head against the back wall.

The man grinned.

And then there was a voice.

"Eh, mate. What are you doin' to our Wolfie, 'ere?"

The bull-man turned.

Whoever it was in the shadows didn't waste any time talking. His fist quickly pummeled the side of the man's shining head, snapping it violently against the wall. Jim's mouth was suddenly liberated. The bull-man staggered backwards, and Jim got a good look at the blade, its point glistening in the murky light.

His rescuer reached out, grabbed the man's hand, and twisted it back. The knife tumbled to the ground. But the man quickly recovered his balance and charged.

Jim watched, rubbing his throat, still getting used to breathing. In a moment it would occur to him to help. But for now, he stood there and watched.

It was street fighting.

The bull-man charged—running right into a swift boot kick to the groin. Then, when he was doubled over, sputtering at the floor, there was another swift boot kick to the head. And then Wolfie's debt collector rolled backwards.

And when he stood up, he didn't bother coming back for any more fun and games.

By now, Manfred Weissleder finally flashed on the fact that there was some trouble near his backstage. He waddled over as the bald guy staggered away, out of the club, cursing in idiomatic German—which Jim understood completely.

Jim turned to face his rescuer.

"Hey, Wolfie, you better watch who you play with. That was one fuckin' nasty sod."

The mystery man stepped closer, into the light of the small lamp. He was dressed in black.

Jim recognized the voice, then the hair, short, just the hint of a bang on his forehead. Piercing blue eyes that caught the light. It was John Lennon.

Of course, figured Jim. There were a lot of stories of John's pleasure in fighting, his nasty prowess . . . tales from the Hamburg days. Before clean, scrubbed, safe-as-soap Beatlemania kicked in.

There were even rumors of John killing someone in a brawl.

After what Jim had just seen, he could believe it.

"Thanks," Jim said.

"Anytime, Wolfie. Just you better take care who you borrow the stray quid from, eh?"

John flashed a grin. And Jim—completely unprepared—didn't have a clue as to what to say, or ask.

God, he thought, what a time to be tongue-tied.

Lennon turned and headed for backstage.

"John," he said, feeling so weird to be standing there, knowing everything that was ahead for him—Beatlemania, Ed Sullivan, *Sergeant Pepper's*, the Maharishi, Yoko, War, Peace, Sean, solitude.

New York.

The Dakota.

That last winter.

"John," he said. "I was wondering . . . I mean, could we talk a bit, I mean—"

Lennon kept walking, pushing open the squeaky stage door.

"Sure, Wolfie." He smiled. "I'll catch you later, at Jurgen's. I'll be there. . . ."

"Right," Jim said. Then, quieter, "Jurgen's . . ."

And then the door shut.

"There's someone else?"

McManus nodded. "Yes. There's a lot I should explain so you can understand just what you—what you—"

"Blundered into would be the proper expression, I believe," a thundering voice commented from the entrance to the lab.

The door to the lab swung open. Ali turned and saw a campus legend walk through it.

It was Dr. Flynn Lindstrom, winner of the Nobel Prize in history, author of five compulsively readable, controversial, noveau classic volumes of interpretative history . . . and the former head of Columbia's esteemed History Department.

The former head because, it was rumored, old Lindstrom started to come apart at the seams. Some of the university's dwindling number of history majors claimed it was demon liquor that caused Lindstrom's fall. Others said it was his unquenchable taste for coeds one-third his age. The more cynical simply argued that whatever brilliance Lindstrom had was gone, lost to age and the onset of untreated Alzheimer's.

And here he was, looking about as incongruous as he could.

His snow-white hair stood up at a dozen different angles. He clearly made no attempt to comb it. He wore a rumpled three-piece suit, an oddly archaic tweed that was the very image of the fading scholar. From the way his eyes squinted, it seemed that Lindstrom had just awakened.

"Lindstrom, this girl and her friend broke into—" McManus started to explain.

"Don't bother," Lindstrom said tiredly. "Your ever-officious thought-police told me all the details of the evening's events." Lindstrom walked over to Ali. He reached out and took her hand in his. He held it a moment. "It's a distinct pleasure to have your beautiful presence grace this misbegotten bunker."

He bent over and planted an embarrassingly full kiss on the back of her hand. Then he looked up. "At least, it won't be all doom and grayness if my keepers permit you to remain here."

"Keepers?" Jacob muttered indignantly.

"Keepers," Lindstrom repeated just as indignantly. "Isn't that what you call those who keep watch over you in a place you can't leave?"

McManus walked over to him. "Please, Lindstrom. Let's not go over all this again. You know the importance of—"

Lindstrom made a shallow laugh, and finally released Ali's hand. "Ah, yes . . . the importance of protecting Western Civilization." He walked over to the monitors. "Except, Doctor, I'm not at all sure it's worth saving. Perhaps a little shake-up might serve as a tonic to the battered planet. A new deal for—" Lindstrom glanced down at the monitors. "Eh, what's this?"

McManus walked over to the desk and looked at the screens that Lindstrom was studying. "The current status of the outside, I'm afraid."

Ali saw a sudden change overcome Lindstrom's face. A few seconds ago he was blithely disconnected from everything, and everyone, in the lab. Now his face dropped.

He looked scared.

"We've lost Texas . . ." Lindstrom said.

"That's not all," McManus said, hitting the computer keyboard. Ali walked over to see the screen.

Lindstrom's face, a ghoulish gray-green in the light of the monitor, went wide with surprise . . . and horror.

"What! A fence? Around the campus? What on earth for? A fence? What is this—an armed camp?"

"And here's Europe," McManus said, hitting some more keys.

"The Euro-Asian Compact? Now, that's a clever one. What on earth is that supposed to be?" Lindstrom asked.

"The documentation is all printed out, over there," McManus gestured to a big pile of paper. "You'd best start looking at it as soon as you can."

"Right. I'd say we were all ill-advised to take that rest, no matter how exhausted we were." Lindstrom was all business now, blinking, rubbing at his eyes. "Can you ask Toland for some coffee? And you, Miss—"

He was looking right at Ali. "Alessandra Moreau," she said.

"Yes, Alessandra . . . could you give me a hand sifting through this data? We have to compare reams of printout . . . reams! That is if they'll let you stay."

For the first time it dawned on Ali that—whatever was going on here—they might need her. And perhaps it was her turn to regain some measure of control over her situation.

She shook her head.

McManus and Lindstrom looked at her, surprised.

"What?" Lindstrom said.

"No. I want to know what's going on here," she said quietly. "What's all this about, this business of 'inside' and 'outside' . . . and why you're here, a historian in a physics lab."

"Why, certainly," Lindstrom said, looking at McManus for approval, "if—"

"And I want to know what we're going to do about Jim . . . to get him back. You tell me that. Then I'll do whatever you want me to do to help . . . anything you want."

Lindstrom smiled, ironic, dangerous. He smiled at McManus.

"Anything?" he asked gently.

It was a cinch for Jim to get Trude to give him Jurgen Vollmer's address, even though she thought it odd. After all, hadn't he been there dozens of times?

But it was less easy dodging her plea to come upstairs to her apartment, just above the Star.

(He saw the room then . . . quite clearly. I must be a regular visitor, he thought. It was a small room, a cubbyhole almost, with a line running across it from which dangled her stockings and oversized undies. A bottle of yellow liqueur with a great elk on the label. The night table was scarred by dozens of unclaimed cigarettes . . . probably put down in that last moment before yielding to Trude's fulsome charms, left to burn themselves out on the cheap wood.)

Jim grinned at Trude.

Wolfie's taste in trysts are different from mine, he thought.

Only bits and chunks of Wolfie's memory seemed to fall into place, lodging uncomfortably with Jim's own consciousness. Could this lead to a Jekyll/Hyde dementia? If all of Wolfie comes back, who calls the shots?

More images, names, words came to him.

He suddenly knew that Wolfie had a mother who lived in a working-class suburb, just outside the city, Hammerbrook.

His father died when he was seven. Died in the war.

(He felt chilled. Someone opened the door. There was a breeze. . . .)

He died at Stalingrad. Wolfie grew up with the story of how his heroic father died in Fortress Stalingrad. There were other men, "uncles" who came to stay with his mother for a while, then moved on. But no other family. Not in Germany.

"What's wrong, Wolfie?" Trude asked, taking his hand.

Jim shook his head.

Wolfie had a sister. She was in America, working as a maid. America. Probably where Wolfie would like to go also.

For a moment, Jim saw the country through Wolfie's eyes. A wonderful place, a place of hope and dreams. Anything is possible. Anything at all.

He shook off Trude's meaty hand as she again pleaded with him to come up and visit her. Then she asked if she could go to Vollmer's with him. But it was clear that she didn't really expect him to bring her.

Good.

He backed away from the bar. But not before Trude leaned forward and planted a big wet kiss on him. He smiled at her.

Don't worry, kid. We'll get your Wolfie back to you.

Then he was outside, wandering onto the still-bustling Reeperbahn. The street was wet, eerily reflecting the garish neon lights of the big clubs and dives. The rain had stopped, but the air was filled with the smell of the wet street, a thick, close smell. Sailors wearing jaunty uniforms from countries unknown to Jim strolled the wide boulevard, stepping into the rainbow colored swirls in the wet puddles.

He stopped to ask directions from two teenagers melted into each other, holding bottles of beer, strolling past the Star. He hoped they didn't know Wolfie.

He told them the street he was looking for. The boy grinned drunkenly and mumbled something completely unintelligible. Jim shook his head and continued to walk the wet street.

He walked past the Panoptikum, an enormous waxworks. Queen Elizabeth and Elvis Presley stood in a window looking outside, cheek to jowl.

"Pleased to meet ya, ma'am."

"Why, thank you, Mr. Presley."

Jim kept moving. In a few years, the museum would feature the same four boys, Hamburg's own Beatles who gigged only a block away.

He was lost again, and he asked directions of some more young kids, a gang that laughed and joked, before one of the older boys told him where to go. He was in the St. Pauli quarter . . . very close. Jim took the indicated street. But it led to what was an obvious wrong turn. He walked down a dark block filled with rapacious streetwalkers, slim-hipped women with full red lips. They eyed Wolfie like wolves spying an errant chicken.

Jim fled back to the safety of the Reeperbahn. He looked for someone more reputable for directions, and he spotted an old man walking alone. Jim asked his help. The man nodded. Jim was near the building, the man told him, just a few blocks north, towards Budapester Street.

"Very near," the old man said, walking away.

Jim took a breath and hurried. Suddenly, he knew where he was going. The streets looked familiar.

As he walked, he noticed that more and more of the lokalen, the bars of Hamburg, were closed. It was nearing dawn. And even this city would stop carousing. . . .

He ran the last few blocks, excited, racing to get there, not knowing how much time he'd have before he'd be yanked away.

He ran, jumping over puddles, dodging cars, seeing people coming out of their houses for some ungodly job that had them up and out before sunrise.

He ran, breathless, away from the Reeperbahn, down a quiet, elm-lined street with neat-as-pin houses and small apartment buildings.

Of course, this was right . . . this was it. He *knew* where to go.

It was *this* building, right here, on the corner.

He saw images in his mind. God, it felt something like a memory. It was this same street. A sunny spring day. He smiled, remembering something that he never experienced.

But Wolfie had. . . .

And Wolfie knew the apartment. He knew what it looked like. Who'd be there. How everyone would greet him.

Wolfie knew it all. And now, like bits of debris floating to the surface after a shipwreck, so did Jim.

And it didn't bother him in the least.

In fact, it almost felt natural.

10

It was three flights up, and Jim ran up the steps full out, taking them two and three at a time, grabbing at the wooden banister, smooth and slippery from years of old people and children guiding themselves up and down.

By the time he got to the third-floor landing, he heard noise. From Vollmer's apartment. Just ahead.

It didn't bother him that he just knew—all of a sudden—which apartment it was. He even knew what it was like inside, with one wall filled with stark, striking black and white photographs, many of Astrid.

And photographs of Stu Sutcliffe and Astrid.

Jim knew Stu had been a member of the band—but not really. He couldn't sing, couldn't really play an instrument. And John didn't argue when Stu said he'd stay behind, after their first gig in Hamburg. Stu was completely and totally in love with Astrid.

The Beatles returned to the UK. Stu stayed behind.

Then he died, a cerebral hemorrhage snuffing out his young life.

Jim reached the door.

On the other side of the door, some of Motown's finest were thumping away. Wilson Pickett. "In the Midnight Hour."

He knocked on the door.

And Jurgen Vollmer, Astrid's friend and a fan of the Beatles, opened it, laughing.

"Wolfie" he said, holding the door open. "Come

in. John told us about your little problem.'' Vollmer patted Jim on the back, still laughing.

And he led him into the room.

Vollmer spoke English. So that must mean, Jim thought, that old Wolfie is bilingual.

The tinny record player was blaring, and a wood-plank coffee table was filled with beer, chunks of sausage, and trays filled with joints. A thin, pungent haze filled the room. Jim took a deep breath.

''Yeah,'' Vollmer said, laughing. ''You've got to watch who you borrow money from.''

There were other people sitting on the floor, people Jim guessed he should know, but didn't. One of them grinned and handed him a joint.

Marijuana. Mary Jane. Pot.

An interesting problem . . . Jim thought.

He was against ingesting any chemical crud no matter what. The Flower Power of the Sixties had given way to a desperate drug culture that nearly destroyed American society. The Government had given up trying to control it. With good reason, too. They were outgunned and outspent by the importers and dealers.

But this . . . this was the Sixties, the birth of the age of psychedelia. It was a time when everyone was going to get by with a Little Help from Their Friends . . . even when mortars were blasting away right next to them.

''Sure,'' Jim said, taking and sniffing the ragged-looking cigarette.

''Go on, smoke it,'' a cute blonde on the floor giggled. ''It won't bite you, Wolfie.''

Jim smiled. No, it won't. . . .

Adrianna. That was her name. It came to him just then, like everything else. Like magic.

Jim stuck the joint in his mouth and lit it, sucking deep. He expected to cough, but the smoke went down surprisingly smoothly. Wolfie must be an old hand at this, he thought. The taste, though, was odd. After holding the smoke for a few seconds, he blew it out—dragon-like. Everyone started laughing. He started laughing too, though nothing seemed *that* funny. Tears filled his eyes. The giggling people on the floor told him to take another hit, when a sudden creepy thought occurred to him.

Bits of Wolfie just keep breaking through. Fragments of memory come drifting by, icebergs in an otherwise deserted sea.

He's still in here. Could that be dangerous? he wondered. Could Wolfie take over again?

The paranoia began to bloom.

Wolfie's in here . . . somewhere. Still here. But then . . . so am I. And somehow, we're starting to come together.

Jee-zus! And what will happen then?

Someone reached up and pulled him down to the floor, to squat with the others. Adrianna reached out and took the joint from him. Jim smiled, the potent smoke kicking in. He felt oddly at home.

"The Midnight Hour" finished, and another forty-five plopped down onto the record player. Jim looked at the machine. He never had seen a record player in operation.

He listened to the music. It was the King. Elvis. Singing "Blue Suede Shoes."

"Put on 'Blue Hawaii,' " a man whom Jim couldn't recall—at least not yet—said, leaning against a threadbare puke-green couch. "Something classic with Elvis and Ann-Margret," the man slurred, and everyone—Jim included—laughed.

Jim turned to Adrianna, still laughing.

"Are they here?" he asked her. "The Beatles?"

She covered his hand with her own and gave it a squeeze. "Sure . . . there inside . . . with Vollmer's friend. You know who . . ."

Jim nodded. Then—feeling a bit like Stan Laurel flashing on an obvious question—he said, "Who are they with?"

Adrianna started to answer. At least her mouth—very pretty, with cherry-red lips that looked even more succulent than the platter piled a foot deep with sausage—opened, about to say something.

But then Pete Best came strolling out of the back room.

"Can't believe it." Best grinned. The drummer—his Beatle days numbered—looked down at everyone on the floor. "I can't fookin' believe them."

Pete Best reached down and unceremoniously snatched up a sausage. He bit off a sizeable piece and chewed, still shaking his head. "I can't believe it."

And since it appeared that no one else was going to ask the obvious question—maybe because they already knew the answer—Jim spoke up.

"Can't believe what, Pete?"

It was easy talking to Best. After all, he wasn't a real Beatle, poor guy.

"They're doing that wacko black magic stuff again."

On the word "wacko" the guy across from Jim stirred. And Jim saw that it wasn't any guy at all, but a tough-looking woman dressed in buckskin.

Jim felt like he was losing it.

Maybe this is all some freaked-out dream, he thought. I'll wake up in my dorm . . . still with no idea how to rescue my thesis.

He quickly looked at Adrianna to make sure that she was a real woman. She looked feminine enough, but that was certainly no guarantee. Jim remembered that Astrid travelled in strange circles. . . . She and Stu had been into a weird sadomasochistic trip.

They had a lot of freaky friends.

Jim coughed. The air was getting a bit heavy in here.

"Yeah, I know, I know," Best whined. "You believe all that malarkey, too. Big waste of time, if you ask me."

The cross-dressed pioneer across from Jim relaxed a bit, reclining on the couch, eyeing Jim.

Not another one of Wolfie's admirers, Jim hoped.

Best squatted down, close by. "Pete," Jim whispered, leaning close to him. "What do you mean . . . what are they doing?"

The drummer shook his head as if he didn't want to bother talking about it.

"Astrid has that bleedin' magic man in there, doin' all sorts of weird shit. They even got George going along with it."

Jim nodded. Is this important? he wondered. Is this some hidden aspect of the Beatles past? The Fab Four as Black Magicians? A deal with the devil for success? A modern Faustian transaction?

Pretty neat if it was true. . . .

"But what are they doing?" Jim asked. He wished his head wasn't so damn foggy now.

Pete Best threw his hands up. "He's telling them they've got the fookin' power. Can you believe it? He's telling them that"—he took another great chew of sausage, and then continued talking—"the Beatles will be the greatest rock band ever. Can you believe it? Tellin' them they will be the greatest songwriters? Might as well tell them how to get to bleedin' Oz, they're so—"

Jim stared at Pete Best. This was wild. Someone was predicting the incredible future of the Beatles—when they were nobodies, nothing—and it was going on, right there, in the next room.

He stood up with difficulty. He had some trouble getting his bearings, tipping forward a bit, threatening the coffee table and Davy Crockett. Finally, he steadied himself. And he took a step toward the back room.

"He says they'll have real power . . . just as long as John and Paul stay together. But if they break up—"

Jim took a step toward the narrow hallway to the back room.

Best looked up.

" 'Ey, Wolfie. You can't go back there. He'll go nuts if anyone barges in, you can't—"

But Jim kept walking. . . .

Dr. Beck carefully wheeled Jim away, off to a side door.

"Where . . . where are they taking him?" Ali asked

McManus. The scientist was at the computer, his head moving from one screen to the other.

He didn't look up at her. "There's another room over there. Don't worry. . . . He'll be safe, out of the way, while we figure out what to do."

"You see," Lindstrom said. "These good fellows"—he indicated the scientists in the lab—"invented this device without any real thought that someone else might be doing exactly the same thing. Yes, no thought that their discovery of Tachyon Degeneration—"

"Tachyon Degeneration," McManus explained turning to Ali. "All matter seeks lower energy states, with inertia—"

"I understand the principle, Doctor," Ali said.

Lindstrom cleared his throat and continued. "Well, there was no thought that there'd be someone else—another team—with the same capability. It was the reverse of the Manhattan Project syndrome. There, everyone was so worried that the Fuhrer was ready to create a nuclear weapon. So billions were spent to beat him to the punch. Only it turned out that Adolph had nothing, just a few very bright, under-financed scientists in a tiny lab. We had the bombs—with no competition. The dawning of a wonderful new age for mankind," he snorted.

"For a while it was," McManus added.

"Sure. But our own frantic race to create a nuclear weapon led to the Russian's developing *their* arsenal. The rest—as they say—is ugly history."

"This isn't the same thing, Lindstrom. Not at all," McManus announced.

Ali saw Lindstrom roll his eyebrows. He was a great bear of a man, with a bushy grey mustache matched by his rumpled, ill-fitting suit. He presented a wonderful antidote to the ascetic atmosphere of the lab.

He continued his lecture. "So this time around no one was worried that there just might be another time machine."

"Temporal Transference Device," McManus corrected.

"Whatever. But there was, oh yes. Not only that, my dear, but whoever was using it started altering the past for their benefit . . . and to our detriment."

"Is that possible?"

"Apparently. Because they did it. And that's when McManus called for me to help them set things straight."

McManus shook his head and walked away from the computer. "No. It's not like that at all, Lindstrom. The whole concept of causality, of before and after—is a human concept. It has no meaning on the plane of quantum physics. But I'm sure you know that, Alessandra."

Ali nodded. That much she knew. An event—something happening in what we called "time"—was just different energy states of the same matter. And each energy state had its own fingerprint, a telltale nuclear tracer. Ali guessed that what this machine did was tune in those states, and then project a synchronized brain wave signal at faster-than-light speeds.

"I'll take your word for it, Doctor," Lindstrom said. "At any rate, Alessandra, someone is tampering with known history."

Ali was confused. Tampering? How could that be? She hadn't noticed anything odd.

Lindstrom continued. "Every time a change occurs in the past, the future—"

"A meaningless word," McManus said, returning to the monitors.

"The future—our *present*— is changed. But here's the sinister part. Everyone's memory of the way things were supposed to be is also altered. They have no memory of the way things used to be."

"Except in here," McManus said, not looking up.

Lindstrom nodded. "Yes, except in this ugly fortress. Thank God for that. At least there was a little bit of foresight going on. It is the one brilliant precaution taken by these rather shortsighted scientists in the Time

Lab. You see, once they realized that events in the past—excuse me, I mean at another point in the continuum—could be altered, they took precautions to shield the building from the effects of the tampering. The red tiles that surround us are identical to those on the Galaxy Probe. Isn't that right, Doctor?"

McManus grunted.

Ali knew what that meant. "Nothing in . . . and nothing out."

Lindstrom smiled. "Precisely. The tiles provide a completely effective shield from any form of radiation or transmission. History might change, but here"—the Professor pounded the top of one of the monitors—"the past lives on."

"Would you please refrain from doing that?" McManus scolded.

"Our computers keep track of the discrepancies between what is history *outside*, and what we have on record here. All the information is fed into the building by shielded cables. Of course, they needed someone who could explain the significance of it all—and how to repair the damage. Which is why they kidnapped me."

"You were invited," McManus corrected.

"With the cheerful help of a squad of heavily armed security guards, I remind you. At any rate, I'm supposed to help them correct the mistakes as they occur."

Alessandra shook her head. "But how? What can you do?"

"We have someone in place," McManus said. "A trained operative."

Ali walked closer to the undernourished scientist. "But I thought you said it was a one-way trip."

"It is . . . for now. Until we find out what's the problem. We had one agent in place, and we were to send another, a volunteer. Except now—"

Ali heard something fall from behind her. She turned. Lindstrom was nosing about near the back of the lab, moving books, peering into drawers.

"Don't bother, Professor," McManus called to him. "We've taken the precaution of removing your, er, normal supplies. I'm afraid that you'll find the entire building completely devoid of alcohol. We need you completely sober for the next couple of days."

"Why," Lindstrom said, spinning around, acting stung, "whatever gave you the idea that I was looking for booze. I was just—"

McManus nodded. "Yes, we found all your hidden 'supplies,' and we'll be glad to return them to you once this is all over . . . one way or another. Damn!" McManus shouted, looking at one of the screens.

Lindstrom jumped at the sound.

"More bad news?" Lindstrom asked. He came and stood next to Alessandra, putting a not-quite fatherly arm around her shoulders. "Do tell us, McManus. Straight out, we can bear up, can't we dear?" He gave Ali's shoulder a squeeze.

McManus gestured at the screen. "I don't understand this. Not at all. You'll have to make heads or tails of this one, Lindstrom."

The professor coughed and cleared his throat.

Then, almost reluctantly, Ali thought, Lindstrom looked at the monitors. "Just what is it? More new borders . . . another new alliance?" he asked.

McManus looked up. "No. It's artwork. Nearly a thousand pieces of art. Masterpieces. All lost—supposedly," he said with derision. "And then found . . . and sold."

"Art?" Lindstrom asked with interest, his bushy, grey eyebrows arching with interest. "What kind of art?"

"Classics. The Mona Lisa. Van Gogh's *Starry Night*. Look . . . Picasso. Klee. Matisse. Look at this list . . . just *look at it!*"

Lindstrom studied the monitor, Ali beside him.

"I don't understand," she said. "What does this mean?"

She looked at McManus. But McManus was looking

at Lindstrom. "We have to do it now, Lindstrom. Everything's happening too quickly."

"Do what?" Ali said, suddenly alarmed.

"Dr. Jacob, could you start working out the correlations? We'll do the shift in five minutes."

"Shift?" Ali said, turning now to Lindstrom. "What is he talking about?"

She heard a high-pitched whine behind her. The tachyon generator—an enormous black box—filled the room with an ear-piercing signal.

Professor Flynn Lindstrom's face was impassive.

Then McManus sighed. "Why don't we see if it works first . . . then we'll tell you exactly what we did. . . ."

Ali looked at the machine, and the wires leading to the nearby room—the room where Jim slept.

And she knew then that all this had something to do with Jim. . . .

11

Jim walked unsteadily—whether from the weed or the bizarre excitement of meeting the mystery person behind the Beatles, he didn't know.

Pete Best still lay on the floor, laughing at him. "Wolfie, sit down. John will be bloody well pissed off if you barge in. . . ."

Jim nodded and said, "Sure. . . ." But he kept on walking. With luck, Wolfgang Prater can take the blame. With luck, my consciousness, or whatever is residing in the waiter's skull, will have already whizzed back to the lab.

With luck . . .

He licked his lips. Damn, this was exciting. This was *history.* He didn't dwell on the implications—the Beatles' involvement with the dark forces of the occult. There might be some tarnishing of their image. But what was the big deal about that? They were just precursors of Shirley MacLaine's Ramfar and all the toothlessly diabolic heavy metal groups.

Who knows? Maybe there are some undiscovered backwards messages on their records . . . something more than the bits of a radio broadcast of Richard III on "I am the Walrus," and the hidden expletive—undeleted—that occurs two minutes and fifty-nine seconds into "Hey Jude."

This might be extraordinary. Real musicological field work!

And, as he steered his unsteady way into the other

room, he felt his pulse throbbing. He was hot, flushed. The excitement was incredible as he entered the dark hall. He smelled incense wafting from the other room. Thick, pungent clouds of overpowering smell—soon to become *de rigueur* in any self-respecting hippy pad. The youth movement would adopt incense, and black-light posters, and a handful of key meaningful recordings—a codex to guide the spiritual explorers of the brave new world of the late-Sixties earth.

A foolish, ultimately sad time.

A time Jim wished he had seen.

(But I *am*, he told himself. Right here . . . right now.)

He took a step and the wood floors seemed to go soft. It felt like his foot had become stuck. He just couldn't get it out in front of him. Was the pot that strong? he wondered. The smells—the pot, the incense—started to fade, as if they were imagined. The music was gone, the voices, all fading, falling backwards behind him. Ahead there was nothing, certainly no continuation of the hall, no room.

Nothing.

Absolutely nothing.

Christ! Jim thought. What's happening? Where did everything go? Did I black out? Then a horrible thought occurred to him.

She's pulling me back. Ali is snatching me away just at the moment I'm about to make my discovery.

Great. Terrific. Seconds away from an absolutely key discovery, crucial to an understanding of the Beatles, and I'm being yanked away!

He remembered the alarms inside the building.

Yes, he and Ali (and maybe, if they were lucky, good old Martin) would all be in deep shit.

Jim decided to test his current status. He raised a hand to feel his moustache, to run his fingers along Wolfie's bristlelike hairs.

He raised his arm. At least, he *thought* he raised his arm. He tried feeling for his mouth, the short back hairs. He felt nothing. For the longest time.

Oh, God, he thought. This may not be good. Maybe something screwed up. Coming here, everything had been quick, instantaneous. This was like being a ghost trapped in a jammed elevator.

Maybe I *am* a ghost. Am I dead? Did I get John Lennon that mad at me?

Then—blessed relief—he felt something. Not at all what he expected, of course. But it was something—a sensation.

Sand. Tiny flecks of sand, hitting his face, his eyes; biting at his skin.

Then he felt the sun, a gentle warmth that took away some of the old blackness of the void he had been trapped in.

Then—with the addition of a brilliant, blinding light—he saw, at last, where he was. . . .

The desert.

Not the desert of Lawrence of Arabia, with beautiful flowing dunes, a golden-bronze sea. This was oddly shaped hummocks and irregular mounds of sand, dotted with scraggly brush. Large boulders and rocks dotted the floor of a sandy valley that stretched as far as Jim could see.

"So, what do you think, Fritz?"

This was another one of those awkward moments, Jim thought. Someone is talking to me, knows me, and I'm expected to respond in an appropriate manner.

He took a quick look around. He was not in the lab. So, he hadn't been yanked back to the Red Building.

But Jim didn't have the vaguest idea where he was. He was sitting inside a large armored car of some kind. It was more like a truck. He turned around, and saw two other vehicles sitting slightly back from a ridge. Everyone had field glasses out, studying something below them, out there on the great rocky plain.

The breeze was dry and cool.

Finally, Jim risked a look at the man talking to him, bringing down his own field glasses.

"So, tell me what you think, Fritz. You've seen the

latest communications . . . the best Berlin can deliver. What do you think?"

The voice was strong, cutting through the air like the call of some great hawk circling its prey, ready to dive.

Jim nodded—not knowing what else to do—and he pulled his field glasses back up to his eyes. He tried to look approximately the same direction as the German officer.

For a while he saw nothing but enlarged rocks, clumps of reedy grass, dry ruts and gullies. Then he saw something else. A jeep, with soldiers standing next to it. They had a map spread out on the hood. One of them was pointing left and then right, gesturing.

Even from this great distance, Jim saw the shiny insignia of a high-ranking officer. A British officer.

Could even be a general, Jim thought.

"Well, Fritz?" the man next to him said.

And Jim turned—having gone from a Wolfie to a Fritz in mere minutes. He lowered his field glasses.

Jim stared at the man next to him—wishing he knew who Fritz was, and where the hell *this* was, and what in the world was going on here.

But then, it all became perfectly clear.

The man shook his head. A massive skull, topped with a fine, thin layer of sun-bleached blond-brown hair. His face was tanned to a ruddy, blackish-brown. But his blue eyes sparkled with wit and intelligence and cunning.

Unless he was terribly mistaken, the German officer speaking to him was Field Marshal Erwin Rommel.

The Desert Fox.

"I . . . I don't know, Field Marshal . . ."

Uh-oh. That might have been a mistake. He struggled to remember when Rommel became a field marshall. It would help if he had some idea what date it was—now that the location was more or less set.

This is North Africa, boys and girls, he thought. But when? In the early days, when the Afrika Korps was unstoppable? Or later, during the hit-and-run battles of El Alamein? Or was it even later, when Rommel was beginning his long retreat back, through Tunisia, all the way back, until the Allies had reconquered Africa?

No. Rommel looked too happy, too carefree, for it to be late in the game.

But Fritz? Who was Fritz supposed to be?

Like all Contemporary Studies majors, Jim had spent a semester studying the different aspects of World War II . . . the economic and cultural basis for the war, the tactics of the major campaigns, and the political fallout.

But his special interest had been Holocaust Studies. Everything else was incidental.

So his knowledge of the battles and the generals was sketchy at best.

God, he wondered, what the hell year is it?

Rommel laughed. "You're much too timid, Fritz. Let's at least give them chase. Who knows? We might get lucky."

The Field Marshal stood up and signaled to the other two armored cars. Then, still standing, he gave Jim an order.

"Let's go."

The idea—patently clear—was for Jim to put the jeep in gear and tear down the rocky slope of the ridge, right toward the British jeep, lost in the desert with a valuable cargo of British brass.

That was the idea. There was one small problem, Jim thought. . . .

The last time I drove a stick shift was on my grandfather's farm in Bucks County. He had an old '92 Nissan in the garage, with a V–6 engine before the new clean combustion turbines became mandatory.

His grandfather didn't let Jim take it on the road, but Jim still had a ball, tearing up and down the dirt road, then across the cornfield after the harvest was over, crunching the yellow, dried stalks.

And his grandfather used to say, "That's what driving *used* to be like, Jimmy."

That was six years ago.

Jim pressed down on the clutch pedal.

"Do you want to sit down . . . ?" he suggested to Rommel.

But the Field Marshal looked at him as if that was a really dumb idea, and then he shrugged the suggestion away.

And Jim thought . . . you might want to sit if you knew how long it's been since I've driven something like this.

(And then . . . he felt the first glimmer, the first chink in this new wall that was Fritz. Jim had a vision of driving the armored car easily, fast and expertly, guiding it down the slope.)

He hoped the image carried over to his actions.

"Here we go," he said quietly.

Immediately he jerked the jeep forward, popping the clutch out. Rommel tipped forward, his hands releasing his field glasses and grabbing at the windshield. The other two armored cars moved ahead, bouncing over the lip of the ridge, and careening down the hill with incredible surefootedness.

"Christ, Wagner, what the hell is wrong with you?" Rommel yelled.

Jim shook his head. The armored car was in gear now, and he gave it a bit of gas as he moved it through the first two gears. The grinding of the gears screamed out, louder than the deep rumble of the engine.

Rommel sat down awkwardly, plopping back into his seat. Jim held the steering wheel tight, his knuckles making Fritz's bronzed hands white.

"What . . . is . . . wrong . . . with . . . you?"

"Something . . . I had . . . for lunch. . . ." Jim said.

Rommel raised his hands to the sky. "We haven't had lunch yet."

Slowly, Jim was getting the big car under control. It was not the same vehicle that the other soldiers were driving. This baby was twice as large, with a nasty-looking mounted machine gun in the back and oversized wheels that gripped the side of the ridge.

He started gaining on the other jeeps.

Rommel stood up again, keeping the British jeeps in his field glasses.

And Jim wondered just what his moral obligations were here. Should he try to stop the Desert Fox from capturing the British? Or should he do what Fritz would have done? And did any of it matter?

"Faster," Rommel snapped, banging a hand on the windshield. Jim put the pedal to the floor. The ridge began to level out.

Then he hit a boulder, camouflaged by the sun low in the east ahead of them, blending into the yellow-brown sand. The car cantilevered to the right. Jim's field glasses bounced out of his lap and went flying out of the vehicle.

"There goes your next month's salary, eh, Fritz?" Rommel said. Then, just as the jeep hit level ground, Rommel said, "Damn, they see us. Faster!"

"Yes, sir. . . ."

And Jim saw the small dots ahead of them—the "enemy" jeep suddenly kicking up a small plume of dust. The other two Afrika Korps cars had manned their machine guns, though, but the target was still miles away.

Was the Desert Fox mad at him? Jim wondered.

Would he say, "Vell, my Fritz, have you ever seen Stalingrad in vinter?"

Instead, Rommel started laughing, a great, full sound, as he lowered his glasses and sat back in his seat.

"We won't get lucky today, not with driving like that."

Jim nodded glumly. It occurred to him that he not only didn't know exactly who he was yet, he also didn't know what he looked like. A weirdly disturbing thought, that.

"You can take us back west. Let's see whether all

that great excitement about Sidi Rezegh, this hush-hush information—yes, let's see if there's anything to it.''

''You want to turn around?'' Jim asked.

''That's where Sidi Rezegh is, isn't it?'' Rommel asked. Jim slowed and Rommel waved to the other two jeeps, calling off the chase. ''Let's go see what the British have planned for us at the airport.''

Jim nodded. Then he asked a question. An embarrassing question.

''Sir, what's the date today?''

Rommel looked over at him and shook his head. ''You must have gotten your head all shaken up. It's November 18th, Oberstleutnant Wagner—''

There was one other question Jim wanted to ask. A really crucial question.

What year is it?

But Jim figured he might be better off waiting to see if he could figure out that one for himself. . . .

12

''He's there. So we use him,'' McManus said. ''It's that simple.''

Ali ran over to Lindstrom. The historian was bent over the printouts. ''Professor, what is he saying?''

''Hmm. Well, you see, if we're talking about a one-way experience here, then it would be crazy to send someone else . . . not if your boyfriend is already, er, involved—''

''He's not my 'boyfriend,' he's my—''

Lindstrom waved away her nit-picking. ''Whatever he is, he's there. And, based on his academic background, I'd say we pretty much lucked out, eh, McManus?''

''We'll see.''

Ali felt overwhelmed by the craziness in the Time Lab. Maybe they were all mad. Maybe Jim hadn't really gone anywhere. She wanted to run from the building and get some help . . . some *sane* help.

Someone to get Jim back.

''I'm leaving here,'' she announced, walking toward the twin doors that led out.

''I'm afraid—'' Lindstrom started. . . .

She grabbed one of the door handles and pulled on it.

''Security won't let anyone out. Not without my permission,'' McManus said. ''Of course, if you need rest, some place to lie down, they can escort you to—''

She turned around. "I'm a *prisoner?* I can't leave?"

McManus shook his head. "Sorry. It's out of the question. For lots of reasons."

Dr. Jacob hurried over to the cadaverous McManus and whispered something.

"What's he saying? What is he telling you? Is it about Jim?" Ali yelled.

She didn't like people telling what she could or couldn't do. Never had. It was—her father never tired of reminding her—her one great character flaw.

She disagreed with that assessment.

"Ah, good news. It's okay, Dr. Jacob," McManus instructed Jacob. "We can talk around her. Ms. Moreau isn't going anywhere."

"That's what you think," Ali muttered. She walked over to McManus and grabbed his arm, holding it strongly, squeezing, just the way her aikido master had shown her. If she needed to, she could hurt the old man severely.

"Please," he said, a thin smile on his lips. "My arm . . ."

She let go.

"What did he say?" she demanded again.

"Dr. Jacob says that all indications show that your Mr. Tiber made the shift."

"Shift? What shift?"

"We had to move quickly," McManus said. He seemed to busy himself playing with the computer keyboard, ignoring her eyes. "But it appears that he's fine."

"He's no longer in 1962, Alessandra," Lindstrom said. "And he's not in Hamburg. You see, we've isolated the source of the problems—all the anomalies we see outside."

"What anomalies? What are you talking about?"

Lindstrom sighed. McManus sat down before the monitors, still acting thoroughly preoccupied, but he started talking . . . slowly . . . calmly. . . .

"We told you that what is going on outside, what

people accept as *history,* is simply not the way things are supposed to be. The past has been altered, and that alters our present."

"But why wouldn't we know that?"

"Because," McManus said, "*your* history has been changed. Whatever was the past has, to those outside, never happened. There can be no memories of events that didn't happen, obviously. The true past is lost forever."

"Except," Lindstrom said, "in here. With all that garish red shielding, this building is protected from any alterations to time. The Red Building is like an enormous memory bank, a protected sanctuary for unimpeachable history."

A thought occurred to Ali. One she was surprised she didn't have before.

"Why is it happening?"

McManus looked up at Lindstrom, as if asking him to tackle that question. But when the portly history prof coughed, McManus spoke up.

"There's someone else—some other group of scientists. And they have a machine just like ours."

"A better machine," Lindstrom added.

"Yes, a better machine. And"—McManus stood up, his eyes aglow, fascinated by the whole idea—"they are changing time, making alterations according to their wishes."

"But why?" Ali asked.

McManus shrugged. "Power. Wealth. Ideology. Who knows? We've been able to determine that they exist, and we've picked up tracers indicating in what time periods and locations they are operating. But that is all."

Ali remembered something McManus had said. "A 'better' machine? What do you mean . . . better?"

"They can come back. Whoever they are, they've licked the insanity problem. We get readings, fluctuations in the background recording of Cerenkov radiation, the radiation emitted by the stream of tachyon particles. And, well, it appears that they can go back and forth.''

''Very handy. . . .'' Lindstrom said.

''Yes,'' McManus agreed unhappily. ''Very.''

It was all too much, Ali thought. Not only did she have to accept the fact that Jim was bouncing around in the past—presumably forever—but now she had to doubt whatever memories she had.

How much of her past was real? And how much was altered?

''Has my past been affected?''

Lindstrom laughed, but McManus shot him an angry glance.

Now McManus became consoling, comforting. He put a hand on her arm. ''Yes. But there will be much more to come, much that you will be protected from . . . as long as you're in here.''

She pulled her arm away. She was in no mood for comforting. ''And I'm supposed to hide in here, safe from the changes?''

''No. Not hide. But we can't do anything to stop them if we're on the outside. In here, with Lindstrom's help, we can know how things should turn out. And we can try to put them right . . . with help.''

''That's what Jim is supposed to do?''

McManus nodded.

''That is what we hope.''

A sudden bleeping sound filled the Time Lab. McManus hurried back to the computer console.

''What's that?'' Ali asked McManus, then turned to Lindstrom. ''What is it?''

''A signal,'' Lindstrom said tiredly. ''Whenever two time voyagers near each other.''

''The other person you mentioned—he's back there, back with Jim?'' Ali asked Lindstrom.

Lindstrom shook his head. ''Yes, but he's not close enough, not yet. No, our boy is too far away.'' Lindstrom pointed at a flashing red light. ''Whoever this is . . . he's not one of ours.''

* * *

The armored car crested a hill, and then Jim saw the gaggle of tanks, in no special formation, their crews sitting atop them. The wind sent small whirls of sand and dust dancing around the impromptu camp.

The other two cars stopped and Jim pulled alongside.

As soon as he stopped, Rommel hopped out. Two soldiers hurried up with a large gas can and started filling the tank of Rommel's armored car.

What the hell am I supposed to do? Jim thought. Pretty soon it's going to be pretty obvious that something is wrong with . . . with . . .

Oberstleutnant Fritz Wagner.

Communications officer . . . and sometime driver for the Desert Fox.

Thank god. A few more bits from Wagner's memory. Already it seemed to Jim that Wagner's secret info was locked up much tighter than Wolfie's. Maybe it has something to do with intellect, or control. . . .

But there. At least I know who I am. It's wonderful how these bits and pieces fall into place. If I can wait long enough, maybe I'll eventually know what's going on.

"Big screw up, eh, Fritz?"

Jim turned. It was another Wehrmacht lieutenant, like him. A tall, beefy man with a vapidly full grin.

"You know, the Field Marshal needs competent help."

The man's accent was thick, loaded with guttural clicks and pops. He's a Bavarian, thought Jim. From the deep south of the German Reich.

Jim waved him away.

An infantryman ran up to the car. His face was pulled tight. He was young—maybe eighteen or nineteen—but he looked as old as the sand. "Dispatch from Berlin," the soldier said, handing Jim a burgundy folder bearing the Nazi seal displaying an eagle. He read the word Reichskanzlei. Jim took it.

And held it.

"Aren't you going to open it, mein Fritz?" the officer asked, still standing there, grinning.

"Look," Jim said, hoping to get the German gorilla out of his face, "I've had a rough afternoon. Surely there's something useful you could be doing?"

The man feigned shock. "What's this? A temper? No more sense of humor from our Fritzie?" He started walking away. "The desert air must not agree with you." He laughed.

Then Jim heard rumbling—like dragons roaring in the distance.

The ground shook, and the air carried the muffled explosions. Rommel stood by a tent, talking with someone in an SS uniform.

This is not good, Jim thought. It's one thing to be hanging out in prepsychedelic Hamburg. But to be in North Africa . . . in . . . in . . .

1941.

Of course. November. 1941. And this has got to be somewhere near Tobruk, near Rommel's obsession.

Tobruk.

The Desert Fox had been determined to take it away from the British, no matter how long his supply lines became . . . no matter how many "skirmishes" sprang up at his rear.

Tobruk. It has to be around here somewhere.

"All set, sir," the infantryman with the gas can said to him.

And then, chilling, eerie words . . .

"Heil Hitler."

And, fighting to sound as natural as possible, Jim raised an arm, desultorily, and repeated the phrase.

"Heil Hitler."

1941. The sun was blindingly brilliant, and growing warmer, hot. The small depression glimmered under the light.

Jim knew what was ahead. The African Campaign made for a fascinating story. Armored Knights of the

Desert. The last bit of civilized warfare . . . before the real nightmare of World War II began.

And the victorious Afrika Korps was due to be dealt its first major defeat. A defeat from which it would never really recover.

And Jim would get to see it.

And hopefully live through it.

Rommel came running over to the armored car.

"All set, Fritz?"

"Yes, sir."

"Good. And please, Fritz . . . not so heavy with the clutch this time."

As the Field Marshal talked, another soldier got in the back of the car, manning the gun. Jim heard him snap open the fasteners to the ammunition box. The soldier brought the string of shells up to the gun, feeding them into the barrel.

Real soldiers, Jim thought. Real guns. Real shells.

The tank crews scurried inside their machines. The tanks—there were two types, both monsters—rumbled to life. Jim imagined how hot and sticky they must be inside. It had to be hell to drive them.

But—God—to be in battle, to be getting shelled while you sweated away your life. That had to be the real nightmare.

He looked up. Rommel was checking the tanks as they rumbled onto the line, falling into an orderly formation. Then the General glanced down at the maroon folder in Jim's lap.

"Ah, more news from Berlin? What does it say?"

Jim cleared his throat. "I didn't look. I thought—"

"Come, come. Let us have a look. I've been promised updates three times a day. Let's see if Berlin makes good on its incredible promise. Read to me . . ."

Jim undid the string on the envelope and pulled out a single sheet of paper. The Wehrmacht eagle was on top of the page, and then, Office of the Wehrmacht, Reich Chancellery, Berlin.

Jim glanced at the page.

What if I can't read the German?

He looked at it. For a second it was a sheet of mile-long words that he would have to translate one at a time—if at all. But then—as if a mist cleared—he understood everything on the page.

"Well?" Rommel said.

"Cunningham's Eighth Army is moving in force to Sidi Rezegh. Montgomery plans to have him push on to Tobruk."

Rommel shook his head.

"I still don't believe it," the Field Marshal said quietly.

"Believe what?" Jim asked, wondering whether it was protocol for an oberstleutnant to ask questions of his commander.

Rommel laughed. His face was beaten and brown by the weather, but when he smiled there was humanity and intelligence.

You'll take poison, Jim wanted to tell him. And you'll die, a fallen hero, before you can make good on your solemn oath to assassinate Der Führer.

This is your time, Jim wanted to say. The days of glory, before the world begins exacting its terrible revenge on the German leader and its nation. In the end, Rommel would know—like so many others—where his duty lay.

But not yet.

"I thought the key was Tobruk," Rommel said. He paused. "I still think so. But this 'new' intelligence is too direct. I must act on it. Especially since Berlin promises to take care of supplies."

Rommel turned away, and waved at the commanders of the long line of tanks, and then at the other armored cars.

"Enough talk, Fritz. Let's join the others—and see what the British really have planned for us today."

Jim eased up on the clutch, amazed at how adept he had become in such a short time. The car barely lurched.

"Much . . . better," Rommel said.

They were in front of the line.

And behind them . . . trailed a long stream of armored cars and tanks, miles of them, leaving a wispy plume of churning dust, swirling against the deep blue sky.

13

Fortunately, Field Marshal Erwin Rommel apparently preferred issuing detailed instructions on just how the line of tanks and armored cars was to cross the great sandy plains. Jim just had to listen to the instructions and figure out what to do.

Then, one hour away from the camp, they hooked up with an even larger force.

This had to be the main body of panzers, and they quickly fell into the long line. Only now, there were motorized artillery, large cannons that Jim could imagine delivering a deafening roar . . . as well as punching some nasty holes in the opposition's tanks.

The terrain was barren, ghostly, Daliesque, Jim thought without any humor. Rommel, sitting quietly beside him, seemed to sense Jim's thoughts.

"I miss my gardens," the Field Marshal said. "There's a special kind of pleasure in watching things bloom . . . in nurturing them. This," he said, gesturing at the sandy wastes, "is a heartless terrain, no?" He paused. The roar of the great army behind them made it an effort to shout each word.

"Yes, sir," Jim said.

Then Rommel said something else, which Jim couldn't hear. Jim thought of nodding his head, feigning agreement with some statement that he didn't catch. But, as that could prove embarrassing if it had been a question, or an order, he said—

"Excuse me?"

"But it's good terrain for war," Rommel said loudly.

Yes, Jim thought. Great for war. Then . . . he had an odd thought.

We're friends.

This Fritz, his aide, adjutant, was more than just a duty officer who delivered and read dispatches, and drove the Field Marshal around. We've spoken about things. About life before the war. About the honorable battle of great opponents. About where this will all lead.

That made Jim feel a bit better. At least if I fuck up too much, I have that.

And as the metal armada sailed the sandy sea, more bits and pieces of Fritz Wagner started to surface.

This Fritz Wagner is a distant cousin to the opera composer Richard Wagner's family. It's apparently something important to old Fritz. And above the endless din of the engines, Jim heard tunes in his head, bits and pieces of melodies that were definitely *not* the Beatles. Little snippets of the Teutonic operas that he must have grown up with. . . .

How about that. . . .

How about—

Wait a second, Jim thought, his hands gripping the ribbed steering wheel hard, holding on, remembering what the dispatch had said.

The British General Cunningham was moving on Sidi Rezegh, just twelve miles southeast of Tobruk. From what Jim remembered of his quick study of the North Africa campaign, that sounded right. This was the most confusing theater of the war. It was nearly impossible to chart the chaotic battles of the campaign. Whole armies made wrong turns, fighting nothing but dust and sand. And when real battles did occur—not just skirmishes but full-blown—it was pretty much a matter of luck.

But General Bernard Law Montgomery? He's not supposed to be here, in North Africa. Not now. The hero of this battle, the iron will behind Operation Crusader, the great British pincer, the first setback to the Desert Fox . . . was General Auchinleck—the Auk.

Not Monty. He wasn't due here until 1942, when Winston Churchill was playing musical commanders, upset by the tenacity of the Desert Fox.

Yet here he was. And it was all wrong. Just as wrong, Jim thought, as my being here.

And there was something else. . . .

Something, Jim thought, that should have been obvious to me from the beginning.

Rommel, with his prize Panzer divisions, wasn't supposed to be here, chugging off to the airfield at Sidi Rezegh.

Not at all.

Tobruk—that was Rommel's concern. . . . Tobruk, until it was too late.

And if there was one thing that historians agreed on, it was this: If Rommel had thrown everything against the British forces at Sidi Rezegh right from the beginning, he could have stomped Crusader into a pipe dream. With a bit of luck—and supplies—he could have turned it into a massive debacle . . . another Dunkirk. He could have pushed the still-reeling British all the way back to the Mediterranean.

Jim turned and looked at Rommel. Then back at the line of tanks.

And he thought, just what the hell is going on here?

This is rewriting history, changing the entire goddam story of the North African campaign. Maybe changing the outcome of the war.

And I'm here, driving the man who's going to do it.

Jim looked ahead, dazed, confused.

And, for the first time since he began this crazy business, scared. On the horizon he saw a cloud. A dark, black, smudgy cloud. Sitting there. Alone, as if awaiting other clouds to join it.

It was smoke from artillery fire, Jim guessed.

The first ugly blotch in the beautiful blue sky.

* * *

Ollie Johnson sat on top of the tank, hoping a stray breeze would spring up and dry some of the sweat off his body. The heat and the smell from the cramped tank were unbearable.

He kept his mouth stuffed with gum, chewing all the time, always sticking in a fresh piece, hoping that the smell and the flavor would somehow keep the stench of sweat and machine oil from filling his nostrils.

His commander stood outside, talking to other commanders.

Everyone was asking the same question.

Where the bleedin' hell was Rommel? Where was this fabled Desert Fox? Was he a ghost, a magician who could make his armies appear and disappear at will?

The Brigadier, old Willy Norrie, didn't seem to have a clue.

Something poked his backside.

"Eh, mate, do you mind popping yer butt out of the hatch? I don't appreciate you scenting my breathin' air before it seeps down."

Ollie looked down, into the shadows. Jack Wright, the driver, was smoking up the main cabin with a fag. Couldn't even be bothered to get his ass out of the tank. He's just happy to be out of the driver's compartment, buried in the nose of the tank.

"If you want some air, Wright, why don't you just come topside?"

"Why bother? Chief is just going to 'op back in and tell us that we're off fookin' huntin' again. Besides," Wright grinned, "it's a damn sight cooler here"—he turned and pointed to his station, buried in the hull of the tank—"than there. You boys got the life of Riley."

"Whatever you say, Wright." Johnson hoisted his body out of the turret and spun around, freeing up the opening for whatever fresh air happened to billow down the hatch.

" 'Ta, mate," Wright said.

Better him than me, thought Johnson. It was a stinking sweatbox in the gun turret. But Johnson knew he'd go absolutely off his bean if he had to sit in the cramped driver's seat, surrounded by all the hot metal and controls, with just a small port for air.

I couldn't handle it, Johnson thought. No way.

He saw the chief nod, and then they caught a signal from the front of the line.

"Moving out," Johnson said, calling down to Wright. Wright was a dour son of a bitch, but Johnson found himself liking the tough Scot with his bushy moustache. The driver seemed totally nervy. Nothing shook him up.

Of course, what have they seen of the war? A few skirmishes? Some shelling when they passed Gabr Saleh?

Nothing to really test our mettle.

Or—Johnson grinned as he looked at the Crusader tank—our metal.

The tank's commander, Lieutenant Ed Collins—a Northern Irishman who worked real hard to swallow his brogue—ran over to the tank, followed by the radio operator, a scrawny kid named Brian Poole who only seemed to speak when he was on the radio. Didn't laugh at the dirty jokes, didn't even crack a smile.

Probably scared shitless.

Probably.

Just like me.

I just want to survive this and get home, Ollie thought. That's all. Hell, I don't even mind a wound, maybe a bad leg, or something to show off to the boys at the pub while I tell them my war stories. The time I chased the Desert Fox.

Just—Ollie Johnson thought coming as close as he could to a prayer—just let me survive.

The chief clambered on top of the tank. The tank commander got the benefit of keeping his head popped out of the hatch, letting the air keep him cool. There was no seat for him, though. He had to stand all the time.

Still, any one of the men would swap his sweatbox seats for that job.

"We're moving on, sir?" Johnson asked.

Collins nodded. Then, smelling the cigarette smoke in the turret he yelled down at Wright.

"Put the fag out!" Collins yelled.

But the driver had already scurried to his seat near the front of the hull.

Poole slipped down, all quiet, into his cramped corner.

"No smoking in the tank! You hear me, Wright?"

"Yes, sir," Wright shot back, his voice almost lost in the surrounding metal.

"We'll run with the cannon hatch open, Johnson," the commander said.

Johnson nodded and slid down, close to the gun that he had no interest in firing.

"Ready," Wright called up.

The commander was able to see the line of tanks slowly fall into formation. They sat there, getting hotter and hotter, with the rumble of the engine and the stench of their bodies growing, filling the war machine.

"Alright!" the commander yelled.

And then the tank lurched forward.

Ali ran a hand through Jim's fine hair. Jim's mouth hung open. A small, whitish pool of saliva gathered in the crease of Jim's lips. She watched the slow, rhythmic rise and fall of his chest, the steady pace of his breathing.

She reached out for a tissue from a box on a nearby table. She dabbed at his lips, thinking, Why . . . it almost looks like he's just sleeping.

She heard a sound. The drip of insulin, falling from the clear plastic sack into a small tube.

The other man was there, too.

Older than Jim.

She hadn't asked who he was, but Ali guessed he was another scientist, or maybe somebody from the government. One week. That's how long McManus said the man had been back there.

That was the funny thing. Time—elapsed time—was skewed. The flow of events, the sequence of cause and effect that we call time—according to the Time Lab's discoveries—linked to the creation and expansion of the universe. Time slows down as the expanding universe slows. A day in the here and now could equal a week one thousand years ago.

This room—set up as a medical lab—was dark, except for the faint glow given off by the monitors keeping track of the time travelers' pulse and respiration.

It's like a morgue, Ali thought.

The two bodies, lifeless, comatose. As near death as bodies could be.

She reached out and touched Jim's forehead, cool and dry. Then her fingers touched his lips.

They were so unnatural now. Jim was always laughing, smiling. He was the last prankster in a world that had become too serious. Now he was like a corpse.

And he might be gone forever.

And when this was over, this great experiment, this great crisis, someone would eventually suggest shutting down the machine, taking out the IV.

That would happen.

Her hand touched his hair.

It was hard to imagine Jim Tiber a hero. She smiled. Yet that was the job they had in mind for him.

And she thought of all the confusing information they had told her. The source of the anomalies was traced to 1941, in North Africa. The beginning of the Allies' counterattack.

She didn't know much about history—at least the way it was supposed to be. Jim, with the help of the other traveler, was to set it right.

It seemed incredible. And impossible.

She put her hand on his chest, letting it rise and fall with each breath. Rise. And fall.

She didn't hear the door open behind her. Some steps. She turned slowly.

"Oh," she said, seeing someone in the shadows. The man came closer.

It was Lindstrom, his greyish-red beard picking up some of the light.

"Sorry," he said. "I didn't want to startle you." He came closer, looking down at Jim. "He's alright?"

Ali nodded. "Yes," she smiled. "Sleeping like a baby."

"Oh, let's hope he's not sleeping. That won't do us any good at all."

She felt Lindstrom look at her, studying her. "You know, you shouldn't think about him, not now. I'm sure they'll work out a way to get him back. It will just take—er, well—time."

She nodded, not believing him.

He touched her elbow. "There's coffee, in the next room. Fresh pot. And some muffins."

Ali pulled her hand away from Jim, thinking—this is like a wake. Standing here, looking at the body. Only he's not dead.

Not yet.

Lindstrom took her arm more firmly, a gentle, guiding hold, urging her away from the bed, the wires, the monitors.

"You said you'd help. . . ." Lindstrom said gently.

She nodded.

"Well . . . we could use that help now."

She took one more look at Jim's sprawling body and turned away, back to the Time Lab.

Ready to do whatever she could to help.

14

How do I get out of here? Jim wondered. And is that even a viable question?

He looked at Rommel, the great tactician lost in his thoughts . . . and in the endless scroll of the desert ahead.

What a place! The only plants were scrubby bushes that a camel would think twice about munching. And though the desert looked flat enough, it hid countless depressions and folds that made the ride jarringly bumpy.

And he had another question.

What the hell do I look like? Jim wondered.

He saw that his body was squat and powerful. No flab on this baby. But what was the face like? Not that it's any vanity, Jim thought. Just that it's nice to know what you look like.

He looked around the armored car for a rearview mirror, but there was only a small mirror suspended out the left side of the car.

And where did Rommel get this armored car from? It was obviously of English origin, with a tachometer from Southampton and a windshield from Shepperton. It resembled an overgrown jeep, more heavily armored and with plenty of room for a gunner in the rear.

Best not ask, Jim thought. It has to be one of those things that I'm probably supposed to know.

Like my family.

Like my—

A wife. Small, blonde. Elsa. And a son, a five-year-old boy with rosy cheeks named Rolf. I can see them! Jim thought. Like a photograph in his mind. Standing in some platz, in a small city, dressed in traditional German folk costumes. Laughing. Eating some big pastries.

An important image, Jim thought. That's why I'm seeing it. Old Fritz is reaching out, trying to push through the intrusion of my mind.

He wants me gone.

Nothing I'd like better, my little Deutschlander, Jim thought. Nothing at all. Except until I find my way back, I'm stuck here.

He rubbed his eyes and shook his head.

"Something wrong?" Rommel asked, looking over at him.

The armored car hit a bump, tipping the vehicle awkwardly to the left.

"No," Jim said. "A small headache. Nothing, really . . ."

Rommel grunted. He obviously wasn't interested in anything as small as that.

The radio crackled to life. The Field Marshal picked up the handset. "Yah. Good. We're about ten miles away." Then he put the receiver back.

"We'll be getting the sun behind us, Fritz." Rommel looked up at the sky. "A bright, beautiful sun. It will be right in their eyes."

Jim nodded. What's he talking about? he wondered.

Rommel stood up and pointed at a small line of hills slightly to the west.

"Go around there," the General said, "and stay as close to the hills as possible. It will be a wonderful surprise for them . . . wonderful."

Rommel stood up and Jim nodded his understanding. The driving of this trucklike car was starting to feel almost instinctive.

So, he thought, a little bit of Fritz's presence was acceptable. Useful.

Just as long as things didn't get out of hand.

* * *

"I don't see anything," Collins said. Poole was sitting on the front of the tank, one arm draped lovingly over the barrel of the tank's cannon. Ollie sat next to the radioman, glad to take the commander up on his offer to ride outside the tank.

The stench inside was unbelievable.

Ollie saw the airport ahead, just a small strip perched on a flat outcrop of rock. Surrounding it were small huts and shacks, and a few British planes that had landed—unopposed—just a few hours ago.

Sidi Rezegh.

While their brothers-in-arms sweated it out in the beleaguered port of Tobruk, the Eighth Army was launching a grand attack on a deserted airport.

No wonder we're losing the bloody war, Ollie thought, creeping up for a better look.

"Johnson!" the commander barked. "Get down. I can't see."

There were a half-dozen tanks, a few infantry tanks for troop hauling—Matildas—in front of them, streaming up the gradual rise to the airstrip.

Lumbering was more like it. Nobody liked those tanks. They were easy prey for the German panzers. But until enough new tanks came along, they needed everything to pull this off—the first counterattack against Hitler's invincible Wehrmacht.

" 'Ey, Poole," Wright said from deep within the cavernous depths of the tank. "Someone's ringing you up."

Poole hurried to the hatch, and Collins let him slip down to his radio.

They waited, the hot air still, stagnant, the greyish metal now painful to the touch.

They waited, ready to climb up to the airfield, for Poole to pop back up.

Collins sat back leaving the hatch free.

Then—a human gopher—Poole was there, looking sheepish, as if embarrassed by his information.

"Enemy tanks spotted, south-southeast of the airfield."

The commander nodded. "Does Cunningham want us to stop?" he asked.

Poole shook his head. "No, sir. Full out to the objective."

Johnson saw the commander nod, none too happily. He'd like to go home too, Ollie guessed.

We'd all like to go home.

"Poole . . ." the commander said to the still-waiting radioman, "did they—"

But the commander stopped. Changed his mind.

"Thank you, Poole, Best stay below." He looked up at Johnson. "You too, gunner."

"Yes, sir," Ollie Johnson said.

He crawled past the taut brown legs of the commander, tanned into human leather by the sand, the wind, and the terrible, incessant sun.

And he thought—I know what question you were thinking about . . . ready to ask. . . .

South-southeast.

That's the direction to Tobruk. Where Rommel is supposed to be holding the city hostage, under siege.

Was this just a small force of German panzers on patrol? Or was it the Afrika Korps ready to meet the Eighth Army head on?

Johnson crawled to the gun hatch, staring out the small sight, seeing nothing but the rubble-filled slope of the hill and wondering . . . like his commander . . .

Do I really want to know the answer?

Ali organized the printouts into three piles. One included changes to the outside that had already been noted and logged. The second included the new material that the computer linked to a "transference" in North Africa.

Then there was the third pile. This included events that—for now—didn't seem to link up to *any* changes in the external history.

"More coffee?" McManus said, smiling. She

looked up and shook her head. "There are cots . . . upstairs . . . if you want to rest." The doctor paused, embarrassed. "I won't have you guarded . . . not now."

"Thank you," Ali said. "But I'd rather stay here and help."

"Good. I have Jacob resting. He was close to exhaustion. I just wish we had some idea what the blazes was going on with all this missing art . . . it has to be important, but I don't know—"

Lindstrom, squatting at an oversized table in the center of the room, leaped to his feet. "I've got it."

"What?" McManus asked.

Lindstrom paced in front of Ali. "It's brilliant," he said to the air. "Remarkable. Foolproof."

"What is?" Ali asked, anxious for the historian to explain.

"I know what they're doing. They're making a good idea better. Just look at it! It's Goering's art heist, his looting of the best Europe has to offer. But the haul is twice, maybe three times as big."

McManus scratched his balding head. "But what would that do?"

"Nothing . . . by itself, that is. But if all that art wasn't recovered?" He looked at Ali. And he repeated his statement, slowly, as if teaching her a lesson from a primer. "If the art wasn't recovered?"

"It . . . it—" Ali said, hoping to flash onto Lindstrom's point.

"Would be worth billions . . . billions!" the historian said exultingly.

"Oh, God," McManus said.

"Excuse me," Ali said, "But I still don't see—"

There was a knock on the door. McManus pressed a buzzer, and one of the security guards came in.

"What's wrong, Toland?"

The guard seemed embarrassed. "The men at the outer gate. They're gone. Ran off . . . just gone."

McManus nodded.

Ali saw Lindstrom run up to the scientist and whisper something to him. "Yes, yes," he said to Lindstrom. Then, back to the guard. "We expected that, Toland. Don't worry about it. Just keep your other men well inside the building and—"

The guard looked even more discomfited.

"But that's the other thing, Doctor. My men are getting spooked by everything they see out there. Real spooked." He cleared his throat. "And I don't know what to tell them."

Ali saw McManus fire Lindstrom an angry glance, as if he blamed Lindstrom for whatever was happening.

"Yes," McManus said. "Well, we'd better walk up with you. We'll see the situation firsthand. I'll talk to your men."

Ali ran over to him.

"Doctor, I'd like to go up with you and see. I mean, I want to stay here, now. But I'd like to see what's going on—outside."

Again McManus looked at Lindstrom, and the historian nodded agreement.

It's curious, Ali thought, but it was seeming more and more like the real control of the project was in the historian's hands.

Ali followed the burly guard to the elevator and they went up the two flights silently.

The elevator opened on the main floor. Two young guards, their faces plastered against the thick glass, were staring out. They were so engrossed in what they were looking at they didn't even hear the group from the Time Lab arrive.

"Ahem," Toland cleared his throat and the two guards spun around.

"It's worse," one of them said, his voice none too steady. "Every few minutes it's something else."

"Yes, yes," Lindstrom said, pushing his burly body between the two guards.

Ali watched him. Even Lindstrom grew quiet when he looked through the thick glass. His face was white and ashy when he turned away from the window.

"Pretty . . . amazing . . ." he said, stepping away.

McManus took a purposely hurried look, feigning a lack of alarm. But even he grew quiet when his face was at the window.

Then he turned and gestured toward the small window, offering a look to Ali.

I'm not so sure I want to do this, Ali thought. But like the box proffered to Pandora, a glimpse was irresistible.

She stepped close to the window, putting her nose up close. For a second all she saw was darkness, and the small eddies of fog on the glass made by her breath.

But there was a moon out on this—what started out as a crisp fall night. The milky-white light cast everything in a frosty metallic color. Everything. . . .

The fence around the Time Lab was gone. In its place there were scraggly trees, bushes, and piles of debris. It looked as if there had never been a fence there.

Because there hadn't been.

Not in whatever was currently passing for history outside.

But then she saw through the bare spots on the trees. Just the faintest images, lost in the half-light of night. Buildings. The Campus of Columbia University.

There were no great dormitory towers in the distance. And the buildings she did see were dark, their roof lines following irregular patterns, bumpy and broken.

And abandoned.

"My God . . . what's happened? It looks like a ruins . . . a slum. What—"

Lindstrom took Ali by the shoulder. "Come," he said. "We have a lot to do."

"Yes," McManus said, turning to the guards. "This is only a taste of things to come. You and your guards should know that, Toland. No one—I mean no one—should leave the building for any reason whatsoever."

One of the guards started to speak. "But we can't stay here for—"

McManus held up a hand. The guards probably have wives, children, Ali thought. And they're standing here watching the outside world—as they knew it—melt away. Had it been explained to them? She wondered. Or were they just told to follow orders?

How mad this all is.

"Do your job," McManus said. "And let us get back to ours."

He hurried back to the elevator, and Ali and Lindstrom followed. The empty elevator awaited them. McManus hit the button, and the door shut slowly.

"*If* we can do our job," McManus muttered, his face twisted . . . angry. . . .

Scared.

"If there's enough goddam—"

No one needed to hear the last word. . . .

15

Time . . . Erwin Rommel thought.

That's what war is all about. Time. Using it. Beating it. Borrowing it. Stealing it.

Time. The morning sun favored the British, flush with tanks and a desperate desire for a success—somewhere, anywhere—against the Third Reich. The morning sun would light up the battlefield for them, blinding the Afrika Korps.

And ten hours later the same sun would help us. The burnt orange light making it so easy to spot the silhouettes of the slowest-moving British tanks, their "waltzing Matildas" that are so easily outdistanced . . . and outclassed by our Mark IIIs and Mark IVs.

So what if this General Montgomery is sending General Cunningham against us with a two-to-one tank ratio? It makes no difference, Rommel thought, not if the other side spreads them out and you can attack them in detail . . . go after each group, one by one, using the desert, and the light.

And time.

He brought his field glasses up to his eyes.

The airfield was ahead. General Ludwig Cruewell was bringing his panzers to the right, ready to stream up the embankment, ready to destroy what was left of the British force—after the artillery barrage littered the airfield with chunks of hot, twisted metal.

The Field Marshal looked left and right. They weren't there yet. The field was empty.

The British would be young, brave boys, like his soldiers were when they first came to save the foundering Italians and their dream of a North African empire. Many of them would die quickly. Consciousness would disappear, as if it vanished in a sneeze.

Others would die more slowly.

And Rommel knew what that was like. He had peered inside the wrecked remains of his own tanks.

Large chunks of brain spattered inside the tank, some of it cooked by explosive fire. There would be twisted and trapped bodies, pinned by the metal walls of the tanks, stranded in hell.

What then for his wonderful Afrika Korps?

There would come an end to the victories, and no great homecoming in Bayern or Prussia. No garlands of flowers and speeches about their service to the Fatherland. Just war. More and more of it, until it would seem like it was the only thing that they would ever know.

But no matter, the Field Marshal thought. Time is running out. For the war. For this new Germany.

I am a soldier, Rommel thought. A planner of strategies, a leader of men. Out here, with all this wonderful open space, this magnificent battlefield, I can do my job.

Until the day when the war won't be in North Africa anymore . . . or even in the vastness of Mother Russia. The time when it will be in Deutschland itself. Not this year. Or the next. Or maybe even the year after that.

But it will come.

And then Rommel spoke—to hear the words, to feel their dark, ancient power. He said them aloud. . . .

"It will come."

"Hmmm," Rommel said. Jim looked over at him.

Without knowing a great deal of the protocol—or even the exact nature of Fritz's relationship with Rommel—Jim found himself responding in an informal way.

The general looked at him. He hadn't said much, and now there was an odd smile on his face. God, Jim thought. Does he suspect that there's something wrong with me? I hope he doesn't give me a pop quiz on German tanks or the infrastructure of the Wehrmacht High Command.

"Excuse me?" Jim said.

Rommel—still smiling—shook away his query. "Nothing, mein Fritz." Then the Field Marshal pointed ahead. "We'll stop just where that small rise begins. You see it?"

Jim looked where he was pointing. There was a gradual slope leading up to a broad plateau dotted with small buildings. That must be the airfield, Jim knew. It was empty . . . undefended.

"Yes, sir," Jim responded.

Then Rommel spoke into the radio, issuing instructions to the Afrika Korps, instructions that had no meaning for Jim.

"Fifteenth Panzer flank left of first artillery . . . Twenty-first Panzer flank right . . . motorized artillery to the immediate front . . ."

Jim looked over and saw Rommel nodding, listening to someone.

"Yes, General," Rommel said testily. "I want them brought to the immediate front." He hung up the radio. "The stupid ass," Rommel said to the wind.

Jim almost nodded, but then he figured that agreement might not be in order.

Rommel stood up, pushing down his goggles with one hand and holding his cap on his head with the other. A fierce wind had sprung up. And it grew stronger as they approached the plateau. Scrubby bushes rolled past them, looking like stilted sagebrush. Once Jim neglected to watch where they were going, and the armored car rolled bumpily into a fat depression. Jim had to hold on tightly to the steering wheel as his fanny went flying into the air.

Rommel, Jim was chagrined to notice, nearly cantilevered out of the car,

"Christ, Wagner! What the hell is wrong with you that you can't drive anymore?"

"Sorry, sir. I—"

"There!" Rommel shouted. "Stop up there. It's perfect."

Rommel pointed at a crease in the ground—the spot where the rise began. Then he picked up the radio.

"Move quickly, Cruewell," he shouted into the radiophone.

Jim stopped the armored car. He waited.

And then, all around him, there was the roar of the tanks and armored vehicles rumbling right and left, kicking up great clouds of dust.

Rommel was still on the radiophone, but Jim couldn't hear a thing.

The great panzer force moved with trained precision to either side of the plateau. Jim looked at the faces of the German tank commanders. They were brownish-black smudges, barely visible in the dust clouds. Their too-white eyes stared out of dusky faces, ghostlike, fierce, determined.

I wouldn't want to be facing them, Jim thought. Then he remembered that they weren't even supposed to be here. Not yet.

Rommel should be at Tobruk.

But here they were.

And Jim felt real bad for the British. . . .

"Hey, Ollie," Wright called back to him. "Could you ask the chief to go a bit slower? I'm getting bounced around like a bleedin' beach ball."

Ollie Johnson leaned down and was able to see just the back of Wright's head. There was a time when Ollie wished he was the driver. You got some bloody air from the tiny portholes in the front. It wasn't so goddam hot.

But then he heard the stories of what happened to the drivers who became trapped in their tin can compartments. They called it the dead-man's slot. If a tank took a hit, the commander might get his head blown off. The radio man might—hah, hah—catch on fire. The gunner—if he was a lucky sod, a *real* lucky sod—might be able to take a blow and scurry out before the tank blew.

But the driver.

Good as dead and trapped.

And if there was one thing Ollie intended, it was to be a lucky sod. I'm going to get through this, live through the whole fuckin' war. I've got a wife, he thought. That helps a fella. Gives you something to live for. The ones who are all alone, the ones who have nobody—they're the ones who always get it.

Sure. That's the way it worked.

The tank tilted back.

"We're climbing, mates," Collins called down. Ollie caught Poole's face, all white and scared. Ollie smiled as if to say, "Hey, it's okay."

He thought of saying something, like—we ain't going to see no Jerries. Not today, anyway. Hell, it will be almost nighttime by the time we get to wherever we're going.

"Now what are we bloody doing?" Wright yelled back.

"Chief says we're climbing," Ollie told him. "Going up a hill."

"Well," Wright said, "I can't tell you the wonderful things it's doing to my butt. There's this piece of metal jamming right—"

"Sir," Poole said, stammering a bit, barely audible over the noisy rattle of the tank. Poole snaked a hand up to the commander's leg, extending the radio.

Ollie caught Poole's wide-eyed stare, and gave him what he hoped was a reassuring grin.

Then the phone was handed back to Poole. And Collins called down to them, "The way's clear, lads. Not a Jerry in sight . . . no one in sight, apparently."

Ollie saw Poole smile. There, thought Ollie, was a boy who wasn't interested in war.

Not today, at any rate.

"Pick her up a bit, Wright. Let's keep up with the rest of the line," Collins yelled.

"Pick her up," Wright grumbled. "Pick her up . . . my baby pram was faster than this piece of—"

"There she is, lads. The airfield's just ahead."

Ollie smiled. He would like to have seen it.

Maybe, he thought, they could get out once they got there. Yeah . . . once everything was secure. They could get out. Take a leak. Smoke a few fags. Let the god-awful sweat dry.

Yeah. Sure. *That* was something to look forward to. Once they had the airfield . . .

"Steady," Rommel said to himself. "Steady. Just keep moving up, nice and steady. That's it. That's—"

The Field Marshal reached for the radiophone.

Jim looked around.

There was a line of cannons—the fabled artillery of the Afrika Korps—stretching in a clean line from either side of Rommel's command vehicle. The crews were frozen into a greyish tableau. Four men for each cannon. No smiles. No bantering. They were, Jim reflected, pros. Something human, something weak and soft, had long ago dried up somewhere in this desert. There were no warming thoughts passing through their minds, causing a momentary flicker of remembrance. No Christmas trees, or long-legged women, or frosty steins of beer. Those terrible, torturing thoughts died a long time ago.

Because, Jim guessed, if you didn't let all that go, you died.

These men were as much machines as the guns they manned, arching up, toward the plateau.

Jim didn't have a clue as to what was going on. Where were the fabled tactics of Rommel's tank corps, the clever maneuvers, the lightninglike pincers of tank warfare in the desert?

This was an ambush.

Rommel held the phone. And then he handed it to Jim. And asked . . .

"Ready?"

Jim nodded.

Take the phone, birdbrain, a voice inside his head prompted. And do what with it?

"Are you okay, Fritz? A bit unwell today, perhaps?"

"No, fine, sir—"

I should tell him, Jim thought crazily. Before I do something so stupid that he ends up putting a gun to my head and pulling the trigger.

Tell him what?

I'm not really Fritzie. You see, Fritzie's buried somewhere inside here—I think. And me—I'm really from the future, where your side—fortunately—lost the war.

And he thought . . . I could tell him more. *So much more.*

You tried to kill the Führer before he trashed Germany forever, before he made the word Germany synonymous with the greatest horrors ever conceived by humankind.

Sure. He could tell him all that.

"Well, snap to it, Wagner," Rommel barked.

Jim took the phone. Rommel jumped out of the armored car and scanned the horizon, looking up at the plateau.

Jim held the radiophone up to his ear.

"All ready, Oberstleutnant!" a voice said.

Jim repeated what he heard. "All ready, sir?"

Rommel nodded, but he didn't bring the field glasses down.

"Just a bit more," Rommel said. "A few more seconds . . . to let them fill the airfield, let them enjoy their prize. Before we shatter their fantasy."

Rommel nodded.

"Just a bit more . . . time . . ."

16

Ali rubbed her eyes and yawned, a long, luxurious groan that reminded her of how really cxhausted she was. The stacks of printouts in front of her were daunting, line after line of minute and major discrepancies in their accounting of historical data.

The material in front of her now was the most curious yet. It was a listing of over twelve hundred works of art "lost" during the war. The best of Picasso, Matisse, Van Gogh, Braque, and Cezanne, as well as hundreds of classical masters. Rembrandt. Breughel. DaVinci.

"Refill?" Lindstrom asked, picking up her cool, stained cup.

Ali shook her head. As tired as she was, she didn't think her nervous system could handle any more caffeine jolts. "I don't get this," she said, tapping her pencil at the listing.

"Yes," Lindstrom said, putting her cup back. "It is rather peculiar. Goering did, of course, steal nearly six hundred pieces of art. But they were almost all recovered at the end of the war. Now, in 'noveau time,' that number has doubled, and nearly half have not been recovered." Lindstrom shook his head and rubbed his scraggly beard. "Very odd indeed."

"I wish I knew more about art . . . or history. I'm afraid my physics isn't much help. Not with Dr. McManus around."

"Tsk, tsk," Lindstrom said. "A bit late to discover the value of a classical education. Still, don't fret. You're invaluable, my dear. Let's see," he said, leaning over Ali's workspace, next to the computers. "What have you done here so far?"

"I've separated the works that remain lost, by country and period. See," she said pointing to one list, "here's what we know was taken by Goering. And here, this is what the nouveau history shows as lost . . . and later recovered."

She look at Lindstrom, who was scratching his beard.

"Hmmm. Yes . . ." Then his eyes went wide. "Wait a second. Yes. That's possible. Let me see. Do you have some more lists?"

Ali shuffled through the oversized papers and produced more columns listing artworks, museums, and countries.

"That just might be it," Lindstrom said excitedly.

"Might be what?" Ali asked.

"Wait a second. I don't want to go off half-cocked. let me check something first. McManus!" he called to the Time Lab professor.

McManus, looking terribly drawn, exhausted, walked over to where Lindstrom stood. "Found something?"

"All our lines to the outside data services—?" Lindstrom started to ask.

"Are useless," McManus said tiredly. "They will all reflect the changes."

"I thought as much."

"What did you want to find out?" Ali asked him.

"Prices. What was the worth of the modern art during the war years . . . and how much did it appreciate over the decades?"

"I don't understand." Ali said.

She saw that Lindstrom was excited by his idea, pacing, walking back and forth. "The classic pieces, the stuff that Goering originally took were considered the most valuable in 1941. But what about fifty years later? If someone went back there with—er—revised price quotes, they'd know just what new pieces to steal.''

Ali nodded. ''But why steal the art?''

''Wait,'' Lindstrom said, holding up a hand. ''I've got an idea. But,'' he said turning to a ruminating McManus, ''is there anything we can find out here, using the lab's computers?''

McManus shook his head. ''Not really.'' But then he looked up, brightening. ''You need an outside data service, some current on-line information. But we might be able to get an approximation of the information you need.''

''How's that?''

''We have a number of CD-ROM information bases. They include typical information on the value of art work for the past hundred years.''

''Great, wonderful, my good doctor! That's just—''

McManus held up his hand. ''But it's not complete. If anything, it would just have typical prices, changes, trends, things like that.''

Lindstrom went over and hugged the gaunt Time Lab professor. Then turned, saw Ali and reached down and encircled her, planting a scratchy kiss on her cheek.

An unpleasant sensation, Ali thought, but the man's enthusiasm was contagious.

''That's all I need. Just a few prices on key pieces. That's all. Then,'' he said winking at Ali, ''Yes, then I'll know whether I'm right.''

About what? Ali wanted to ask, but Lindstrom hurried McManus to one of the computer/CD-ROM stations, while Ali tried to wait patiently for the rest of Lindstrom's brainstorm. . . .

There has to be a way out of this, Jim thought.

There probably were plenty of WWII freaks who

would sell their soul for a chance to watch the Desert Fox in action. But the only thing Jim felt was a terrible anxiety that was getting worse every minute.

What's it going to be like when they start firing? he thought. What kind of effect will *that* have on my nervous system?

He sat there, staring ahead, up at the enormous plateau, when someone tapped his shoulder.

"Ey, Fritz . . . what's wrong? You look like you've just seen a ghost."

Jim turned and saw the man—an officer. Then—as if by magic—there was a name. Erich Volkmer. Colonel Erich Volkmer. Colonel Erich Volkmer. He's in charge of . . . logistics.

A bit more of Fritz broke through. . . .

This Volkmer doesn't like old Fritz at all.

"Just waiting, Volkmer," Jim pointed at the plateau. "For the British to arrive."

Volkmer laughed. "Well, they'd better arrive. You gave the general the information."

Jim turned back to Volkmer. "What?" he asked.

"Trying to back out already, Fritzie? Get your coordinates wrong?" Volkmer clicked his tongue. "It would be a shame if the Field Marshal abandoned Tobruk because you got the message wrong from Berlin." Volkmer walked away, laughing. "Very sad."

I gave him the message, Jim thought. Something came from Fritz that made him change his plans . . . changing history.

Or rather, it came from Berlin.

The thought—of history changing, shifting, like the sand under his feet, gave Jim a chill. We're not in Kansas anymore, Toto. . . .

Rommel's hand shot up in the air.

Jim looked over at him. He was a short man, solid, squat, not at all imposing. He stood a few yards away, his field glasses locked on the plateau.

"Ready!"

Rommel's voice, clear and powerful, cut through the desert air.

"Now!" he brought down his hand.

For a fraction of a second nothing happened. Then the Field Marshal's hand brought his field glasses back up. Immediately there was a succession of clicks, running left and right like falling dominos. Metal slapping against metal. Followed by the roar, the tremendous, earthshaking roar of the artillery firing.

Jim felt the armored car vibrate.

Dozens of puffy clouds belched from the cannons, then lingered above the open desert, drifting away, dreamlike.

Jim felt like throwing up. His stomach tightened. He felt cold. Then hot. His ears rang from the first barrage. But then there was another succession of clicks, and more artillery fire. Again, and again. He held the steering wheel of the car as if it was moving a hundred miles an hour.

Rommel looked over at him, his face angry. The Field Marshal shook his head. He pointed. And then he yelled something completely inaudible.

Shit, Jim thought. I'm supposed to be doing something. But what? After one more barrage, Rommel ran over.

"Why aren't you—" Rommel yelled, a bloodcurdling sound right in Jim's ear—

(Another barrage, and the general waited. . . .)

"—calling Cruewell?"

Jim was tempted to try to explain. You see, Herr Rommel . . . to yell back—"I don't really belong here! And as much as I might want to help you—which I don't really want to do—I haven't the foggiest idea what the hell you want me to do . . . or how to do it."

Rommel shook his head angrily and grabbed the phone.

"Yah," Rommel said. "Good, Ludwig. How many meters short? Yes . . . yes . . . good."

He replaced the radiophone. Volkmer came running over and Rommel said something to him.

Then, before he went back to studying the battle scene, Rommel gave Jim a look—a terrible, deprecating look that would wither a weed.

I'm in big trouble, Jim thought.

But hey . . . what a story to tell my grandchildren. . .

A few minutes before the shelling, Ollie had his head out of the tank. And his commander stood next to the tank, talking.

If this was war, then it was nothing to write home about. A few more battles like this, Ollie had been thinking, and then back to the UK for some R&R, some healthy pub crawling with the love-starved dollies.

The thought—so tantalizingly sweet—made Ollie smile.

What a rotten bloody trade war was, Ollie had been thinking. They take away your women and give you big machines and guns and bullets and food that can make you puke.

A bloody 'orrible trade.

That was what he'd been thinking when he heard the first blasts.

There was that second when he didn't know what caused the noise. Did a hundred trucks just backfire? Did a gigantic thunderstorm just break? Then, with a sticky sick feeling in his gut, he knew.

It was war. Arriving. At last.

The commander took a step. Raised an arm. He said something to Ollie. Probably said get down below, back into the bowels of the tank. We're going to button up.

But the shells landed. One fell only ten feet from where their chief, Collins, had been standing. Ollie watched the commander's body blown in half, cut down like a reedy stalk of straw. Snapped in two, one half smashed against the right side of the tank, the other blown to the heavens.

A whistling piece of metal flew past Ollie's ear. He heard it hiss as it missed his head by a centimeter.

That's my break, Ollie thought. My one fuckin' break. From now on I'd better make my own luck.

He let himself slide back into the turret, pulling the hatch down behind him.

"The chief's out of it!" he yelled as more shells exploded outside. Johnson was readying the ammunition for the hull machine gun. The tank lurched forward.

"Which way?" Wright yelled.

Good fucking question, Ollie thought. And why ask me? Just because the chief is gone, why the hell ask me!

"Can you see the rest of the Eighth Army . . . what the hell are they doing?"

"I can't see bloody nothing!" Wright said.

"Take her west," Johnson said. Yes, west. Off the plateau, away from the bloody German artillery.

Wright wasted no time, pushing the tank at full speed. Once Wright braked, and Ollie and the others were thrown against the turret walls, slamming into them hard.

"Nearly fuckin' crashed," Wright said. "Can't see anything out here. It's all smoke and sand."

A shell exploded near them. The concussive explosion rocked the tank.

Ollie thought of a girl he knew. The way she laughed. The way she smiled.

Poole squeezed past him, loading a shell into the Matilda's cannon. Poole slapped the cannon shut with a jarring clank while Ollie thought. . . .

There are no girls here. No tall glasses of stout. No greasy chips and chunks of cod.

The turret was filled with the smell of cordite, burning oil, and other choking fumes. The tank lurched forward again.

Poole looked at him. Poole, now so steady, calm almost. Tapped his shoulder.

"It's ready, Ollie."

And Ollie nodded as he bent down to look through the narrow sight of the cannon.

17

"There you go," McManus said as the data flashed onto the screen.

"Good . . . good . . . ." Lindstrom said. "Now, Ali, can you enter the names of some of the pieces of art on your list . . . and then we'll compare the prices?"

Ali moved through the list on the screen and highlighted items that were on the printout. Each work was—according to the "outside"—stolen by the Nazi high command, most under the direction of Goering. After Ali had picked about a dozen pieces, Lindstrom tapped her shoulder.

"That's enough. Okay, show us their current value."

For this, McManus accessed a datanet from the outside. The information would be tainted—historically inaccurate. But it would reflect the value of the art in the current world market . . . and the current situation.

And that's what Lindstrom wanted to know.

The results flashed on the screen. And they were staggering.

"Incredible," McManus whispered.

"I thought as much."

The paintings—the ones that had been stolen and "lost" according to the outside history—had appreciated incredibly. In some cases, their value had gone up ten, twenty, and even, fiftyfold. Forget the old masters. Here were Picassos selling for forty and fifty million dollars. The looted paintings were worth billions of dollars.

"Some very informed investing," Lindstrom said wryly.

Ali turned to him.

"But why? Why steal art . . . hide it . . . and then sell it? What's the point?"

McManus walked away, nodding to himself.

"A war chest . . ." he muttered. He stopped, looking up at the great black wall of the tachyon generator. "It can be expensive to rewrite history, Ms. Moreau. Just going back isn't enough." The scientist turned around. He looked defeated, Ali thought. Small, shrunken, caving in on himself. And, as she saw his hope vanishing, she felt scared.

"Exactly, Elliot. We should have seen this coming. You can't," Lindstrom said, looking at Ali as if he was delivering a lecture on symbolism in Moby Dick, "buy loyalties cheaply. They probably had to purchase whole governments, leaders, everything. . . . They certainly have outstripped your budget, eh, McManus?"

And then there was quiet.

The computer made small tweeting sounds as new updates arrived. Something called the "U.S.S.L.A.," they learned, had been formed a decade ago—the United Soviet States of Latin America. A naval embargo was thrown against the U.S. a few years later, crushing the already shriveled democratic republic. And more strange information, hot off the press. There were rumors that the United States—with Canada—was ready to follow South America into a close alliance with world communism.

And worse . . . hunger, poverty, and exploitation by the rest of the world had turned the U.S. into a chaotic, violent country. The cities—outside of the lavish and heavily guarded playgrounds for the rich and jaded—were degenerate, abandoned places.

And this was going on right outside, Ali thought. It's reality. Right outside the doors of the Time Lab.

She stood up, wanting to say something to the other two men, to get them to start thinking. There had to be *something* that could be done.

"Can you contact Jim . . . or the other man you've sent—"

McManus laughed. "No, but don't think that I haven't thought about it . . . wished for a way—but no, it's impossible. Of course, if we could bring them back it would be a different story. We could tell them about this, tell them what's going to happen. Stop it—" his hands, thin, tapered, almost feminine, fluttered helplessly in the air. "But no, there's no way we can send a message there."

Lindstrom laughed. "They could send one to us though, isn't that right, Elliot?"

Ali saw McManus nod. "What do you mean?"

"We have prearranged a drop in the Bavarian Alps . . . near the German-Italian border. Any message left there will turn up in the historical record."

Ali's eyes flashed. "You mean if Jim were to leave a message in one of those places, it would just . . . appear?

"Not exactly. It would be found, and it would enter the historical record."

The idea that she might actually hear from Jim thrilled Ali . . . for a moment. Then she remembered where he was. And who he was with. The Alps were a long way from the Libyan desert.

But then . . . she had an idea. Perhaps, she thought grimly, the only idea left.

"Dr. McManus . . . Professor Lindstrom . . . I—"

She started to speak, not really sure she wanted to say what was on her mind.

A high-pitched sound suddenly filled the Time Lab. High, piercing.

McManus looked at Lindstrom. "It's happening!" he yelled.

The sound kept shrieking, echoing in the small lab. The sound, Ali thought.

An *alarm* . . .

* * *

The artillery barrage stopped, and Rommel, his face rigid, intent, hurried back into his armored car. Already his tanks were streaming up the ridges, climbing up to the smoky netherworld of the plateau.

"Get a move on!" he snapped at Jim.

The car climbed the rubble-strewn slope easily, outrunning the tanks. Though Jim was sure that he didn't want to get up there before the Afrika Korps arrived in force, he thought it best to follow the Desert Fox's instructions to the letter.

There was a stale taste in his mouth. Something from Fritz's breakfast, a bit of dried meat.

I'm not handling all this too well, Jim thought.

The armored car tumbled into a small hole, tilting left, threatening to dump Rommel and the machine gunner in the rear right out. But they were obviously getting used to Jim's erratic driving.

He eased up on the accelerator—just a bit—and the tanks, all spread out behind him, a wave of fierce-looking metal, caught up to the command vehicle.

They neared the top of the plateau. And then Jim saw the madness created by artillery.

The airstrip was *gone*. In its place was a pock-marked expanse of holes and rubble. There were dozens of tanks on fire, bodies hanging half in, half out, the oily flames licking at the dead bodies.

The smell made him gag. His stomach heaved.

Without stopping, Jim turned to the side and tried to spit up—something, anything. But he just hacked at the air as the dizzying, sick smell filled his nostrils.

He glanced at Rommel, to see if the Field Marshal was looking at him, disgusted at his weakness.

Jim looked around, scared, numb from the sound, the smells. This was glory! This was war! The last gasp of chivalry before the ovens and the A-bomb forever made this war humankind's most sick creation.

But Rommel's face was set, impassive. Thoughtful.

He said something to Jim. Something Jim couldn't really hear, not above the sound of the tanks' treads digging into the sandy slopes, clawing at the rocks, sending up showers of grit.

Couldn't really hear it, Jim thought. But it sounded like—

"Steady, Fritz."

Steady.

More Allied infantry tanks were scurrying west, hurrying to get off this airstrip which had turned into a skillet for cooking British armor.

Then—darting in between the burning hulks, ignoring the lost, confused tanks that were missing their retreat, scurrying in the wrong direction—Rommel's tanks moved in for the kill.

"Waltzing Matildas . . ." Rommel said.

"Excuse me, General?" Jim yelled back.

"Those British tanks. Look how slowly they move, and turn. So they outnumber us two to one, Fritz, Maybe even three to one. It will not matter."

Rommel's tanks didn't fire. The smoke and dust obviously made the idea of finding a target nearly impossible. So they streamed on, grim, blackish-grey, clambering over bits of metal and chunks of young men, pursuing a more powerful enemy, now in full rout.

More German tanks appeared to the south . . . a pincer closing in on the fleeing British.

Then, with a commanding position on what was once the airfield of Sidi Rezegh, Rommel's tanks began firing.

And the British tanks, looking more like trapped animals, hunted, cornered, scurrying away in full panic, began exploding under the trained cannons of the Afrika Korps.

Ollie peered out of his gunner's slit—a small metal opening that showed him only a tiny piece of the mayhem outside.

His unit—maybe the whole bleedin' Eighth army—was retreating, all of it. An organized retreat? Perhaps, Ollie thought. But more likely, everyone was just trying to get to some cover, stop, and perhaps return some fire.

We'll never make it, Ollie thought. We were one of the first tanks. So, we'll be one of the last tanks off the slope trailing down, catching every shell Rommel cares to throw at us.

It was as if they knew we were coming. As if they knew all about Operation Crusader, Ollie thought.

He laughed, angry, hollowly. He turned and saw Poole looking at him.

"I'm going to fire a few shells," he said to Poole.

Poole—ever the conversationalist—nodded.

Then Ollie yelled down, "Stop her, Wright. Let's see if we can do the Jerries some damage."

The tank kept moving. "I said to fucking stop her. Do you have ears?"

Still the tank moved. But then it jerked to a sudden stop.

"Go have your fun, Ollie," Wright called back.

Ollie grabbed the controls of the heavy cannon. The turret moved slowly, as if it had all the time in the world to turn and find a target. No rush. Just slowly . . .

Turn.

Then there was the sun. Not quite on the horizon. But low enough to make the tanks of the Afrika Korps barely visible. They were just shadowy smudges on the horizon.

A shell landed to the side of Ollie's tank, sending up a spray of sand and dust.

He saw a target.

He worked the two hand controls to raise the cannon barrel up a few degrees.

"Come on!" Wright yelled. "Don't take all day."

Another click, and the angle seemed right.

The tanks were heading right toward them.

(He thought about his last night in the UK. How about a nice beer, she had said, slipping into the stall beside him. She wore lipstick—too much, he thought at the time. But now, seeing her in his mind, she seemed just perfect.)

"Got 'er," he said.

He fired a shell.

And, through the slit, he watched the smoke, and saw the shell lob into the air, before it crashed a few feet ahead of the target tank.

"Damn bloody hell."

Poole was already loading another shell, slapping the hot cannon shut.

"I'm getting the hell out of here, Johnson!" Wright yelled from the bowels of the tank.

"Just hold on," Ollie said.

The tank lurched forward, picking up speed.

The German tank, his target, had spotted them, its own turret turning slowly, menacingly, as if pointing at them. *There. There they are. Now, everyone fire at that tank!*

Ollie brought the cannon down a bit.

Should be about right, he thought.

He fired the shell. And he watched it hit the other tank. The German tank ruptured, spouting fire and chunks of metal.

"Got her, lads. She's popping open like a bottle of champagne."

Poole patted his back.

Wright had their tank moving full-out.

And that's when they caught the shell with their names on it. . . .

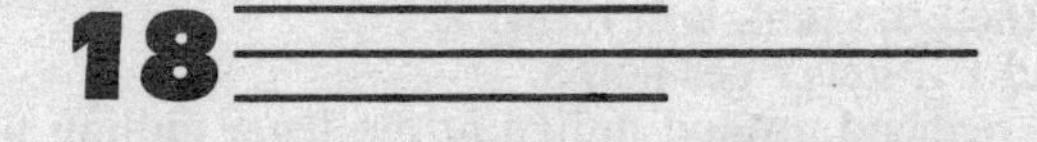

18

It was as if it were happening to someone else.

Someone else's bad luck, Ollie thought. Someone else caught one. Someone else won't be going home with the boys for a couple of pints and rippin' war tales around the dart board.

That was the dream. The hope. The desperate prayer . . . before the inside of his tank went from a noisy, cramped place to a chaotic hell.

The exploding shell was muffled by their armor. But the force of the explosion gouged enormous holes into the turret walls. Ollie turned to Poole—about to ask, stupidly, What happened? What's wrong? But half of Poole's face was gone. Half of the radioman's face still wore that same, grim, sullen expression. His glasses—also blown in half—dangled from one ear.

Ollie felt liquid on his face. Bits of bone and jelly-like material. A bit hung on his lower lip. Near his tongue.

He tasted the blood.

Then he couldn't see anything. The turret was filled with smoke. He called out the driver's name.

"Wright! Wright! You okay, Jack?" But there was no answer, not even a groan. In the dense smoky haze Ollie tried to climb up to the hatch. The whole tank might blow any minute.

Okay, man, get a move on, Ollie thought. We've got

to get the hell out of here. Before she blows. *We have to get out.*

Ollie pushed at the dead commander's legs until he realized that that's all there was . . . just legs. Like some theatrical prop. Two stumpy legs. Ending in . . .

Ollie pulled his hand back. The smell of cordite and gasoline was making his head ring. I'm going to black out, he thought. The fumes are going to knock me out. And then the tank will blow.

And I'll never get home.

He reached up and pulled at the legs, pulling them down and away from the hatch. They jammed against the side of the hatch opening, getting stuck on latches or a hook. Ollie was grunting, pulling at the legs, talking to himself.

"C'mon . . . c'mon. Out of the way, you bastard," he said, speaking to the commander's trunk as if it was some stubborn officer wanting to go down with his tank.

He grunted. And pulled again.

Come . . . on.

He heard something tear. He couldn't see anything. He pulled harder and they came loose, tumbling back onto him, as he fell into a small pool collecting on the bottom of the tank. He didn't waste any time to see whether the pool was blood, or gas, or his own piss. He clambered back to the hatch, knocking his head against the upper part of the turret.

It was then Ollie realized that he'd been hurt. One leg. And it was bad.

It bore a wound, about the size of a saucer. He touched it gingerly, as if it didn't belong to him. He felt the moistness there.

And then he reached up, his hands flapped around, trying to feel the rim of the opening. Where the hell is it? his mind screamed.

Then he felt the smooth metal of the hatch. He saw light, and billowing smoke belching out.

I'm going to make it, he thought. I'm going to get the hell out. I'm going to be okay. And he kept saying the word over and over and over in his mind. Okay. Okay. I'm going to be—

He pulled himself up. He felt the wound tear. It sent a shaft of clear, demanding pain jabbing into his leg. He whimpered like a baby even as he pulled himself out.

His head popped out of the hatch. He smelled the air—still filled with smoke and powder and oil. But there was something to breathe out here, at least. Then he hurried on.

Thinking . . .

The tank's going to blow. The Matildas always do. Bad design, they always joked. The fuel tank is too fucking exposed. It's right there, right in the back. Why, one good shot to the hull—

He swung his legs out, and over, and slid down the right side of the tank as if it was a children's toy. Down, down, until he hit the hard macadam of the airstrip. He crawled. A baby leaving the playroom. Hand over hand. One knee and then the other.

Okay. I'm going to be okay.

He looked over his shoulder. He was well away from the tank, but still he kept crawling.

The tank exploded. Ollie went flat against the fragments of macadam. He felt heat. The hot breath of smoke billowing around him. He heard chinks of twisted metal landing noisily nearby.

But he was okay. Alive.

He looked forward. And there, in front of him, were two boots, scuffed and worn by months on the desert.

He looked up, still a baby, still on all fours.

A soldier. An Italian soldier holding his carbine down, the barrel just inches from Ollie's head.

The soldier gestured with the rifle. He wanted Ollie up. "*Presto! Fretta!*"

Ollie smiled.

"My leg," he said. And then, craning around, looking around to see the burnt orange wound, Ollie repeated. "My leg, *signore.*"

But the soldier merely put the barrel of his gun right up to Ollie's head.

"I will talk with you later," Rommel said to Jim, making no mistake that it wasn't going to be a friendly chat.

Too many screw-ups, Jim thought. Fritz Wagner was a trusted aide to the Desert Fox, and here I was acting like I flunked Driver's Ed.

But now Rommel was out talking to some of his generals. The battlefield was starting to clear, the westerly wind blowing away the clouds of smoke. Some of the British tanks still smoldered on the airstrip.

The British survivors—the few there were—had been rounded up and put onto a truck. Italian infantry strolled rather casually amidst the carnage, checking for any movement, searching the dead bodies for some souvenir of the great battle.

And what a battle it was!

At first it appeared that Rommel had been outgunned. The plateau had been filled with English tanks and, behind them, infantry. But Rommel's hidden artillery had caught the English completely unawares. Their losses—in the first few minutes—were incredible.

Then Rommel's tanks danced around the British tanks, moving with a speed and precision that made the confused British machines look like they were standing still.

And when the British began their retreat—which only added to the debacle—the Crusaders couldn't put any distance between them and the Germans. On the western down-hill slope the German panzers picked off the sluggish Matildas like they were sleepy hedgehogs in winter.

It was a great victory.

But Jim knew there was something wrong with it. He didn't recall the name Sidi Rezegh from his studies. If there had been a battle there, it had been small, inconsequential. A footnote. But this had to be a major blow to the British. Their Eighth Army had been routed.

If Rommel wanted Tobruk, Jim had no doubt that now he could claim it. And that—Jim knew—never happened.

Not in the real world.

Stretchers passed Rommel's command car. British soldiers—most from the tanks—groaned and cried out, sounding more like boys than men. The blood soaked their clothes. Their bandages turned a brilliant maroon as the ineffectual help of the German medics worked to stem the tide. Jim was surprised to see the care given to the enemy soldiers. It's not what he would have expected. He thought rules went out the window during World War II.

When Rommel came back he had someone else with him. He brought a soldier over to where Jim was sitting.

"Your replacement," he snapped to Jim. "You can ride in the back . . . until we find out what's wrong with you."

"Yes . . ." Jim said. it was better than facing a firing squad for erratic driving.

The Afrika Korps was turning around, the tanks streaming off the plateau, leaving the airfield.

Why isn't Rommel chasing the British? Jim wondered. He has them on the run. He could wipe them out.

One answer suggested itself. The sky, a brilliant blue all day except for the shower of clouds made by the battle, had darkened. Night obviously took a long time to come to the desert. But there was, Jim guessed, only about a half-hour of good light left.

The Field Marshal wants to get back to his camp.

As they joined the line of tanks, trucks, and foot soldiers moving back east, he saw a sight . . . repeated over and over. Tank crews filling fuel tanks with clunky grey gas canisters. And he saw men sipping water, passing around a ladle carefully.

Fuel. Water.

Supplies. Rommel was at the end of his tether. He could travel only as far as his supply line would let him. They could only go so far . . . held in check by the supply lines maintained by Berlin. Like a rubber band being stretched more and more, eventually it must snap back . . . or break.

They drove in silence. It became dark. Rommel seemed to sleep. The air turned cool, and then cold. Jim pulled his thin jacket tight against his body. He rattled around in the back of the armored car, trying to doze too, but all too often banging his head against the stock of the mounted machine gun.

I'm hungry, Jim thought. And, as he licked at his lips, thirsty. Cold hungry, and thirsty.

But I'm alive.

At least, Fritz is alive.

The ride seemed to last forever. An endless expanse of desert, with no landmarks in the distance, just more blue-black sky, more cold winds, and the interminable sound of the tires scratching at the sand. He had just dozed off for the twentieth time when the car stopped abruptly.

"Get a move on, Oberstleutnant!" Rommel said, tapping the side of the car.

Jim shook his head and scrambled out of the car, nearly tumbling onto the ground. Rommel turned and walked away.

Jim saw lights. The outline of tents. The sound of soldiers talking, relaxing. He saw lights dangling off dozens of tanks and people working on them. An airplane flew overhead, low. One of ours, Jim guessed. Or theirs. He was having trouble figuring out whose side he should be on.

The new driver was still at the wheel.

"Where are we?" Jim asked.

The driver looked at him like he had just asked a very stupid question.

"Our night lager, Lieutenant."

"Oh, of course," Jim said. And he hurried to catch up with Rommel . . . wondering . . .

What the hell's a night lager?

19

McManus stood at the door of the lab, talking to Toland.

"What is it?" Ali asked.

McManus turned around, looking confused. Overwhelmed.

"There are people outside. All around the building. Poking at the walls. Trying to get in. I don't—"

"Can't you do something?" Ali said. "The building's self-sufficient. Can't you keep them out?"

"I—I don't know. We have the guards," he said, looking at Toland. "But if too many people come, trying to break in—looters—and if they have weapons . . . I just don't know."

"We'll do what we can," Toland said as he backed out of the room.

McManus looked shocked, like he was going to faint.

Ali stood up.

"Are you okay, Doctor? You look—"

And then McManus collapsed. Like a balloon deflating, he crumpled to the floor.

Ali yelled, "Dr. Beck! Professor Lindstrom! Come here!"

Beck hurried from the other room. "I knew this would happen," she said. She looked right at Ali. "He's had no rest, he eats nothing. He just keeps pushing himself. This whole project has been on his shoulders and he won't stop until—"

She had an electronic stethoscope up to McManus's chest. In seconds she had a pulse reading and an analysis of his irregular rhythm. "This is not good," the doctor said. "He's had a heart attack before. Now he's exhausted. Hold him up a bit, please."

Ali cradled McManus's head. His eyes fluttered open. "What? . . . What's happened here? Why am I lying on the ground?"

Ali watched Dr. Beck stick a small penlight up to McManus's just-opened eyes. "You're flat on your back, Elliot, because you won't take care of yourself. What good will it do if you die? Will you tell me that?"

"I must," he said, struggling to get up, "get back to—"

"No," Beck said. Like a magician producing a rabbit, she whipped out a hypodermic needle. "You have to rest. If only for a few hours. Three hours . . . and then I'll wake you."

"No," he said, looking up at Ali, pleading for her to intercede. "I can't—"

But Beck jabbed the needle into McManus's arm. His face twisted in an angry snarl. But then the quick-acting drug made his eyes go heavy.

"Help me get him into the other room," Beck said to Ali.

The scientist was incredibly light. It felt as if they were lifting a child.

Ali thought of the man's responsibility. Of his bravery. If history survives, it will be due to this small man.

McManus was still protesting, his words growing slurred, as they shuffled him into the dark room. She passed near Jim's body, his shallow breathing the only sound. And she saw the other man, curled up in his chair, looking so peaceful and comfortable.

They eased McManus into one of the beds. Ali took off his shoes, while Beck checked his pulse again. Then Ali pulled a thin blanket up to his chin.

She saw Dr. Beck smooth back some strands of McManus's hair. The doctor stood there, in the near dark, and watched McManus.

And Ali backed away.

Just then she heard a yell from the Time Lab.

"I've got it!" Lindstrom's voice called out. Then he was at the door. "I've—"

"Quiet!" Dr. Beck hissed at him.

Lindstrom gestured at Ali. "I *know* what's happening. How they did it . . . and why. . . ."

"What?" she said.

Dr. Beck came out of the room, shutting the door behind her. Lindstrom guided the two of them over to his table.

"Here," he said, handing Ali a yellow pad. "The outside computer has records of the missing art . . . when the pieces turned up . . . who bought them . . . and how much they paid. But I also came up with this!"

He flipped over a yellow sheet.

"It shows exactly when they were lost. And how it happened."

Lindstrom's excitement was lost on Ali. "I don't understand. The Nazis stole the art. We know that. It's—"

Lindstrom nodded, his hand bobbing up and down with excitement. "Yes, yes . . . of course they stole the art. Two, maybe three times as much as history records. But don't you see what this shows?"

Ali took the yellow pad. There were names there. Places. Dates.

"But the Nazis didn't get to keep it. This is what really happened to the treasure." He put a great bear arm around her. "Here's where the other Time Lab got their money from."

"They?" Ali asked.

"Oh, yeah," Lindstrom said, grinning. "I know who they are now." He paused, watching her face react. "I know who's running the other Time Lab!" He paused, his grin growing even larger. "I even know their names. . . ."

Jim followed Rommel into a large tent. The Field Marshal brushed aside the door flap, and Jim immediately heard the sounds of moaning, of men calling out . . . some in English, some in German.

Naked light bulbs dangled from struts near the top of the tent.

He walked up to the bed of the first man. His face was almost completely covered in red-soaked bandages. Just one eye was visible, and it darted wildly, left and right.

Rommel looked at the tag at the bottom of the bed.

"How are you doing, boy?" the great tank general said in slowly, carefully enunciated English.

The young soldier's eye widened.

The Desert Fox was a legend . . . and here he was visiting the enemy's wounded. It was past midnight.

The soldier nodded—ever so slightly. He opened a hand.

"Good," Rommel smiled. He reached down and grabbed the hand. "You get better now."

Then he moved on to the next bed. It was another British soldier, his chest and one arm wrapped in tight bandages. He was smoking a cigarette.

Rommel stood at the foot of his bed, nodding. "Anything you need?" Rommel asked him.

"No sir," the soldier said.

Rommel nodded, and moved to the next bed. And the next. And the next. Until he had stopped at every bed, looking at the wounded, the sleeping, the ones poised near death. The field hospital was filled with the smell of dried blood and alcohol. Sudden moans and yells for help brought the attention of one of the medics—who quickly stuck a syringe in one pain-wracked soldier.

One side of the room was filled with British and Australian soldiers . . . the other with a scattering of

German and Italians. It had been a bad day for the UK's Operation Crusader.

It was near one A.M. when Rommel finally finished his tour. He turned to Jim. Rommel's eyes—bright and piercing—were now hidden under lines and creases of fatigue. "This is what war is really about," he said to Jim, sighing. "Eh? Young men. Hurt, maimed. Brave men who would rather be out with young girls. They are brave without knowing why they are fighting. So ignorant . . . and so courageous."

Jim nodded. He imagined that, despite all his screw-ups, Fritz was someone Rommel could talk to, a confidant. He felt like telling him who he really was, to end the charade.

"I—" he started to say.

"Yes?"

"I know. It's hard to see this and think that it's all worthwhile."

Rommel laughed. "Worthwhile? For the Fatherland, my young Bavarian? What has happened to your love of country? . . ." Rommel's voice was heavy, biting in its sarcasm. "Your love of the . . . Führer!"

Rommel's voice bit off that last word. This was the disenchantment, Jim knew, that would lead to Rommel's plotting Hitler's death.

A plot that would lead to his own poisoning.

And in a nasty ugly war, where the death and carnage reached incredible proportions, Rommel and his Afrika Korps would stand for something a bit different, for a last gasp of chivalry before the apocalypse.

Rommel shook his head. A sad grin crossed his face.

"Walk with me, Fritz, to the doctor. We must keep the Field Marshal of the D.A.K. in good health, eh?"

And Jim followed him, to the back of the tent, and then to a smaller tent. It glowed burnished yellow from small lamps. Rommel walked right in.

"Field Marshal," the doctor said, standing quickly and clicking his heels together, "congratulations on today's impressive victory. All the Fatherland will rejoice to—"

Rommel held up his hand.

"Please, Dr. Bock . . . I'm much too tired for any long salutations."

Jim looked around the tent, filled with trays of medical equipment, and brown jars of medicine. He heard the doctor apologize. And then he felt the doctor looking at him.

Staring at him.

Jim was just looking around when he felt the heat of the doctor's stare, studying him. Jim looked up. He felt as if he was exposed, as if all of a sudden someone could see who he really was.

The doctor was talking to Rommel, but looking right at him.

The field marshal rolled up his sleeve. The doctor rubbed a swab dabbed in alcohol on the general's arm.

Jim looked up at the doctor.

At first, Jim thought he was just being paranoid. Sure, after one of the great battles of World War II that never happened, it made sense. He's a bit on edge, a bit shaky.

Sure.

But when he looked in the doctor's eyes, he had no doubt that something was wrong . . . something about the eyes, and the way the doctor talked as he positioned his syringe and then—drove it home.

Looking at Jim, studying him.

Jim felt light-headed. How could this doctor know about me? he wondered. I'm just feeling paranoid, that's all. It's just paranoia . . . shell shock. . . .

"There," Bock said. "That should help your system stay strong. Now," he said, putting the needle down, "I recommend that you get some rest. Immediately. My orders now, Herr Field Marshal."

Rommel rolled down his sleeve. "Yes. After I give my aide here the plans for Berlin." Rommel slipped on his jacket. "Tomorrow, the British army will be completely defeated and Berlin can have its precious Tobruk back."

"Wonderful," Bock said, but again he studied Jim.

God, Jim thought. He knows! He knows that there's something wrong with me.

"*Guten-nacht,*" Rommel said, hurrying out of the tent.

Jim nodded.

And leaving the tent, he felt Bock's eyes watching him.

Ollie Johnson snaked his hand down toward his wound.

Of course it was all bandaged now, all covered in white cloth. But it was a bad wound. He knew that from the ugly faces the medics made when they changed his bandages. How bad? He wanted to ask them.

Bad enough that I'll lose my leg? . . . Bad enough that I'll have to lie here and watch you kill any feeling in it with your bleedin' wonder drugs before you start sawing away at it? Cutting, back and forth, through the skin and muscle and—oh, God—the bone.

What will I be then? Will I still be a soldier if I have one leg?

Will I still be a man? Yes, and will the pretty dollies still like sitting with me, talking with me, when I have just one bloody leg?

And—here's the amazing part, he thought—I got to meet the man who did it. The bloody Desert Fox himself. Everyone said he was goddam unbeatable and—hah—they were right. He sure beat us. Got all me mates, didn't he? Maybe he'll even get my leg.

Someone moaned from the other side of the tent.

He's singing an old war song, Ollie thought, grinning at his grim joke.

And my war's over.

He reached out to a small table and grabbed a crumpled pack of German cigarettes. He dug one out and lit it, in the darkness.

His leg throbbed.

Better the pain, he thought. Better that . . . than nothing at all.

20

"Sit down, Fritz," Rommel gestured to Jim.

Rommel's command tent was spartan. A small field table, a cot, a small basin for washing. The only symbol of Rommel's importance was the pair of guards outside the tent.

It was cold in here, but Rommel had stripped to the waist and started sponging off his body.

"The plans are there," he said, pointing to a maroon folder sitting on the table. "Keep using the new code until Berlin tells us otherwise." The field marshal raised a finger. "And make sure you get the location of at least two of the British depots. We can't go chasing them back to Egypt with empty tanks and thirsty soldiers." Rommel snatched a plain robe off a small clothes tree behind the cot. "You've still not heard from your wife?"

"Er . . ."

Wife! Jim thought. He thought on the word.

And then, there was a clear picture. A woman. Pretty, in a straightforward fashion. He saw her outdoors, bright blonde hair catching the light. Behind her, there were jagged, jutting mountain peaks limned in snow. And a small girl.

And then Jim felt this pain . . . this anger.

"No?" Rommel said. "Look . . . these things happen, Leutnant. Especially in war. But—don't worry. She'll be there when we finally get to leave this desert and go home."

Jim nodded. The feelings he felt were sudden, incomprehensible.

This is Jekyll and Hyde stuff, Jim thought. Names pop up. Faces. Now feelings. How long can I keep this Fritz repressed before he takes over his life again?

And when he does, where does that leave me?

Jim went to get up.

Rommel came up to him. There was warmth and strength and a humanity in this man. But there was also fierceness.

"Is that what was wrong today? You weren't there today, Fritz."

Tell me about it, Jim thought.

"You can't let it happen tomorrow. No matter what you're feeling or thinking about. We all want to go home." Rommel walked back to his cot and sat down. "No one more than I."

"Yes, sir."

Rommel pointed at the maroon envelope. "You'd best go."

"Yes, sir." Jim took a step to leave the tent.

"Leutnant . . . aren't you forgetting something?"

Oh, shit. Now what? . . .

Jim made a confused grimace, hoping to elicit a clue.

Rommel opened his eyes wide, the thick eyebrows arching with obvious amusement. He cleared his throat . . . "Heil? . . ."

"Heil Hitler," Jim said quickly.

I didn't click my heels, he thought. Was I supposed to click my heels?

"Get out of here, Leutnant," Rommel laughed . . . a laugh Jim continued to hear as he walked out into the darkness.

Heil Hitler.

Rommel poured himself a small brandy. It's nearly 2 A.M., he thought. In three hours I will wake up. And try to finish this desert war.

He took a sip of brandy.

It felt warm and wonderful. His lips were permanently dry and cracked. Desert lips, his men called them. The body gives up trying to keep moist. The dust and grit fills every pore, every crack.

He took another sip, letting it linger, burning his tongue.

Tomorrow I'll win the desert war. And why? To let my Führer, the great Adolph Hitler, send my men and my tanks to Russia.

Where we'll all be defeated. The German nation, to be sure. But also the Russians, as they feed their hordes into the meat grinder of the German war machine.

And what is it for?

Lebensraum?

There was a time, in the Sudetenland, when I believed that. I was under his spell, proud to be in charge of his cadre of bodyguards. He was reclaiming the historic German birthright . . . reclaiming ancestral lands. It was a great moment.

But National Socialism wasn't about reclaiming anything. Or building anything.

It was about death and murder.

Which is how it will end for Germany.

Unless . . .

(Another, last sip. The brandy was gone. He was tempted to have another. But he put the small snifter down.)

Unless someone stops him.

Rommel lay back on the cot. He didn't bother taking his pants off. Not for a three-hour nap. Maybe it's superstition, he thought. I'll stay in the same clothes. Continue my luck. Incredible luck. Helped by equally incredible intelligence from Berlin.

He closed his eyes, thinking about the question that played in his mind all day long as his Afrika Korps streamed westward.

How did they know? How in the world did Berlin know that the Eighth Army, the Army of the Nile, would end up as sitting ducks on that airstrip?

And with that thought still teasing him, he fell quickly and soundly asleep. . . .

Outside, away from the light of the tents, Jim felt lost. He clutched the maroon envelope tightly.

What am I supposed to do with this? he wondered.

He understood that somehow Rommel's plans for the next day were to be radioed to Berlin. And Jim was supposed to bring back information, the location of enemy supply dumps. Jim could see how crucial they would be.

There must be a radio tent somewhere. But where?

He stopped and asked two soldiers who were standing by a tank, smoking cigarettes.

Jim looked at their faces. They appeared to be tired, with sunken eyes and dusky skin. The tank soldiers would get three, maybe four, hours of sleep if they were lucky. And it looked like most of them had to put in some kind of guard duty.

Some crews were working on their tanks.

It would be bad news to get stranded in the middle of the desert.

The soldiers gave him an odd look when he asked directions to the radio tent.

"Verbindung?" one of them said.

Right, Jim nodded. *Verbindung* . . . Communications. They directed him to a distant tent, near the eastern edge of the camp.

Jim walked away from the soldiers, away from the rows of tanks and trucks, sitting idly now, waiting for the dawn.

He walked through the dark. And he felt like he was being followed. It was a step he heard. The faintest footfall landing after his own.

He stopped walking in a dark valley made by two large supply tents. He waited, pulse racing. It was cold—the desert night. And though his jacket was buttoned tight, all the way to the neck, he shivered.

He took some more steps.

Again he heard the sound of feet, just behind him. The scattering of sand. The stray rock kicked away.

He spun around quickly, in the darkness. He saw no one.

He called out, "Who's there?"

Feeling ridiculous, he repeated it . . . louder. "Who's there?"

I have a gun, Jim remembered. Of course, I never fired a gun before. But why should that stop me? I never drove an armored car before either.

His hand unbuckled the flap of the holster. "If someone's there, you'd best come out now."

But it was silent. He heard only the sound of the wind puffing at the tents, tugging at them.

I've got to get some sleep, he thought. My nerves are shot. I'm going crazy. I'm hearing things.

He shook his head and turned away.

He saw the communications tent, a large antenna reaching to the black sky. He saw three splotchy dots of light inside. It looked very welcome indeed.

He took a step. And he heard more sounds . . . more steps. Running toward him.

But before Jim could turn around, before he could try to whip out his German handgun, someone flew on top of him and he went crashing to the ground.

"How's McManus?" Lindstrom asked Dr. Beck, who had taken a seat next to Ali.

"He'll be better once he's had some rest."

"Good," Lindstrom said expansively. "We can't do without him. Now then," he said, leaning over his pages of notes and printouts, "here's the art that we know was stolen by Goering for his private estate, Karinhall, and for Hitler's Führer Museum in Lindz."

Ali looked at the list of art. It was a Who's Who of classical paintings. But it was devoid of modern masterpieces.

"A very select grouping," she said.

"Yes," Lindstrom said. "The Nazis wouldn't have anything to do with decadent art. And they certainly didn't foresee the phenomenal prices that the Cubist and Dadaist works would fetch. But''—and here Lindstrom grinned—''someone did.''

He showed her another list. ''These pieces were—according to tainted history—also stolen, over twelve hundred pieces in total. And they remained lost, only surfacing on private markets a decade ago—or so the outside computer tells us. More classic works, but also Chagalls, Kandinskys, Klees. Phenomenal works . . . that fetched phenomenal prices.''

''But for whom?''

''That was the hard part. The art market is nothing if not secret. But cash flow is cash flow, and certain patterns emerge . . . especially when you're dealing with billions and billions of dollars. Even the Swiss banks have to register the transfer of funds, the tremendous debits and credits. Enough money could be tracked so that I know where it went.''

''And that is?''

Lindstrom slipped a map out from under his pile of papers.

''Here. A small town in Georgia.''

''In the south?'' Ali asked, before she saw the map.

''Yes,'' Lindstrom said. ''The south of the gold old U.S.S.R. Right''—his finger floated above the map and jabbed at a tiny dot—''here.''

Ali leaned over the desk and read the name. . . .

''Krasnodar.''

Lindstrom beamed. ''Yes, Krasnodar!''

Ali didn't know why he was so excited. ''So . . .'' she paused, searching for its importance, ''what?''

''So what? Do you know what Krasnodar is?''

She shook her head. Lindstrom looked at Dr. Beck, who shrugged.

''Krasnodar is the head of the Iron Men, the KGB hard-liners who were drummed out of the government after Glasnost. They're hardcore Stalinists, tough, nasty Commies like your grandma knew. They went underground, here, in Uncle Joe Stalin's homeground. They were tolerated, ignored, and—guess what?''

"What?" Ali asked.

"They must have their own Time Transference Device and"—Lindstrom whistled, sitting back, pleased with himself—"and enough money to buy the world!"

Lindstrom acted delighted with his detective work. But Ali was frightened. She wished McManus was here, to tell them what to do, how to stop what was happening. Every hour . . . every minute . . . made the Iron Men's hold on history all that stronger.

"This other man . . . back with Jim . . . can he do something about the artwork?"

Lindstrom shook his head. "No. There's nothing he can do. Not without new information. You see, this only happened *now.* Jim Tiber doesn't know about it, nor does—"

A thought crossed Ali's face. An unpleasant . . . unnecessary thought.

"Then," she said quietly, "there's only one way to stop the Iron Men.

Lindstrom's smile evaporated.

"Yes . . . I'm afraid there is."

Yes, thought Ali. Someone else has to go back there.

And she knew who it would have to be. . . .

21

Whoever it was felt like a dead weight on top of Jim, knocking him off his feet. Suddenly Jim found his lips pressed into the crystalline sand. His attacker's arm was levered against the back of Jim's neck, pressing hard.

What is it with this time travel thing? Jim wondered. I'm always getting attacked! Does Fritz owe some Reichsmarks to someone?

The man on his back was big, dressed in smelly, oily garb that was nearly as overpowering as his bulk.

This is not real, Jim told himself. If I thought it was real, I'd be scared. But everything that's happened has got to be just some kind of dream, an illusion. A remarkable simulation, like the Hall of Presidents in the old Disneyworld.

Jim twisted his head left and right, trying to make eye contact with this man. Instead, he felt his head even more firmly pinned to the ground, and the man leaning close, bringing his face right up to Jim's ear.

"Who was elected President . . . after the Quayle impeachment?"

Jim's tongue snaked out and tried to lick away some of the grains of sand threatening to enter his mouth. Jim started to answer.

And then he realized the obvious.

The man was speaking English. With a trace of accent, but English nonetheless.

It almost sounded foreign.

Jim hesitated another second, and the man pushed Jim's cheek into the glassy sand.

"Hey," Jim said, speaking English. "It was Kean. He—"

"No, stupid. Who was elected?"

"Oh . . . John Kennedy Junior."

Yes. Simple question. After all, young John did go on to carry his father's torch . . . in all respects. Simple question. Except—

Who the hell is asking it and how could they possibly know? . . . Unless . . .

Unless they were from the future.

Jim felt the arm releasing his head. Jim knelt up, and he rubbed the back of his neck. He twisted his head left and right, just to make sure it still worked properly.

He stood up.

"Thanks for the adjustment. I can give my chiropractor a vacation for the next month."

"Why the hell didn't you wait? . . ." the man hissed, whispering in the shadows. The area was filled with the smell of oil and gasoline.

Jim looked at the man. He was dark, almost black in the half-light. Only his teeth and eyes were visible. He wasn't a soldier. He wore the ill-fitting clothes of a peasant, baggy pants, and a rough, sloppy shirt.

If he wasn't a soldier, what was he doing here?

Jim took a step backwards. No telling when the man might decide to play pin the Nazi to the ground again.

"Wait . . . wait where? What are you talking about?"

The man's eyes squinted to slits, unsure, cautious. "You're from the Time Lab, aren't you?"

Jim grinned. That's it. Of course! It's someone else from the Time Lab, someone sent to rescue him from the North African desert. Ali and he must have done something wrong. Sure, that's it . . . and this guy came too.

"Yeah, I used the machine. But I was in Hamburg to study the Beatles and all of a sudden—"

"The Beatles? What are you talking about?"

"For my thesis. We, Ali, Martin, broke in—sort of. And I was doing great, real fine, back in 1962. I met Lennon, and even—"

"The Beatles?" the man said again, shaking his head. "Oh, Christ, then you don't know what's going on, do you?"

"Sure I do. Somebody screwed up and I got bounced to 1941. But that's no problem." Jim took a step toward the man. "You're here to get me out, right?"

"Wrong," the man said sullenly. "That's not why I'm here. And—I hate to break the bad news to you—there is no 'out.' "

"I'm going."

Ali looked Lindstrom in the eye, fixing him with that same "I'm-not-to-be-denied" stare that she usually reserved for her father.

"That—that—" Lindstrom sputtered, looking around to Dr. Beck for support—"is impossible. We're better off waiting until Dr. McManus awakens. Then he can decide—"

Ali shook her head.

What was going on outside? Riots? War? Revolution? Anything was possible. Waiting didn't seem like a viable alternative.

"Didn't you say that every minute here is four or five minutes in the past?"

"Something like that," Lindstrom said without conviction. "Perhaps more. I don't have the exact numbers. If we wait until McManus—"

"If we wait until he's up, we might not even be here anymore. Do you know—or understand—everything that's going on outside?" She pushed her long hair off her forehead.

Lindstrom looked down at his stacks of printouts. "No. Not exactly. It seems—"

"We can't wait. Someone has to let Jim and your

agent know what's happened . . . and help them stop it."

"Then I should be the one to go," the history professor said. "If someone has to go, it should be me. But I still—"

But Ali dismissed the idea with a quick shake of her head. "No. You're the one person who can keep track of what has been lost . . . and what's been changed. I'm expendable." She took a step toward him. "You tell me what to do, Professor. What to do, and how to do it. And—if I fail—you can take the next trip yourself."

"I don't know—it's—"

"Can you send me to North Africa . . . to meet Jim?"

"Yes. But he won't be staying there. Besides, the problem can't be fixed there. Your going to North Africa won't help this problem at all."

"Then where should you send me?"

"Berlin, to start with," he said with a sigh. "It's the only way . . ."

"Okay." She nodded. She sat down at his desk. "Can you quickly tell me what I have to do—"

"Yes . . . I've had some ideas since I've been following the changes."

Lindstrom pulled out a list of places, people, dates. . . .

"One thing, Professor Lindstrom . . ."

"Yes?"

"I don't want to be left back there. I think I've figured a way to come back. I'm surprised you didn't think of it yourselves."

Lindstrom looked at Ali with interest.

"Oh, really."

"It makes me a bit worried," she said. "If you didn't think of that . . . what else have you missed? . . ."

The man pulled Jim through the maze of dark, sleeping tanks. They went quietly, turning left and right, stopping to listen if anyone was on guard, moving farther and farther until Jim saw that they were well away from the Desert Fox's night lager—his night camp. The man climbed into a small depression, one of the countless sinkholes that seemed to fill the desert. And he gestured to Jim to sit.

Jim sat down, facing him.

"My name is Steven Port," the man said. "This body is on loan from an Algerian partisan . . . one tough hombre, judging from all his knife scars. I apparently have free passage through all the desert camps. The bedouins know me, share their food. They hate all soldiers, and not just the Germans and the Italians."

"What are you, CIA?" Jim said.

"Something like that," Port nodded.

"So what's going on?"

"I have to be quick. I thought they'd send someone completely briefed . . . maybe McManus himself."

"McManus?"

"The project head, the father of the Time Transference Device. The man who is trying to save history."

Save history? Jim thought. Sounds a tad more important than researching the Beatles.

And he listened to Port's story.

Of course, Jim had a hard time swallowing certain things . . . that the Columbia campus didn't have a fence around it, that there was no Mexican Conflict. These were just the tip of the iceberg. As the path of history was changed, the true future became almost unrecognizable.

Jim's being here was a mistake. But since he was here, he'd be used. Besides, Port laughed, there was no way back.

And then—just to make things more interesting—there was the other side. The friendly folk who were twisting history to their own ends. And they had one great advantage.

They could go back and forth.

Port paused in his story and rubbed his grisly cheek.

"I don't know about you," he said, grinning for the first time, "but I'm having a hard time getting used to this body. Ever ride a camel?" he asked Jim.

Jim shook his head.

"A real bitch. I've been here two days, and I've lost two meals from riding one. And this guy has something wrong with his back. Hurts every time I get up."

Jim nodded. It's funny, he thought, talking to someone who wasn't the person you were looking at.

"Is there any way to recognize these others?"

"Not that I know of." Port looked around. "They probably have someone here, in North Africa. And where you'll be going . . ."

"Going? What do you mean?"

Then there was a sound from behind Jim. He spun around, the scattering of sand and rock incredibly noisy in the quiet night.

"There's someone—"

Port leaned over, covering Jim's mouth.

The agent grabbed Jim. And Jim smelled a revolting mix of sweat, dirt, and grease.

"Shh . . ." Port whispered.

Then they saw the invader, walking toward them. Slow, deliberate steps.

A small person. No taller than three, four feet.

He grew more tentative as he approached them. Port released Jim's mouth. And then he barked an order in what Jim supposed was a flavorful local dialect of French.

It was a kid.

The boy stepped closer, with his short cropped hair glistening ever so slightly under the starlight.

"Papa," he said, his voice trembling—from fear or cold? Jim wondered.

"Papa?" Jim repeated, turning to Port.

"I'm afraid so," Port said.

Rommel waited for Bayerlin to show up.

All of these doubts I have are silly things, he thought. A sign of age, eh?

Tomorrow would be the proper finish to the wonderful victories of the spring. So what if Montgomery had Cunningham equipped two to one for every Axis tank . . . four to one if only German tanks were counted?

So what?

Isolate the British in detail. And finish them off. And it should all happen tomorrow.

Still . . .

(And Rommel permitted himself another small sip of the brandy.)

Yes. Still so much depends on Berlin. The near-miraculous information. Logistics—the very-real prison of supply lines—could hold his forces back. But Berlin promised the exact location—the *exact* location!—of the enemy depots. That, and the British plans for the next day's stand-and-fight defense.

The British can't afford a full rout. It would destroy their confidence. Perhaps crush it. It could—and here Rommel permitted himself a small, self-satisfied smile—destroy British resistance completely.

He sipped the brandy.

And that would be a good thing. Eh?

Perhaps. But, perhaps not. Would that make the German nation strong, proud, restored to its ancient glory? Or would it be—

(He searched for the right word—what the French call *"le mot juste."*)

Yes.

Possessed.

And if it was possessed, should he be helping the country debase itself?

The tent flap opened and Bayerlin stuck his head inside.

It was past two A.M.

"Yes, Major. Thank you for coming. I'm sure you were resting—"

"No, mein Field Marshal. I was just checking that you had another driver for tomorrow . . . as you ordered."

"Yes . . . that's why I asked you to come. Oberstleutnant Wagner has not returned. He's been acting very—" Rommel indicated Wagner's state with an airy wave of the hand. "He seems preoccupied. Not himself. But," Rommel turned on his heels. He caught Bayerlin looking at the empty snifter. "He hasn't been himself. Perhaps the strain . . ."

"I doubt that, General. Oberstleutnant Wagner has been completely unflappable."

"Yes. Perhaps you're right. Still, I'd like him watched. See if anything's wrong." Bayerlin clicked his heels, saluted, and turned to leave the tent.

"And, Major . . . bring some men with you. Just in case."

Bayerlin nodded and left.

And Rommel looked at the warm glow of his lamp. "Just . . . in . . . case . . . ," he repeated quietly.

22

"He's yours?"

Port nodded. "We didn't know about him. I tried leaving him back near the Libyan border with some nomads, but it was no go." Port stared at the thin boy. His skin was a burnished brown and his face was grim and grown-up.

"No mother?"

"Dead. The village was strafed."

"Luftwaffe?"

"Who knows? I couldn't dump him. And, besides, I didn't know what plans his father had for him." Port paused, reached out a hand, and ran it across the boy's closely cropped head. "I know he loves the brat." Port nodded. "I *know* that."

"Yeah, I understand those feelings. Man, it's weird, like—"

Port's head turned suddenly, sharply, as if he heard something. Once again his hand shot out, covering Jim's. They sat there, in the shadows of the depression. Jim heard nothing.

"I thought I heard something," Port said. He repeated the words to the boy, and then said something else in his heavily accented French. The boy scurried away, climbing up the gentle ridge.

"I'll have Tomas—that's his name—watch out. But we don't have a lot of time. Listen. You've got a lot to do, Tiber. A hell of a lot. And we don't have time to give you a nice, neat explanation. So listen up."

Jim nodded. Though he found it hard to muster up any enthusiasm. If I'm trapped here, what does it matter to me what happens in the future? It didn't seem like things were going all that well anyhow. How much worse could it be? He tried to think of a reason to give a damn about it all.

And he found one.

Ali. Sitting in the Time Lab.

Or better yet, Ali sitting with him under one of the last old maples left on campus, lean and sleek and too beautiful to be wasted on a yellowed patch of grass and a battered old tree.

Good enough reason, Jim thought.

"You're Rommel's adjutant . . . almost a friend. He's been getting the Brits' plans direct from Berlin, courtesy of the time bandits. That's what you're going to pick up tonight. And when you get them, swap them for these."

Port dug into a big leather satchel hanging from his side.

"They're identical, even down to the Reich Chancellery stamp. Rommel will go into battle tomorrow with all the wrong plans. They'll also give him the location of the British supply depots. These too will be all wrong. It will make Operation Crusader the German's first major upset in this war . . . like it was supposed to be. But worse than that, it will make the Desert Fox fallible. His Afrika Korps will never recover."

"Sure. This is the start. . . ." Jim said, remembering more of his WWII studies. "El Alamein was the big battle, but Rommel went on the defensive here."

"Right. You've got it. But not unless you do the switch. And you've got to give the code operator these."

Jim took another stack of papers from Port.

These were just typed pages . . . with a signature on the last page.

"Rommel's plans?" Jim said.

Port nodded. "Part of the arrangement with Berlin.

They need to know what route he'll take so that they can lead the Brits astray. The time bandits obviously are onto ULTRA, using the code breaker for their own purposes. You give them the phony papers, and—with a bit of luck—they'll feed Montgomery the real route Rommel takes to Gabr Saleh."

"And if I'm caught—" Jim said, easily picturing some horrible death dreamed up in the Nazi manual for traitors.

"You won't be. And—"

Tomas came running down the slope, a spray of rocks announcing his arrival. He rattled some quick French to Port.

"Damn. He says there are soldiers over by the tanks, nosing about." Port grabbed Jim's arm. "Listen up. You're getting out of here tomorrow."

"I am?"

Port leaned up, looking over the ridge of the depression. He urged the boy to keep watch.

"Somehow, they've got Monty here so that he can be embarrassed by the debacle they're setting up."

Jim heard voices, clear in the distance.

Port continued, hurrying, whispering. "Then they get Monty out and General W.H.E. Gott in." Port grabbed Jim's wrist. "Except Gott is out of ideas. A routiner. He'll retreat all the way back to Gibraltar. If Monty is out—and there's nothing we can do about that glitch—we have to get Auchinleck, the Auk, to show up, on schedule, to put some starch into Cunningham's shorts, to push Rommel back when he's out of supplies and reeling from the British counterattack."

"You're losing me."

Port dug into his satchel and handed a piece of paper to Jim. "I've written it down. For Christ's sake, don't lose that paper. Study it later. Because you have to get Gott's plane shot down."

"What? Are you—"

Port muzzled Jim's mouth again. "Keep it down, bozo," he hissed. "Gott's plane is *supposed* to be shot down . . . but not for months. You have to make sure that happens now.''

Port stood up.

His unexpected son came back.

''Read the notes. And meet me here tomorrow night. By then you should be scheduled to go to Berlin.''

''Berlin?''

''Yes. . . .'' Port stepped back into the shadows. ''Don't be too surprised when he tells you. It's been planned for a while. Just meet me here tomorrow night. . . .''

Port turned and disappeared, swallowed by the darkness. Jim heard the voices. He made sure all the orders were in the satchel. And then he carefully climbed up, wondering what he'd say if he was seen climbing out of a big hole in the desert. . . .

''You feel alright?''

Lindstrom patted Ali's hand, and all the suspected lechery seemed to have vanished from his touch . . . replaced by a concern that Ali tried not to think about.

Dr. Jacob walked over, his glasses precariously balanced on the end of his bulbous nose.

''Everything is ready, Professor.''

Dr. Beck had her stethoscope on Ali's chest. An IV bottle was just behind the contoured chair, ready for her.

Lindstrom leaned close. ''There's still time . . . to reconsider. No one will think any the worse.'' He patted her hand. ''McManus will be up soon. We can let him—''

She shook her head.

No. After all, she thought, adventure has always been my goal, hasn't it? From schussing down closed ski trails to sailing a choppy ocean all alone, fear wasn't something she admitted.

Because that's what they'd expect, isn't it? Daddy's little girl, spoiled, growing up with everything except a real family . . . real love.

She had to show it didn't matter. That nothing mattered.

"No," she said quietly. "Let's get going."

Lindstrom smiled. "Yes." He turned to Jacob. "Okay, let's start."

The whine of the tachyon generator began, its thousands and thousands of miles of optical coils buried in the wall, speeding the subatomic particles, accelerating them past the point of matter to pure energy and light.

To the point where everything is energy.

Ali winced hearing the sound. This is worse than going to the dentist . . . listening to the archaic drill, the gurgle of the thing that sucks up water. A medieval torture instrument, an anachronism.

The whining sound rose in pitch.

The electronic stethoscope beeped. And she saw a frowning, disapproving Dr. Beck jot down something. "You haven't even had a proper physical," the woman said, shaking her head.

"Are you okay, Alessandra?" Lindstrom said. "Alessandra, are you—"

The voice changed, deepened.

Alessandra. Alessandra.

Calling to her, from across the great lawn of their East Hampton summer house. The grass was still wet from the sprinklers. It was perfect grass, blue-green, soft on her bare feet.

She was in her bathing suit, all pink and green, with cartoon shells circling around and around. She held one of the new puppies in the air, laughing at its goofy grin. It growled, so small and fierce.

"Alessandra!"

It was her father. Calling to her from the great deck. Dressed in a bright summer suit, resplendent, brilliant, a glowing vision of strength standing there. She sat up.

"Alessandra!"

I was five. The beach house that summer seemed to be the whole world. Didn't everyone live like this? Of course. The world was made up of small girls and their puppy dogs, a perpetual vacation of sun and water and—

"Alessandra!" her father took a step off the deck, down onto the grass. She tilted her head, looking at him. He seemed mad or upset. Had she done something? Forgotten something? Why was he walking over to her?

She stood up. Holding the puppy tight.

(Tighter. As he came close. It made a soft *grrr* against her chest.)

He came to her. But stood away. His eyes looked foggy, milky. Farther away than even usual. He started to talk.

She saw other people on the deck. Her aunt. A friend of her father's. Other people watching.

Someone was missing.

"Alessandra . . . something has happened. . . ."

Her father crouched, low to the ground. They were eye to eye.

He's crying, she thought. Seeing those coral-blue eyes up close. Crying. There were red lines and small trails running down his cheeks.

He's crying.

She looked back at the deck. Someone wasn't there.

Mom.

As beautiful as he was handsome.

"Back after lunch, sprite," she had said, getting into the sleek silver car that made Ali hold onto her seat belt.

It was the name of an animal. That car. An animal.

After lunch.

Her mother waved.

And vanished down the twisting road to town.

Lunch was a long time ago. Such a long time ago.

Her father reached out, trying to take her hands.

"Ali . . . I—"

But she pulled away. And she searched the deck, shielding her eyes from the sun. She checked each person, sure that she had missed her, standing there, waiting for her to come.

But Ali didn't see her.

"Mommy?" she said. She took a step toward the patio. "Mommy?"

"Ali, no—"

But now Ali ran.

She ran. Crying. Screaming, her voice mingling with the startled cries of the gulls swooping over the house.

"Mommy! Mom-e-e-e-!"

Each call more desperate, more pleading. Until it was a harsh yell, begging, demanding that it wasn't true. That it never could be true.

Until she stood on the smooth stones of the patio, her protesting puppy still held tight under one arm.

She looked at the adults. Hating each one of them. Hating them, now and forever.

Because they were here. Alive.

And her mother was gone. . . .

23

As soon as Jim popped his head above the edge of the small depression, he saw a group of soldiers looking at him.

"Ah, Lieutenant! We were worried about you," one of them said. "In fact, the field marshal asked me to come and see what in the world could have possibly happened to you."

Jim struggled out of the gully, ungracefully crawling on the sand.

"Yes," he said.

Thinking, what can I tell them? Needed some air? Took a wrong turn by the panzers?

"Is there something wrong?" the officer in charge said, stepping close.

(I should know this guy, Jim thought. That's another trap ready for me to fall into.)

"I'm not feeling well," Jim said. "In fact—if you want to know the truth, I've been sick as a dog all day."

The major nodded. There was no clue on his face as to how the story was going over.

"I came out here . . . to—you understand—"

The officer nodded.

Get the picture? Jim wondered. I needed to toss my cookies, Jack. Didn't want to gross out the entire army.

"Oh," the officer said with exaggerated sympathy. "That is too bad. Perhaps Doctor Bock could help.

Here," he said, snapping his fingers, "my men will escort you."

The officer saw the maroon folder clutched in Jim's hands.

"And I'll take care of this for you. The field marshal is waiting—"

The officer reached out for the folder but Jim pulled it away. "No. Please. I just needed to get away. I'd rather take this to Communications myself."

The officer nodded. And he stood there as if he was thinking over what he was going to do next.

Then, abruptly, he said, "Very well. I will tell the field marshal that we found you, that you're not . . . well. And that you chose to bring him the information yourself."

"Yes." Jim smiled. "I'd appreciate that."

Just as they were about to leave, there was a sound. In the distance. A squeal.

The officer stepped close to the edge of the depression. "Did you hear that?" He raised a hand, and the soldiers came up beside him. "Did you? I heard something out there. Just . . . that way—"

Jim turned and looked into the darkness. Gray-black clouds had snaked in, filling the night sky. And it was completely dark out there.

"Perhaps it was an animal. A bat. Something—" Jim offered.

The officer stood there, poised. Then, after an interminable wait, he said, "Perhaps. Well, maybe I'll send some men out there later." The major sniffed the air. "Maybe it was some filthy bedouin nosing about for something to steal." He turned back to Jim. "Good night, lieutenant. Heil Hitler!"

Despite the sand, the major deftly clicked his heels. Jim returned the salute and walked away, back to the sprawling night lager of the Afrika Korps.

Standing next to the radio operator, it finally dawned on Jim just what was happening here.

He handed the young soldier the stack of papers.

The radio operator looked at them, then passed them on to another man. He was probably the code officer, Jim guessed. Whoever he was, he checked the papers carefully.

Jim hoped that the forgeries were as perfect as Port said they were.

When he got to the third page the code officer's eyes went up. He showed something to the radio man.

"Everything is in order, I trust," Jim said, trying his best to sound imperious and impatient.

"Yes," the code officer said. "There was a name new to me. That's all, sir."

Jim nodded.

"You have the reports from Berlin?" Jim asked.

The code officer nodded, and reached down to a small file cabinet by his side. "I was about to send them to Field Marshal Rommel by courier."

Jim nodded and took the stack of papers.

There, he thought. That should about do it. He turned and started out of the tent. He reached the opening.

"Heil Hitler," the two men said behind him.

Jim nodded. Thinking . . .

Go fuck yourselves.

He darted between two tanks, two sleeping monsters, and crouched in the darkness. He took the real Berlin reports out, folded them into a small square and stuck them into his back pocket. Then he inserted Port's phony reports.

That's it, he thought. Tomorrow's battle has been changed by a handful of papers.

Men who wouldn't have died will die because of what I've done. And instead of becoming the unvanquished Lion of Africa, Rommel and his fabled army will taste defeat for the first time.

Jim stood up.

I'm putting history right. Pretty incredible, he thought.

He headed back to Rommel's tent. The clouds were

thicker, the sky pitch black. A small, ominous wind whistled through the alleyways made by the panzers and the tents. Some soldiers still struggled and fussed over their machines.

And as he walked, he wondered what else he'd have to do.

The memory faded.

And Ali felt freed of the terrible grip of that moment.

When it was over, when she finally stopped crying, she promised herself that she'd never feel that much pain again.

Nothing—and nobody—would ever hurt her like that again.

But now as the memory melted like dirty icy snow lingering into spring, there was nothing but a feeling of floating, spinning in the air like a dandelion thistle. Streams of white light passed her, moving so fast.

She could reach out and touch one—if she had anything to touch with.

But when she thought of doing just that, she didn't see her hand, or her arm. She just drifted in that direction, joining the blazing white stream, sailing along with it.

It was cool, refreshing.

White, then whiter. Like an explosive flash, unfolding in slow motion. A universe of white.

Until she felt something again.

Warm. And there was a smell. Sweet. Like fruity wine.

And noise. Distant. Voices laughing. A piano playing. And the white faded to black.

"Oh, so very, very sweet."

She looked at this man.

She was on his lap. He had his hand up near her thigh, touching her skin, toying with the elastic of her garter belt.

His face was buried in her shoulder, nuzzling her.

All she could see was a skull on his epaulet. And twin lightning bolts—in the shape of SS.

His hand, thick and fumbling, started a creepy-crawl up, along her thigh.

Heading toward home plate, Ali thought. Bad timing for my little time jump.

There was some laughter, just outside the door.

"No," she said.

But she heard herself say, "Nein."

Interesting, she thought. I'm thinking in English but speaking in Deutsch. But of more immediate concern is this SS gorilla pawing me.

Ali squirmed back, edging away from the relentless hand.

"No," she repeated. "There are people coming."

The man surfaced, his hair all askew, wearing the giddy expression of someone lost to lust. "Don't worry about them," he cooed. "It is dark in here. . . ." He took a quick nuzzle of her neck. "No one"—another wet lick—"will bother us."

It would seem, Ali noted, that a more direct approach was needed. Not too direct, though. She didn't know who this bozo was, and what kind of revenge he could wreak on her.

"No," she whispered huskily, kicking away. She slid to the side, off the officer's lap, onto the couch. Her legs ended up sprawled across the man. She quickly swung them around onto the floor.

"Later," Ali said. She reached out and pinched the man's cheek. And she suddenly knew his name.

Sturmbannführer Henrik Klotz.

She saw a wedding ring on his left hand. That might prove useful.

She stood up.

"Let's rejoin the others," she said, backing away.

But Henrik didn't look too pleased with the proposal of deferred gratification. His face was folded into a grumpy mask and he stood up, snatching a glass from an ornate table.

Ali smiled. But Herr Klotz wasn't about to be charmed.

"Yes," he said, pushing his thinning hair back into place. "Later," he snapped. "I'm sure my wife would love to have you join us." And he walked away.

Ali stood there, taking a deep breath.

There was a taste on her tongue. Champagne. And cigarettes—a not altogether unpleasant burr on her tongue. She felt a craving for something.

She saw her purse.

She opened it, and there was a pack of Drei Pintos, black cigarettes. What the hell, she thought. She tapped one out, put it in her mouth and lit it, expecting to hack away the foul smoke. But it tasted rather pleasant, soothing.

The party sounds swelled again. There was another song playing on the piano.

Alright, she thought. The time has come to make my entrance.

I know I'm in Berlin . . . November 24. Inside the Reich Chancellery. I work here . . . I live in one of the dozens of apartments upstairs.

And that is about the sum total of my knowledge.

But then—she started for the noise outside—I like meeting new people. . . .

And I *love* a party.

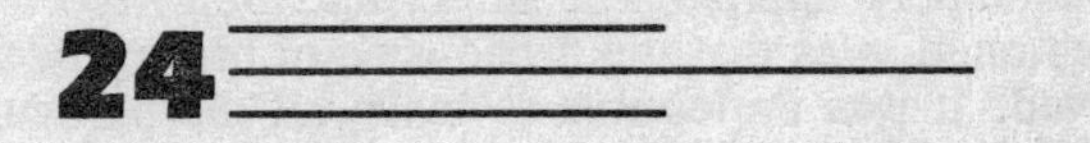

It was near dawn when Jim read the notes for the third time.

And each time he hoped that they would change . . . disappear. But as the black night gave way to a blustery, overcast dawn, he saw that his wish wasn't going to come true.

The North African campaign was all out of whack. General Bernard Montgomery was in charge of Operation Crusader instead of General Auchinleck.

That was disastrous for two reasons. First, the Auk, as Auchinleck was called by everyone from Winston Churchill on down to the lowliest foot solder, saved Crusader. When General Alan Cunningham faltered, afraid to pursue the battle, Auchinleck came down and put some starch in the old boy's shorts.

Rommel's depleted panzer army was reeling, ready to be pushed into a complete rout. And the Auk knew it.

But somehow, Monty was here. Already he had suffered a major defeat at the airstrip—a battle that the Brits should have won. In a few days, Monty would be replaced by General W.H.E. Gott.

Just about the worst person for waging the desert war.

Gott was supposed to die in a crash months later, when he first came to Africa. That's what was to bring Montgomery to Africa in the first place.

The phony plans would help. Rommel had accepted

them without question, standing in the yellow light of his tent. In the half-light, the man looked older, unsteady. Jim had seen the bottle of brandy. The field marshal seemed concerned about the weather. Jim had to fight the urge to shake.

If all went well, Rommel would walk right into a British attack. Not only that, he wouldn't find the precious supply dumps. The important thing, the notes mentioned, was that the broad arch of history be preserved. It was impossible to make all the particulars right. Nothing could be done about that.

But it was the other thing, the stuff on the last page, that made Jim just want to slap himself to wake up from this desert nightmare.

Rommel became sick many times during the campaign, flying back to Berlin, leaving less imaginative officers in charge.

But lately, somehow, he was very well. His health had never been better. Someone was taking care of the commander of the Afrika Korps.

And Jim was supposed to kill him.

Right, he thought. Me, who has trouble taking a hook out of a fish. I'm going to kill someone.

Wrong.

It's not my problem. I just want out of here.

In fact, when he saw Port that night, Jim would tell him just that.

Jim crumpled up the papers and tossed them onto the ground. Then, thinking better of it, he bent down and scooped up the incriminating pieces of paper. He stood up and put them in his pocket.

Outside he heard the sound of engines starting. He opened the flap and heard voices. German voices, tired voices, making jokes about women who took on whole regiments. Jokes about one-armed soldiers. Jokes about the stupidity of the British soldier. How bad their tanks were.

The night lager—after just a few hours sleep—was coming to life.

And Jim rubbed his grizzled face, wondering . . .

How would the day's battle go? With the wrong general. In the wrong place.

Would the broad arch of history be preserved?

And if not . . .

What would he do about it?

Ali took a second flute of champagne from a silver tray held by a waiter wearing a starched white jacket. And she tried to act like she belonged in this very grand room.

The reception room of the Reich Chancellery was garish and powerful. It recalled Versailles, but without any sense of age and taste. This was pure rococo ostentation.

And though she stood alone, sipping the wine, she couldn't help notice all the men paying attention to her, some in dark suits, some in Wehrmacht uniforms, and others, brazen in their black SS uniforms. They complimented her, kissed her hand.

And Ali thought she was going to be sick.

She smiled and went to get some hors d'oeuvres.

Now what do I do? she wondered, standing alone at the party. I know my name. And that's about it.

Elizabeth Stolling.

She could see that she was a blonde. Interesting. Not that she wanted to be a blonde. It's such a direct, brassy hair color.

What do I do here? she wondered. Besides service the swine of the Third Reich?

Then another young woman walked over.

"Elizabeth, are you okay?"

The women was short, a bit pudgy, but with a warm, open face.

Ali tipped her champagne glass. "A bit too much Dom Perignon, I'm afraid."

The woman nodded. I wish I knew her name, Ali thought. It would be helpful.

Her friend leaned close. "What did you do to Sturmbannführer Klotz? He came out of the drawing room *very angry.*"

"It's not a case of what I did. More a case of what I didn't do."

The woman laughed. "Oh. I see."

Then there was a flurry of activity near two large doors at the west end of the great hall.

The Reichkanzlei was decorated with flowers, great vases filled with red and white roses, and a classical quartet was playing Mozart, very quietly, very discreetly, in the corner of the room.

The doors flew open with a theatrical suddenness and the guests fluttered close to the doors.

Another SS officer sidled up to Ali and the other woman.

"Coming, ladies? Erika . . . Elizabeth?"

This woman—this friend's name—it's Erika. *Of course,* she thought. It was suddenly so familiar.

Ali shook her head.

Erika turned to her. "Come, Elizabeth," she said, pulling on Ali's arm. "It would be good for us to be seen with Dr. Goebbels."

Oh, Christ, Ali thought. This is like visiting some demented Disney exhibit. Third Reich Land, with animatronic Nazis.

Erika tugged, and Ali let herself be pulled along. The guests became subdued, expectant. Someone signaled to the musicians to stop. Waiters and liverymen stood at the outer periphery of the ceremonial group, trays of champagne and petits fours in hand.

"What's happening?" Ali asked.

"He's bringing news . . . from the East. . . ."

They stepped closer.

Goebbels was a small man. At first, she couldn't see the infamous Propaganda Minister. But then she saw him move, and the crowd parted. A beautiful woman walked behind him, a model or an actress. The man who would inflame the hatred of a nation limped, struggled as he entered the room.

A twisted, ugly little man.

Well, Ali thought, you didn't have to be Freud to

figure out where he was coming from. Talk about over-compensation . . .

"To Dr. Goebbels!" someone said. Ali turned and saw Henrik Klotz holding his glass up, proposing a toast.

The crowd responded, in unison.

"To Dr. Goebbels!"

A nice mid-sized incendiary device. Yes, Ali thought, that would take care of this whole room.

Goebbels took another few awkward steps.

And Ali felt someone's hand on her ass.

She reached behind and, with a move taught to her by Sun–yen, her aikido master, she gave the poor soul's wrist a nasty twist. Then the man collapsed to his knees with a painful grunt.

Erika turned and looked down. Then she looked up at Ali.

"You have someone at your feet."

"Yes," Ali hissed, "and if he touches me again I'll push his nose in."

Erika leaned back, studying her, impressed.

One of the Wehrmacht officers took a step closer to the Propaganda Minister.

"Tell us . . . is there any news, Dr. Goebbels?"

The minister stopped. Ali saw him scan the crowd. He looked around, smiling.

And then his face seemed to stop. He looked at Ali. His smile broadened.

Oh, Christ, she thought. I'm going to be sick. Not Goebbels.

She leaned down to Erika. "Excuse me, Erika . . . this might sound like a dumb question, but do I . . . know Dr. Goebbels?"

Erika laughed. "You're asking me?" She giggled again. "Not unless you've been keeping something from me."

"Good," Ali muttered, and she finished her glass of champagne.

"News?" Dr. Goebbels said. "Yes, there is excellent news. I have just come from receiving the Führer's report from the Wolf's Lair. The war in the East is all but won. The Red crooks have fled Moscow, yes. And even now, General Haape's men are at the outskirts of Moscow."

Everyone applauded. Erika squealed and clapped her hands next to Ali.

Goebbels nodded and grinned. "Once again, we will have the most excellent caviar."

The crowd laughed, and Goebbels signaled to someone. The music began, the waiters circulated. And once again the Propaganda Minister's eyes fell on Ali. Chilling her. Her stomach heaved.

Ali thought of this master liar, killing his blonde children and his wife in the bunker, four years down the road. Then taking his own life.

Was that all to be changed?

She was alone for now. Alone and scared.

She eagerly took another glass of champagne when the tray floated by. . . .

Ali lay back on the bed, her head throbbing from too much champagne.

Please stop, she asked the anvil chorus in her head.

But the banging kept up, incessant, obnoxious, and so terribly loud.

If only she had enjoyed drinking all the bubbly, it wouldn't have been so bad. But she had kept drinking just to calm down.

She pulled the pillow tight around her head, trying to make the noise stop.

Thank god Erika had spotted her in distress and guided her to their room. It would have been peculiar if she had to go around asking where her room was.

I shouldn't have drunk so much, she thought. Nerves or no nerves, it wasn't the best place to lose control.

She lay there, the pillow pulled tight.

Her body—this loaner—didn't feel like it was in as good shape as hers. The legs—though trim—lacked muscle tone. And she could feel her arms were spindly things.

I have to remember that, she thought. I'm not the same person.

She heard another thud. She thought it was coming from inside her head. It grew louder and louder. And someone was calling.

"Fräulein! Fräulein Stolling!"

Ali sat up, the dark room weaving before her. "Fräulein! Will you please open the door?"

She staggered to her feet.

"Who—who is it?"

"Sturmbannführer Klotz."

Groan. I thought I was rid of him, she thought. "I'm sorry, Herr Klotz, but I—"

"We have some questions for you. Official questions. Please, I must demand that you open the door."

Shit. What did I do? I've got the Gestapo at my door. She undid the lock and sat back on the bed.

Henrik Klotz walked in with two young, sheepish lieutenants.

"This won't take long, Fräulein Stolling. But I'm afraid we have a few questions for you."

"Go ahead," Ali nodded.

"One of my men happened to notice that you didn't applaud Reich Minister Goebbels's announcement of the coming victory in the East. It was very direct, he said . . . very clear." Klotz paused.

The bastard enjoys scaring people. The little sadist . . .

"Your explanation?"

"Yes," Ali said. "I think I had already drunk too much." She smiled. "I don't know if what Dr. Goebbels said even registered."

"You were drunk?" Klotz laughed, and looked at his two cronies. "Drunk?" He stared at her. "That might explain . . . many things." But then his smile faded. "What about the toast? You didn't see everyone's glass raised?"

"Yes . . . I mean, perhaps—"

There was a glimmer in Klotz's eyes. The bright light that comes into a cat's eyes when he has his mouse cornered.

Klotz nodded. "I think I want you to come to my office. For some more questions. Such behavior . . . concerns me."

Klotz reached down and pulled her to a standing position. He smiled. "It shouldn't take long."

Ali tried to think of a way out of this.

"Can we wait until the morning?" she said, forcing a smile. "I feel terrible and—"

But Klotz shook his head.

"No. I'm afraid I'd like to question you now." He kept pulling her toward the door.

"I do hate unfinished business. . . ."

25

Like the great wagon trains that braved the West, the tanks—the Mark IIs and the powerful Mark IV Panzers—lumbered to life in the early morning bleakness.

And it was made even more bleak by the incessant wind that blew—unfettered, powerful—sending a constant spray of sand and grit showering over the German and Italian infantry who fell into line behind the great armored force.

The tanks spiraled around, each knowing its place, like circus elephants forming a great circle.

And at the front, standing, his goggles on, riding in his captured vehicle, a modern Hannibal, stood Rommel.

Jim ran up to Rommel's vehicle.

"And it is completely overcast to the north and west. . . ." A lieutenant was shouting at Rommel, trying to make his voice rise above the din of the roaring wind and the unmuffled tank engines. Rommel nodded, and used his ever-present field glasses.

Jim started to climb into the driver's seat.

How am I going to see in this mess? he wondered. The desert was alive with dust storms, small tornados that whizzed left and right, as if daring the great Panzer army to come out onto the desert.

Rommel put a hand out. Flat. To the side.

A signal to wait.

"Sir?" Jim said.

Wondering . . . Was there something wrong with

the information I gave him? Did Port somehow screw up?

Rommel's hand stayed there, waited, until he brought his glasses down.

"No, Oberstleutnant," Rommel said. "I will use another driver today."

Jim turned around. A smart-looking soldier stood at attention near the back of the heavily armored car.

Jim backed away. Relieved.

But worried.

Is there something wrong here? he fretted. Or is it just that the Desert Fox has had enough of my driving?

"Get some rest," Rommel said. "Take this battle off."

Jim nodded, stepping back from the vehicle.

Rommel looked at him, a small smile on the general's weatherbeaten face. "Visit my doctor. Tell him . . ." Rommel's grin broadened, and Jim's heart did a weird flip-flop. ". . . tell him that you haven't been yourself lately."

The sand beat into Jim's face, a shower of fine grit. His eyes watered. The temperature was dropping, actually getting cooler with the sunrise.

It was not going to clear by sunrise. Not from the looks of things.

Rommel signaled the other soldier, Jim's replacement, and he quickly slipped into the driver's seat. Rommel remained standing. Jim backed up farther. He could see the line of tanks behind Rommel. Tanks, and armored cars, and motorized artillery, and the hapless infantry, streaming behind him, and then around and around.

All of them being sent to a trap, Jim thought. If all goes well. A major defeat for Rommel. History set right, I hope to God, set right. . . .

Rommel picked up the radiotelephone.

He grabbed the windshield of his armored car. He raised a hand, probably lost in the maelstrom. And then he yelled. Loud, primitive, carrying over the terrible roars of the wind and the engines. . . .

"Nun! Nun . . . !"

Now.

And this modern Napoleon led his forces farther into the wilderness.

McManus awoke in total darkness.

He heard other people sleeping near him. Muffled snorts. Small gasps. It was black, completely black. Like being buried alive.

He took a breath, and blinked, remembering where he was. And what was happening.

Can't afford to sleep, he thought.

"Can't afford to sleep," he said aloud.

One of the people nearby, one of their two time transference subjects, sniffed in answer. McManus blinked again, and then he slid off the small cot, his feet touching the cold lab floor.

Then he heard the noise. Little pops. Sounding almost like firecrackers. Far away. Over and over. Pop. Pop. Except he knew that they weren't firecrackers.

He stood up and looked for a sliver of light to tell him the way out. He saw the thin line of light outlining the door and he ran to it, pushing it open.

Jacob and Lindstrom were together, looking at something on the table. Dr. Beck was nowhere in sight.

"What's going on?" he asked.

Lindstrom looked up, rubbing his unkempt beard. He looked worried, embarrassed.

"It appears that we're . . . under siege."

"What?" McManus yelled. "By whom? What's going on?"

Dr. Jacob backed away from the table.

"An attack. On the building. The guards are returning fire."

"Well, who the hell is it?"

Lindstrom looked over at Jacob. "We don't know. . . . Dr. Beck—she just went up. To see who it was. We thought it best if we monitor—"

"An attack!" McManus fumed. "If they get in here

. . . if they do anything to the machine, or the subjects—''

He turned and started for the door leading out of the lab, unaware that he was still in his stocking feet. He reached the door just as Dr. Beck came back in. She was upset, her eyes puffy from worry and fatigue.

''What is it?'' McManus snapped.

''There are some people. They have guns. Nothing too powerful. Toland says he can take care of them . . . he'll come to talk with you just as soon as he's sure they've stopped. . . .''

''Are they police? Soldiers? Come on, woman—who are they?''

She shook her head. ''Just looters. Crazy-looking people. Laughing and taking shots at the building. The guards are able to keep them away—for now.''

Lindstrom had walked closer to them. ''For now. Doesn't sound too auspicious.''

McManus shook his head. ''I could damn well not afford that little nap.''

''You were exhausted,'' Dr. Beck offered. ''You're still exhausted.''

McManus waved the idea away. ''Exhausted or not, the guards won't save us. It's all in the hands of—'' McManus stopped. ''Where's the girl?''

No one answered.

''Where is that girl? You haven't let her leave, have you? Because that would be stupid, really—''

But when everyone was quiet, McManus's eyes darted from one to the other.

''I—I figured out the source of the art anomaly, Elliot.'' Lindstrom took a cautious step closer. ''Not only that, I found out what they did with the art. It's all over here.'' Lindstrom gestured, pointing to the table. ''The figures, the amounts, every—''

''Where is the girl?''

Lindstrom sighed.

''She volunteered to go, Elliot. She wanted to find her friend and—hope to God—stop them.''

''Them?''

"The others, Elliot. You see, I know who they are now." He paused taking a deep breath. "And it's worse than we thought . . . much worse."

McManus sniffed the air. "Yes. Then show me everything you have, but first"—he looked around the lab—"where the hell did you put my shoes?"

Klotz pulled Ali close.

The creep was obviously enjoying his little display of power, grabbing her arm, poking her, pushing her toward the door.

I guess, Ali thought, you don't tell a Gestapo colonel to take a hike.

"Look," she said, trying to pull away, "I'm sorry. Can we do this in the morning, Colonel? My head is hurting something fierce."

"Nein," Klotz snapped.

The man was not to be denied.

His two officers stepped out of the room, and Klotz took Ali's bare arm.

No goddam muscle tone, Ali remembered. And this Elizabeth Stolling obviously wasn't much of a drinker, not from the way her head was aching.

"Please," Ali said, raising her voice. "If only you'll—"

Some people were walking in the hall. A woman and a man.

Ali looked down the dark hall, and she saw Klotz turn and look also. She saw her roommate Erika walking toward her, accompanied by a Wehrmacht officer.

"Erika!" Ali called with great relief.

Her roommate came running over to her.

"What is this?" she said loudly, with just the right amount of exaggerated histrionics. "What is this?" She looked at the SS Officers, Klotz, and then—with her powerful eyes flashing—at her big, burly Wehrmacht officer.

"Herr Klotz wants to ask me some questions," Ali explained. "And he says he can't wait until tomorrow. . . ."

Erika's mouth went wide with horror. "Questions? At this hour? Who asks questions at this hour? Who?"

She said the last word staring right at Klotz's puffy face. The insinuation was clear. Only a depraved bastard hauls a young German girl out of bed in the dark early morning hours.

Then, with perfect timing, she saw Erika turn to her Wehrmacht officer. "Can you believe this, Oberst? Is this what the SS is supposed to be up to?"

Her Nordic-looking officer cleared his throat and took a step closer to the fray. "Yes, Colonel Klotz . . . what is this that you're up to here?"

"This woman acted suspiciously during the party. She didn't toast Reich Minister Goebbel's speech and—"

"She looks like she had more than enough 'toasts,' " Erika snapped.

"I rejected his . . . attentions," Ali muttered.

On cue, Erika took a deep breath. "Ah-h-h!" she said in mock horror.

"So that is it, mein Klotz, eh?" The oberst grinned.

"It is most certainly not. I have no intention of—"

"Then"—the officer put an arm around the SS colonel—"for appearance's sake perhaps you'd better conduct your interview at a more"— He smiled.

Erika hugged Ali's free arm.

—"more reasonable hour."

Klotz nodded and waited. "If you suggest. I was just trying to do my duty . . . as precipitously as possible."

"I'm sure," Erika's officer said.

Klotz signaled his two soldiers to follow him, and he clicked his heels.

"Heil Hitler!"

The Wehrmacht officer returned the salute with an even louder click.

Klotz turned and walked back down the hall, his dumpy body comically poised between the two young soldiers.

And the army colonel waited until Klotz was out of

sight before he burst out laughing, hugging Erika and Ali both close.

And Ali, whose skin was still icy cold, who felt like she had just slipped through the hangman's noose, managed a small smile.

"Now that is surely worth a small nightcap, eh?"

And he walked back to their room, his laugh a great rolling sound, like the ocean breaking against a stone jetty.

"A drink," he said, as Erika pulled out a bottle of brandy, "to the perils of war!"

And Ali laughed.

He was only miles from the depot.

A six-mile drop of British fuel, water, weapons, and ammunition.

A treasure trove, Rommel thought.

And absolutely essential. The farther they moved from their own desperately stretched supply lines, the more essential this poaching became.

It could, Erwin Rommel thought, determine the battle. Only miles away.

And yet . . .

He saw nothing.

It could be the weather. It was easily the worst day in weeks. And with the air this cool—almost *cold*—it could even rain.

That would be bad. The panzers, especially the Mark IIIs with their clumsy gear ratio, could lose half their speed as the dry sand turned into a thick concrete, clutching at the tracks, sucking at the tires.

And we're not just facing sleepy Matildas today, he knew. There'll be—what did they call them? Yes . . . Crusader Tanks . . . and something they called Honeys—an American tank.

But no matter. My artillery can win half the battle before even one tank fires.

The new 50mm cannon had tremendously improved penetration over his 88s. And they were much faster.

He could trap the enemy and let the artillery completely debilitate them. Before even one tank fires.

It has worked so far. And it would work today.

But still the weather worried him.

How would we get the range? What if the British split into groups? Two, maybe three armies? They could try to outflank us.

Rommel looked behind himself. His armored line stretched for miles, back into the distance, lost in the sandy windstorms.

Two-to-one, he thought. Nothing to worry about.

Four-to-one. Forget the Italians. They just want to go home. They've had enough war.

He raised his field glasses. And so have I . . . he thought.

So have I.

26

Jim walked into the hospital tent.

A few German medics were still cleaning up from the simple breakfast . . . bowls of cereal, some dates and raisins, bitter coffee, and milk.

And he stood there.

I have to see him first, Jim thought, this doctor. I have to look him in the eye. Then I'll know. Then I can plan—

What I'm going to do.

You must kill him, the note said.

The doctor was a key. For reasons that Jim didn't completely understand. Rommel couldn't stay in North Africa, healthy, overseeing each battle.

And the doctor was just like Jim. Someone from the future.

Will he be able to tell by looking at me? Jim wondered. Is it something in the eyes? A way of smiling? A way of walking?

Do I speak Fritz's German using modern phrases?

And if he recognizes me for what I am, will he kill me first?

Jim walked down the aisle separating the German soldiers from the scattering of British and Australian soldiers. A few beds were empty. Newly empty.

Jim clenched his fists.

One of the medics, carrying a full bedpan, turned and saw Jim.

"Need anything, Oberstleutnant?"

Jim shook his head. He walked past the medic, now closer to the end of the long tent, close to the curtained-off cubicles at the other end.

Then he was there.

He took a breath.

(God, he thought. I'm not cut out for this. And he had another thought. Maybe this is all wrong. Maybe I'm the one who is messing up history. Oh, jeez, what if I'm the one helping some maniacs fuck up history?)

And the longer he thought about it, the more likely it seemed. Yes, his anxious, panicky mind screamed. Of course, you're being suckered. Someone's using you.

He decided, quickly, with the assurance born of crazed fear, to turn and leave the hospital tent.

Then someone emerged from one of the cubicles. It was Dr. Ernst Bock. He had a clipboard filled with papers. But he stopped and looked up.

And said, "Lieutenant?"

Jim nodded.

"Is there something wrong? Something I can help you with?"

Jim looked at him, then just as quickly looked away. He looked down at the ground. But he felt Bock's eyes on him, studying him.

"Not . . . well?" the doctor asked again.

"Yes," Jim said, whispering. He was aware that they were alone. The medics seemed to have all vanished. There were just the soldiers, most of them medicated, sleeping.

"No . . ." Jim said. "I haven't been feeling well. Field Marshal Rommel suggested I come—"

The doctor smiled.

"Well, what is wrong? Your stomach, perhaps? Your head?" The doctor's voice fell to a confidential whisper. "Your nerves?"

Jim looked up . . . to face the man whom he was supposed to kill.

"Yes," Jim croaked. "My nerves."

And Bock nodded, his eyes not leaving Jim's for a moment. "I have just the thing. Come with me."

And Bock led him back to one of the closed-off areas, where, Jim realized, no one could see them.

She found her desk by process of elimination.

It was the only one vacant in the large office filled with the clattering of mechanical typewriters—such a quaint sound—and the clicking of the secretaries' shoes moving across the smooth, stone floor. Great window panels lined the east wall, but there was no sun today, just a gloomy, gray sheet that cast a sepulchral gloom inside the hall.

Ali recognized most of the faces from the party. She didn't know their names, but they nodded to her.

Her head was still beating a crazy tattoo and she realized that, for as long as she was in this body, she'd have to watch the bubbly.

(And how long is that going to be? she wondered. She knew what she had told—ordered—Lindstrom to do. But would he do what she had asked? No matter what, she had said . . . no matter what.)

"Feeling okay?"

Ali looked up with a start. She expected to see Klotz, ready to have another go at her nether regions. He was a comic-opera Nazi who was using his position in the only way he knew how.

But this was an army officer, tall, thin, not unattractive. He smiled at her.

"Okay?" he repeated.

Ali smiled, waiting for a helpful name to be supplied from whatever corner of the brain the real Elizabeth Stolling controlled. But either the champagne had rendered her host incommunicado, or the officer was too unimportant; there was nothing.

"I've felt better."

"You have to be careful of those Chancellery parties," he said. "At least during the week . . . when you have to work the next day."

She smiled at him. And he handed her a piece of paper.

"This should be attended to first. Type three originals and get them back to me. . . . I'll see that they get to Herr Luther."

She took the piece of paper. It was a handwritten letter.

"And take some aspirin." The officer smiled.

The officer turned on his heels, and Ali looked at the piece of paper.

It was a short letter. Saying something about agreeing to the change in plans. The new conference date was acceptable. January 23rd. The location—unchanged—was also noted.

Wannsee.

The note was signed by Martin Luther. Foreign Office Minister. It was addressed to Heinrich Himmler.

She held the paper. Looking at it. Reading the words over and over, until they started becoming nonsense syllables. Meaningless babble.

Wannsee.

She knew what the name meant.

Wannsee. Where Himmler would outline the Führer's master plan, his "Final Solution" to what he called the Jewish Question.

She touched the paper.

A direct link to—

(How many millions would die? she thought. How much pain? How much horror? And I'm part of it—part of—)

"Still under the weather, Lisa? You must be more careful."

Ali turned. It was Erika, leaning close.

"Especially with nasty Colonel Klotz waiting around and—"

Erika came closer. She brought a hand up to Ali's face.

"What is it?" Ali said, feeling like she was in a masquerade and her mask had just slipped off. She'll see who I am, she'll know I'm not from here—

"You've been crying. Why? Has anything happened? Is anything wrong?"

Ali shook her head. She sniffed, and the runny sound confirmed what Erika said.

She rubbed at her eyes.

"I—I don't know. I just—"

(This is mad, she thought. It's some twisted nightmare. It can't be real. It can't . . . be.)

"Here," Erika whispered. She dug into a pocket of her skirt and then slipped something into Ali's free hand.

"Take one now—and one later." She smiled. "They're good for calming you down." She gave Erika a reassuring squeeze on her shoulders and then walked away.

Ali rubbed at her cheeks.

When was the last time she was in temple? she wondered. When she was seven . . . maybe eight? Her father had brought her up to be aggressively agnostic. His house was one where the only truths, the only realities, were hard and physical. Money, power, reputation.

There was never any sense of her being a Jew.

That conjured up too many comical images, images from another century, images that her father ridiculed. The Twenty-first Century can't afford religion, her father had said. There are enough things to divide people. Things like intelligence and talent. We don't need religion. Any more than we need nationalism . . . or terrorism. . . .

The Bible was one of the great mythological books of all time.

And when they talked about the Holocaust—which they did two—or was it three—times, her father railed about the victims. Six million! And where did they fight back? he asked. Where did they take a stand and turn on their keepers, overwhelming them with their sheer numbers?

They were sheep, he said angrily.

(She remembered he had been drinking. They were

talking about his father . . . about his family. About old people and old beliefs . . . an old world.)

Sheep, he had said.

And Ali grew up to forget that she was a Jew. It was unimportant. Not relevant.

Never—

Until—

She touched the piece of paper.

What can I do? she wondered. I'm here. Now. Knowing what I know. What can I do?

But she knew the answer.

She wiped her eyes again. And took Erika's pill. . . .

27

"Stop," Rommel ordered the driver. And he held up his hand to the line of armored cars and tanks directly behind him. The driver picked up the radiotelephone and passed the order on to the rest of the serpentine Panzer Army.

Rommel brought his field glasses up and scanned the horizon.

Desert. Covered with a thin veil of swirling motes of sand. He could taste the dust on his lips. It gathered in the folds of his collar, buried in the thin cracks and lines of his neck, filled in every line on his exposed skin.

Visibility was poor, and getting worse. And yet the depot should be right here!

"The map!" he snapped at the driver. And the driver handed him the cumbersome map, with the two depots circled.

This was it. There had been no mistake.

The British depot should be here. A tremendous cache of supplies. Fuel. Water. Even ammunition.

Enough for his army to extend its run hundreds of miles, chasing the British into the sea. If only the weather hadn't been so bad, he would have had some air reconnaissance.

But it was bad. And growing worse.

For the first time, he thought of going back. Perhaps tomorrow would be better. The weather might clear. Berlin might tell him where the supplies really were.

But he thought of his long-armored column, the tank commanders, on edge, ready to complete their defeat of the enemy. The artillery crews, young and proud of their sleek new cannons, fast deadly machines that were writing a new page in armored warfare. And then there were the Italians. Tired of the war they began. Just as happy to turn around. To leave North Africa forever.

He couldn't risk it. It would be too demoralizing. His hands gripped the windshield tightly. We must maintain the momentum, he thought.

"We must . . ." he said aloud.

"Sir?" the driver said.

Rommel shook his head.

So then, he thought. No supplies, no booty. Not here, anyway.

No matter. My panzers have large fuel tanks. We can travel all day, if we have to. Like the camels we see, who watch us, unconcerned, amused by our desert folly.

It is not—he convinced himself—all that important.

But when he sat down, he felt that the seat of this British armored car—O'Connor's own Mammoth!—was damp from a fine mist. The beginning of the rain? he wondered.

Battles can turn on small decisions. Like the one I just made. And on battles, campaigns can turn. And a lost campaign can lose a war.

He thought of that, as he turned to his driver and said—

"All right, west now." He nodded. "West. To Gabr Saleh . . ."

General Alan Cunningham reread the telegram.

> Today is a historic turning point in the war. The enemy stands poised to drive us from the continent. But it shall not come to pass! When the story of this war is written, this day and your inevitable victory will forever be remembered by all free peoples.

He looked at the name at the bottom.

Winston Churchill.

After yesterday the old boy's trying to inspire me, Cunningham thought. Already Montgomery was expected to be relieved. General Gott—a routiner if there ever was one—was scheduled to arrive tomorrow.

It wasn't intended to be a slap in the face to Monty. But yesterday's debacle at Sidi Rezegh had horrified the PM. Operation Crusader, begun with such overwhelming confidence and superiority in numbers, had nearly turned into a rout.

And Cunningham wondered whether it would have been different if Auchinleck had been in overall command.

After all, the Auk had been scheduled to replace Sir General Archibald Wavell. But then there was that freak accident in Tripoli. Failed brakes, and Auchinleck was lucky to escape with his life. Doctors aren't sure if he'll walk again.

The misfortunes of war.

You'll outnumber Rommel, Monty told him.

Very reassuring, Cunningham thought. Then why don't I feel reassured?

He looked up at the dark mass of clouds overhead. Steel grey, and growing greyer.

He felt the first tentative drops of rain. Oversized drops, plopping on the brim of his cap. Bouncing off the dry desert floor.

A rarity.

Rain.

Should make it a wonderful day for a tank battle, Cunningham thought. All I have to do is sit in this trap . . . and wait.

Wonderful. . . .

Jim stood close to the doctor.

He had the flap to his gun, a clunky luger, open and ready, even though he knew he couldn't use it.

Why? Because then I'd be killed in minutes. Just as soon as the sentries heard it.

That left the knife, a squat blade with a serrated tip. Port had told him just how to do it.

You drive the knife into the doctor's stomach, then twist it hard and bring it up.

Sure, Jim thought. Should be no problem. So what if I'm inexperienced? Didn't sound any more difficult than changing a light bulb.

Now he stood in this enclosed area, trying to listen to the doctor and quiet his mind—which mostly screamed—

Get out. Get out of the tent now. Leave. While you can. Just turn around and—

"Nerves. Well, there's not much I can do about war, Oberstleutnant," Bock said.

(Only it's not Bock, Jim thought. It's someone else. Like me. Someone from decades away. That's what Port said. If this whole thing isn't crazy, if this isn't something out of a nightmare . . .)

"Yah, nerves. Well, these should keep your hand steady . . . at least when you're driving the field marshal around, eh?"

He handed Jim a vial of white pills. Jim reached out to take them.

The knife was strapped to the back of his belt. He felt the sheath, heavy against his body. And then he felt something else.

Bock was looking at him, staring at him.

Jim looked up. The doctor's eyes were a piercing blue. He studied Jim, as if bothered by something.

Jim's skin was ice cold. His breathing went shallow.

God, he thought. I'm going to faint. I'm just going to tumble backwards and fall on the ground.

The wind pressed the sides of the tent together. Like it was breathing. Growing anxious.

Just like me.

"You are sure," Bock asked, "that there isn't anything else wrong?"

Jim tried to smile. But he knew it came out all wrong, kind of lopsided, twisted. An assassin clown.

He fumbled with the vial of pills, trying to put them in the pocket of his Wehrmacht jacket.

"No . . ." Jim said, stammering.

Bock's eyes narrowed. Jim saw a hint of something there. Something dark. A look of confusion.

Concern.

The knife was there.

"Well," Bock said, recovering, nodding, "if there is anything else, come back and see me."

Jim nodded, and without knowing, he turned and started to walk away. Out to the main tent, past the wounded, the sleeping, the moaning, the dying.

He walked out.

Barely able to see in front of him. Gasping at the air. So cold, so horribly cold. And when he stepped outside, he felt the rain.

Coming down hard, vengeful, an angry rain that attacked the dry desert floor.

Bock smiled.

So, he thought, There is someone else here . . . some other *voyager*. It was easy to see, in his face, in his eyes. Fear, confusion. He was shaking, just standing there.

Well, if that's the best they can do, then we'll have no problem. None at all.

We knew that they'd send someone. That wasn't unexpected. But why had he come here?

To kill me? Very possibly. So then . . . what stopped him?

He closed the case—Bock's blank cases filled with syringes and three rows of vials. This field hospital was surprisingly well equipped . . . surprisingly.

The real Bock would never have figured out how to take care of the great Desert Fox. Rommel's strange fevers were nothing more than a persistent viral attack that flared up at the most inconvenient times. It was a virus that responded well to specific vitamin and antibiotic therapy.

I'll be able to keep him on his feet. Rommel won't

have to go to Berlin. He smiled. And that should change things considerably.

He closed the case and snapped the latches shut.

Then Bock pushed aside the flaps of his white lab coat. And he felt the gun. He unbuckled the holster.

There, he thought. I'm ready. The next time, I'll just shoot him, this Fritz, and be done with it. I'll say he attacked me, that he went crazy.

And, since the real Fritz will die too, why—he laughed—it will be like killing two birds with one stone. . . .

Jim sat in his tent.

A soldier, young, but with a distant, lost look in his eyes, asked him if he wanted something. Some tea. A schnapps. Something . . .

Jim shook his head. And then he said, loudly, speaking over the pounding of the rain on the tent, "No."

Then Jim sat alone.

How long before he sees Port? He checked his watch. More than seven hours. By then Rommel should be coming back. And I'm going to leave.

For Berlin.

Won't that be fun, won't that—

(Daddy!)

A small boy. Blonde, curly hair. A pink, puffy-cheeked smile. Fritz's son.

Jim blinked, as if the thought, the memory, was an illusion. As if he could make the slow swelling of memories from this other persona stay away.

Instead, he saw something else.

A woman. With a pleasant, sweet face. Simple, unadorned. And Jim felt a weird feeling. Uncomfortable, then angry.

And he knew that Fritz and his frau were on the outs. And that was okay with the lieutenant. That was fine. Except, yes, except for his son.

Jim shook his head. Just be glad, Fritzie. Yeah. Be

glad that the boy will be too young. Too young for the Hitler Youth. Too young for the war.

Jim stood up. The rain's incessant tattoo was maddening. The plops seemed to grow louder, annoying and oppressive in their steady rhythm.

He thought of the doctor, the imposter—the supposed imposter. I can't kill him. God, I've never killed anyone.

And he thought of Rommel.

Somewhere out there. In the vast desert. And the massed Afrika Korps moving through the rain, searching for a final battle to win the Afrika Campaign. . . .

28

Rommel shook his head.

"Nein," he said softly. Then louder, almost barking it, *"Nein!"* He turned to his driver. The water cascaded off his face. It was a warm rain, foul-smelling, like stagnant water.

"There is nothing," he said.

The driver had the radiotelephone at his ear. He passed the General's words along.

Rommel brought the field glasses back up.

Perhaps we should go back, he considered. How often did it rain here? Ten, maybe twenty days a year? It would be hell for the panzers, and worse for the trucks and armored cars. Already the infantry was struggling to keep up with the main force.

And there was nothing ahead. No great British force, with their Crusaders and their American Honeys, moving right into our trap.

I should call it off, he thought.

"Give me the phone," he snapped to the driver.

Rommel took the phone, never letting his eyes move from the horizon, visibility shrinking every minute.

"General Cruewell, do you see anything?"

Ludwig Cruewell was a good tank commander. A bit too cautious, perhaps, a bit too conservative . . . like most of the old Weimar Generals. The new methods of this new war sometimes left them feeling dazed, struggling to keep up with lightning advances and daring breakthroughs.

Cruewell's force was coming from the east, ten miles away. With one panzer division—mostly PZIIIs—and two light infantry divisions, he was moving more slowly. Still, they were to meet up . . . just ahead.

If they were to keep on going.

"No, Field Marshal," Rommel heard Cruewell say. The rain soaked the phone. It was like breathing water. Rommel wondered whether it might damage the instrument. Without communications, they could be in trouble.

"There is nothing, nothing at—"

Rommel looked out at his artillery, his row of 50mm guns, poised, ready to decimate the British. The gunners, in their shiny grey rain ponchos, waited by the guns, waited for the orders, waited for the enemy.

"There is—" Cruewell continued.

Rommel heard the sound of a cannon blasting. Through the radiotelephone.

And again.

"Cruewell!" Rommel shouted. "What is it? What is happening?"

"I—"

But Cruewell's voice was lost in the terrible barrage that Rommel heard over the phone. Terrible, and incessant, like the phone was broken, filled with a crazy, garbled static that blocked out Cruewell's stammering.

Cruewell's forces were under attack.

By whom, Rommel wondered. By how many tanks? All of Cunningham's forces? Or are the rest still coming here?

Rommel held the receiver to his chin, thinking . . .

If it was only a small armored division attacking, then Cruewell would be able to deal with that himself. There would be no reason to break away from the plan. Not yet.

But if it was the main force, then Cruewell's soldiers would be wiped out in hours.

It would be a loss I could ill afford, he thought.

Every tank is precious. Every soldier—every German soldier—is absolutely vital.

"Cruewell, report. What is happening?"

Through the hiss and crackle of the battle, he heard Cruewell, sounding distant, overwhelmed.

"We're being attacked . . . from the sides. We're in a depression . . . the British are on—"

He stopped as a shell exploded noisily near the phone.

"—a hill." Cruewell paused. "We'll need help, Herr Field Marshal. It would appear to be—"

Another shell interrupted Cruewell's report.

"—a trap. . . ."

Ali looked out the window. It was a beautiful clear fall day outside.

Not very much different than the day she had left, some sixty years from now. Except by then this building, this Reich Chancellery, will be gone. Destroyed, like all of Hitler's mad dreams.

But not yet. That was the weird thing. This—right now—was the present. And all bets were off. Anything could happen. And that would be history.

She stood up.

I don't have a lot of time, she thought. She walked over to her friend Erika's desk, which was filled with papers and a massive mechanical typewriter.

"Feeling better?" Erika asked.

Ali smiled. "A bit. . . ."

Erika looked around. "Shouldn't you get back to work? You know how Herr Luther hates his fräuleins taking unscheduled breaks."

Just as Erika said that, a door opened near the back of the large office and a small man came out. He handed something to another secretary and looked over at Ali.

"See what I mean?" Erika asked, lowering herself to her desk, acting busy.

Ali nodded, biting her lip.

But the man—Martin Luther, minister of Internal Security—hurried back inside his office.

Ali turned back to her friend. "Erika . . . who is in charge of the trains . . . assigning them?"

Erika smiled. "Trains?" She laughed. "Are you looking for another job, liebchen? Believe me, you don't want to work for the Reich Ministry of Transportation." Erika leaned across the table and rolled her eyes, grinning wildly. "The fräuleins there have a very hard time of it . . . *very hard.*"

"No, I don't want to be reassigned. I just—"

She looked at Erika and noticed that her friend was giving her an odd, questioning look.

"Yes?" Erika said.

"I need to find something out. About a shipment . . . moving to Bavaria . . . through the Alps."

"Oh, you do, do you? And what on earth for?"

I'm in trouble, Ali thought. Erika was looking at her very strangely. I'm probably asking for classified war information.

"A friend," she said. "He wants to—"

Oh, that was probably worse, Ali thought. Now it sounds like I'm giving information to someone. Maybe helping the Russians or the British—

Which was true.

In a strange way, true.

But then Erika smiled. "Oh, you want to see when your officer friend is coming back from Paris, huh? If he comes back. . . . From what I hear, they are having too much fun with the wine and the mademoiselles to ever return to the Fatherland!" Erika laughed.

And Ali smiled. "Yes," she said. "That's it."

Erika leaned across the table, conspiratorially. "Well, I have a friend in transport, Colonel Albert Weitzel. Tell him you want to see when your 'friend' is coming home. Be sweet to him, and maybe he'll show you the lists."

Ali smiled. "Thanks, Erika."

Erika reached out and patted Ali's hand.

Funny, Ali thought. In my world, Erika is probably long dead. Maybe she never survived the Armageddon of Berlin. But here, she's so young and fresh. A bit bubbleheaded, but that must have made working in this building possible.

"Thanks," Ali said.

And she walked back to her own desk.

We'll move, Rommel thought. And quickly. Before Cruewell gets chewed up by the British.

Damn, this was all wrong. Completely. No supply dump. No massive fuel depot, no ammunition. And now Cruewell was in a trap, a British pincer that was supposed to be right here. What the hell was wrong with Berlin's intelligence?

But no matter. I've fought without their help before . . . and I can again.

Already the large artillery were moving to the side. The gun crews were hurrying, confused by the strange orders. But the big wheels of the guns were getting caught as the rain transformed the sand into thick sludge.

The artillery will lag behind, Rommel knew. And so will the troop carriers, and the trucks.

I will just have the tanks and the armored cars.

His soldiers slipped in the sand, falling into the rapidly multiplying puddles.

Hurry, Rommel thought. Every minute another tank could be lost.

Hurry. . . .

Finally the guns were moved to the side, and Rommel picked up the radiotelephone.

"Schnell," he said.

He remained standing, waving his hand to the line of panzers behind him.

And he headed east into the maelstrom.

General Alan Cunningham watched the confusion on the depression below.

Just as Whitehall had told him—though Monty had doubted it—the Germans were streaming toward Gabr Saleh. And just who did they expect to find there? Cunningham wondered.

The battle—a terrible blur of guns, smoke, and rain—was going well. Almost too well. The German panzers were caught.

Cunningham watched them turn, confused, some heading west, into even more of Cunningham's Crusaders, while others tried to loop around and attempt something like a retreat.

That was most disastrous.

They couldn't fire while turning tail so quickly and they were, for those few moments, as good as dead in the water.

Only when it seemed like Cruewell was restoring some sense of order to the rout did Cunningham finally let some of his tanks stream off the hill, down to the depression.

Then the battlefield became truly nightmarish.

Tanks would face each other and blast away. The Crusaders, with their heavy guns, usually won any blow-to-blow contest. But there was enough disorganized firepower down there to leave dozens of the British machines burning hulks.

Cunningham lowered his glasses. Rumor had it that the plan wasn't Monty's at all. No, it came from Winnie himself. Something borrowed from his American cousins . . . from The Battle of Little Big Horn.

And we're the Indians. Cunningham grinned.

Rommel saw a different kind of cloud on the horizon. Blacker, darker than the overcast sky that sent down the hard rain.

His panzers—fast in good conditions—were struggling to keep moving. When he looked back, he saw tanks spin left and right, as one tread or another clawed at some sludge, trying to get some traction.

As they moved, Rommel spoke into the radiotelephone, giving explicit instructions to his Panzer Division.

They would have to fan out just as soon as they reached the depression. That was clear. Then, they'd need to pick their targets carefully . . . very carefully.

It would be just as easy to blow up a German tank as a British one. It would be just as easy to do some damage rather than help.

And once the heat of the attack was off Cruewell, Rommel could link up with Cruewell's main force and push the British back.

And what, he wondered, if that didn't happen? What then . . . ? The artillery was still way behind. It would be tank against tank. But the numbers were all wrong . . . all wrong. I have a little over three hundred tanks, no more than half of them German. Against what? A force of six hundred, maybe seven hundred British tanks?

If all of them are here. . . .

And how many of those British tanks are new, heavy tanks . . . fast tanks . . . better than what I have?

For the first time since he arrived on the African continent, Rommel felt like everything was slipping beyond his control.

He opened his mouth. Small rivulets of rain streamed in, not really refreshing. He spat, off to the side.

Damn Berlin, he thought.

Damn Berlin . . . and Hitler. . . .

29

There was a hearty babble of voices ahead of her, laughing, echoing through the massive halls of the Chancellery.

Her heels—damned uncomfortable—clicked noisily as she made her way down the dim corridor.

Ali tried hard to avoid looking around, gawking at Der Führer's nerve center, this new Chancellery, a gaudy fortress for the Thousand Year Reich.

She kept walking.

It had been easy to ask one of the other fräuleins where the Transport Office was—though the girl laughed, as if it were a joke. That had been simple.

But walking there now, alone . . .

It was scary.

She just had to concentrate on making her legs keep moving, one after the other, nice and steady. It was cold here, and her arms were coated in gooseflesh. The laughing voices were closer now, just around the next corner. She forced herself to keep moving bravely ahead. She reached the corner.

They were officers, moving in a slow, haphazard fashion, more interested in enjoying whatever was making them laugh.

She kept walking.

Then she saw some black uniforms ahead. More SS, she thought grimly. And then, from the corner of her eye, she saw a well-stuffed man in a powder-blue uniform. She didn't look at him.

"Fräulein," the man in the blue uniform said, accompanied by a distinct but muffled click of the heels.

They have that routine down, she thought.

Ali turned slightly, still moving, and nodded. She saw the fat man's face. It was familiar. A face she had seen in books . . . in old documentaries. . . .

She saw the Reich Eagle insignia on his uniform.

That face . . .

Then she remembered.

Not from the war, though. Later. A photo from Nuremberg. The Nazi War Crimes. Speer, Doenitz. Rosenberg. And, slumped in his chair, Goering.

Before he hanged himself, Ali remembered.

Another Nazi suicide, boys and girls. Like some naughty children, all the head Nazis checked out before the parents of the world had time to punish them. Such a pig face, she thought.

And the irony . . . the weird irony, she thought . . . is that I have to help him. Lindstrom was clear on that. Everything must be as it was, before the KGB maniacs, the Iron Men, started playing God with history. Everything. Even Hermann Goering's private art cache.

She kept on walking.

And she felt the men standing there, watching her. Then they burst into laughter, rude, obnoxious laughter obviously at her expense.

In my world . . . in my time, Ali thought . . . I'd spin around and dump them on their Teutonic asses.

But here, now, all she could do was ignore them and hope that she could keep moving toward the Transport Office.

The voices of Goering and the officers faded, and the halls were quiet again. Walking through here was a foretaste of the bombed-out sepulchre it would become, she thought. A gigantic mausoleum, the death of Germany's humanism. A stone and marble monument to hate and madness.

More steps, and she heard the hungry pecks of many typewriters. And some voices. . . . She saw two soldiers posted outside a pair of massive double doors. She slowed, took a breath, and then kept walking.

What if they stop me? she wondered. Perhaps I'm already in trouble for even being here. But if that happened, then she hoped that being a secretary for Luther would carry some clout.

She arrived at the doors. The guards took no notice of her. She grabbed the gleaming, gold-plated door knob and opened one of the doors. She walked into the room.

The room was a sea of desks. Men and women—civilians—moved busily from one desk to another, a frantic, frenetic activity that belied the deathly calm outside the room. Ali felt her pulse throbbing in her skull. She had begun breathing in short, nervous gasps. God, she thought, I'm going to faint. This lady's nervous system can't handle all the excitement. Wish I had a—

Cigarette?

Incredible. The idea sounded so good, so soothing.

Sorry, honey, she thought. Today's the day you quit.

Ali took some tentative steps into the room. No one took notice of her.

What now? she wondered. Stand here and wait for someone to wait on her? Go look over everyone's shoulders . . . maybe talk to them?

Excuse me, do you know when Field Marshal Goering's trainload of art is leaving Paris? And could you tell me exactly what route it will take?

What if there's no record of the train here? Then things would be even more difficult.

No, not difficult. Impossible.

She spotted a young man with wire glasses and the pinched expression of an emaciated starling. He looked up at her, curious, concerned.

The wall at the rear of the room was filled with a massive map of Europe—Der Führer's playground. Colorful magnetic squares dotted the map, obviously giving some information about train movements. But it was nothing she could understand.

She saw someone looking at her. A Wehrmacht officer. He saw her, and she turned away, casually, as if she might be looking for a friend.

But the officer walked toward her, slowly, deliberately. She took some steps back, edging to the door leading out.

An excuse popped in her head. Thought it was the toilette. So sorry. . . .

But then the officer hurried to her side, swooping down on her, grabbing her elbow, gently. But grabbing it nonetheless.

"You seem lost, fräulein. Is there anything I can help you with?"

She made a sick smile. And then tried to answer the officer's question. . . .

General Alan Cunningham waited.

Not an easy thing to do, he thought. Not for me. Always too bloody impatient to get on with it. Didn't take enough time, his public-school masters told him. Do slow down, Cunningham. And the way he used to run all over the rugby field, as if he was playing the game by himself.

And now he had to wait and watch.

It was impossible to make out what was going on down below. The small rain squalls mixed with the black clouds of smoke that just hung there, suspended. Just one armored brigade and one infantry . . .

While behind him was the rest of his British tank corps.

It was Monty's plan. Even though he was already in Tripoli, ready to fly back to England. By tomorrow afternoon Gott would be here. And that didn't inspire a great deal of confidence.

But Winnie was shaken. They couldn't afford to lose Africa. It might signal the end. There were rumors of a negotiated peace, a diplomatic term for an easy, painless surrender. Hitler keeps Europe and the UK keeps the Atlantic.

For a while, Cunningham guessed. Until Adolph felt strong enough to launch his cross-channel invasion.

Africa was the key. The UK can't afford another "Miracle" like Dunkirk.

So he waited.

Either Rommel would arrive soon . . . or he wouldn't.

And if he does, Cunningham thought, then we'll be ready.

Jim picked up the knife, a long, clunky Wehrmacht blade sheathed in handsome brown leather. He took the blade out.

In. Twist. And up.

Hard.

Jim hefted the knife, imagining what it would feel like to use it.

It was heavy in his hand.

How did I get so lucky? he thought. One day I'm a grad student, and the next I'm an assassin, saving the world from time wars.

With his other hand he touched the cold metal. The blade was razor-sharp. It would cut through cloth, through leather, through skin, with no trouble at all. None at all, he thought.

Except.

Except I can't bring myself to use it.

Perhaps Port can do it, he thought. Yes, Jim thought, sliding the knife back into its sheath. Port can do it. He'll understand.

And Jim thought he heard something then. Something more than the wind whipping the tent, making it swell and breathe like a bellows. A distant crack. Maybe thunder. Maybe gunfire.

But then all he heard was the steady fall of the heavy rain.

"Where are the PAKs?" Rommel shouted into the radiotelephone.

The answer was expected. The Panzerabwehrkanonen were still trailing behind the tanks.

Rommel looked out at the battlefield.

I can't wait any longer, he thought. My hand is forced.

He nodded to himself.

It's all wrong. It's right there in my book, my "classic," as the Führer was fond of saying. It's right there in *Infantry Tactics*.

Never commit your entire force to an engagement unless you know that the enemy has committed its entire force. Otherwise, you will have no reserves, no response.

Good advice.

Yes, very good . . . when you can stay back and let your smaller force test the enemy's strength . . . its resources. But that was impossible now. If I wait, I'll lose Cruewell. And all his army.

"We go," Rommel said grimly.

And then, when he noticed that his driver had taken no notice, he spoke more loudly, hating the rain, and the desert that changed from being an expansive highway for his Afrika Korps to—

A trap.

"We go!"

And immediately the order was passed along, and the tanks began flanking Rommel's command vehicle, captured from the hapless English General O'Connor. Rommel wore O'Connor's goggles also, enjoying the booty, the captured loot from his defeated enemy.

But this time the tanks didn't fall into position so easily. Some fell into muddy ruts and gullies that had their treads slipping. The tank commanders were constantly yelling to their drivers, screaming at them over the thunderous rain, to avoid this stray rock, that hole.

They moved down to the battlefield, a grey smoky vision of hell.

There would be no tactics down there, Rommel knew. Just a horrible, deadly brawl.

He waited, and watched the tanks swooping down

to the depression. Some of them had begun firing, a practice tolerated by Rommel. If a commander felt he could sight and hold an enemy while advancing, there was nothing wrong with firing.

Except that we're already low on ammunition, Rommel thought. Ammunition . . . and fuel . . . and water. . . .

And where were the damned depots? What did Berlin do?

His tanks fired. And he saw some of the sleek new British tanks explode in brilliant flares that dispelled the yellow-grey gloom of the storm. He tapped his driver to follow.

His tank crews—hardened and comfortable in battle—made good use of each shell. Then some of his Panzer IIIs, barreling down to the plain, started catching some fire.

At first, Rommel didn't notice anything odd. Some shells exploded in the sand around the charging tanks. But then there were more shells, and a hit, and Rommel saw one, then another, and another tank explode, popping like metal balloons on their way down the ridge.

The shells weren't coming from the battlefield!

He took his field glasses and scanned the horizon. It was nearly impossible to see anything. The rain was too heavy; the clouds made it like dusk.

But then he saw the dark shapes low on the horizon, across the depression, on another ridge. A long line of armor. Tanks. Trucks.

A classic error, Rommel thought. How clever of Cunningham to have waited.

How clever!

As if he knew we were coming.

Rommel looked at his own tanks, joining what was obviously a diversionary skirmish below. While there, on the crest of the ridge, three, maybe four hundred tanks were ready to pounce.

There was only one thing to do, Rommel knew.

One thing . . . if he had time to do it. . . .

30

"Now, this is *interesting. . . .*"

Lindstrom handed a piece of paper to McManus.

"What is it?" McManus asked. "What does it mean?"

"It means that something is happening back there. You see that—" Lindstrom stood up, away from his console, and pointed to the paper. "Those are some changes that were undone. Corrected, if you will. Monty will get his chance to finish Rommel after all. And look, all the stuff in 1944, the invasion, the Ardennes, it's all starting to shift back."

McManus smiled.

"Then we're out of the woods?"

Lindstrom's face sagged a bit. "Not exactly. You see, we still have a whole pile of things," Lindstrom said, thumping his stack of notes. "The Euro-Asian Compact—God spare us—and that new god-awful Co-Prosperity Sphere run by the Nipponese Marxists. Oh, there are plenty of things awry. But here's the thing, Mac. Whatever our people are doing there, Port and our two amateurs, it seems to be working. Now if only—"

"Dr. McManus!"

It was Beck, calling from the doorway to the other room, where she monitored the unconscious bodies.

"Yes, Eleanor, what is it?"

Dr. Beck's face was all twisted with fear and worry.

"It's one of them, Elliot. I'm getting strange life systems readings. Erratic pulse, shallow breathing."

McManus walked to her, with Lindstrom following.

"What does that mean?" McManus asked.

"It's the preliminary warning signs of coma." She looked at the two of them. "I'm afraid something's happened back there . . . we're going to lose one. . . ."

Lindstrom took a step forward, cleared his throat, and asked, "Which one?"

Rommel directed half of his tanks to turn east and face the British advance.

For a few moments he admired the new British and American tanks.

The tanks rolled off the hill in an endless wave, the hardware of the Allies overwhelming his depleted forces.

This is the way things will be, he thought. Some of his panzers stopped, preferring to dig in and pick their targets from the horde streaming off the ridge. But it was obvious—clear—what had to happen.

Now.

Before the loss was so total . . . so complete . . . as to end the Axis presence on the continent.

I must retreat, he thought.

He picked up the radiotelephone and started giving the division commanders their orders. Cruewell would need heavy fire support to get his surviving men out.

And as Rommel spoke, he saw the main body of the British operation, the Seventh Armored . . . and the Fourth . . . pressing down with everything they had.

How much fuel do I have left? he wondered.

He watched one of his tanks take a hit. A shell blasted the left treads. Then—unlucky break—the fuel tank caught. The panzer exploded in a thunderous clap. Then another tank was hit. The commander was blown right out of the tank, pieces of his body flying through the air. The driver and the gunner tried crawling out of the smoking hulk. But machine-gun bullets from the ridge cut them down as they scurried off the dead tank.

Retreat.

Toward El Agheila.

Then, east.

And if they follow?

What then?

Rommel nodded. They won't follow. Not now. They were too new at this, too inexperienced. They will take their victory, savor it . . . and wait for another day.

He would have a chance to punish the British for this. That he was sure of.

His tanks—haphazardly, like soldiers drunk on beer—started pulling away from the battlefield, many of them taking hits even as they tried to scurry away.

Rommel grabbed the windshield of his armored car—his warlord's price, so hollow now.

But it begins here, Rommel knew. Inevitable. Inexorable. The Allies have begun the game in earnest.

And where will it end?

In Italy . . . France . . . ?

At the Rhine?

Or—mad thought—in Berlin itself?

Rommel tapped his driver.

"Quick," he said. "Get us going." And Rommel sat down on the soaking seat, his uniform stuck to his soaking body.

And the car spun around, turning its back on the great battle.

Ali couldn't back up fast enough. The short man with small wire-frame glasses was at her side, a wide-eyed look of concern on his face.

"A problem, fräulein?"

Ali smiled. He didn't use my name, she thought. Good. That means that he doesn't know me . . . and I won't be expected to know his name.

"I'm sorry—it's just that my friend suggested—"

As she spoke she saw someone go to the large map board and, with a long stick, move a few of the markers from one point on the map to another.

"She said—"

The officer's eyebrows arched. "You are not here on official business?"

Ali shrugged sheepishly. And she thought . . .

I must have been crazy to think I could just walk in here and say, Excuse me, could I see all the scheduled trains out of Paris for the next three days?

"No," she said softly. "It's my friend—a soldier. He's been in Paris. But he's scheduled to come back before this weekend. But with all the secrecy . . . I'm sure you understand."

From the look on the portly officer's face, there was every indication that he didn't understand. Not at all.

He folded his arms in front of him. Licked his lips.

"I haven't seen him since last year," she said. "I thought if I got a look at the transports leaving Paris, I could meet his train at the Friedrichstrasse Bahnhof."

The transport gnome stroked his chin.

After an interminable wait, he nodded and said, "You realize you're asking me to share classified information." He gestured to the outer doors. "There's a reason those guards are there."

Ali took a step backwards.

Just thought I'd give it a shot, Ali thought. She smiled, but the officer seemed impervious to her charm. She backed up another few feet, ready to turn and get out before the man summoned the guards to throw her in whatever dank dungeon lay at the bottom of this glistening Chancellery.

He raised a hand, palm out, signaling her to stop.

"Field Marshal Rommel is back!" a young soldier announced to Jim, opening the flap to his field tent. Jim stood up, knocking the sheets Port gave him to the floor.

How long have I just sat here? he wondered. Sat here. Frozen. Waiting for what . . . ?

"He wants to see you immediately, Oberstleutnant!" the soldier said.

"Yes," Jim answered. And he left the tent. The rain had slackened somewhat, but still the bad weather kept up. With nightfall only an hour away, it was turning cold. Jim followed the soldier, stepping into great muddy puddles.

And as he walked, he watched the return of the Afrika Korps.

It was so different from this morning, the streaming line of panzers and armored vehicles. Now, some were chugging through the wet sand at half speed. A few carried wounded soldiers, riding on top of the tanks. It was a nightmarish vision, the disorganized arrival, the yells of the soldiers asking the overwhelmed medics to hurry here—save this soldier, my friend.

Some of the panzers stopped dead just as soon as they reached the perimeter of the camp, their crews probably exhausted, unable to go any farther.

The young soldier led Jim to Rommel's tent. He pushed the flap back for Jim.

"Oberstleutnant Wagner . . ."

Jim went in.

Rommel turned to him. His face glowed red in the flickering light.

"It was a trap, Fritz. A trap. Berlin cost me—what? Just this battle, or—" Rommel laughed. "Maybe all of Africa. A trap . . ."

Rommel shook his head as if he couldn't believe it.

"I can't fight this way. And since I can't go to Berlin, to explain the importance of supplies to them, the absolutely crucial matter of logistics, someone else will have to go."

Another soldier covered in a grey rain poncho popped his head into the tent.

"Field Marshal, the southeast corner of the lager is completely flooded. Where do you want—"

Rommel waved the soldier away. "Put the panzers anywhere for now. We can't stay here for long . . . not now. . . ." He looked at Jim. "You must explain the situation. You must," Rommel said, slapping a fist into his other hand, "see that I get accurate information. I need water. I need fuel."

Jim nodded. "Er, yes. When do I go?"

"In three hours," Rommel snapped. "I've made the arrangements."

Jim heard the water splattering against the side of the tent. "In this weather?"

"Yes, in this weather," Rommel barked.

And then . . .

(Strange moment . . .)

The field marshal seemed to stop and stare at Jim. He froze, looking at him, as if—

As if Rommel was seeing him for the first time.

Rommel took a step closer. His eyes trailed up and down.

"Field Marshal," Jim said. His voice cracked on the last syllable, giving him just the wrong kind of adolescent whine.

He senses something, Jim thought.

God, he knows. *He knows!*

Rommel tilted his head . . . and smiled.

Toland, the head security guard, came into the lab.

McManus turned to him.

"So what's going on upstairs?"

Toland looked confused, overwhelmed by phenomena that he was unable to understand. The guard's voice was low . . . confidential.

"It's very curious, Dr. McManus. We were firing warning shots at the looters. But there were just too many of them. I mean, it was only a matter of time until they overwhelmed us."

McManus looked over at Lindstrom, to see if he was listening.

Then he said, "Yes, go on."

"Then—all of a sudden—they weren't there. They just—I know this sounds crazy. I know you explained about things happening outside . . . and things inside, but—"

"They're gone?" Lindstrom asked, walking closer to Toland.

The guard nodded.

McManus felt a sudden rush of excitement. It's turning around, he thought. We're stopping them. . . .

"And the fence?" he asked. "The other buildings, the campus and—"

But Toland shook his head.

"No, that's all the way it was before. It's still a ruins outside, Doctor. That's still the same. . . ."

Right, thought McManus. It was best not to hope for too much too quickly. And besides, it could just as easily change back again, like switching channels on a TV set.

He looked at a nearby clock, thinking . . .

That's an ironic instrument in this lab if there ever was one.

31

"Ah . . . an affair of the heart."

The officer reached out and laid his pudgy hand on Ali's shoulder. She tried hard not to tense.

"Such stories move me." He pinched his face into the shape of an earnest persimmon. "Really move me. War can be so destructive to one's emotional life."

He used his draped arm to pull Ali closer.

And Ali thought . . . I've been manhandled more in the past twenty-four hours than during the rest of my entire adult life.

He started walking her toward the back of the room. The workers at their desks rather pointedly took no notice of Ali's tête-à-tête with their boss.

He led her to a large table in the back and gestured at a large black book.

"Here is a list of all the trains from Paris, fräulein . . . for this week, at least. You may see if your friend is there."

His fingers gave her collarbone a little squeeze, and then he backed away.

Ali walked over to the table and pulled the book close.

The man kept watching her, a bemused smile on his face, as Ali flipped it open. She started looking at the first pages.

"Oh," the officer said, "don't bother with those first few pages. They're just transports, no soldiers I'm afraid, and—"

Ali nodded. But as she flipped through the pages she saw something. A transport, leaving Paris on Friday . . . the very next day. Paris, to Nice, and then on to the Alps, to someplace called Toplitz See.

Fifteen cars long.

One car—

(She could just glance, as she turned the page. . . .)

—occupied by a brigade of Waffen SS, commanded by Gruppenführer Alfredo Arussie.

She turned another page. There was no indication of what was in the train. Nothing.

Then, the last page.

Special Shipment. RM, H.G.

That was it.

Reich Marshal Hermann Goering.

She looked up and smiled at the transportation officer.

And Ali—trying to control her breathing—kept flipping through the pages of the book, pretending that she was checking for something, running a finger through the list of names.

"No," she said. "I don't see it . . . not here . . ."

"Keep looking." The man grinned. "It may be near the back."

Ali nodded.

And she went on turning the pages. Repeating in her mind the information about the transport. The time it was leaving. Its route.

And—most important—its destination.

"What has happened to you, Fritz? What did Dr. Bock say?" Rommel was nose to nose with Jim. "There is something wrong with you? . . ."

Jim cleared his throat. And backed up a step.

"I'm not sure, Field Marshal. . . . Perhaps it's the weather—or something."

Rommel shook his head. "I don't think that's it, mein Fritz. I think—"

Rommel pursed his lips as if he just had an odd thought. "Something else. Anyway, you'd best be gone,'' he said at last, waving his hand. ''Three hours and you fly to Berlin.'' Rommel stepped close and poked Jim's chest. ''And I expect you to keep me informed. Make Goering's fabled Luftwaffe find the damned British supplies.'' The Desert Fox made a fist. ''Get me the fuel, Fritz, and I can win this campaign.''

Jim nodded.

Then, almost without a thought, he clicked his heels. ''Field Marshall . . .''

(You'll take the poison, Jim wished he could tell him. Because Count von Stauffenberg's assassination plot will fail and Hitler will have all of the plotters killed, hanged. He will have their gruesome deaths filmed for his own amusement. All of them. Except for you—because of your great battles in Africa.)

Rommel turned away, dismissing him. And Jim walked out.

The cloud-filled sky darkened early. A busy, chaotic gloom filled the camp.

Jim hurried to the eastern edge of the lager, to the depression where Port would be waiting. He ran past the battered, smoking tanks, their scars still fresh, the metal newly twisted by the craters of shells. He saw soldiers collapsed into sandy pools, smoking cigarettes or eating a tin of food, eighteen-year-old-boys who looked like old men, ancient zombies.

And this war was only beginning for them.

He kept moving. He was late. Port was waiting.

And I have to tell him, Jim thought. Tell him I couldn't do it. And what the hell am I going to do in Berlin? And am I ever going to get out of 1941?

(And he had an answer to that one. Sure. Yeah. Hah, hah. You'll get out of 1941, Jimbo. Just wait until midnight, December 31. . . .)

The farther away he got from the center of the camp the faster he ran, full-out now, breathless. Port was his only link to reality. Port was some verification that he hadn't simply gone mad, that he wasn't really Rommel's aide suffering a bizarre delusion.

He came to the depression, another of those endless scooped-out hollows of sand and stone. He nearly tumbled over the crest, jumping over small rocks, slipping in the sand, sliding down to where Port would be waiting.

It was black and cold. The rain was tapering off, but still—incredibly—it was coming down. And he thought of his flight to come.

He looked ahead, looking for someone standing in the darkness, waving at him. But he didn't see anyone. There was no one.

"Where the—" Jim said in English.

(It sounded strange, with a trace of an accent.)

Maybe I should call out for him, Jim thought. Maybe I got the place wrong. It sure as hell would be easy to do out here. It all looks pretty much the same, and the landmarks he picked . . . a supply tent, some barrels, a few tanks . . . I might have the whole thing wrong, all—

He saw someone.

It wasn't Port, though. It was someone shorter.

It was the boy. Tomas.

And he was standing by himself.

"Where is your father?" Jim asked the boy, first in German . . . then in English.

The boy was shivering. Jim pulled off his poncho and placed it over the boy's head. It dwarfed him, and he now blended into the grey-black night.

The boy reached out and took Jim's hand and tugged on it.

He wants me to follow him.

Okay, Jim thought. Maybe it isn't safe here. Maybe Port wants to meet somewhere else.

But that didn't make sense. He wouldn't risk the boy's life . . . if it wasn't safe there.

Tomas pulled him along, much more surefooted than Jim. He led him out into the desert, away from the lights of the lager, the sounds of trucks getting into position and soldiers talking. The boy led him into the darkness.

Once Jim stepped on a rope.

He thought it was rope. But it was suddenly alive, a black coiling snake trying to escape the flood. It turned on him, but he was already leaping into another abyss, pulled by the constant tug of the boy.

Until he stopped.

They were at a rocky overhang, a pile of three large boulders that seemed out of place on the desert floor. But they made a small cavelike opening, the smallest shelter from the storm.

The boy gave Jim's hand one final tug. Guiding him to the opening.

And Jim saw someone lying there—just inside.

It was Port.

And Jim saw his eyes, a faint glow. His mouth opened. But Port coughed.

And Jim saw something else catching the light, farther down, near Port's midsection, trailing down, off his body, onto the rocks.

It was blood, a lot of it.

Jim stared at it.

Until Tomas pushed him into the makeshift cave.

Port said something. It was a faint whisper, unintelligible, lost in the wind that buffeted the rocky cavern. Jim crouched down to him.

Seeing the blood, streaming from his wound, dripping down onto the rock.

"What happened?" Jim asked.

Port tilted his head, trying to point somewhere to the west. "A German saw me. . . ." Port coughed. "They're always taking potshots at the bedouins." He looked up at Jim, his eyes half-closed. There was another red smear at the corner of his lip. "I was hurrying . . . I thought I'd miss you." Port grinned, and then coughed some more. He tried to turn to the side and spit something out.

The wound, all the blood, scared Jim. "I . . . I've got to get you help."

And he thought . . . Who dies? Port . . . or his host? Is this like a pretend death, like when I played war when I was a kid? Or was this for real?

But Port's eyes told the story.

"I'll get you some help. . . ." Jim repeated.

"No," Port said. Then the boy came close with a skin-covered canteen. He held it up to the lips of the man he thought was his father.

"Poor kid," Port said, opening his cracked lips as the boy gently and slowly tipped the canteen, and the water wet Port's lips.

Jim stood up. "I'll get some medicine . . . some bandages. . . ."

Port shook his head, making the water dribble to the side. "No," he croaked again. He tried to smile, a weird, ghastly sight in the gloom of the small cave. "I'm afraid it's too late for that. . . ."

And Port moved his hand, exposing the full extent of his wound. Jim saw the open gash, surrounded by brilliant red pockmarks, like burst blisters glistening red. But there were also stringy pieces of white sticking out.

The gunshots had just about gutted Port. He was dying.

Jim stood there.

Port raised a hand, searching for Jim, the fingers making small wavelike motions, urging him back down.

Tomas sat back, close to his father, protective.

Jim knelt down and leaned close to Port.

"You killed the doctor . . . you killed Bock?"

Jim licked his lips. "No. I mean, I tried—"

Port's sleepy eyes opened wide. Jim knew that—if he could—Port would grab Jim in anger. Instead, he spoke, working hard to say each word. . . .

"You have to . . . damn, why didn't you, why—" Port coughed some more.

"I tried," Jim said. He felt the boy watching him,

not understanding what they were saying, but hovering close to his father.

"I tried. I walked in. I had a knife. But—"

Port's fingers snaked their way to Jim's right hand. And they closed around him, holding tight. Strong, rough fingers, covered with a lattice of calluses and cuts.

"Listen . . . " Port croaked. Jim came close to Port's dry lips. "If you don't do it . . . if you don't kill him, it will all be on your head. . . ." Port paused, and looked right into Jim's eyes. "Don't be an . . . asshole. . . ."

Jim pulled away.

"The whole"—Port stopped to cough—"fucking mess could by your damn fault." Port's hand squeezed Jim's, pinching it. "Kill him, for Christ's sake."

Jim saw the boy looking at him. Tomas's dark eyes glowed, tiny points of light in his dark face.

"Say you'll do it. Say it!"

Jim nodded. "I'm leaving for Berlin. I have to go in two hours. God, I—"

"Say it!"

"I'll do it."

Port seemed to relax, his body slumping against the stone. "Good. There's something else. They're sending Gott over . . . to take Monty's place. . . ." Port shook his head left and right. "Gott is supposed to die . . . in a plane crash. . . . But if he comes now . . ."

Port moaned, a terrible sound, deep, from within his chest. The sound of intense pain. It was so loud Jim thought it might carry on the wind and they'd hear it in the camp. So loud and terrible it made Jim want to throw up. Port moved his hand.

His wounds—his red craters—were freshly bleeding.

"He can't come here. It would screw everything up."

Right, Jim thought. And what am I supposed to do about it? Send him back?

Port said something to Tomas in his hurried Algerian patois. The boy dug through a small satchel strapped around his neck. He pulled out a piece of paper and stuck it out, handing it to Jim.

Jim freed his hand from Port's grip and took the piece of paper.

"Wh—what is this?"

Port moaned again. "It's Gott's flight plan. It's all there. He's leaving from a small airstrip in Dartmoor, then over the Bay of Biscay, down to Gibraltar, all the way to Tobruk."

Jim looked at the paper and then at Port. "What do you want me to do about this?"

"His plane must be shot down—"

Jim laughed. "Oh, come on. It's one thing to kill some Nazi doctor, but—"

Port's lips curled in disgust. "Everything has to be put right . . . the way it's supposed to be." Port tried to raise himself up, agitated. "Don't you see? That's why I'm here . . . you're here. And Gott is never supposed to be here. He can't be here. Auchinleck has to take over. Auchinleck has to replace Cunningham, bring in General Ritchie. . . ."

More coughing.

Tomas hurried to bring the canteen up to Port's lips.

"Just give the information to Goering's office in Berlin. Let the Luftwaffe handle it." Port turned away, looking to the side. "He'll die in a plane crash. The way he was supposed to."

"And after that?"

Port shook his head, very slightly. "I don't know. Maybe the Time Lab will be able to get you back. Maybe not. Maybe they'll send someone else, someone to—"

Port seemed stuck on the last word, looking at the stone wall, as if thinking hard. Jim leaned close.

"Port?" he said, tapping the man's shoulder.

But Port's eyes kept staring, unblinking.

"Port . . ." Jim said quietly.

And then Jim felt it. The boy's eyes were locked on him. He's looking at me. Jim turned slowly and met the boy's stare. Tomas's shiny dark face was tight, impassive.

Waiting for me. To tell him that everything's okay.

Jim shook his head. Then, he said a word . . . in English. "No." Then, in German . . . *"Nein."*

He shook his head and reached over to Port's open eyes. And—grisly moment—he closed the two eyelids, so rubbery under his fingertips.

Now the boy moved, putting his head tight against his father's chest. "Papa?" he said, whispering. Then louder.

He tapped his father's body.

"No," Jim said. "Tomas, no. He's dead. He's—"

"Papa!" the boy yelled. "Papa!" The boy grabbed his father's rough hand and squeezed it, saying the same word over and over, his drum-tight face melting, tears pouring down his cheeks.

Jim hesitated a moment, and then reached out and pulled the boy close. Tomas resisted at first, wanting to hold the dead hand. But then he let go, crawling close to Jim, crying on his shoulder, heaving.

And Jim thought . . .

Such terrible spasms from such a small body.

Jim knew he didn't have a lot of time. Not a lot at all. But he knelt there with the boy, until—at last—Tomas's body was still and quiet.

32

It was his second dinner of the night.

Yes, sitting down earlier in the evening with Halder and von Brauchitsch to discuss the air war in the East did nothing to improve his appetite. Besides, Reich Marshal Goering preferred eating alone.

Good food, well prepared, deserved one's full attention. It was a great pleasure, a supreme pleasure, to eat and savor each forkful of an excellent meal. A fine wine. Perhaps two—to complement each other, of course. To keep the palate alive, awake!

The dining table was no place for war.

He wiped his lips and then pushed away the plate of pickled pig's knuckles, a specialty of the Chef de Maison, the Chancellery's own culinary wizard. It was no secret that the best meals to be had were right here, right in Der Führer's Chancellery. There were many private dining rooms.

This one, with its two walls covered with tall mirrors, was the most beautiful. Goering had ordered that it be lit with candlelight only.

Within a moment, a waiter appeared and removed the empty plate.

Goering shifted in his seat. There was to be no wait between courses—another order from the Reich Marshal.

As soon as one waiter left the room with an empty plate, another appeared with the next course, a creamy mushroom soup flavored with brandy.

It was hard for Goering to avoid smacking his thin lips when the waiter put the bowl in front of him and removed the silver corner.

"Ahh," he said, sniffing the steam. "*Wunderbar.*"

The Luftwaffe commander wasted no time scooping up the soup, slurping it down. It was delicious, ambrosia . . . absolutely wonderful.

The air war in Russia . . .

Such an obnoxious question from that obnoxious General Halder, Chief of the General Staff. Besides, thought Goering, I had told Der Führer that the Luftwaffe stood ready to supply the great German army anywhere in the East. Anywhere!

I have the planes, and it can be done.

He kept shoveling in the soup, not too hot, but just warm enough to make the exquisite flavor even more wonderful.

Moscow will fall in days anyway, Goering had told them.

But then Halder had looked at von Brauchitsch, Army Commander in Chief, exchanging uneasy glances with him. They had come from the East and were due to go back at dawn.

I must warn the Führer about them. Goering thought. Like most of the General Staff, they are weak, timid—ineffectual.

Perhaps, even traitorous.

The soup was gone. And a waiter brought the entree, a steaming rack of lamb, enough for two or three people, surrounded by clever rosettes of potato and pureed carrots, sprigs of parsley, and dollops of a candied apple butter.

Nice and pink. The way lamb should be.

He couldn't wait, and he picked up one chop and bit the whole succulent meat down, picking the thin bone perfectly clean.

Delicious.

Then Goering scooped up his utensils and attacked the lamb chops in a more methodical manner, pausing only to take great swigs of a spicy Gewurtztraminer, his favorite. The sweet wine went wonderfully with the meat.

No, the East didn't concern him. Even Himmler—the pinched-nose ascetic, the busybody schoolmaster—*even Himmler* said it was only a matter of days until Russia fell.

There was only one matter that concerned him, Goering thought. And it had nothing to do with the Luftwaffe, or the East. Nothing at all to do with the Great German Victory.

It was his train.

Everything was completely arranged.

The Führer Order had established the Alpen Base near Lake Toplitz, an underground warren that housed an abandoned mine. Goering had convinced Hitler that a scattering of these hidden bases was necessary, vital.

Just in case, Mein Führer.

(And Goering had seen an odd glow in Hitler's eyes, as if he could see farther than the rest of us . . . much farther. To the possibility of actually needing an alpine redoubt, some mountain fortress to defend—)

But no. It was just good planning, nothing more. And the Führer Order gave Goering everything he needed to order the hidden command posts to be built.

Except that Goering had another purpose completely.

He abandoned the cutlery and picked up another chop with his hands.

Too much art from the Louvre, from the Rijksmuseum in Amsterdam, had filled Goering's own play palace, Karinhall.

He was out of room . . . without stuffing masterpieces in every closet, in the basement.

It was the Waffen SS Gruppenführer Alfredo Arussie who came up with the other idea. Hide the treasures away. For later, he insinuated.

Should anything happen . . . to Hitler . . . to Germany . . . why, then Goering would have the means to finance a new regime. A new Reich, Arussie had suggested.

But then came the odd thing. . . .

Goering picked up his last chop, sad to see the great platter empty.

The list of painters Arussie gave him contained over five hundred paintings, by artists unknown to the Reich Marshal. Artists like Chagall, Kandinsky, Klee, Ernst . . . some of them Jews.

Why all this Jewish art, Goering demanded, this decadent art? Why not more masterpieces?

And Arussie, with a brazen confidence, put an arm around him. Trust me, he had said. These will be worth more than you could possibly dream, a treasure beyond value. They will make a treasure chest to support your bid for power, Reich Marshal.

A waiter hurried over and removed the platter.

Goering licked his lips.

Should he order more food . . . perhaps more lamb? He thought a moment. No. Enough. There was still dessert, perhaps a gigantic Lidzertorte, or a dark Black Forest Cake layered with cream and cherries. That would be enough. That, and the rest of the wine.

And so the train leaves tomorrow, guarded by Arussie himself, with a brigade of crack Waffen SS.

I trust him, Goering thought. But why? Why do I believe what he says?

Goering shook his head.

It was instinct. Something about the Oberführer, the look in his eyes, his voice.

Something.

The door to the private kitchen opened, and the waiter glided over. Even from across the room, Goering could see the pile of cakes, so tall, like a mountain with a snowy powder of sugar.

And he stopped fretting about his train. . . .

Jim left the radio operators, neither of them acting at all confused by his message to Berlin.

If it works, he thought, I'll be responsible for a British general being shot down.

(And how does that make me feel? What other

creepy stuff will I have to do? I'll go insane if they yank me back to the Time Lab. But I might just as easily go crazy if I stay here.)

He walked out and then Tomas darted out from the shadows of a PZIV. He took Jim's hand.

I've got to get the kid to leave. Back to his own people. Even if he has no one.

He walked the boy away from the center of the camp, hurrying. It would be hard to explain if anyone saw him walking with the boy.

Jim stopped walking and crouched down. He grabbed the boy's shoulders.

"Allez!" Jim said, looking at the boy's face. Jim knew about a dozen French words, and he hoped somehow his meaning would get through. *"Allez . . ."* Jim waved to the west, to the empty desert.

How tough was this kid? he wondered. Tough enough to get himself home? Tough enough to stay alive?

He pushed the boy away.

"Dangereux . . ." Jim said. *"Allez . . . maintenant . . ."*

And then—hard moment—he pushed the boy away.

And Jim stood up.

They were in the dark. No one could see them. The camp light was well away. But there was enough reflected light for him to see the boy's face.

Don't cry, Jim begged.

"Allez!" he said loudly, ordering the boy away.

Don't cry.

Because if you do, I won't be able to scare you away. It won't be possible.

But the boy moved his mouth. His small face went tight and hard. He pursed his lips.

And then he spat at Jim's feet.

And before Jim could say anything, Tomas turned and ran away, vanishing into the maze of sleeping panzers.

Good for you, Jim thought.

You're tough. You'll live.
Good for you.

Ollie Johnson couldn't sleep. It was his leg, hurting him more every hour as the wound dried and stitched itself.

The Kraut doctors gave him something for the pain, but they only came every few hours and ignored him the rest of the time.

Like now.

And then there was the bloody noise, the moans of the new boys in the tent. Cots were lined up cheek to jowl, with no attention paid to whether the Germans were on one side or the Tommies on the other. They were all mixed up.

The guy next to him—a Kraut—was sleeping. Knocked out. He had a white, red-stained bandage where his forearm should be.

What kind of sound is he going to make when he comes to? Yeah, too right . . . what will he say when he comes to and sees a chunk of his arm gone?

It must be late, he thought. Everything that could be done for the day's wounded had been done. Most of them were Germans . . . a bad day for the Jerries.

And what did that mean? Ollie wondered. Yesterday Rommel had danced circles around us. But today? . . .

It looked as if something different had happened today.

Ollie heard a sound from the other end of the field hospital. Someone came in and started walking past the cots, past where Ollie lay in the darkness.

A German officer.

Heading toward the back, heading to where the doctor was. . . .

33

"Ready, General?"

Brigadier General W.H.E. Gott stared out the filmy window, watching the slowly shriveling trails of rain run down the glass. He saw the small Dartmoor airstrip and there, lurking in the dark, black and ominous, the plane.

It looked too big, he thought. Oversized, as if it made a mistake by landing here.

He turned to the R.A.F. lieutenant who addressed him.

"Yes . . . the weather is clearing?"

"Yes, sir. Gibraltar reports only some clouds. And the skies over the Mediterranean appear good."

Gott nodded. He was a land soldier, always had been. Though he didn't admit it to anyone, flying wasn't something he did too easily.

"Let's be off, then," he said.

And, truth be told, he didn't much appreciate coming onto the North African scene in this way. It wasn't quite cricket. Auchinleck was unaccountably ill, and Monty—always a bit of a hot pistol—summoned home to explain the almost immediate setback to Operation Crusader.

It was . . . peculiar.

Even as Monty was leaving, the first cautious reports came in about a victory, maybe a major victory, this very day.

And if that was true, why am I going there?

But Gott knew the answer to that.

He followed the lieutenant out to the airstrip. A cool, damp breeze blew the misty air into his face. It sent his jacket flapping back.

The general saw the crew in the cockpit and the nose gunner, his face illuminated by the gentle glow of some small lights.

At least it's not raining, Gott thought . . . not hard, anyway. And good thing my stomach is empty.

The lieutenant walked fast, hurrying to the big, twin-engine plane. The lieutenant turned and helped Gott up to the entrance door in the underbelly of the plane. Gott reached up and grabbed the lip of the door.

"Wood?" he said, surprised by the feel.

"It's a Mosquito, General," the lieutenant said.

Gott nodded. He had heard about these new planes, with their spruce and balsa and plywood. They were fast and maneuverable, doubling as effective bombers and fighters. Painted black, they were even being used for photo reconnaissance.

Still, he would have preferred a metal plane.

Gott pulled himself up into the cabin. It was warm, with the mixed smell of oil and wires and sweat.

The crew—a pilot, a copilot/navigator, and a gunner—turned in unison and saluted.

"All right, gentlemen," Gott said. "Now where do I plant myself to stay out of your way?"

The engines started, two powerful Rolls Royce motors whose roar drowned out the pilot's answer.

The lieutenant peeked his head up through the entrance hole. "Have a good flight, General." Then he slammed the small door shut.

"Right back there . . ." the pilot yelled. "There's a small seat."

Gott turned, seeing nothing at first, and then noticing a paddle-sized chair next to what looked like a radio. This was no transport plane. Every inch of space was being used.

Gott squeezed past a protrusion from the bulkhead—more wood—and slid his too ample bottom onto the paddle.

"Sorry, it's not more comfortable, sir," the pilot yelled.

"It's fine, Captain. Don't worry about a thing. I'm—"

The plane started moving. A small jump, and then it was rolling, turning onto the small Dartmoor airstrip. There were no lights, so the pilots were flying by dead reckoning.

What a comforting thought. . . .

From his vantage point, all Gott could see was the sky, still a murky black, still with no stars. He tried to settle back. The plane stopped.

Gott took a breath as the engine's low rumble turned into a high-pitched whine. The two large propellers created their own rhythmic sound, a steady vibrato. Gott's stomach tightened.

Then the pilot let go of the brake, and the plane was moving. Gott felt every crack, every split on the tarmac. He saw the crew's heads outlined by their instrument lights.

He took another breath. And then, because no one could see him, he closed his eyes.

The Mosquito seemed to jump into the air, suddenly, without warning, and the pilot banked left, out to the Atlantic and south toward Africa.

Jim looked in one of the curtained alcoves, quickly pushing aside the draped material to see if the doctor was there.

He felt cold, frozen. Almost rigid with fear.

What the hell am I doing? he wondered.

But then he saw Port's borrowed face, the eyes determined, even as he was dying. This was serious business. No mistake about it. And like it or not, Jim thought, the ball is in my court.

He looked at the empty room, some medical instruments on a table, a roll of white bandages, lit by a single naked bulb overhead.

He stepped out and moved along to the next curtained area. He heard something. The soft clink of metal touching metal. A foot shuffling on the wooden slats of the makeshift floor.

Jim took a breath. Someone was in there. Probably the doctor . . . probably Bock.

Jim reached behind to feel for his knife. A gun would have been better. But then I'd be dead, Jim knew. This way I at least stand a chance of getting away . . . of staying alive.

Maybe they'll yank me back.

I've learned my lesson. No more time traveling for me! No, sir. No—

He grabbed the curtain, gathering the sere material in his fist, ready to yank it open.

On three, he told himself. One. Two.

Three.

He pulled. And there was Bock, standing at a tray of instruments, cleaning them. The doctor didn't turn around.

Jim felt for the knife behind him.

Then Bock spoke. "I've been waiting for you."

Jim started to slide the knife out. And something weird occurred to him. The doctor had just spoken English.

English.

"Took a while to build up the nerve," the doctor went on, turning now.

Jim hurried to get the knife out. Should have had it ready, he thought. But then—stupid thought—how would I have explained it if someone stumbled upon me, skulking around with a—

The doctor turned around.

"But I knew you'd come—"

And just as Jim had the knife out—

(Straight in, twist, and then bring it up—hard! That's what Port said. That's what Jim kept telling himself.)

Bock was there, with a luger pointed right at him.

"—so I made sure I was prepared."

The gun was leveled at an area Jim believed to contain his heart. Anatomy wasn't his forte.

"You knew . . ." Jim said.

"Of course I knew. It's something you can see in your eyes. A bit of understanding . . . of things to come. It was obvious something was wrong with you. Too bad you got cold feet when you first came to me. Too bad."

Jim heard the slightest mechanical sound. The gentle pull of Bock's finger on the trigger.

I could run, Jim thought.

Sure.

About two inches, before the gun cut him down.

Out of blind panic, Jim asked Bock a question. "Why are you doing this?"

Bock laughed. "You don't know? I would have thought they would have briefed you before you left."

Jim shook his head, relying on his interest to gain an extra few minutes of life.

"No. I just used their stupid machine. Then they sent me here—"

"To kill me," Bock announced.

Jim nodded. "But I don't know who you are . . . why you're doing this . . . changing history. . . ."

"Curious?"

Jim licked his lips. Nodded. Anything to keep the pressure off that finger.

"Too bad you'll have to die with that intriguing question unanswered. . . ."

Now, Jim thought. He's going to do it now.

And he thought he heard Bock's finger tense against the trigger. . . .

The Mosquito was up. Well, Gott thought, that was a good thing. At least in the air there wasn't all that horrible bouncing and rumbling along the airstrip. Still, the noise from the engines was maddening.

I shouldn't even be here, Gott thought. Of course, you don't say "no" to Winston Churchill. Even if he has lost faith in Monty. It was to be Gott to the rescue, to get Cunningham in line.

You can do it, Gott, Winnie said, blowing cigar smoke into his face, clapping him on the back. Give us the great victory in Africa that we need.

And Gott didn't have the heart to tell him. My ideas are old. They're tired, stale. My ideas have had their day. Let the new boys take over, the ones out of the military schools, young, fired up.

The ones who don't mind flying.

But Churchill wasn't to be denied.

But if yesterday's battle was a great turnaround . . . if Cunningham's success was as great as it appeared it might be, why, Bernard Law Montgomery might be back in a few days.

I'll just sit tight, Gott thought. Hold the positions. Keep any ground won.

Gott wiggled in his tiny paddle seat. It was damned uncomfortable.

"We're over water," the pilot said, as if that were cheering news. God, water. Wouldn't that be bloody wonderful? To tumble into the icy November sea and bob around, hoping some Portuguese fishermen might stumble upon us.

At least the plane is made of wood. Maybe it would float. Wouldn't that be handy, wouldn't that be nice?

"Coffee, General?"

The copilot extended a thermos and small metal cup to Gott.

"Yes, thank you," the general said, taking the proffered items. He wedged the cup between his knees and then proceeded to unscrew the thermos top. A small vapor cloud escaped, and he poured half a cap . . . just a mouthful. Just enough to put some taste back on his dry lips.

The plane bumped.

"Wait a second . . ." the pilot said.

Gott looked up, startled by the sound of the pilot's voice. The plane banked to the left, and then the right, jerking around as if it were avoiding potholes. The coffee in his cup sloshed back and forth until finally a small spray shot over the lip, burning his thigh.

"Ow, damn it," he said. "What's—" he began to ask.

But he saw both pilots pointing to the left, seeing something in the sky.

"Can we outrun them?" the copilot said.

Gott saw the pilot shake his head.

"They're coming straight at us . . . as if they knew—"

Gott leaned forward, as far as he could with the strap holding him tightly to his seat. "What is it?" he asked.

The pilot turned around. "Sorry, sir. Luftwaffe . . . Stukas, I'd guess. Kind of slow . . . kind of clumsy . . . but they have the advantage. . . ."

The pilot turned away.

And Gott sat back. Helpless. Unable to command any troops to leap to their rescue, or beat a hasty retreat to some higher ground.

This was a new war. No retreat. No higher ground.

And a general could just be another soldier.

34

Ollie Johnson heard the English voices.

They were coming from the back, behind the curtains.

English voices!

He struggled to the side of his cot. He put some pressure on his wounded leg, all wrapped in bandages. There was an instantaneous sharp pain. It sent a brilliant flash of light into his brain. But then it subsided to a rhythmic, throbbing intensity.

He stood up with a groan and quickly looked around to see if any of the dozens of other wounded patients, Germans, British, Italians, Australians—brothers in blood—were watching him.

But no one stirred.

He took a hobbling step. Another.

The voices were still talking.

Don't go away, he thought. Just don't go. I want to talk with you. Maybe get the bloody hell out of here. Make plans.

Like they taught us in the UK. Disrupt the enemy, they preached. Try to escape. Make things difficult for the bastards.

More steps, and the voices were louder, clearer.

And Ollie stopped. They sounded like they were arguing about something. One voice sounded angry . . . one of them was scared.

Ollie stood there . . . listening.

* * *

"They'll wonder why you killed me," Jim said quickly.

Anything to buy a few seconds of time. Just a few more moments of life.

"Not with a knife in your hand. Perhaps you wanted drugs. Perhaps you were suffering from battle fatigue. It happens. . . ." Bock smiled. "What is your real name, for my own curiosity?"

"Jim Tiber."

Bock nodded.

Now it was all over. Jim thought of rushing him. Maybe startling the creep before he blew a donut-sized hole in him.

Then there was someone else there.

Jim turned and saw one of the patients . . . one of the Tommies. He hobbled into the makeshift operating room.

"Get back to your bed," Bock snapped.

(And Jim saw the gun waver, move away from his vital regions.)

But the soldier took another clumsy step into the room. And he shook his head.

"Pretty good English, Doc."

"Get the hell back to your bed!"

The gun moved another few centimeters off target. Jim felt the knife heavy and purposeful in his hand.

"So you can kill this bloke, Doc? Seems to me," the tank soldier said, hobbling closer, gesturing at Jim, "seems to me like this Kraut may be working for the good guys, eh what? And if that's true—"

"Get back now!" Bock hissed.

And Bock had his luger aimed at the soldier who kept coming closer, lumbering, like the Mummy intent on revenge. He was distracting Bock.

Now, Jim knew. I have to do it now. Before he blows both of us away.

Now. But nothing happened. He didn't move, didn't budge. Oh, Christ, he thought. C'mon. Don't let me freeze up.

And then—as if he were someone else, as if he were

watching a movie, "The Adventures of Jim Tiber"—he moved.

The blade was in front of him.

Bock turned, bringing the gun back, to point at Jim. Too quickly, too damn quickly.

But the soldier had something in his hand . . . that's why he was shuffling closer and closer. He held a scalpel, small, shiny, catching the light of the ugly bulb overhead.

The soldier moved with a more sure hand. He quickly jabbed the scalpel into the back of the doctor's hand. Bock recoiled, involuntarily snapping back.

And that's when Jim drove his knife home.

He was off target, missing the man's midsection completely, cutting to the side. The blade hit bone—horrible feeling—and then slipped into the gap between the ribs.

Jim stupidly tried pulling the blade up, but it was impossible.

But the soldier grabbed Bock's wrist and held the gun hand tight. The grizzled soldier turned and said, through clenched teeth—

"Finish the bastard off . . . finish him!"

And Jim nodded. He dumbly obeyed, pulling out the knife and then sticking it in again. Bock moaned.

(He remembered the pitiful sound of a frog pithed in his high school biology class. Jim had missed the frog's spinal cord with his needle and the frog moaned out its protest when Jim awkwardly started his live dissection.)

Except that this was no frog.

He twisted the blade. Another terrible moan from Bock, muffled this time by the hand of the soldier.

And Jim brought the blade up. He saw Bock's eyes go wide with terrible horror and then—like windows with shutters—they closed.

Bock slumped to the floor.

Jim stood there, looking at the body.

"Drop the knife. . . ."

Jim stood there, still staring. "Drop the knife," the soldier said.

Jim turned to him. "Why did you do that . . . why did you help . . ." Jim gestured to his uniform. "I'm a German—"

The soldier grinned. "The hell you are. I heard that stuff you were saying. You're some kind of spy, or something. And I figure that we need you just where you are."

Jim looked back at the doctor's body. A pool of blood was spreading onto the floor, staining the planks.

"But what about—"

"And when they find him, I'll make up some story . . . something about a nasty bedouin. I'll tell them I heard the struggling . . . and I saw some native type rush out."

Jim nodded.

Only later would he realize who'd get blamed for Bock's death.

"Best get the 'ell out of 'ere, mate. Can't tell when some real Krauts will come along." He smiled at Jim, the first friendly thing Jim had seen in a while.

And then Jim reached out and squeezed the Tommy's shoulder.

"You know, I wish I could explain what this was all about. You deserve to know—"

"That's okay—just doing my bit. . . ."

"But just believe me," Jim grinned. "Your great-grandchildren will be mighty appreciative. . . ."

And then—knowing that a plane was waiting for him—Jim walked out, hurrying to the camp's airstrip.

Gott looked around for something to grab, anything to give some illusion that everything was okay.

His hand felt along the smooth wall of the Mosquito, searching for a strap, a handle. Then the plane banked sharply and suddenly to the left, and Gott's hand flapped at the air.

The pilots were talking to each other. Staccato

bursts, incomprehensible to him. They seemed in control, in charge, everything's okay.

The first bullets hit the plane.

They ripped into the cramped cabin somewhere to the back, whistling and pinging. The Stukas' engines roared overhead, so close that Gott thought that they'd crash into his plane.

The Mosquito leveled out. And there were more bullets, this time coming from his plane, coming from somewhere up front, near the snub nose of the Mosquito.

It was a long, angry burst, surely powerful enough to blow a dozen planes out of the sky.

"Are they—" Gott started to ask.

Then he was surrounded by the sound of rapid machine-gun fire, engulfed by it. He heard shells slice through one part of the hull and crash into the other side.

It kept up, a constant din.

They're on our tail, Gott figured.

The Mosquito dived, and Gott was held into his small paddle seat only by the strap, clutching him around his stomach like an overwhelmed mother holding a porky infant.

He wanted to scream.

I'm so helpless, he thought. Absolutely helpless.

Some glass shattered in the cockpit. And Gott, still facing down, looked up. The copilot was slumped over his seat, sitting like a drunk. There were new lights on the console. Red lights. And still he heard the sound of the shells smashing into the Mosquito, chewing the plane up.

He waited for the plane to pull out of its dive. The nose was still pointing down.

More shells.

And Gott felt something sticking into his back. He felt behind him, expecting to feel a buckle or a piece of stray metal poking him. He reached back, and he felt that it was wet.

In the darkness, he brought his hand in front of him. Looked at it. Knew what it was.

The firing stopped.

But now the captain was slumped over too. From behind him, Gott smelled something burning, the stench of rubber and airplane fuel.

The plane wasn't pulling out.

How could it? Gott thought . . . in those last few seconds.

After all, the pilot is dead.

Gott reached out, as if there were some switch he could throw to stop this ride, to get off.

Just as a brilliant ball of flame exploded in front of him.

"Port's gone," McManus said to Lindstrom.

"Too bad. He was brave, very brave. When this is over—"

"Yes," McManus interrupted. "We'll see that he gets his proper memorial. But where do we stand now, Lindstrom? How do things look?"

Lindstrom looked down at his papers. He scratched his head and rubbed his beard. He seemed to take forever to answer before he turned to McManus with something close to a smile on his face.

"I think things are going well. I mean," he said, pointing to the printout, "look at this. We just got the Africa Campaign back. And Rommel lived to face the Allied Expeditionary Force in Normandy. . . ."

"But—" McManus prompted.

Lindstrom shook his head.

"But we're not out of the woods yet. There are too many other screwy things popping up. New things, I'm afraid." He pointed at one line. "Just what do you suppose the Protectorate of Switzerland is supposed to be?"

McManus's face fell. He had hoped that everything would be all set right by now, especially with Port—their one trained agent—gone. Now, perhaps one of them would have to go back.

McManus didn't like that idea at all.

It wasn't just the distressing idea of making a one-way journey. He had come to terms with that option weeks ago.

No, it was something else, something Dr. Beck had passed along to him. The stress connected with the Time Transference Device was tremendous. The machine taxed every physiological system to the utmost. It was clear, Beck had told him, that only someone extremely fit could survive the experience.

Death, if it did occur, would be quick.

No. Neither he nor Lindstrom could go. There were the security guards, but that was just a case of more untrained people.

"What do you think?" he finally asked Lindstrom.

"You mean about this? I don't know. I hope it has something to do with the billions of dollars of stolen art, the war chest from the Iron Men's Time Lab. And if that's the case, well, we still have Ali . . . and her boyfriend."

McManus shook his head. He sighed. "So that's what protecting the future comes down to . . . a young physicist . . . and someone who wanted to meet the Beatles."

Jim touched the side of the plane. It was corrugated, like a cardboard box, and emblazoned with a great swastika on the side. The door opened and the pilot stood there. He smiled and handed Jim a piece of gum.

Jim took it but gave the pilot a questioning look.

"Why the gum?"

"It helps with pressure," the pilot said, pointing at his ears. "We will be very high, Oberstleutnant."

The pilot stood holding the door and Jim crawled into the small cabin. It looked as if he was to be the lone passenger. As soon as he sat on the hard bench seat in the cabin, the small corrugated metal door slammed behind him, latched tight. And the twin engines started, a throaty coughing that Jim found completely disconcerting.

Propellers, he thought. How quaint.

He fumbled around for the seat belt even as the plane began moving. It wasted no time taxiing into position on the small desert runway. Then it stopped, and the engines began a loud, anxious whine before the plane broke free and bobbled down the runway.

God, Jim thought, as the plane rocked left and right. It will never fly.

But then the bumps and ruts of the desert floor disappeared.

And he was soaring north.

Into the heart of Fortress Europe.

35

Incredibly enough, Jim slept. Lulled by the steady hum of the engines, he dozed fitfully.

He dreamed of the desert, of tanks, and explosions, and people looking at him, staring at him, chasing him.

He dreamed of the doctor, writhing at the end of a knife. Spitting out words, screaming at Jim while a froth of blood gathered at his mouth.

And then Jim would snort, wake up a bit, and fall back to sleep.

The plane landed once, coming down hard. Jim stirred, and one of the pilots came back and told him that they were just refueling on some island.

And then the plane was back in the air.

And Jim dreamed of Ali.

They were walking the campus, like they usually did. He was talking a mile a minute and she was listening, smiling. In his dream he saw her hair flying behind her, a golden stream of light-brown that just begged to be touched. He stopped talking.

"You're beautiful," he said.

So beautiful, he thought.

And she turned to him, still with that same smile on her face, and she took his hand and squeezed it. He dreamed of coming close to her face, kissing her cheeks gently, tiny kisses that she accepted as her proper due before turning to him and kissing him back, no fooling now, hard on the lips, hungrily—

Something shook him awake. He sat up. The smell, the taste, of Ali vanished. He looked out the oval window of the plane.

The sky had a hint of color on the horizon. And though it was dark below him, dark, except for the occasional glimmer of headlights moving through the streets, Jim saw that it was a city. The plane dropped some more.

We're landing, he thought.

Good God, what am I going to do now? Live the rest of my life as a German lieutenant? Most likely I'll die . . . in the East . . . or in the Ardennes.

A terrible despair, a hopelessness, settled on him.

The plane dropped some more, and in the dim morning light Jim made out the outline of the airport. Templehof. Gateway to the Reich's capital.

Jim tried to think of whether Der Führer was here. Hitler. Just the thought was enough to make his skin cold.

But no . . . Hitler would be in his eastern headquarters, his Wolf's Lair. Watching his Eastern Campaign just beginning to come unglued.

The plane leveled out and began a smooth glide down to the tarmac. Jim awaited the screech of the wheels when the plane landed. He looked out the window and—as the plane landed, bumpily—he saw some cars ahead, near a building. Big black cars . . .

Like they were waiting for someone, he thought.

And then, belatedly, it occurred to him who they might be waiting for. . . .

Gilbert Moreau was an engineer.

He built bridges. Tunnels. Dams. His work dotted the countryside of southern France.

Years from now, he always thought, my children . . . and their children . . . will come here and be able to see what I did with my life. *I built things!* I made things that will last for centuries.

That was what he used to do. Now he had a different job.

He stood up on the rock, watching the sun beginning to crest the horizon, a thin yellow line, a miracle that seemed to offer the possibility of hope and cleansing.

But reality was his gun, a stocky British rifle. Slow, cumbersome, with a pronounced tendency to jam. And there weren't even enough of them for his men. One gun for every two men. The rest made do with knives and homemade bombs.

Such was the army that he brought to fight the Germans. They had their few weapons . . . and they had time.

(He reached into a small satchel and pulled out a piece of dried mutton. It was salty, biting. But with a long gulp of cool water from his gourd, it was breakfast.)

Time. To let the British return. Because he had to believe that the British and the Russians would reclaim Europe.

And the Americans? Perhaps they will wake up and see that it is their war too. . . .

He had to believe that.

Gilbert Moreau looked around, checking the trees, the nearby hills, and—in the distance—the now nearly bare valley for any signs of movement.

And, farther in the distance, the train tracks.

One more day. That's all he and his cell, his small secret army, had. Then, yes then, we will at last get to strike a great blow for *Le Resistance*, for France.

For humanity.

He stretched his arms over his head, holding his heavy gun high. And then he turned and walked back into the wide mouth of the cave to awaken his men.

"Heil Hitler! Wilkommen auf Berlin, Oberstleutnant Wagner."

The guy holding the door open was dressed in a black uniform. Bad news . . . Jim thought. As Jim got out, he tried not to stare at the art deco SS on the collar of the uniform.

With all his sleeping, Jim hadn't had any time to think about what he was going to do.

(There was Fritz's wife . . . and his child. But the thought—the strangeness of it all—was too much. He had money. He'd find a hotel.)

Jim smiled at the SS officer, wondering . . . Does he greet all the new arrivals?

"Oberstleutnant," he said as Jim got out, pulling a small bag behind him, "there is a car here waiting to take you. . . ."

The officer grinned. Not a good sign, Jim thought. Take me where? Did they find out what really happened to Dr. Bock? Were thumbscrews already being prepared for extracting any information he might be reluctant to share with the Third Reich?

Jim nodded. And said, "A car?"

"Yes. Over there, by the main gate."

Jim looked in the direction the cheery officer pointed. And sure enough, there was a big black Mercedes waiting, its lights off, but a steady stream of exhaust billowing from its rear.

"Good," Jim tried to say with some feeling.

He started walking, expecting the SS officer to follow him, chortling about Jim's predicament.

But he didn't. Instead, he called to Jim. "Enjoy your visit to the capital, Oberstleutnant."

Jim kept walking.

Now there was some real light in the sky, and the east had a rim of fiery red-yellow, outlining the buildings of Berlin.

In about three years, one-third of the town would be rubble—check and mate in the demented wargame launched by a psychotic . . . a failed artist.

Did the world ever pay so heavily for frustrated ambition?

He walked to the gate, and he saw the car door open.

Jim licked his lips. Each step was harder than the last. He would have liked to stop. Turn around. Run away.

The door opened wide just as Jim reached the gate.

A solemn, grey-faced soldier stood guard, seeing nothing, as Jim passed him.

Someone was getting out of the car.

Someone.

A woman.

She stood up, by the open door. She was pretty, with reddish-brown hair, in the shadows, the light behind her.

My wife? Jim wondered. But no . . . there would be some kind of reverberation from the Fritz part of him. Sure, there would be some recognition.

The woman smiled. Very pretty. Fresh and clean.

I don't know this person, Jim thought. I don't know her at all.

He stopped just a few feet away from her. Her smile broadened.

(Something familiar about that, he thought. Damned familiar. . . .)

And she spoke.

In English.

"Hello, sailor. Need a lift?"

And he knew who the strange woman was. . . .

Goering was having his nails done when he heard the knock on the door.He put down a chunky brioche, fresh from the Chancellery bakery. Who else could be up at such an early hour?

"Yah?" he said.

It was Halder. Tiresome. Such a worrywart.

The Luftwaffe chief signaled the girl to stop, and she paused in mid-brush.

"Yes, yes, General Halder. What is it?"

"I felt you should know, Field Marshal Goering . . . Rostov has fallen."

Goering picked up the roll and waved at Halder. "Good. Now, on to Moscow . . . eh?"

Halder shook his head. He came closer. "No, Field Marshal . . . you don't understand. Our army has lost Rostov. Von Rundstedt has evacuated the city. The Russians have recaptured it."

Goering had bit into the roll, but now he chewed slowly, deliberately. This was confusing. Goebbels had told him that the war in the East was almost finished. The Russians were just about out of it. Now this—this—

"Thank you, General," Goering said. "I appreciate—"

"The Führer has ordered all staff officers to report to Wolf's Lair this evening."

Goering's face fell.

The Wolf's Lair. East Prussia.

He didn't like leaving Berlin . . . especially for the hinterlands of the new Reich.

I won't be here to watch over my train. . . .

"Yes, Halder. I will be there for Mein Führer."

Halder nodded and left.

The girl was still at the field marshal's feet.

"Should I continue?" she asked.

And Goering nodded as she once again attacked his fingernails with admirable fervor.

36

Jim took the woman's hand and followed her into the car.

Her face was catching just the faintest light. In the east, right past the control tower of the airport, the sky was giving way to a brilliant sun in a clear blue sky.

The woman leaned close to the driver. "*Vierzehn Prinzenstrasse, bitte,*" she said, and the car pulled sleekly away.

Only then did she turn back to Jim and smile. Warm, radiant, the first really friendly thing he'd seen in days. For a second her face seemed to cloud over, as if she was suddenly unsure of something . . . Unsure of me, he thought.

Finally, after sitting an eternity, just staring at her, staring at this strange woman he knew so well, he spoke.

"Ali . . ." he said, thinking that maybe he was crazy.

The car turned out of the Zentralflughafen Templehof.

She smiled and nodded. And then she reached out and took his hand. Her voice was quiet, a whisper. "Jim . . ." She looked nervously at the driver, who was well within earshot.

He nodded. "What are you doing here?"

She smiled. "Picking you up, of course." She pat-

ted his hand. "I'm taking you to a cafe . . . we can talk . . . catch up on old times." She grinned.
"That would be nice," he said. "Very nice."
Then, as she turned away for a moment, to see the route the car was following, Jim thought he saw something. A cloud of anxiety crossing her face. He covered her hand with his, patting it.
He laughed. "How do I look?"
She turned back, once again smiling. "Different . . . very different."

The cafe was called Die Taube—The Pigeon—and from the droppings that littered the outside tables, it was aptly named. Already workers filled the tables, talking animatedly in the dawn while they drank dark, strong coffee and dipped chunky hard rolls into the sweetened mixture.
Ali pulled him along to a table near the road. She nodded to the waiter, signaling that they had found a satisfactory spot.
A breeze sent strands of her shortish auburn hair across her forehead.
She ordered for them both . . . two coffees, two schnapps, and a basket of sweetbreads.
"Tired?" she asked.
"Exhausted. Ali . . ." he reached across the table and grabbed her hand. "I don't feel the same. I killed someone last night, a—"
She nodded. "I know . . . they know."
"They?"
"The Time Lab, the—"
The waiter appeared with his tray carefully balanced with coffee and sticky buns. Ali smiled at him and waited until he was gone. Then she looked right at him. "They know you had to kill the doctor." She squeezed his hand. "You did good, Jim Tiber. But we're not out of the woods yet. That's why I'm here."
Jim reached out and picked up the delicate glass that held the pale schnapps. "I knew there had to be

a reason . . . bottoms up,'' he said, downing his drink.

Ali followed suit.

She shivered from the sting of the alcohol.

''What the hell happened, Ali? What's been going on?''

''There's so much to explain, Jim . . . too much. And not a hell of a lot of time. Funny, how even here, now, time holds us hostage. You'd think we'd have all the time in the world. Okay, here it goes, but you'll just have to take what I say on faith, okay?''

Jim nodded.

''I know you were told about the other Time Lab—the baddies. They've been screwing around with history to change the world . . . to change everything. God knows what they're grand plan is. But here's the weird part, Jimbo. Half the stuff you and I grew up with isn't even real . . . it didn't even happen. Not really. Things aren't the way they're supposed to be.''

''Like what?''

Like the closing of the UN . . . the Euro-Asian Compact of '98 . . . The United Soviet Socialist States of Latin America. . . .'' She stirred her coffee. ''All of it is brand new. When we blundered into using the machine, the scientists at the Time Lab were already trying to put things back together again. The time bandits had selected North Africa as their field of operations—''

Jim reached out and took one of the hard rolls. ''Makes sense. The first crucial theater of the war. Very clean, manageable. A good choice. But what were they trying to do?''

Ali—this other woman, with a fuller, far less patrician face—smiled. ''Rommel was to win the first battle of Alamein and push the British right back into the Mediterranean. There was going to be no General Auchinleck to press back on Rommel's stretched supply lines. Montgomery would be a failure. General Gott would take over—tired and worn out. At least, that's how Dr. McManus explained it."

Jim asked who McManus was.

"He heads the Time Lab. He looks a bit like Peter Cushing from those old horror movies," she said, grinning.

"So that's why they plucked me from Hamburg."

She nodded. "They needed someone else. And since you were there already—"

"Because it's a one-way trip . . ."

He watched her bite into the bread. It's a pretty face, he thought. Clean, simple, but not unattractive.

"Yes . . . you were already back there."

The street started filling with cars as Berlin started to come awake. The waiter reappeared to see if they needed anything else. Ali asked for more coffee . . . and more schnapps.

"The plan—at least as much as they understood before I left—runs like this. Make Rommel a national hero, the unquestionable successor to Hitler. Then, Hitler was to be assassinated."

"Hitler was assassinated," Jim said matter-of-factly. Everybody knew that.

But this German fräulein shook her head. "No, he wasn't. It's bogus history, Jim. The plan was for Rommel to head a powerful, unvanquished Germany to pursue a negotiated peace. Russia would be weak, Britain's power almost gone, and the U.S. would not have entered the war."

"Who the hell was doing all this?"

Ali held up a hand as the waiter resupplied them. She waited a few seconds—and then—

"A disenchanted group of KGB hard-liners based in Georgia. They call themselves the Iron Men. They disliked the real turn of events in the '80s and '90s, so they decided to do something about it." She picked up her schnapps and tilted her head back. *"Prosit!"* she said, finishing the liqueur in one gulp.

"But things are still goofed up. God, Monty was

in North Africa too early, and Auchinleck is sick and—''

''It doesn't matter. Those are details. They may have some impact on history . . . but nothing major. The important thing is to preserve the overall outline of history. And that's what you've done . . . so far.''

Jim shook his head. ''Right. By killing someone . . . and arranging for a British general to be shot down.''

She leaned close to him. ''It was supposed to happen . . . had to happen.''

He looked at her. ''I don't even know your name.'' He smiled. ''Your new name . . .''

''Elizabeth Stolling,'' she said pertly.

Then his smile faded. It was a one-way trip. He knew that. One way.

''Why are you here, Ali?'' he said solemnly. ''Why did you come?''

''Because, cher James, something new started happening. The other side is limited in how many people it can have in the past—just like we are. But there's someone else here . . . and we're not done.''

''I was afraid you'd say that.''

She brought Jim back to her room, through the labyrinthine halls of the Reich Chancellery, to the wing filled with the private apartments of the staff. No one looked up or questioned her appearance with an officer of the Wehrmacht.

She led him into her small room, empty, after another night when her roommate didn't come back to sleep.

She shut the door and bolted it.

''This is likely to be a bit weird,'' she said.

Jim touched her cheek. The skin felt smooth against his large, unfamiliar hand.

''I've never been afraid of strange things,'' he said in English.

"Best you use German . . . you never know," she said.

"Yah."

He leaned forward and kissed her lips. For a second it was like kissing a stranger. Then her mouth opened, and she pressed hard against him. He pulled her body close. The sensations were new and exciting.

When he stopped kissing her and looked at her face, he saw that she was finding the whole experience amusing too.

"It's like living another life," she said. "Finding each other years later . . ."

"Or earlier," he said.

"Too strange for you?" she asked.

"Not at all." He smiled.

And to prove the point, he reached out and traced a line from her cheek, down to her neck, and then down to the buttons of her serious-looking white shirt. He undid each button while keeping his eyes locked expectantly on the surprise treasure to be revealed.

"Very nice," he commented, pushing away her blouse and then gently caressing her breasts through the thin material of her bra.

"Yes . . ." She grinned. "One of the advantages of my new body."

He pushed at the straps, and pulled her close. He kissed her, tasting her, devouring her as she tugged at his uniform.

They made love twice. The first time was filled with all sorts of unexpected discoveries. Different curves, different bodies. It was crazy, exotic, and, Jim thought, absolutely the most erotic time he ever had. They made love with the directness and familiarity of old-time lovers, but nothing was the same; the smells, the tastes, the rubbery feel of skin against skin.

When she reached an orgasm they both laughed to discover the apparent lack of reserve built into Elizabeth Stolling's compact body.

And Jim's own moment of bliss brought a shuddering reminder that he'd been a long, long time in the desert.

The second time was more leisurely, just for fun. Ali took charge, sensing Jim's fatigue. He was just a friend from grad school. But he was also a soldier.

And she wanted him to just lie there and do nothing.

Finally, when they were resting, both of them feeling strange cravings for—God!—cigarettes, she said, "How did you know it was me?"

"I didn't. Not at first. A strange, beautiful woman with a car. How could I resist? But then it was easy."

"Hmmm?"

"Your eyes. You looked right at me, locked on my face, and didn't even blink. I've only known one person who did that."

Ali laughed. She slipped out of bed and started getting dressed.

"What are you doing?" Jim asked. "Come back to—"

But she turned to him and shook her head.

"No. That's it for the reunion, I'm afraid. I told you that there was another problem. A new problem."

"Yeah . . . so we'll deal with it. But not now, I need—"

She slipped on her skirt and walked over to Jim. She ruffled his hair.

"I'm sorry. But you don't have the time."

He sat up in her bed. "I don't? Why the hell—"

"Because," she said, quickly buttoning her now-wrinkled blouse, "you have a meeting in forty minutes . . . in the Chancellery. And I haven't told you anything."

"A meeting? With who?"

He watched her awkwardly step into her not-too-sensible shoes.

She pushed some errant strands of hair off her face.

"You'll be meeting with Reich Marshal Hermann Goering."

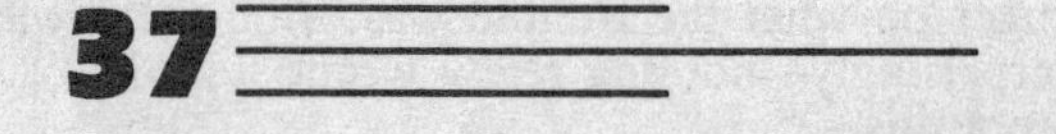

Gilbert Moreau led his sleepy-eyed resistance fighters down the slope of the hill. They were spread out in a winding line, darting from the cover of one evergreen to another.

It was best to be as careful as possible, Gilbert thought. There was always a chance that some plane might swoop down for a look at the hills and discover them.

Their work was too important to be discovered this time. It was too important, this information . . . this mission.

A train, filled with artwork, bound for the heart of Germany. Centuries of art treasures from the Louvre . . . the Jeu de Paume . . . classic pieces . . . modern art. To be gobbled up by the Nazi monster.

There were many reasons to stop it, Gilbert thought. Pride. The honor of France's cultural history.

But there was a more important reason. There were many people who would buy stolen art, pay millions to own a priceless treasure that once graced the walls of the Louvre. The Nazis would pay. And if the Germans owned it, they'd collect the money. It was just one more way for them to keep their war chest filled.

It was an important job ahead of them. Stopping the train. Hiding the art.

Still . . . there were odd things about it.

Never before had they received such detailed information about a secret transport. It was incredible. And outside of a small contingent of guards, the train was to be undefended.

The plan had Moreau and his maquis hiding the art in chateaus and farmhouses throughout Vichy France. It all sounded reasonable.

Still . . . something bothered Moreau about the plan.

He thought about it for a long time, trying to put his finger on what the trouble was. And there was—not surprisingly—nothing really wrong with it.

Except this—

He felt as if someone was manipulating him, guiding him and his maquis into position. As if we were figures on a chessboard.

There's more going on here than meets the eye, Gilbert Moreau thought.

But, *tant pis*, he didn't have a clue what it might be. . . .

Jim sat stiffly outside the Reich Marshal's office. Every now and then the secretary looked up at him. He smiled, but she merely returned to look at her typing.

Exhausted, Jim seemed to wait forever. He tried to practice his speech to the head of the Luftwaffe. And he thought of what Ali told him.

It was a brilliant plan. The KGB group, the Iron Men, would finance their adventures in rearranging modern history by ripping off the best of Europe's art. It was artwork stolen by Goering, with the best classics destined for his massive Karinhall estate, and others bound for hidden strongholds near Lake Toplitz.

Historically, most of the art was recovered.

But someone had convinced Goering to add great stockpiles of the best modern art . . . Klee . . . Kandinsky . . . Chagall . . . Matisse. Pieces that would be worth billions of dollars in the future . . . which was their true destination.

But using the maquis . . . the French underground . . . that was true brilliance. They already had close ties to the Communist Party. Once they stopped the shipment and removed the art—to protect it for La France—it would be an easy matter to smuggle it east, to the strongholds of the Iron Men. And there it would remain hidden until the KGB group was ready to act.

The rest—he thought with grim humor—would be history. Unlimited funds to finance unlimited power.

The intercom buzzed.

The secretary looked up.

"You may go in, Oberstleutnant."

Jim smiled, an unreturned gesture. And he stood up to face the overstuffed Nazi Lion of the Air.

Goering gave him a great bear hug and then—most disgusting—a great kiss on his cheek. Jim smelled perfume, a flowery smell that was decidedly at odds with the Reich Marshal's corpulence. You know, Jim thought, if this guy wasn't so fucking bad, he'd be comical.

"A bit of refreshment, Wagner?" Goering gestured at a table filled with bottles of liqueur—wine, schnapps, and a freshly uncorked bottle of champagne. It was always party time in the Third Reich! There was also a tray of small sausages, cheese wedges, and crackers. From tiny bites and chew marks, they had the appearance of already being heavily nibbled.

"No?" Goering said, making a moue of disappointment. Then he turned and poured himself a rather full snifter of brandy.

This is Hitler's personally selected successor, Jim thought. What a judge of character.

"Your information, Wagner, was—" Goering fished for the right word—"exact. My Stuka squadron found Gott's plane right over the Mediterranean . . . just where you said it would be." He walked over to Jim. Goering squinted his eyes. "How did you come by such remarkable intelligence?"

Jim cleared his throat. There were great, heroic tapestries on the wall. Some fabulous German princes celebrating a great triumph over medieval Mongol hordes.

Wishful thinking at this point.

"We captured an aide . . . one of Cunningham's men."

Goering grabbed a sausage finger and bit down, sending a sharp snap echoing in the too-large office. "You must have used some of Himmler's excellent interrogation techniques. Well done, Wagner. Well done."

Goering draped an arm around Jim and pulled him close. The smell of perfume was at odds with the spicy sausage aroma. Goering held the pose for an uncomfortable few seconds, with his bullish, rouged face only inches from Jim's.

Jim cleared his throat, and Goering—getting the message—ended the clinch.

"So—what did you want to see me about?" As directed by Lindstrom, Ali had arranged the meeting for Jim.

"More intelligence," Jim said, "but not anything I wanted on the radio waves." Goering nodded while refilling his snifter. "Delicate intelligence. It's one reason Field Marshal Rommel wanted me to fly to Berlin," Jim lied.

Goering arched an eyebrow. "Go on."

Jim licked his lips. "There's a train leaving Paris tonight . . . bound for—"

But Jim watched Goering turn quickly, the snifter shaking in his pudgy fingers. All the *joie de vivre* had vanished from the Reich Marshal's face. He obviously didn't expect the secret train to be brought up.

Dangerous territory, thought Jim.

"It contains art . . . to be guarded by you, for after the war."

"Yes," Goering said cautiously, a half-eaten sausage held in one hand, like a chunk of a finger.

"It will be stopped."

"By who?"

"The maquis. They will stop it and remove the art . . . and they will hide it throughout France."

Goering threw the sausage bit into a corner of the room.

"Damn!" He stormed up to Jim. "How do you know this is true? How the hell—"

"Cunningham's aide was working with the Algerian underground," Jim said, thinking of Port . . . and the boy. "He knew all the details of the train. And he knows where it will be attacked."

Goering picked at his teeth with a fingernail. "It is not undefended," he said.

Jim nodded.

"But is it defended enough?" Jim asked.

Goering backed away. He looked out the giant windows of his office, out to the gleaming white stone of the Brandenburg Tor.

"Perhaps not," he said slowly. "Perhaps . . . not . . ."

Jim started to back toward the door, ready to salute, ready to do the Heil Hitler shit, and leave. But Goering raised a hand.

"I'll send a full detachment of Waffen SS . . . under Arussie." Goering grinned. "Yes, that should do it."

"Very good, Reich Marshal," Jim said, still backing away.

But just as Jim was at the door, ready to issue his parting salute, Goering turned to him.

"And—since you revealed the plot to me, Wagner—you will have the honor of accompanying Gruppenführer Arussie. You will travel with the train, from Paris . . . to Lake Toplitz."

Jim walked passed Ali's desk without paying her any notice.

Then, after a few wrong turns, he made his way back to her small room. He waited for her, only now his breathing was starting to pick up a normal rhythm. Ali came in.

"How'd it go?" she asked.

"I can't believe I'm helping that fat slob rip off—"

She put a finger to her lips, trying to quiet him. "But at least if he gets it, then it will be recovered . . . after the war is over. It won't finance the Iron Men."

"I can't believe it . . . I'm going to get on the train in Paris. With some SS officer named Arussie."

"When do you leave?"

"Now. As soon as I'm ready. I'll tell you how things go when I come—"

Ali turned away from him. "I may not be here when you come back."

Jim walked to her and turned her around.

"What do you mean . . . not be here? Where are you going, Disneyworld? It's a one-way trip, babe, isn't it? We're stuck here. Right?"

She shook her head. "McManus said they weren't sure why people come back insane. They couldn't figure it out. Then . . . I had an idea—I don't know why it didn't occur to them."

Jim didn't like what he was hearing. "Go on."

"I wondered what would happen if the tachyon stream was reversed—even for a second. Maybe the damage done by the Cerenkov radiation might be eliminated. It seemed logical . . . besides, I didn't want to stay here. Not forever. Hell, I didn't even know whether you'd show up. Being a secretary for the Third Reich wasn't my idea of the good life. So—"

She paused, and Jim felt her studying his face for a reaction—

"I told them they could test it on me."

"Oh, God. You didn't."

She nodded.

"When?"

"Tomorrow. After the train arrives . . . safely. If you hadn't shown up, I was going to try and feed the information to Goering . . . to stop the French underground."

"I can't believe you. It's bad enough you're here. But it will be a hell of a lot worse to end up a vegetable. I thought you were smarter than that. And there's no way to stop them?''

And, to his surprise, she nodded yes.

''There is.''

His face brightened.

''Sort of. I mean, it's crazy, but if we had more time. But it's impossible.''

But Jim kept staring at her.

''Go on. I'm getting used to impossible things.''

And then she told him how.

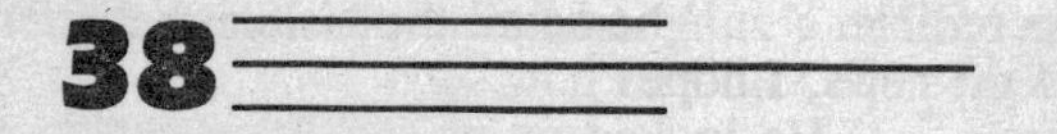

38

"How long before we can pull her?" McManus asked, standing at Dr. Jacob's shoulder.

Jacob turned to him, his face strained, dotted with sweat.

"I don't know," he said petulantly. "I didn't design the machine, McManus. And I wish she never had the idea." He looked back at the massive tachyon generator. "I don't know if the blasted thing is possible."

McManus nodded. "Don't get upset with yourself." He patted Jacob's shoulder. "It's a damned good idea. Let's just keep our fingers crossed that it works."

But McManus wasn't really all that confident. He could just forget Dr. Jacob's promise to her. They could forget that Jacob told her he'd pull her out—no matter what. After all, chances were it *wouldn't* work.

But there was something else.

This was a chance to try the idea. If it worked, well, then they'd be on an equal footing with the other Time Lab. They could come and go through time.

If it worked.

Ali had volunteered to be the guinea pig. She was there, in place . . . ready and willing to let them experiment with her.

In a way, he had no choice but to use her.

He put a hand on the other scientist's shoulder. "How long, Julian? Just tell me that?"

Jacob shrugged.

"I don't know. Twelve hours. Twenty-four. Maybe more. I can tell you more when it's nearly ready."

McManus tried to smile. He patted the man's back and turned around. Lindstrom was flipping through yards and yards of scanpaper.

"Incredible. . . ." he heard the historian mutter.

"Good news, I hope?"

"Yes . . ." He looked up at McManus. "But still nothing from the Bavarian find."

McManus rubbed his chin thoughtfully. "I'm not surprised."

Lindstrom smiled at him. "Have you looked outside yet this morning?"

McManus shook his head.

"You should." Lindstrom grinned. "You really should. . . ."

The bus—Ali had to ask where the autobushaltestelle was—left Berlin at eleven A.M.

It was scheduled to arrive in Fussen at 4 P.M., deep in the heart of Bavaria, the land of gemutlichkeit, dirndls, schnitzel, and a lot of less savory things.

I might have enough time, Ali thought.

She looked at the map in her jacket pocket. It was a cool morning, and she hoped the thin coat was enough.

I must have warmer stuff, she thought, but who knows where?

With Teutonic punctuality the yellow-and-green bus pulled up to the bus stop. One man waited with her, but he looked at the bus number and strolled back to study a pastry shop window. And Ali took a breath and got on, hoping she had enough Reichsmarks stuffed into her coat pockets.

"Bestimmung, fräulein?" the driver asked with almost comical imperiousness.

"*Fussen, bitte,*" she responded.

Then she handed the driver a twenty RM note. And as the driver issued her a ticket, she looked at the other passengers. A few soldiers, sitting together, smoking, looking so young. A pair of nuns in the back wearing their black-and-white starched habits. A chubby, red-cheeked fellow easily filling two seats.

The driver handed her some change and as Ali made her way to an isolated seat, the green-and-yellow bus pulled away from the stop.

Despite his bewilderment, his feeling that he was trapped in some weird World War II freak show, Jim fell asleep.

He fell against the back seat of the grey military car rumbling westward to France and slept deeply.

It could have been minutes. It could have been hours. Jim slid down onto the padded bench of the back seat, wanting only to sleep for as long as he could, forever if possible.

Once he woke up when the car came to a jerking stop. He shot up, not knowing where he was, what in the world he could be doing.

A Wehrmacht corporal was in the front seat, talking to him. The corporal gestured out the window.

"They seem to be moving east," he said, pointing to a long line of armor and troops. "They'd better hurry up or they'll miss the war." The soldier laughed.

Jim looked at the slowly moving line, blocking their way east, to the mountains of Alsace. He rubbed his chin, feeling a surprisingly heavy beard after only a few days without shaving. This is real, he thought with a sick feeling. Real. And there's nothing I can do to make it go away.

He wanted to lie back down. To give himself over to sleep again, to forget all of this in the only way open to him. But he watched the line, watched the infantry trudge past. Most of the soldiers thought the war was nearly over. Their faces seemed light, untroubled.

In the end, how many of them would be alive? How many will live to see old age, to play with grandchildren? How many will live to see the new Germany?

What did they think about their Führer now? he wondered. And what would they think at war's end, with the Russians thundering through the streets of the deserted capital?

The line ended.

"Ach, finally," the driver said.

He turned and grinned at Jim, who could only turn away, hungry for sleep and forgetfulness.

And the car sped east.

Toward the town of Bar-le-Duc.

Moreau brought two fingers up to his mouth and made a shrill whistle.

"*Non!*" he screamed at a group of men across the ravine, on the opposite hill across the railroad tracks. They were rolling boulders into place above stacks of freshly cut logs.

"*Non* . . . you must move the stones higher! They will just crash through the logs like that."

He saw the men look at each other, disgusted with the hard work Moreau was asking of them. It was one thing to live like some romantic bandit. Quite another to spend all day cutting trees, rolling heavy rocks around.

"Should I go over there, Gilbert?"

Moreau looked at the young man next to him. He was the son of his best friend. More of a boy then a man. But brave, and incredibly loyal. Moreau shook his head. "*Non,* Pierre. I think they understand." He laughed. "They may not like it . . . but they understand."

Moreau looked back at his side of the ravine. The logs were lower, held in place by massive stakes pounded into the ground. Up above, another group of maquis was struggling with boulders that threatened to run away from them.

There were so many things that could go wrong.

So many things.

But there was one thing that worried him more than any other.

What if another train, an unexpected train, came by? And they discovered them? Could the whole thing be a trap, something to capture his men?

"Gilbert!" someone yelled to him from across the ravine. "Is this what you want?"

Moreau smiled. "Yes," he said, seeing that they had brought the logs down lower, while rolling the stones farther up the slope. "Good work!"

And he waved his gun—his English rifle that sometimes jammed, and sometimes didn't. He waved it, knowing that their real work was still hours away. . . .

The leisurely, meandering bus trip south, to Bavaria and the German Alps, was filled with a quaint postcard beauty that seemed at odds with the horror of the war unleashed by Hitler's Germany. Though the leaves were long gone from the trees, the evergreens grew ever more dark and lush as the bus made its way from Prussia and North Germany down to the Black Forest.

Ali found herself looking out the window—a tourist.

But she was unprepared for the beauty of Fussen, the picture-book town with its peaked roofs and cobblestone streets set above a gleaming lake that was aglow with the sun, just beginning to dip below the nearby hills. The town seemed built on a spit of ground rising out of a gorge, like some welcoming fortress standing guard at the gateway to the Alps.

The bus stopped. The driver called out Fussen.

Ali—snapped out of her reverie—hurried to the front.

"*Guten abend, fräulein,*" the driver said.

Ali smiled and nodded as she got out.

The door closed behind her. The bus pulled away. She looked at her watch.

Four P.M. Right on time.

Would she have enough time to get to the castle, to find the spot, to leave the message? Would it work?

She looked around for someone to help her.

She saw a man dressed in a light brown uniform . . . a policeman of some kind, she guessed. But he also had a swastika on his arm. The symbol was everywhere, like a plague, growing, spreading, devouring the country. She walked over to him, smiling sweetly.

"Excuse me," she said, "but could you tell me how to get to Neuschwanstein?"

The policeman turned. He arched an eyebrow and—he looked as if he might ask her for her papers. A strange, unreasonable paranoia ran through her body. I have nothing to be scared of, she thought. But it didn't put her at ease.

"Ludwig's castle?" the officer asked. He rumpled his face and made a big show of looking at his watch. "You'll have to hurry, fräulein. It's very late. . . . You don't have much time. . . ."

I know, thought Ali.

I know.

The car stopped with a suddenness that sent Jim rolling against the back of the seat.

"What?" he said, confused, speaking English.

He shot up, afraid the driver heard him, but the corporal was already opening his door, hurrying outside. Jim rubbed his eyes and got out of the car. It was cold here, and the wind icy, with the taste of winter on its lips.

Jim saw the train.

He had expected the car to drive up to some station, some civilized place where he would board, and sit down with the good old boys of the Waffen SS. But the train, stretching in both directions around a tree-lined bend, farther then he could see, was just stopped dead in its tracks.

"I believe," the driver said cautiously, "that they are waiting for you."

Jim nodded and took a step.

And suddenly the side of one of the train cars opened.

There were a dozen soldiers standing there at the opening. And probably a dozen more inside.

And standing in front was their commander. The man Goering called Arussie.

And Jim knew the name.

Gruppenführer Alfredo Arussie. A colorful character. Arussie was one of Goering's personal errand boys. He oversaw the stockpiling of much of the stolen art. He was in charge of the SS contingents at Lake Toplitz and Lake Wolfgang, and other hidden stockpiles, some forever lost to history.

But Arussie was much more than that. He became one of Hitler's factotums.

This wasn't the last train Arussie would supervise. No, the Waffen SS officer would go on to make quite a name for himself. And there was something else—something Jim read years ago . . . in his undergraduate work on the Holocaust. Something . . .

"Welcome, Oberstleutnant. You must have been delayed?"

Jim nodded and looked up at Arussie. He was a dark, swarthy man. Decidedly un-Nordic. But powerful-looking . . .

Scary.

"Yes, Gruppenführer. Some troops delayed our movement."

Arussie shook his head and then broke into a wide, unappealing smile. He extended a hand down to Jim.

This is where I take his hand and get on, Jim thought. And as he reached out and let Arussie clasp his hand, he didn't look at the man's face.

Didn't feel Arussie scrutinizing him.
Which, of course, he was.

Ali stopped for just a second and looked at the magical castle before her.

Neuschwanstein. Mad Ludwig II's last and most fabulous castle. The model for Uncle Walt's Fairyland spires. Set on chunks of rock, surrounded by trees, with incredible views from every direction.

She walked up the stone road to the castle's entrance—half expecting a fire-breathing dragon to be slouching there, guarding the portal. Instead, she met something almost as good.

"I'm afraid," a wizened old man said at a gothic ticket booth, "that all the tours are done for the day. The castle is due to close in fifteen minutes."

The man was struggling with badly made dentures and he had some trouble pronouncing *"funfzehn minuten."*

"I know—" she said, letting her voice plead in a way that normally she found completely reprehensible. But under the circumstances—"but I'm only in Fussen for this one day. I just want to see the Great Hall . . . and the views from the castle's windows."

A small, appreciative twinkle gleamed in the ticket seller's eyes. "Yah, yah. Well, okay then, but don't go wandering upstairs. The schloss guides will get very mad at me if they find you just wandering about."

Ali beamed, and exchanged some money for a ticket. Then she entered the storybook castle. Let me have enough time, she thought. She wasn't exactly sure how much time passed in the Time Lab for every minute here. It wasn't quite a one-to-one relationship. She knew that.

If she didn't get to the hall in time . . .

She took a breath, walking into a great hall covered with tapestries and wood paneling that gleamed.

I'll make it, she told herself. I'll make it. . . .

* * *

''There!'' Jacob said.

''You've got it?'' Lindstrom asked from his desk.

Jacob backed away from the tachyon generator cautiously, as though he might disrupt some delicate balance.

''I think so.'' He turned around. ''Where is McManus?''

Lindstrom hooked a thumb and gestured up. ''He's looking outside.''

Jacob turned back to his machine. ''Well, I'm not too sure how long I can hold it like this. I mean, the stream is running backwards and—''

''Alright,'' Lindstrom said, getting out of his chair. ''I'll go get him.''

Lindstrom hurried out the lab doors and up to the front entrance of the building. He saw McManus and Toland standing by the doors, looking out the glass window.

''It's something, isn't it?'' he heard Toland say to McManus.

McManus nodded.

''I wouldn't have believed it,'' Toland said. ''I wouldn't believe that the whole thing could change . . . just like that. Overnight.''

McManus said, ''And it could change back just as easily.''

Lindstrom came close to the window and peered between the two men.

There were students walking past the Time Lab, bundled up against the wind. Errant leaves swirled around their feet. Two guards stood on duty near the fence girding the Red Building.

''It looks perfectly normal,'' Lindstrom said.

McManus turned to him. ''Perfectly, Lindstrom. Normal. It means that we've turned the tide.''

Lindstrom nodded. ''So far . . . The machine is ready.''

McManus arched his eyebrows. ''Oh . . . then we'd better hurry.''

And Lindstrom took another look outside the window at the pleasant fall scene, so brisk and collegiate. Then he turned and followed McManus back to the Time Lab—and their risky experiment with Ms. Moreau.

39

It was done.

Moreau's men had covered the newly cut logs with clumps of evergreen branches. The heavy boulders—just above the logs—were wedged into place by bundles of thick stakes pounded into the ground.

His men had been told to spread out, to lie close to the ground . . . to stop their usual jabbering.

Moreau crouched low to the ground, listening for a sound, faint, in the distance. Something different from the chirping of the birds, different from the wind rushing through the trees.

It was done. And all that was left now was the waiting. . . .

The train lumbered forward, reluctant to get moving, ridiculously slow at first. Each chug rocked the SS detachment, again and again, until the train began to pick up speed and the time between each great push forward shortened.

The large sliding door of the car was shut tight. Only thin cracks of midday light sneaked through the wooden slats.

Jim thought of other trains, other trains moving east, an endless succession of trains, destined to stop at civilization's nadir. He thought of old men, ripped from the simple comfort of their homes, old easy chairs, and plain kitchen tables. And children, still clutching some precious toy, a doll, a rabbit, a wood truck, a talisman against the real-life nightmare.

The train jostled him, and Jim imagined standing here, for days on end, as the car filled with the stench of people packed in like human cattle.

Faster now. The train was starting to glide over the tracks. The yellow-white sunlight flickered, strobed, catching the sullen faces of the soldiers, their expressionless eyes.

He saw Arussie looking at him.

And Jim turned away. As if the Gruppenführer could see who he was. Knew it.

"You feel alright?" Arussie called to him from the other wall of the car.

Jim nodded.

Arussie held up his watch to catch some rays of light. "If your information is correct, Oberstleutnant, it shouldn't be long . . . not long at all."

No, not long at all. From Bar-le-Duc onto Nancy, and then climbing through the Vosges Mountains until—almost at the German border—the maquis would strike. Somewhere near the town of Saverne.

And they'll be cut down. Because of me.

(Gotta keep things in perspective, Jim thought. I'm not doing this. They shouldn't be here, shouldn't be stopping this train, shouldn't—)

But there was no comfort in that thought.

Not now.

Ali heard voices, coming from the end of a long corridor. A tour, she thought.

She looked ahead. There was a staircase, wide to the point of excess. The rich, shiny wood was polished to a brilliant luster.

She had to get up to the third floor, and quickly. Before they chased everyone out of Ludwig's garish schloss.

And she dug the piece of paper out of her jacket, crumpled now from so many rereadings. She hurried to the bannister and started up.

She looked at her note, though she had each word memorized.

"To My Friends in the Red Building:
I wish to stay here.
A.M."

Short, obscure to anyone who would discover it and read it.

(But it would be there, over the decades, a strange message that would only have some meaning to the future, to McManus . . . and Lindstrom in the Time Lab. It would have meaning to them, if she was in time. If she—)

"Fräulein . . ."

The voice came from behind her, not terribly excited. "Fräulein, the upper rooms are closed now, bitte. I'm afraid—"

She didn't turn around. She wasn't even aware that she started taking the steps faster, two at a time, running.

"Fräulein!" the voice yelled, angry now.

And she knew that whoever it was—some tour guide, a guard, whatever—was chasing her, running up those stairs too.

Please, she thought, let there be time. She was growing more and more afraid of going back. The idea of being stranded in 1941 had been unacceptable . . . especially when there was a possibility that there might be a way out.

But none of it had seemed real to her. Now, with Jim here, alive, it was a risk she wasn't prepared to take.

What does it feel like to be insane? she thought.

She ran full-out.

"Fräulein!"

At the top of the stairs, she faced a grand hallway lined with rooms, all with great doors adorned with carvings and ornate handles.

It's not here, she knew, still running. She had to go

up another long staircase, to the throne room. . . . Ludwig's throne room. Where he sat and stared at his Wagnerian murals . . . Tannhauser . . . Lohengrin . . . while the bureaucrats plotted his downfall.

She came to two immense white doors, and for a second Ali thought for sure that they'd be locked. The footsteps were just behind her.

"Alt!" the guard screamed.

She tried one handle. And the door popped open. . . .

"All set, Elliot," Dr. Jacob called to him.

McManus looked over at Lindstrom. The bearded historian was staring intently at the computer screens.

"Anything new?" McManus asked him.

Lindstrom shook his head. "Nothing at all." The historian looked up. "Everything seems to be on hold . . . at the moment."

McManus hesitated.

If the train was going to be stopped . . . if the art was going to be saved . . . well, that was already in progress. Either Tiber and Ms. Moreau would be successful.

Or not.

And if they hadn't been successful, then McManus knew that they'd best start looking for some other way to derail the Iron Men.

At any rate, this idea of Ali's—as risky as it sounded—was something he needed to try. If it worked, it would be so important.

He rubbed his eyes. So damn tired they throbbed with pain.

"Alright," McManus said. "Let's do it. . . ."

Gilbert Moreau heard it. A whisper. A breathy puffing noise in the air. One could miss it mixed in with the breeze and the other sounds. But it was there. Steady, rhythmic, closer . . . and closer.

He craned his body forward, popping out of the

shelter of the brush. He brought two fingers to his mouth and made a shrill whistle.

Some distant raven screeched back an answer.

But—from across the tracks, on the other side of the ravine—he saw his men wave, signaling that they heard . . . that they were ready.

Moreau crept down to one of the chunky pegs holding the logs in place. He rested a hand on top of it.

And in his other hand he held his gun.

"Schnell!" Arussie said to his soldiers. They all had what looked like nasty automatic weapons. With a great clatter of metal rattling against metal, they jammed cartridges into the guns and stood at a rocky attention against the wall of the train car.

The train rolled them to and fro, and Arussie walked down the erratic line, talking—

"You will split into two groups," he said. "You"—he indicated one line—"will fan left, get cover and move against the eastern ridge." Arussie turned around. "You others will use the train for cover and move against any maquis to the west."

Jim wondered just what he was supposed to do.

And Arussie turned to him, a big smile on his face.

"Join in whenever you feel like it, Wagner. I'm sure this won't be much excitement for a hero from . . ." He took a step toward Jim . . . "North Africa . . . Someone who has fought with the great . . ." Arussie paused. His whole face seemed to sneer scornfully. . . . "Rommel."

No love lost between those two, Jim guessed.

Arussie was right up to his face. "You know, there are those in the SS who question Field Marshal Erwin Rommel's loyalty . . . to the Führer. He's a great general. No doubt. But"—Arussie smiled—"is he dedicated to the leader of the German State?"

Arussie seemed to be waiting for an answer.

"I don't—"

The SS officer came closer. "And what of you, Wagner? Who holds your loyalty?"

Jim took a step back. ''My loyalty has never been questioned before. I—I brought Reich Marshal Goering the information about this raid. You'll be able to reach Toplitz safely—''

Arussie laughed. ''Toplitz? Yes, I imagine you still think that's where we're headed.''

Jim looked at the soldiers. They stood in the half-light, looking away, ignoring the bizarre scene being played out before them.

''B-but this train is supposed to—''

''No. Not Toplitz, Oberstleutnant Wagner—''

(And Jim was chilled. The way Arussie said his name, *Wagner.* As if he—)

''I have convinced Reich Marshal Goering to seek another—repository. Someplace farther . . . east.''

Arussie laughed again.

And Jim understood what had happened.

They found out. The Iron Men. They found out . . . about my warning Goering. About stopping the maquis raid. And they changed the plans. They were still going to get the art. And Jim knew who had done it.

''You—''

Jim started to say.

But the train made a sudden violent lurch, a sharp turn, as it fought its way up the mountain pass.

40

Ali ignored the gloomy wonder of Ludwig II's Byzantine sanctuary, the walls brooding with an ancient somberness that belied their relatively recent origin. She heard her steps echoing as they hit the stone floor, as she hurried, breathless—from smoking, no doubt—to the great apse.

It was here that Ludwig was to have his monumental throne. But it was never finished . . . never ready.

Still, he hid secrets here. Secrets that remained hidden long after his death.

She moved to the left wall, to a small alcove, with mythical images—great knights, dragons, beautiful princesses—cut into the dark grey stone.

She started counting blocks.

Up from the floor.

One. Two. Three.

(She heard other steps now, way back at the end of the hall, hurrying to the open throne room.)

Four. Five. Six.

There. She thought. Hoping she hadn't misunderstood, that she hadn't somehow gotten everything all mixed up.

She grabbed the stone, the sixth stone in the corner and she tugged.

The footsteps were closer, almost at the door.

"Come on," she said. "Damn . . . it . . . come on!"

The block wouldn't move. And she knew she had made a mistake. She had gotten it all wrong.

And the note—her note to the future—was on the floor. Wrinkled. Maybe—if she didn't get the damn stone to move—useless.

She tugged one more time.

And the stone slid out, as if giving up the battle.

Her heart was racing. She made a small moaning sound. And grabbed the note, bringing it up to the opening.

To put it with other papers and notes . . . Ludwig's mad scribbles. All of them to be discovered in 1953. A surprise find during restoration of the room.

Now, her cryptic note would be there too . . . part of the historical record.

She started shoving the note into the hole when she felt the air go stale, dead.

"No," she mumbled.

And someone was yelling at her, shouting—

"Halten!"

The long train took the curve awkwardly. Moreau waited until he could see one, then two, then three cars. And then he stood up. He waved his hand and whistled, the sound lost in the deep growling of the train's engine.

He grappled with one large stake while Patrice pulled at the other. They were hammered deep into the loamy dirt of the hillside. But he rattled it back and forth, and it started to reluctantly come loose.

Above him, more of his men stood by the boulders, ready to remove the wedges that held them in place.

"Pret?" Moreau asked Patrice. The young man nodded. And together they pulled the stakes out of the ground.

The logs started rolling down the slope, slowly, then gathering speed, rolling over bushes, unstoppable, bouncing giddily into the air.

Moreau turned just in time to see the other group send their logs down to the tracks.

They won't meet perfectly, Moreau thought. But close enough.

He waited until he saw the piles of logs crash together, that noise finally louder than the train. He looked at the train. There was no way the engineer could stop it in time.

No way.

And as soon as it was secure, Moreau would have the trucks brought up, trucks from all around the valley, to haul away the art, the treasure of his conquered nation.

Moreau stepped out of the way and raised his hand. He waited just another second and again brought the hand down quickly.

And now the boulders were freed, and they tumbled down the slope, even more maddeningly than the logs. They raced to join the jumble of broken logs that cluttered the tracks.

Moreau smiled.

But he heard something. The train had slowed. Even before it reached the ravine.

It had slowed!

As if someone knew they were there.

He took his gun and—signaling his men to follow—he led the way down to the tracks. . . .

"I have her. The generator has located Ali in the stream."

McManus nodded.

And the scientist waited. Dr. Beck had wheeled Ali's body out to the Time Lab. So they could see—right away—if it worked.

Ali was beautiful, McManus thought, smiling at his belated awareness of that fact. She slept peacefully. He nodded to Jacob, standing near the tachyon generator.

He saw Jacob hit a button.

When Lindstrom shot up out of his seat.

"Wait a minute! Wait!"

* * *

Moreau watched the train screech to a halt. The wheels locked, rubbing against the rails, straining to stop before the jumbled pile of debris.

"Wait . . ." Moreau whispered to himself. "Wait . . ."

He studied the train, the cars filled with art, priceless booty for the Nazi coffers. He looked at the freight cars, the long line curving to the right, following the slope of the mountain.

The train slowed, sparks jumping from the rails. Until it finally stopped.

And Moreau stood up, waved his hand.

His men moved down the slope and he followed, excited, enjoying the moment.

But bothered.

There was something not right about this.

He kept looking at the stopped train, its great steam engine wheezing like a tired streetcleaner. The engineer stepped out of the train.

There'd be guards, he knew. A few for each car. But they would be no problem, none at all. No, it was—

And then he saw it—how stupid of him!—as he ran down the slope.

So stupid . . .

One car—right in the center—was different. As if it had been sandwiched between all the others. It was larger. No markings on it, but it was different.

"Attention, Messieurs . . ." he hissed.

But most of his men were already halfway down the slope, advancing toward the train. And he had said it too quietly, too unsure.

Then, a nightmare made real, the door to the car opened.

And Moreau screamed out a warning.

Much too late . . .

Jim stood there, staring at this Arussie, whoever he was, when the doors—on both sides of the car—flew open. Two machine guns were moved into position and began spitting out a heavy covering fire as Arussie's men leaped out of the train.

Jim's hand came to rest on his own gun.

Arussie screamed out some orders to his men. Then—as if an afterthought—he turned to Jim.

"Of course, we won't announce the change in our plans until we get to the border." The Gruppenführer grinned. "It's all been kept very secret."

Jim felt his gun, right there, brushing against his palm. Insistent, demanding.

Do something. . . .

But the look in Arussie's face didn't show any fear.

"Surely," he shouted over the firing guns, "they could have done better than you." Arussie laughed. "Were you some kind of mistake . . . a clown, perhaps?"

The two machine-gun teams ignored Arussie's rantings.

Jim felt his gun.

A clown.

He felt it, and he closed his hand around the gun, and pulled it out.

But Arussie brought his own luger around. He looked happy, as if he wanted this.

Jim didn't even have time to aim his gun.

Arussie fired and the bullet blasted into Jim's left shoulder, kicking him backward. He collapsed into the darkness. For a second there was no pain, just a dull throbbing, as if someone had jabbed him right near the collarbone. But in seconds he felt the pain grow, blossom, and—God!—he felt the bullet lodged in the muscle and bone of his shoulder.

He dropped his gun.

Arussie stepped toward him, standing near the opening.

The guns outside sounded unreal, like popguns. Less like fireworks and more like children's toys. But one of the machine-gun teams was silent, the men sprawled over their weapon and its belt of ammunition.

Arussie took another step.

"A clown . . ." he whispered, leveling his gun at Jim, taking aim for his head.

Sorry, Fritz, Jim thought. And he wondered . . . What does this mean to my body? Will that die too?

The pain was constant. He put his hand up to his wound, to feel the blood and the terrible opening there.

And he saw bright yellow flashes before his eyes as Arussie made ready to blow a hole right through his skull.

Moreau saw his men being cut down, saw them blunder into the German soldiers with their sleek automatic weapons, while their own guns misfired and jammed and—Christ!

He had to get them out of here.

"Arrêtez!" he screamed. He yelled again, hoping that the men on the other side of the train would pull back.

It was hopeless, completely hopeless.

Moreau began to steady crawl back to the woods, watching the Germans crouch and pick off anyone who let his head pop up too far from the ground.

And then he saw the German officer. Saw him and his SS bars. Right at the doors to the freight car.

And—funny thing—the officer was turned away looking into the darkness of the car, his gun pointed into the darkness.

A bullet cracked into a tree trunk just a few feet from Moreau.

He watched this officer. Who was he aiming at? Who could be in there?

No matter, Moreau thought. It was worth a shot. He raised his British rifle and took aim. His men were already behind him. If he didn't move fast, he'd either be dead or captured.

He took aim at the officer's skull. . . .

And he pulled the trigger.

More yellow flashes. Maybe I'm being pulled back, Jim thought. Maybe they're getting me the hell out of here. But—if anything—his pain felt stronger. And he knew he wasn't going anywhere.

I'm just blacking out. That's all.

He could barely see Arussie through the brilliant spots that danced on his retinas. Arussie was saying something, and he took another step, the gun just a black smudge.

It will be fast, Jim thought. I might hear the explosion, but that will probably be all. Then . . .

Who knew what?

And then he heard the sound of a gun. But not close, not here in the train. But farther away.

And somehow Arussie collapsed, falling to his knees. The SS officer turned and looked away and Jim saw a hole, and all this stuff leaking out of the man's head.

A hallucination, Jim thought, as his own vision was completely taken over by the yellow spots, and the pain, and he let his head fall back . . . crashing against the wood floor of the freight car.

EPILOGUE

Jim stood in a long line of other wounded soldiers, some on crutches, some with their heads almost completely covered in bandages, to use the single phone the hospital provided for the patients.

It was old Catholic Hospital in Nancy, a brick fortress surrounded by skeletal willow trees. The nurses were nuns with head gear that looked aerodynamic. But the care was excellent, and the food edible. While Jim tried to avoid getting involved in any conversations, he listened to the soldiers. Some of them had been here since the first days of the Western Blitzkrieg. A few had been on the train with him.

One soldier finished on the phone, and another, with his one crutch, hobbled forward.

Until Jim was next.

His own wound still hurt anytime he moved his right arm. He even felt the wound pull painfully if he just clenched his fist.

But somehow I'm alive, he thought giddily. *I'm alive.* And my wound was just one of many that occurred in the attack on the train. After he came to, he learned that all the wounded were removed at the next town, as were the dead . . . including Arussie.

And the train continued on.

To Lake Toplitz?

That was his first question. Did the train get away? Did it get to Lake Toplitz? Arussie's plan called for no change in plans until the train entered Germany. And with Arussie gone, the train would just continue to the original destination.

Strange. The art would be in German hands until the end of the war. Goering would have his precious plunder, his masterpieces for Karinhall.

But they would be safe.

Jim licked his lips. He felt weak, standing there. He shouldn't be out of bed. If the head nurse, a battleship of a nun named Soeur Cecile, caught him, he'd get a good scolding.

But he had to call. He had to find out what had happened to Ali.

The man in front of him seemed to take forever on the phone. Talking quietly, smoking a cigarette.

Jim cleared his throat. It did nothing to hurry the man.

Then the soldier hung up, just as Jim caught Soeur Cecile out of the corner of his eye. On the prowl. Whenever she hectored him, he pretended that he didn't understand any of her French.

The phone was free. And Jim walked to it.

He felt chilled. More scared then when he was looking at Arussie's gun. He dug a crumpled piece of paper out of his pocket and picked up the receiver. He cleared his throat and asked the operator, in rehearsed French, for a German connection.

There were primitive buzzes and clicks as the long distance line was cleared.

And finally he heard someone answer.

"Heil Hitler! Reich Chancellery."

"Fraulein Elizabeth Stolling," Jim said.

He happened to look back and Soeur Cecile spotted him. She made a dramatic grimace, shook her cone-head, and hurried over.

Oh, not now, he thought. Keep the vengeful penguin off my back until—

"One moment, *mein herr,*" the voice on the other line said. There was more static and buzzes.

And he thought of Ali.

Did she make it in time? Did she stop them from

pulling her back? It seemed like a crazy idea, but it was the only way to get a message to them—in the future—to tell them not to do it. If she hid the message in Ludwig's castle it would be found with the other documents uncovered in 1953. It would be part of the official record.

Dr. McManus had promised to keep checking it before trying the experiment to get her out . . . in case she needed more time . . . wanted more time.

Jim waited.

And there was one thought that scared him more than any other.

If they pulled Ali—and it worked—well, they would then pull me out, wouldn't they? In fact, I'd be gone now. *If* it had worked . . . if Ali made it back—

Sane.

But if she was gone . . . and I'm still here. Well, that meant—

"Yah, bitte?"

Jim recognized the voice. It was her.

"Yes," he said, almost too scared to say anything. "Yes . . ." And then finally, he took a breath and—

A strong hand grabbed his arm, and tugged at him.

"Non, monsieur, c'est ne pas bon pour vous—" Soeur Cecile had swooped down on him, an avenging angel insisting on pulling him away from the phone. *"Il est faut—"*

He waved her away.

"Who is this, bitte?" the faint voice on the phone asked.

Jim felt his heart beating. He was cold. Too scared to say anything, to ask—

Then, he just said it . . .

"Ali . . . I—"

He waited.

"Ali—"

"No, *mein herr,* you must have the wrong office. I am Fräulein Stolling and—"

"Ali—" he whispered . . . and again. "Ali . . ."

"No," the woman was saying. A wrong number. A bad connection. A wartime mistake.

So sorry.

He cradled the phone against his cheek.

"No," he said to himself. "God, no . . ."

"*Monsieur,*" the nun was saying. She grabbed his wrist holding the phone, trying to pull the phone away from his cheek.

He barely heard the woman speaking in the receiver. "I am sorry . . ."

He heard the click as she hung up.

Too late, Ali had been too late. And he thought of how they had made love, each in someone else's body, the feelings so weird, yet somehow the same.

The nun took the phone away.

He looked up at the woman. She was all blurry. Jim felt an itching on his cheeks. He reached up. He felt the wet trails of his tears.

"She was too late," he said in English. Then, he sobbed, "too late."

The nun—a black-and-white blur, looked startled. Then, slowly, she came closer. She held his arm even tighter, this time holding him up.

He brought his good hand up to his eyes, rubbing at them, pinching the sockets, crying full out now, not giving a damn what anyone thought or saw. Not giving a damn that he kept billions of dollars worth of art out of the Iron Men's hands, not giving a damn that he helped save the British in North Africa, not giving one good goddamn about history.

It was McManus who spoke first.

"Well?"

Lindstrom seemed to be confused. He scratched his head, shook it, then flipped angrily through the pages of printout.

Finally, Lindstrom looked up. And smiled.

"You did it, McManus. Everything looks fine. We just got Texas back into the Union. And the Euro-

Asian Compact is, er, history.'' Lindstrom laughed at his joke.

McManus turned to Toland. ''Quick,'' he said. ''Go look outside. See what it looks like.'' The guard hurried out of the lab.

''Of course,'' Lindstrom said, his brow furrowed just a bit, ''there are discrepancies. Lots of them, actually. But nothing major, nothing that a hearty, intact history can't absorb. I never believed that poppycock theory of small changes irrevocably screwing up the grand scheme of things.''

McManus grinned. ''It worked. It's incredible.''

Dr. Jacob, standing by his trusty tachyon generator, cleared his throat.

''Elliot, I shouldn't keep the girl in the flow much longer,'' Jacob said. ''If we're going to try to bring her back, we should—''

''Yes,'' McManus said. He kept looking at Lindstrom. Thinking—

We won. We beat the Iron Men.

''Just a few more seconds. Let's here what Toland reports.''

The guard came bursting through the door, a big grin on his normally impassive face.

He stood there, smiling, waiting for someone to ask him—

''Well?'' McManus said.

His smile widened. ''It looks beautiful. Absolutely beautiful. No fence, and the campus is alive with coeds.''

Impulsively, McManus clapped his hands together.

''Great. Then, Dr. Jacob, we can try—''

It was wonderful, that moment. When it all had been put right. McManus would look back on it as a special time. When they thought they had won the game.

Once . . . and for all.

But immediately a small bleep signaled a data input from the outside. A red light in the corner flashed.

''What—?'' Lindstrom muttered.

Set to automatic printing, the computer started spitting out sheets of laser-read scanpaper.

McManus's smile faded.

What a fool, he thought in that moment. Stupid. Overconfident.

Lindstrom got up from his desk.

The scanpaper was tumbling to the floor, making a great pile that spread like a stain.

Lindstrom crouched on the floor. He ripped through the sheets, flicking them back and forth.

His voice was a whisper. Hollow. Scared.

"No . . ."

And McManus took a breath. It was starting again. It wasn't over.

"What about the girl?" Jacobs asked. "I can't—"

"Where are they?" McManus asked, walking reluctantly to Lindstrom, knowing what it meant. "Where the hell are they now?"

Lindstrom looked up. "The worst possible place," he said quietly. "And the worst possible time. . . ."

Ali thought she felt stone touching her fingers. It was her last sensation, the crumbling, gritty stone against her fingertips. Then it faded.

There was nausea . . . as if she was about to go over the top hump of a roller coaster. She wanted to scream, to cry out. Don't.

And then she waited to be jerked forward, to see if her theory worked. And if not, well it wouldn't concern her much. Not if she was insane.

She waited. And waited. Floating in a diaphanous ether. Feeling, hearing, smelling nothing. Aware of light, a strangely colored stream that swirled around her.

She waited.

And for a long time nothing happened.

This is death, she thought. No. This is insanity. This is what it feels like to lose your mind.

Then there was movement. Everything was black. She realized that she had her eyes closed. And even as she opened them, she tried to check her mind, to see if it still worked.

What's my name? When was I born? What's the complete resolution to Hawking's Paradox?

And then—when she opened her eyes—she saw that she wasn't in the lab.

And she wasn't in Germany.

She looked around, amazed, thinking—

And I'm sure as hell not in Kansas.

It was later. Weeks . . . days . . .

Only minutes.

Jim lay in his bed, on top of the starched white linen, looking up at the pale yellow ceiling of the hospital.

What hadn't I said to her? he wondered. What should I have told her that I never had the chance—or the balls to say?

And now he was trapped here forever, and Ali was—what?

He pictured her then, pulled back to the Time Lab, an experiment that didn't work. Her beauty twisted, marred by the terrible contortions of her face, her insane face.

Jim tried to turn over on the small bed. It pulled at his bandages, his wound. But he welcomed the pain. At least it was another sensation, something else to feel.

He stared at the white sheets. And staring at the expanse of crisp whiteness, he felt a faint glimmer of hope.

Maybe it worked. Maybe she was okay. Maybe they were waiting for some reason before bringing me back.

He reached out to touch the white bedclothes. *He reached out.* But he didn't see his hand.

"What?" he said. He turned—with difficulty—to look around, expecting to see the yellow ceiling, a nurse, soldiers sitting up in bed smoking cigarettes.

But he only saw more white, until it was all around him, engulfing him like a summer breeze that seems to come from first one direction and then another.

He tried to say something. Anything.

(I've been here before. Yeah, he thought. I know what's happening. And then—another thought—I know what it means! It worked. They got Ali out, and now they're getting me out!)

The fog began to lift.

The whiteness turned muddy, resolving itself into gray-black blotches. Buildings. A street. People.

He took a breath. There was the rich smell of hot oil. And voices. He turned to his left.

He blinked. And he could see . . .

People selling things. Wearing peaked hats. Oriental people, standing at stalls, with rings of glazed ducks hanging from lines. And wicker baskets filled with green vegetables . . . and rice.

There was music behind him. He turned around.

It was a bar, murky dark, lit by purple and red lights. He saw some small dark women looking out, hungry eyes glowing in the darkness.

And he heard Mick wailing.

"I can't get no . . . sat-is-fac-tion . . ."

"Hey, McShane what's wrong with you, good buddy?"

Jim spun around. He looked at someone talking to him, someone with a southern accent as thick as molasses.

He was a GI.

Then, Jim looked down at his own uniform, at his combat boots. And back to the guy talking to him . . .

The grin had faded. "You okay, Mac?"

And not knowing what else to do, Jim nodded.

(Where the hell am I, he wondered. Where the hell am I now?)

"Well, fucking-A, then let's go have some beers, buddy." Jim watched the soldier, apparently his friend, walk into the bar.

And not knowing what else to do, Jim decided to follow. But first he looked up, at the neon sign, some of its curving magenta letters flickering halfheartedly.

The sign said, "Saigon Louie's."

And Jim walked in, knowing where he was.

And wondering . . . *just what am I supposed to do now?* . . .

About the Author

Matthew J. Costello is a Contributing Editor at *Games* Magazine, and writes for *Sports Illustrated* and *Writer's Digest.* His interviews have regularly appeared in *The Los Angeles Times* and *Amazing Stories Magazine*.

Costello lives in Ossining, New York with his wife and two children.